D0189659

Also by Max Byrd

JEFFERSON
JACKSON
GRANT

SHOOTING THE SUN

Max Byrd

BANTAM BOOKS

SHOOTING THE SUN
A Bantam Book

PUBLISHING HISTORY
Bantam hardcover edition published January 2004
Bantam trade paperback edition / November 2004

Published by
Bantam Dell
A Division of Random House, Inc.
New York, New York

Book design by Glen Edelstein
Map illustration copyright © 2004 by Laura
Hartman Maestro

Library of Congress Catalog Card Number: 2003052403

Bantam Books and the rooster colophon are registered
trademarks of Random House, Inc.

ISBN 0-553-58369-7

Manufactured in the United States of America
Published simultaneously in Canada

BVG   10 9 8 7 6 5 4 3 2 1

For my friend Oakley Hall

The Somerville-Babbage Expedition

MONTANA
MINNESOTA
WYOMING
IOWA
UTAH
N. Platte River
NEBRASKA
Platte River
COUNCIL BLUFFS
Green River
Colorado River
DENVER
COLORADO
KANSAS
INDEPENDENCE
Bent's Old Fort
SANTA FE TRAIL
KANSAS CITY
MISS
Arkansas River
TAOS
Cimarron
Arkansas River
SANTA FE
ARIZONA
Continental Divide
Canadian River
Red River
ARK
NEW MEXICO
Brazos R.
OKLAHOMA
Here be Dragons
Pecos River
Red River
EL PASO
Rio Grande
TEXAS
LOUIS
Rio Grande
Colorado River
Brazos River
MEXICO
SAN ANTONIO

2003   Map Illustration by Laura Hartman Maestro

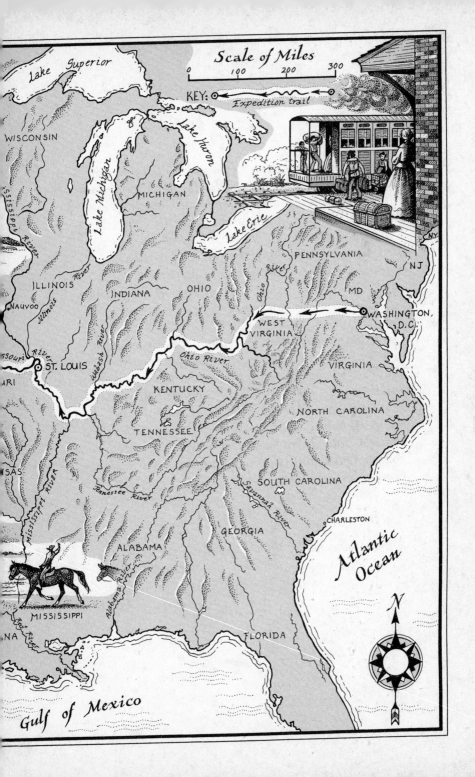

Scale of Miles

0   100   200   300

KEY: Expedition trail

Lake Superior

WISCONSIN

Lake Michigan

Lake Huron

MICHIGAN

Lake Erie

PENNSYLVANIA

NY

NJ

ILLINOIS

INDIANA

OHIO

Ohio River

MD

Nauvoo

WEST VIRGINIA

WASHINGTON, D.C.

Illinois River

Wabash River

Missouri River

ST. LOUIS

Ohio River

VIRGINIA

RI

KENTUCKY

NORTH CAROLINA

Mississippi River

TENNESSEE

SAS

Tennessee River

SOUTH CAROLINA

Savannah River

GEORGIA

CHARLESTON

Atlantic Ocean

ALABAMA

Alabama River

MISSISSIPPI

N

FLORIDA

NA

Gulf of Mexico

Brass and iron have been invested with the function of brain, and instructed to perform some of the most difficult operations of mind. In what manner so ever there is place for addition and subtraction, there also is place for reason, and where these have no place, there reason has nothing at all to do; for reason is nothing but the reckoning of consequences.

—Thomas Hobbes

The wandering whites who mingle for any length of time with the savages have invariably a proneness to adopt savage habitudes; it is a matter of vanity and ambition with them to discard everything that may bear the stamp of civilized life, and to adopt the manners, habits, dress, gesture, and even walk of the Indians. You cannot pay a free trapper a greater compliment than to persuade him you have mistaken him for an Indian brave.

—Washington Irving

America was where the money was.

—William Henshaw Pryce

INTRODUCTION

Mr. Babbage
Lived entirely on cabbage.
He used his head, rather than his thumbs.
In inventing his machine for doing sums.
E. Clerihew Bentley

IT IS EASY ENOUGH, A HUNDRED AND THIRTY YEARS AFTER THE fact, to see why Victorian England regarded the great Charles Babbage as an impossible crank.

He was, let us be clear at the outset, for all his oddities a genuinely impressive figure.

Babbage was born just outside London in 1791 and died in that city in 1871, and in his nearly eighty years of life he published six books and some eighty-six scientific essays; he invented the British "penny post," the railroad locomotive cowcatcher, and the ophthalmoscope; he wrote a ballet and devised a new and practical system for theatrical lighting; and from start to finish, in all of his projects, he displayed quite possibly the most brilliant mathematical genius in English history since Isaac Newton. And yet from boyhood on, he was one of those irascible and colorful eccentrics that the damp, unweeded garden of England seems to throw up in endless profusion.

Any visitor to his famous workshop at 1 Dorset Street, London—and there were many scores of them over the years—would certainly have known of his peculiar reputation.

For one thing, such a visitor would have had to thread his

way up to the front door through a milling and uproarious crowd of minstrels and itinerant organ grinders, who gathered daily to play outside the house in retaliation for Babbage's constant lawsuits against noise in the streets. From time to time, like Mr. Dick in his friend Charles Dickens's novel, Babbage would simply rush out the door and charge wildly among them with a cane, scattering musicians and monkeys in every direction.

Once inside the workshop, however, a visitor would find, not eccentricity, but calm, serious, obsessive perfectionism.

Its two stories, each fifty feet long, had been built to support a large collection of lathes, cutting equipment, and heavy machinery for working with metal. At the rear of the building, overlooking a neighbor's cow-yard, was an office with drawing tables and literally hundreds of rolls of mechanical plans and copper plates for printing them. Next to the office was a locker and storage room for Babbage's half a dozen assistants. A covered passageway connected the workshop to his private residence next door. And on the right-hand side of the building's first floor, just before the passageway, an entirely closed room had been constructed, as fireproof and dust-free as Victorian science could make it, which housed the visitor's chief reason for coming to Dorset Street in the first place: the one and only working model in existence of the Difference Engine.

For intuitive reasons that Babbage would have appreciated, our modern academic historians are very much given to measuring time in decades ("Having ten fingers explains a great deal of human nature," he liked to say). There is as yet no generally agreed-on name or label, like the Roaring Twenties or the Gay Nineties, for the decade of the 1830s, but there is a strong case to be made that these ten amazing years mark the real Birth of the Modern, the true coming of the Technological Age that we still live in today. And in the thrilling sense they gave contemporaries that the world was being transformed moment-by-moment by science, that a curtain was finally being lifted and a miraculous revolution in human life was taking place, no other decade in history more closely resembles the last ten years of the twentieth century.

To begin with, it is the decade of the 1830s that sees the astonishing and seemingly instantaneous appearance everywhere of railroads, a form of rapid, safe (mostly), and cheap transportation that almost literally rearranged the world. The first regular commercial train line, the Liverpool & Manchester, began operation in September 1830; by 1838 the L & M was carrying some six hundred thousand passengers annually, a total larger than the combined populations of the two cities it served. By the end of the decade, four thousand miles of iron track crisscrossed England, and a predominantly rural culture had suddenly become a vast network of interconnected urban centers.

In the same decade, in 1831, a rudimentary electric telegraph was invented by an obscure professor at Princeton, and a few years later Samuel F. B. Morse began to perfect it.

By 1838, with dramatic consequences for emigration, steamships had reduced the crossing from England to America from two months to fifteen days and the fare to under five pounds.

By 1839, photography (usually in the form of daguerreotype) was becoming a widespread art, transforming in the most radical sense the world people saw. The application of steam power to tools and industrial and mining engines of every description began to level and alter nature itself. And if only he had known to work with silicon and plastic instead of brass and mahogany, Charles Babbage would have introduced in the 1830s the world's first digital computer.

It would have helped, of course, if he had been a less disagreeable eccentric. (*Saw Babbage today. He continues eminently unpleasant to me,* wrote the equally unpleasant Thomas Carlyle in his diary, *with his frog mouth and viper eyes, his hide-bound, wooden irony.*)

The idea for the Difference Engine, which in later years he actually took to calling a "computer," had come to Babbage one afternoon in 1812, in a single flash of inspiration. He was a student at Cambridge, sitting at a desk before a book of logarithmic tables commissioned by the Royal Astronomical Society and computed by hand. But page after page showed one mistake or another—an eight instead of a three, a transposed line, a simple error in multiplication. According to his memoirs, Babbage (already unpleasant) muttered something under his breath. Across the table, his friend John Herschel looked up. "What are you dreaming about, Babbage?"

"I wish I *were* dreaming," Babbage said and slammed the book shut. "And I wish to God these tables had been produced by a *machine*!"

And then he sat back and stared at the ceiling, and the first astonishing vision of the Difference Engine floated like a specter into his head.

There had been other modern computing devices, of course, before Babbage. A sixteenth-century Scotsman named John Napier invented logarithms and a set of calibrated "bones" to calculate them; shortly afterward an English clergyman named William Oughtred invented the slide rule. A German, Wilhelm Schickard, devised a cast-iron calculating machine to do basic arithmetic; while still a teenager working in his father's tax office, the French philosopher Blaise Pascal constructed a desk calculator that could add a column of eight figures. And in the latter half of the seventeenth century the mathematician Leibniz built a machine that partially employed the binary system of 1 and 0. But for the purposes of commerce and science, all of these devices were painfully slow, and either they or their operators made frequent errors.

Babbage's machine, however—first the Difference Engine, then its successor the Analytical Engine—could solve complex mathematical problems, it could be "programmed" by means of punched cards to calculate endless and variable algebraic formulae, and it could print the results, without error, on sheets of paper. In effect, Babbage's genius had conceived of the mainframe computer more than one hundred and fifty years ahead of his time.

But he *was* ahead of his time. And he therefore faced three perhaps insuperable obstacles.

First, he had to create a language of symbolic notation to operate his engine, a language, as he said, "of signs rather than words."

Next, in order to manufacture the extraordinarily tiny levers, wheels, and gears necessary for the Difference Engine, he had first to design and build the machines to build his machine.

And finally, because designing and building this way was very expensive indeed, he needed *money*.

Babbage was himself a well-to-do man, thanks to an inheritance from his banker father, and at first he invested a considerable sum of his own in the Difference Engine, which in 1822 he estimated he could bring to perfection in three years. But the three years quickly passed, he was unable and unwilling to invest more, and he began to look about for subvention.

One source was obvious. The British government, unlike the French, was not accustomed to subsidizing scientific research. But in this case the practical importance of Babbage's engines was enormous—the British empire was founded and sustained by its maritime fleets, commercial and naval, and these in turn depended upon quick, accurate calculations and reference tables for their navigational efficiency and, above all, their safety. Yet the relatively simple French Board of Longitude tables on the sun and moon, used by ships everywhere, contained at least five hundred typographical errors, and many more errors of calculation.

Supported by John Herschel and the prominent female astronomer Mary Somerville, Babbage pointed this out to the Royal Treasury. He added that the French series on sines, tangents, and logarithms of numbers—likewise standard for the British Navy—was contained in no fewer than seventeen clumsy folio volumes, difficult to transport, hard to use on a heaving deck in the open sea. It had been produced by 916 clerks working under the supervision of the Académie

Française—one table alone included eight million figures—and its human errors were conservatively estimated to be in the tens of thousands. Every month, ships were wrecked, cargo was destroyed, and money was lost because of these errors.

What Babbage did not add in his request to Parliament was that the newly created life-assurance industry also desperately needed such a machine—Babbage had worked one year for such a company and learned to calculate actuarial tables with great ingenuity and some profit. Babbage's silent partner and underwriter, William Henshaw Pryce, had come to him from "life assurance," he was an experienced and ambitious businessman (but also constrained in the matter of available cash), and he surmised, though the pure scientist Babbage did not, that they were sitting on a gold mine.

But Babbage was *so* slow. And he offended *so* many people with his blunt manners and grim ways.

The British government granted him small sums, but grudgingly. Babbage spent them quickly on his workshop, yet made little visible progress, and in a short time the combination of his quarrelsome temper and scant results guaranteed that no proper or satisfactory grant would ever be forthcoming.

To these problems we may add that Babbage was a genius easily distracted. When (so his partner Pryce thought) he should have been at work on the Difference Engine, Babbage ran for Parliament; wrote a play; planned a novel; devised a new kind of submarine; went to Italy to study volcanoes; and, most curious, became friendly with beautiful Ada Byron Lovelace, the great poet's legitimate daughter, who was at once a brilliant mathematician herself and a compulsive gambler on horse races. Babbage spent a good deal of time making tables and calculations for predicting race-course winners (with, alas, the usual dismal results).

There remained one other possible source of money.

Babbage's frail and elderly great-uncle Richard had been an enormously wealthy man. But in the family tradition of eccentricity, Richard Babbage had some years ago gone off to America and, without a word, disappeared from view. His fortune was still tied up in the Court of Chancery, in a real-life version of *Jarndyce v. Jarndyce,* the interminable lawsuit in Dickens's *Bleak House.* In 1840, eight years after his uncle's vanishment, Charles Babbage was the potential heir to an estate worth at least four hundred thousand pounds—a staggering sum for the nineteenth century, more than enough to build a hundred prototype Difference Engines. But before it would distribute a shilling, the Court of Chancery required, like the Queen of Hearts, to know several impossible things, including where and when precisely Richard Babbage had died, and whether a qualified English citizen had witnessed his death. Without such testimony, Richard Babbage's huge fortune would rust away forever, just a few pieces of paper out of Charles's reach.

Of all this, Pryce, as Babbage's partner and confidant, was completely aware.

PART ONE

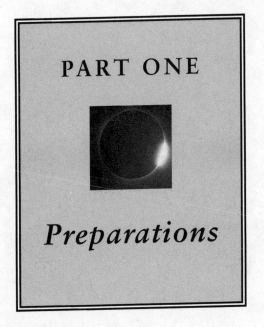

Preparations

CHAPTER ONE

Miss Selena Cott

IF YOU WERE MY DAUGHTER," SAID THE COMTE DE BROGLIE, taking Selena Cott's hand and kissing his own thumb, as was the Continental custom, "I would put you across my knee and paddle you."

Selena, who had known the comte since she was a baby, smiled at him and in her mind's eye pulled his great red French nose till it honked. "Well, of course you would," she replied, and retrieved her hand and used it to shade her brow. The docks of Baltimore City, where he had come to greet her, were astonishingly hot for the month of June, deafeningly noisy. She hardly knew whether to look at them or the disapproving comte, a small, foppish man of sixty or so, much given (as she now recalled) to the old-fashioned eighteenth-century ways. He had evidently doused himself in cologne, and unmistakably he had coated his face with rouge and white powder. Under the blazing American sun, with his black silk parasol held stiffly over his head, he looked like an exotic and demented Robinson Crusoe.

Because he disapproved, the comte was silent for a full twenty paces up the wharf, but because he was French he was constitutionally unable to keep it up.

"One young girl and two dozen men," he muttered as they reached the Customs building.

"*Seulement cinq ou six*," Selena said mildly. "Only five or six men."

"And in the middle of the burning desert!" The comte signalled briskly to a hatless black stevedore whose arms and face were gleaming with perspiration.

"Mr. Babbage made a calculation."

"Ah, Mr. Babbage," began the comte, and then apparently thought better of where his sentence was going. "The lady's telescope," he commanded the stevedore.

Inside the Customs building it was even hotter than outside. Selena fanned herself with her baggage ticket and followed the comte across a crowded reception hall toward a rank of queues and official desks at the other end. On every side, knots of busy merchants and sailors turned to stare as she passed by.

As indeed they might.

Selena Cott was twenty-three years old just that month, and even though she had worn it six of her seventeen days at sea, her blue taffeta travelling dress still clung to her figure with Parisian style. She was slender and five feet six inches tall, four inches taller than the comte. She had striking blonde hair, worn unconventionally short and without a bonnet, and a quick, dancing smile which caused the comte unconsciously to stretch to his full height and rise on his toes as he walked beside her, and which from the cradle on had quite unfairly disguised, as the comte had almost forgotten, her absolutely maddening obstinacy of purpose, whatever that purpose happened to be.

He glowered at the staring merchants and sailors. Selena ignored them and concentrated instead on the reception hall. There were four desks and queues in front of them now, and high overhead, suspended by ropes from the ceiling, the biggest American flag she had ever seen. Sunlight poured in on either side of the flag through a series of tall dirty windows like golden lava (in the heat she allowed herself to be fanciful). The room was lined with barrels and stacks of crates and smelled of fish scales, raw cotton, pine boards, and something she identified after a moment as linseed oil, and while the comte guided her into the shortest queue, reserved for disembarking passengers, she tried to remember the triangular trade routes that her father used to draw on his old sea charts on the Rue Jacob.

"The lady is American," the comte informed the clerk and flourished Selena's neatly folded passport. "Born in Massachusetts, America."

Whatever the clerk answered was lost in the growl of a steam-driven winch starting up on the docks outside. He spat on the floor, stamped her papers, and stabbed a thumb to his right, and thus, Selena concluded, the democratic formalities were over.

Selena was not a sentimental person. From her sea captain father she had inherited, along with her height and smile, an indisputably New England directness. She prided herself on being objective and self-controlled; to describe herself she liked the crisp, cool new word much in use, "scientist." Nonetheless, she thought she would have liked to stand there for an instant or two of quiet exhilaration, to drink it all in— her return at last to her native soil, the twenty-eight bright stars glittering on the beautiful flag above her like a good omen, the rich liquid sounds of American voices, American accents. But the comte's hand was on her elbow, the black stevedore was holding a door open, and she found herself unceremoniously whisked outside, onto a tilted brick sidewalk under an awning.

Next to her, the comte seemed to have been suddenly transformed from eighteenth-century fop into brisk nineteenth-century man of business.

He rattled off a volley of orders to the stevedore. He opened his gold watch, then closed it with a snap. The parasol waved imperiously, and a hackney carriage detached itself from a row of wagons half a block away and clattered up. Yet another black man heaved her trunk into the back. Selena had time enough only to notice the horses—unfamiliar buff-colored drays with hooves the size of soup plates—and then they were lurching and swaying up the street.

"Your mother, dear unhappy lady, says you're as reckless and terrible as ever." The comte smiled maliciously and leaned close to make himself heard over the racket of the wheels. "Still the same"—he searched for a word, reverted to French—"same old *gamine*."

"Tomboy."

"Tomboy," the comte agreed. Outside the carriage, the city of Baltimore was rolling past like a strip of badly painted theatrical scenery—wooden storefronts with patched roofs and slanting porches; weedy vacant lots; an occasional two- or three-story red-brick building. There were signboards everywhere, stray animals, odd abandoned wagon parts, a pervasive sense of clutter: *Gen. Mdse., Dry Goods, Jos. Parker Hatter, Jowett and Pitts Fairly Honest Stables.*

"So I wrote the poor woman I would go with you as far as Cincinnati, or perhaps Louisville in the Kentucky."

"A mature *chaperon*," said Selena, with a touch of the comte's own malice, "just what a girl needs."

And the comte, who perhaps thought of himself as more gallant than "mature," gave an untranslatable but dismissive Gallic shrug. "And after that," he said, "the whole world goes black, no?"

"Not exactly that, no. What actually happens—"

But before she could say a word more, the carriage came rocking and bouncing to a halt, and the comte held up one flat palm like a traffic policeman.

"And I *also* told her I would give you a modern comfortable trip, too, before you start in with all your mules and pirogues and covered wagons. Look out the window, there. They have the *chemins* in Europe, of course, your friend Babbage is an expert, but over here they blow up all the time—*boom*!"

With a cheerful cackle he jumped to the ground and held out his hand for Selena. Behind him, in the scorching, shimmering heat, she could barely read the sign: *Baltimore & Washington Railway Company.*

She took a step forward and felt the full, amazing sun slam her bare face and scalp like a hammer. A lady, as her mother insisted, should always travel in a bonnet.

Beyond a grill fence, a steam whistle blew. The comte lifted his parasol and led her ruthlessly up a set of stairs to the station entrance. Her telescope, he explained in French as they ducked inside, and all her other instruments had to be passed separately through Customs. He, the comte de Broglie himself, would go back to the docks and arrange it. Meanwhile the railway would take her thirty-six miles south to a place called Wheaton Mills—the ride was his treat (the malicious smile again) because his favorite tomboy was known to love all things scientific. And since they were repairing the lines into Washington, at Wheaton Mills the railway company would transfer her to a stagecoach and she would proceed on to the hotel as inscribed on her ticket—no other arrangements required, females travelled alone all the time in America. He, the comte, would rejoin her tomorrow morning, with the instruments.

As he said all this he was guiding her through the station lobby and outside again to a high-roofed platform, where passengers were already clambering aboard a green and yellow three-car railway train.

In England and France, railway carriages were divided into first- and second-class compartments, and uniformed ushers stood at the doors to keep them separate. Here, shopgirls, filthy laborers, men in tall hats, children, matrons, Negroes all pushed ahead, shoulder-to-shoulder, indivisible, like one great sweating Hydra-headed body.

An Irish family with carpetbags and a wicker basket of live chickens squeezed past Selena, then a whiskered man in buckskin breeches and a derby. Somebody's valise slapped into her leg. The locomotive whistle screeched again. The comte thrust the ticket into her hand and made a courtly bow, only partially spoiled by another basket of chickens passing between them. "In America," he said as the train gave a mighty shudder from front to rear, "they call a railway wreck a 'concussion.' *Bon voyage!*"

The train gave a second lurch. Selena climbed aboard the nearest carriage and worked her way up the aisle to an empty seat by a window, and the wheels began to turn. A shoeless boy on the opposite bench gravely offered her a slice of green apple from his knife. She watched the comte on the distant platform, growing smaller by the second. He raised his parasol, the train entered a long, sweeping curve, and he vanished.

"She ain't American," the boy's mother told him. "Look at her clothes." The boy cut another slice of apple and put it in his mouth. Selena smoothed her skirt. "She was talking Latin back in the station," the woman added as the train passed into a vast open field of dark green leafy stalks, which after a moment Selena identified as the first actual tobacco plants she had ever seen in her life.

At the eight-mile signpost, they pulled into a siding parallel to the main track and waited while another passenger train clanged by, Baltimore-bound. On impulse Selena stood and walked up the aisle to the very front of the carriage, then stepped through a door and out onto an observation platform.

Two months ago Charles Babbage had taken her to the Liverpool Street Station in London, and together they had witnessed a demonstration of the famous locomotive "Rocket," reported to reach a straightaway speed of forty miles an hour. She could see at once that the American locomotive was far more compact, certainly less powerful. On the other side of the fuel car, a single driver stood on a narrow exposed shelf, gripping a handrail, with no roof or wall for protection. In front of him was a bell-shaped furnace topped with a polished whistle that blazed under the relentless sun like a brass ball of light. In front of the furnace was the boiler—a brilliantly painted green cylinder about six feet long—and then a tall black smokestack. Four small wheels, two big ones in the rear, jointed pistons. Even at rest the whole contraption hissed and trembled; it radiated heat back in palpable, scalding waves, as if it might undergo a concussion at any moment. She smiled at the fireman sitting in the fuel car and leaned over to study the T-shaped design of the rails, which was still uncommon in Europe.

She was, Selena told herself, quite as American as anyone else on the train, in the state, in the whole strange, enormous, unfamiliar country, where she had, after all, been born. And she was *not* a tomboy, not "reckless." She thought of her father's bemused farewell, her mother's tears. In the carriage door window she adjusted the knot on her French scarf. Greasy smoke had already given her two black raccoon rings around her eyes, and as the locomotive abruptly began to roll again and pick up speed, her hair was blown straight back by the wind like a flag. Well, she thought, matching the fireman's huge grin and starting to think more kindly of the comte— maybe a little reckless.

Wheaton Mills proved to be no more than a dusty collection of wooden shacks beside a ramshackle tin-roofed granary. In the fields on the other side of the railway tracks, farm workers weeded rows of tobacco plants that seemed to flap and pant like big green tongues in the heat.

The railway passengers filed over a culvert and began to distribute themselves into three flat-topped stagecoaches waiting in a grove of pines. Black porters shifted their baggage. Selena took one glance inside the dank overcrowded passenger compartment of the nearest coach: then, holding her skirt with one hand, to a few jeers and catcalls, she climbed up to the open seat next to the driver.

He spat between his boots and looked at her. "Hot," he said, though for all the resemblance to the English Mr. Babbage spoke, or she spoke, for that matter, it could have been Bantu. *Haw-ut*.

"I like it haw-ut," she told him.

From Wheaton Mills to Washington City was still another six miles, though usually, according to the driver, the railway tracks were in use all the way in to the Second Street terminus,

Washington, just the way you could take a steam engine train from Boston to Providence right now without a stop.

Selena rocked and swayed on her perch above the road. On her father's maps Washington City had always been marked with a large red star for "Nation's Capital," like London or Paris, and on those same maps the whole eastern seacoast of North America looked densely populated, a long printed necklace of impressive city names: Boston, Providence, New York, Philadelphia, Charleston. But in fact the three stagecoaches might have been rolling across the empty plains of the Auvergne or the Massif Central. They passed a farmhouse or two, some barns. Twice a solitary rider went by in the opposite direction, and once, over a distant gray horizon of trees, she glimpsed the stately white topgallant sails of a square-rigger gliding south on Chesapeake Bay. But the general impression was one of emptiness, openness, endless space; scarcely inhabited or cultivated land.

Selena felt the faintest sensation of fear in her throat, like ice. What it was like a thousand miles to the west, she couldn't begin to imagine.

The sun had dropped below the trees when their coach crested a hill, and for a few moments Washington City spread out beneath them in a panoramic grid of rooftops and streets, bounded on the far southern edge by a curving band of bright brown river. Then they were plunging downhill, entering the village of Georgetown, and speeding at last up an unmistakable city street, even shabbier than Baltimore but busy with wagons, pedestrians, a horse-drawn omnibus on wooden rails. They crossed into Pennsylvania Avenue, which was muddy and wide and seemed to contain a remarkable number of pigs.

Her driver pointed to the right. The stagecoach passed a two-story white building, one wing unpainted, where gas lamps could be seen glowing in all the windows and a cow grazed on the lawn.

"Van Buren's house," the driver said succinctly, and then a

minute later as he pulled back on the reins and kicked the brake lever, "Willard's Hotel."

Inside the lobby Selena followed the top-hatted bellman who had seized her trunk the instant the coach had skidded to a stop. At the desk she presented her ticket and opened the registration book. The clerk propped his elbows on the blotter and read aloud upside down: "Miss Selena Cott, Somerville-Babbage Western Expedition."

He wiped his nose on his sleeve and turned around to a pigeonhole cabinet of room keys and mail. When he turned back he had a crisp brown vellum envelope for her, and also a square packet of American newspapers, *Niles' Weekly Register* on top, folded and underlined so that she could see her own name in bold print at the head of a column. He replaced his elbows on the desk, gave her a friendly leer of appraisal, and drawled in a thick, barely intelligible United States Bantu, "Whole town's been waiting for *yew,* little lady."

CHAPTER TWO

Mr. Pryce and Mr. Searle

A S INDEED IT HAD.

"The population of Washington Metropolis," announced William Henshaw Pryce next morning in his sharp, authoritative City of London voice, "is 30,200 souls exactly."

He paused and turned his profile toward the window of Willard Hotel's suite 23 as if all 30,200 might have gathered in the street below to pass by and be counted. "And that population is served, Miss Cott, by no fewer than four daily and two weekly newspapers, every one of which has published a story"—quick, small, undeniably charming smile—"about *you*."

His right hand made a sweeping gesture toward the long table next to the breakfast things. There, six white crisply folded newspapers lay in two rows like trout in a box.

"Miss Selena Cott," intoned Pryce. "Mr. James Searle."

With the other hand he indicated the second gentleman in the room, who now stepped forward, removed his hardshelled Indian solah sun hat, and bowed.

William Henshaw Pryce she already knew, of course. They had met in London months ago at Mr. Babbage's house. Pryce was a handsome, beak-nosed man in his early forties, with a wiry red beard and moustache in the closely trimmed style made fashionable recently by the Prince of Wales. His habitual expression was one of mild, slightly ironic amusement. Men and women both found him "intriguing." His origins were faintly mysterious—north of England, it was said, or possibly the Isle of Wight—and his parentage was completely unknown. But he was thought to have attended Rugby and Oxford. His circle of acquaintance included bankers, Members of Parliament, and "sporting gents." And it was a matter of fact that, before he allied himself with Mr. Babbage, he had formed and managed the first successful life-assurance company on the London Exchange, now regrettably bankrupt.

"The *explorer* James Searle," Pryce told Selena, and James Searle, having bowed and replaced his hat, bowed again and with obvious reluctance shook (once) the hand that she extended toward him. "Explorer," of course, was unnecessary. Nobody could have possibly looked the part more. Unlike the elegant cologne-dabbed and frock-coated Pryce, James Searle was dressed in white trousers, black boots, and khaki-colored many-pocketed jacket with the finishing touch of a gleaming leather bandolier across his chest. He could not have been older than thirty. He was clean-shaven. He had a Roman nose, a blue-dot jaw, and a deep, rich tan, and the hot-wax smell of his leather boots and straps reminded Selena, oddly, of a short-haired Welsh pony her six-year-old self had once been in love with.

"I disapprove completely," James Searle said, "of females on an expedition," and Selena decided that she was not in love after all.

"Even so lovely and talented a female as Miss Cott?" Pryce asked, amused. Behind them, summoned by some invisible signal, a Negro servant in a red and blue Willard uniform entered with a fresh tray of coffee. "Miss Cott's given name, you know—Selena—means 'moon' in Greek. Mrs. Somerville tells me that Miss Cott has won three times the Lanet Prize in Paris for mathematics and astronomy. A younger man would add that she has golden hair and splendid blue eyes that would eclipse the sun—and what could be better for our Somerville-Babbage adventure? I approve of Miss Cott," said Pryce, sitting down and accepting a cup of coffee with another of his urbane, sensual smiles, "completely."

Searle snorted and remained rooted just where he was in the middle of the carpet. "Women are not allowed in His Majesty's warships or his army or marines. Women disrupt the men, are the source of certain tensions, and are altogether too fragile physically and mentally to endure..."—he worked his jaw, frowned hard, and ended lamely, "what we are about to endure."

"I shall do my best," interposed Selena, who had heard this speech so often (beginning with her own beloved and backward-looking mother) that she scarcely even listened to the words anymore, "not to excite any tensions."

"It is well known," said Searle, "that you have lived in France," at which William Henshaw Pryce burst out laughing, Searle flushed deeply under his tan, and Selena, to hide her smile, likewise sat down and accepted a cup of coffee.

"And now to business," Pryce decreed. "We are due at the United States Coast Survey auditorium at eleven A.M. I shall give a short and inspiriting talk to the assembled multitude— mostly journalists and soldiers—entitled 'Where We Are Going and Why.' And then Mr. Searle, who is, I hardly need add, an expert practical astronomer, will give a heliographic demonstration with the telescope."

"It is ten thirty-one," prompted Searle, consulting a fat repeater watch with hunter's case.

Pryce sat back in his chair, recrossed his legs, and lifted his cup of coffee to his lips. "I like to make an entrance," he said serenely.

CHAPTER THREE

The Somerville-Babbage Expedition

THE SOMERVILLE-BABBAGE EXPEDITION, AS EVERY NEWS-paper reader in Washington City now knew, had been conceived by the celebrated English scientist Charles Babbage and the astronomer Mrs. Mary Somerville and organized by Babbage's enthusiastic business advisor, William Henshaw Pryce.

The international party was to comprise eminent persons of science, including, at the insistence of Mrs. Somerville, Miss Selena Cott, and also, at the insistence of Babbage, one artist and landscape painter, Mr. Bennit Cushing. After a short period in Washington City, intended to generate public interest, the Expedition would travel down the Ohio River and up the Mississippi to St. Louis, over the famous Santa Fe Trail southwest toward the Rio Grande and Mexico, and then due west into the vast, fabulous, and unexplored deserts beyond the borders of the Independent Republic of Texas.

And there in the trackless waste, at latitude 37 degrees, 13 minutes north, longitude 103, 15 west, they planned to set up camp and await, at 2:15 P.M., on September 5, 1840, the first total solar eclipse visible in the northern hemisphere since 1831.

There were a dozen reasons why nobody thought they would succeed.

In the first place, the southwestern deserts of America, notoriously and literally *terra incognita,* lay a good five hundred miles from the last outposts of civilization—no more than a handful of white men had ever ventured into them, Indian tribes were violently hostile, and such maps as existed at all were works of imagination and fiction rather than science. For all anybody knew, latitude 37, longitude 103, was at the bottom of an immense inaccessible canyon or the top of an unscalable mountain peak.

In the second place, nobody could really be sure where the exact and very narrow "belt" of total darkness would fall. That determination depended on accurate maps, and also on laborious calculations and extremely good tables of logarithms, both subject to human error and imprecision. Even then, the best science in the world might still miss the area of maximum shadow by as much as forty miles.

And in the third place, nobody but Mr. Babbage and his friends thought a total eclipse was going to happen at all.

At precisely 11:06 their hired hackney carriage rattled to a halt in a cloud of dust. Selena stepped down and adjusted her skirt, then shaded her eyes against the fierce Washington sun.

In front of her rose a whitewashed wooden two-story building, glittering in the heat, flanked on both sides by grassy vacant lots. On its roof was a small black observatory dome and over the door a blue and white sign: *United States Army Topographical Corps—Coast Survey.*

"We're running late." The curt and unapologetic Searle bumped her in the back with a satchel of something angular and iron and promptly disappeared around the corner of the building. William Henshaw Pryce took her arm more tightly than she liked, straightened his top hat, and led her up to the door. "I thought I might begin," he said, "with a sprightly quotation from the blind but visionary poet Milton, something about the 'dim eclipse that nations terrify' "—another crinkling smile as he released her arm—"or then again, perhaps not. Go right in and take a seat."

The inside of the Coast Survey Building was cool and dim and smelled, as apparently every American building did, of stale tobacco. The auditorium, she surmised, following the hum of voices, was on the second floor. She removed her bonnet, climbed the stairs, and slipped inside just as two military ushers were closing the doors. She saw a podium, a lectern, and a tripod holding a large *affiche*-sized placard covered with a purple cloth. Three walls were hung from ceiling to floor with black-and-white maps, colored charts, survey graphs of every size and description. The fourth wall had a fine double bay window with a view of the handsome Corinthian pillars and broad marble steps of the distant Capitol.

She took a seat in the last row and noted that there were at least fifty whiskery, expectorating men, soldiers and civilians, sitting in front of her. As usual at scientific gatherings, she was the only woman in the room.

Some of the men turned and studied her; turned back again. Slowly the hum of voices died down. A clock amid the maps and charts ticked loudly. Selena twisted the band on her wrist and looked at her own small, fashionable chronometer. Eleven-eleven.

"Mexico!"

Pryce made an entrance indeed, striding at full speed down the center aisle from the back as if he had been shot from a cannon. His right hand clasped a wooden pointer. He reached the lectern and slapped his top hat on it. Then he pivoted on his heel, and with a matadorial flourish swept the tripod cover to the floor, revealing a very large and colorful map of the western half of North America.

"Texas! Missouri! Gentlemen of the Press, the Corps"— Pryce inclined his head toward the front row of benches— "distinguished invited Members of the Senate. Here is Spanish California." *Rap.* "Oregon." *Rap.* "The great Pacific Ocean. And here"—the pointer circled ominously over a wide blank space north of Mexico, west of Texas—*"here be dragons!"*

There was a smattering of applause. Pryce beamed and smoothed his beard. He made another half-pivot and raised the pointer. From the corner on his right an army officer in shako hat and blue dress uniform sprang forward. He wore great gold epaulets the size of hairbrushes and carried a second oversized, oddly thick map. At Pryce's signal he lifted it to the tripod.

This, Selena could see as she leaned forward with the rest of the audience, was a much enlarged version of the blank space north of Mexico. Unlike the other map, it was crisscrossed with grids of latitude and longitude and filled in with sharp-toothed representations of hypothetical mountain ranges; in several places it did indeed show fancifully drawn and colored medieval dragons spouting flames from their mouths. At the top of the map was the simple caption "Great Southwestern Desert."

"Here," Pryce rapped the pointer resoundingly against the blank center of the map, "is the final destination of the Somerville-Babbage Western Astronomical Expedition. Here is where we are going!

"The first report," he said, balancing the pointer expertly between two fingers as if he were about to make it twirl, "I hardly need remind *this* audience, the very first report about these fascinating lands reached civilization in 1810, from the pen of the great explorer and mountain man Zebulon M. Pike. Pike told the world, you will remember, after two months of incredible solitary trekking down from the Rocky Mountains, that everything north of the Rio Grande Valley all the way up to the Missouri River basin was a sterile wilderness and waste. Another mountain man, the intrepid Henry Breckenridge, confirmed this report in 1817. In 1823 the ex-soldier Stephen Long said the same thing. And just one year ago, in the spring of the year 1839, the pathfinder Thomas Farnham returned to Washington City after a circuit south and west of the Oregon Trail and filed this report with this very body, the Army Topographical Corps."

With his left hand Pryce pulled a sheet from his inner

coat pocket and snapped it open. " 'The Great Southwestern Desert,' " he read, " 'stretches five to six hundred miles east of the southern Rocky Mountains, a scene of desolation scarcely equalled anywhere on the continent, or anywhere else on the planet, a burnt and arid alkali desert, whose solemn silence is seldom broken by the tread of any other animal than the wolf or the starved and thirsty horse that bears the dispirited traveller across its wastes.' "

There was a long and impressive silence. Heads nodded judiciously. Tobacco arrived at a thoughtful velocity in several spittoons.

"Why go?" Pryce banged the pointer against the floor. "Why *go*? Why send a small and nearly defenseless expedition to such a desolate, uninhabited, *godforsaken* place as this?" He lowered his voice to a penetrating whisper. "For knowledge, my friends, for *Science*!"

A murmur of approval swept through the audience. And then Pryce straightened and added, "And because Mr. Babbage's wonderful Difference Engine tells us to go!"

The murmur instantly rose to mutter, grumble, questions. Pryce raised his hand and pressed rapidly forward. It was true, nothing could be truer, that the scientific world disputed Babbage's prediction—the *Nautical Almanac* said there would be no eclipse whatsoever, the *Olbers Observatory Table* of Germany said an eclipse would take place, but partial and of short duration, of no scientific interest. Even in these modern times, he knew, the calculation and prediction of a total solar eclipse—the rarest and most spectacular of all astronomical phenomena—that calculation depended on a truly daunting series of mathematical operations. Pryce was well aware of the doubts. He touched his rakish red moustache and smiled. He was well aware that the *Gentlemen's Sporting Book* of London and Manchester gave odds against the Expedition's success at nine hundred to one.

"Yet, as Mr. Babbage says, 'The human brain is weak and fallible. But the machine *knows*.' "

The auditorium was growing hot. Selena fanned herself

with her bonnet. Her mind began to drift. The Expedition would have to cut across the borders of three sovereign nations, Pryce said, studying his map: the United States, the newly minted Republic of Texas, and the recently independent Republic of Mexico, not to mention the domain of the Red Indian west of the Mississippi. The Southwestern Desert was an unknown, unexplored world—no more than a handful of white men had ever ventured into it, its nomadic Indian tribes were violently hostile. He hooked his thumbs in his waistband and nodded at the tripod, and the slightly mischievous twinkle in his eyes made it seem as if nothing could be more fun, more amusing. Such maps as had been published, he agreed, would be perfectly useless beyond the Arkansas River.

Selena's gaze wandered to the bay windows and the view of the great white marble Capitol on the hill. She wondered where James Searle was, and exactly what kind of heliographic demonstration he had devised; wondered as well where the other members of the Expedition were, and when they would arrive in Washington City. All men, of course.

"Six minutes and ten seconds," said Pryce, and Selena's attention returned at once. Six minutes and ten seconds was the length of time that Babbage's Difference Engine had predicted the sun would be in the moon's umbra, close to the maximum theoretical duration. If the Engine was right, the North American eclipse of 1840 would be the longest total solar eclipse in two hundred and forty years. And in that extraordinarily rare and marvelous interval of total eclipse, Pryce was now reminding his audience, it would be possible—then and only then—to see the sun's magnificent hidden corona, to study the great arching prominences of fire on the solar "limb," to observe the eerie phenomenon known as Baily's Beads, even to search with their telescopes for the legendary intermercurial planet Vulcan.

Selena felt her throat grow tight and her skin tingle. At an age when most young women discovered their sensual life in more conventional places, she still possessed the remarkable gift, present since childhood, of responding to abstract ideas with her whole physical being. Those who thought her too cool and cerebral, the young, hopeful Parisian gallants who drifted away from the Rue Jacob either bored or baffled, would have been amazed at the extent to which something like Pryce's word-picture of the eclipse stirred her inmost feminine nature.

"And beyond all that," Pryce exclaimed, wheeling around. "Beyond all *that*—"

The soldier picked up the bulky map. Underneath it, now exposed, was a brilliantly realized painting of the sun in total eclipse, the thinnest possible ring of light around a central blue-black disk, a blazing golden corona, and in every inch of the canvas hundreds and hundreds of fat white oily dots, like a field of exploding angels.

"Everyone in this room," Pryce said, "has heard of Monsieur Daguerre of Paris. The inventor of the printing of images by chemical process. 'Photography.' "

The audience nodded. Washington City, it was obvious, was a place devoted to the creation of impressions. Even during the hasty carriage ride over, Selena had counted three shops on Pennsylvania Avenue that sold nothing but daguerreotype prints.

"The great theme of the nineteenth century," Pryce said solemnly, surveying his audience, "is the triumph of Science over Nature."

Someone in the back applauded; the whole first row joined in.

"Miss Selena Cott," Pryce said in slow, breathless tones and extended his arm toward her. Every face turned. "The gifted Miss Selena Cott has actually devised a method," Pryce said, "of taking a daguerreotype of a total solar eclipse— think of it! A 'photograph' of light when there is no light! Where our artist has painted an imaginary picture, a beautiful but untrue flight of fancy, Miss Cott has made it possible for us to have a permanent record, a true, permanent scientific record of that wonderful astronomical event predicted by Mr. Babbage's Engine, certain to occur four months from now, in the Great Southwestern Desert." He paused and made a second long survey of the room. "Her photographs will be *everlasting proof* of the Difference Engine's astounding powers."

Then he clapped his hands together briskly and broke into a still more rakish smile. "Time for the demonstration," he said.

CHAPTER FOUR

The Demonstration

THE NOONDAY SKY WAS BRIGHT AND TAUT AS STRETCHED blue silk, hot as flame.

In what was evidently the back garden of the Coast Survey Building, a half-acre enclosure of ankle-high grass and weeds, James Searle, the comte de Broglie, and nearly a dozen perspiring soldiers were in the final stages of assembling their equipment.

The comte himself, despite the heat and his age, was actually engaged in the physical labor of unpacking the last tubular sections of a long silver spider-legged refracting telescope that Selena recognized as one of her own, brought down from the Baltimore docks just as he had promised. Uncharacteristically, the comte had removed his linen jacket and rolled up his sleeves. Uncharacteristically, too (but Selena had been told that he was once a boy courtier at pre-Revolutionary Versailles, and so perhaps the posture came naturally), he was down on one knee. His right hand was on his hip. His left arm was thrust deep into the packing straw of the shipping crate, and his eyes were squeezed shut in such a moue of concentration that he looked for all the world like someone who had dropped a ring in a commode.

"A man of your word," Selena told him. "*Bonjour, mon comte*, thank you for the railway trip and the telescopes."

"I was told to find a box of lenses," muttered the comte. He opened his eyes and scowled in the direction of the laboring Searle. "By your large-jawed astronomical friend."

"These are red and blue telescope filters." Selena picked up two heavy rings with colored glass centers and adjustable metal screws that could attach the rings to the eyepiece aperture of a telescope. "Didn't he want them too?"

"He said emphatically *non*." The comte closed his eyes again and plunged his arm back into the straw.

Still holding the filters, Selena laid her free hand on the silver telescope barrel and stroked it back and forth. Her very first telescope had been a foot-long nautical spyglass, a gift from her father when she was four years old and convinced there was a little old lady who lived in the moon. She had slept curled up with it the way other girls slept with a kitten.

A shouted order to the soldiers made her frown and look to her right. There, Searle, a solah hat taller than anyone else, was steadying the legs of a collapsible tripod. Behind the tripod the soldiers were holding another telescope ready, its tubular sections already connected. Others were moving boxes and crates aside, setting up a field table, fitting still another small telescope on a tripod. From the side door of the Coast Survey Building, the audience for Pryce's lecture flowed out in a steady stream. Pryce himself stood to one side, talking with animation to the epauletted soldier and a large clean-shaven older man who had been sitting in the senatorial row of benches.

"I don't like the look in your eye," the comte told Selena.

"I'm merely thinking."

"Merely don't think, please. When you get that look, wise men steal away. Your instructions are to stand to one side."

"And be ornamental and silent, yes, I know." As far as she could tell, Searle's plan for a scientific demonstration was quite uncomplicated and elementary. The large refracting telescope would be trained on the sun, which was now blazing fiercely almost straight down on their heads. Then, judging from the equipment on the field table, Searle would fasten a special optical prism onto the eyepiece. The prism would reflect a weakened solar image sideways onto a small adjoining table and into a shaded viewing box, which was really nothing more than a three-sided wooden carton big enough to hold a slanted ten-inch mirror. A cloth hood would block the outside light. A spectator could simply bend, insert his head under the hood, and see the sun as it really was.

The surprise, of course, would be the size of the sun as it really was—you could win a good many bets if you asked people at random the dimensions of the sun as seen overhead at noon: as big as an orange? a peach? a grape? The correct answer, unbelievably, was the size of a pea. The great eternal Sol had an angular diameter on earth of only half a degree. It was the brightness, she thought, tugging her bonnet forward and looking up, the glorious cascading diffusion of light in the atmosphere, that made it seem so large.

And yet, she thought, after Pryce's stirring and passionate speech, how dull and conventional just to glance in a wooden box at the diminished sun! How exactly and precisely what you would expect from a masculine slab of beef like James Searle. She turned the blue filter over in her palm.

By now Searle had nearly finished organizing the telescope and box. The soldiers were guiding the lecture audience into a single queue. Searle looked back, nodded once to himself in curt approval. Then he removed his hat and flipped back the tails of his jacket and bent to inspect the viewing box. When he straightened again he had his gold repeater watch in his hand.

Thirty seconds, he loudly announced, was the maximum safe length of time to view the sun, even in the special apparatus provided. Otherwise there was grave risk of damage to the eyes, irreparable burns to the retina. During the eclipse in September, of course, it would all be different; they would have numerous protective devices, they would take quite elaborate precautions. Today he would merely time and monitor each person and stand beside them to answer questions.

Murmurs and grumbles again, some nervous stirrings and backings. The first gentleman in the queue wore an absurdly tall black stovepipe hat. Searle folded his arms across his chest and lifted his big jaw. The stovepipe hat came off, its owner dipped his head like an obedient shorebird, and the demonstration was under way. Well behind the telescopes, Pryce strolled arm-in-arm across the grass with the same clean-shaven, big-chinned individual, who did indeed have, Selena could see as they passed by, senatorial importance collected into his face.

With apologies and nods, she stepped forward and through to the other side of the queue and began to poke among the numerous wrenches, metal rods and clamps, spare lenses, and general clutter of equipment on the long field table. She found a square-shaped magnifying glass on a metal handle, a flexible rod, and a black metal disk about the size of a large coin.

Even a simple blue filter over the telescope aperture would have been more dramatic, she thought, than Searle's unimaginative plan. A blue filter snapped into place would instantly transform the sun's image on the mirror into a floating spectral saucer, mottled and grainy like blue rice in a bowl, and you would be able to see—as you could not in Searle's plan— the tiny black spots on the sun's surface that moved in eleven-year cycles and that appeared, the longer you looked, more and more like living creatures.

Red filters were even better.

"Gentlemen." Selena moved to the front of the queue with her armload of equipment. "Gentlemen, please!" Searle turned and looked at her sharply. "To give you another idea, just an idea of how wonderful the sun truly is, and how still more amazing the eclipse will make it—" She leaned in front of Searle, forcing him to take a step backward. Two small C-shaped clamps would attach the magnifying glass to the prism. The red filter would fit into place without a screwdriver.

"I don't know what you're doing," hissed Searle. "There is real danger to the eyes."

"Back in ancient Greece," Selena told the men at the front of the queue, who were now actually breaking ranks and gathering curiously around her. She swivelled the wooden viewing box and lowered the black cloth hood across its front like a miniature stage curtain. "The Medes and the Lydians were at war, and the great eclipse of 585 B.C., which of course nobody knew how to predict, suddenly turned the sky black and frightened them so much, they threw down their arms in the middle of a battle and made peace right on the spot."

"An unreliable weapon of diplomacy," rumbled Pryce's senatorial friend. He now stood with Pryce just behind the viewing box table and regarded her not unkindly.

"And in the days of King Arthur," Selena continued, "the terrified peasants stampeded through the streets beating drums and shooting arrows into the air, to drive away the dragon they believed was devouring the sun."

In what she knew was an unladylike gesture, she wiped perspiration from her brow with the back of her hand. The black metal disk was ordinarily used, when their equipment was being moved about, to protect the eyepiece hole in a telescope. Held (ladylike) between tweezers extracted from her purse, it would cast a perfectly sized shadow. She extended the red filter toward the top of the telescope and was pleasantly surprised to find that the little comte had anticipated her. Without a word he took the filter from her and snapped it into place.

One last adjustment.

Selena pulled the black cloth of the view box tight and anchored it under the box's weight so that it made a rigid screen.

"As it normally is," she said, straightening and looking around at her distinctly puzzled audience, "the sun is extremely hard to study. It can damage the eyes"—a nod to the unblinking, unsmiling Searle—"it requires certain special apparatus; there are always clouds, and rain, and dust. That's why an eclipse is so important; though, of course, the sky around us today won't go dark, as it will in September. I've done this experiment a dozen times, at my home in France. This disk can throw a shadow exactly like the moon's umbra—you can see the sun in true form, without distraction, so to speak."

She turned the telescope slightly, moved the prism, and suddenly the sun's great image appeared on the stretched black cloth, but red this time, not white, a shocking, pulsating, angry red circle the size of a man's fist. At the same instant, she extended the tweezers and disk between the eyepiece and prism. The disk's shadow slid into place, and she nudged the telescope half an inch.

"An eclipse!" said the comte.

"And when we see the real eclipse," Selena said, "four months from now, out on the trackless desert, without any artificial red filters—" On the backdrop cloth now the disk's shadow covered the entire center of the sun, leaving only a glowing red ring of fire around the circumference. "Solar prominences," she said, and used a pencil to indicate jets of crimson light leaping from the black circle of the sun to the very edges of the cloth.

Then she took the magnifying glass by its handle and inserted it between the prism and the cloth, and the solar prominences all at once filled the whole cloth from corner to corner, living, dancing fingers of flame eighty million miles from earth, ten thousand miles long, so much more unimaginably hot than Washington City or the trackless desert that nobody had yet figured out how even to measure their temperature. There was a gasp of astonishment from the men behind her, a general crowding forward and crush of shoulders, elbows, hats. She should have stepped aside, she knew, a good showman would—Pryce would—but instead she remained just where she was. The thrill was absolutely palpable; it made her heart pound and her pulse race and it left her always, every time she turned her full attention to the Apollonian wonders of the sky, breathless.

When she finally stepped back to let the Senator and the others crowd into view, William Henshaw Pryce materialized at her elbow and took her left arm in a grip so tight that she could feel his knuckles against her breast.

"*Fiat nox,*" he said dryly, "Miss Cott. Very well done. I fear our poor Mr. Searle is not as happy as the audience and I. Still—" He gave a good imitation of a Gallic shrug.

"Exactly like her father." The comte squeezed by them to assist with the viewing box, muttering. "Hotheaded, rash, *tête de cochon.*"

Pryce was indeed a handsome man, Selena realized. His closely trimmed red beard gave him a vigorous, satyrlike air and made him appear ten years younger than he was. But in the harsh light of the Washington sun, Selena noticed for the first time, the corners of his eyes were crisscrossed by intricate silvery lines like a spider's web, and his shoulders were rounded and stiff with strain. His voice, however, when he released her arm, was as urbane and amused as ever. "Poor old Mr. Searle," he repeated. "I've clearly misjudged. As soon as we return to the hotel, I suppose I shall have to revise my lecture."

Selena blinked up at him in puzzlement. "How so?"

"The theme of the nineteenth century," Pryce said, "is quite evidently, if you, Miss Cott, are a sample, the triumph of the Female over the Male."

Which felt somehow, until he flashed his quick, ironic smile, as much a threat as a compliment.

CHAPTER FIVE

The Thomas Arnold

As Washington City had learned, and Selena well knew, there had never before been an expedition like the Somerville-Babbage Expedition.

Almost eighty years ago, in 1761, the French Academy of Science had sponsored an ambitious series of voyages to observe the transits of Venus across the sun, an event that occurs only about every one hundred and five years, in pairs eight years apart. Their purpose was to measure the transits from different points on the globe at the same precise instant and thereby calculate the elusive solar parallax and thus, by a few simple operations of geometry, the true distance from the earth to the sun. But amazingly enough, since 1769, although geographical exploring expeditions had become as common as omnibuses, no other astronomical expedition had ever been organized anywhere outside France. And there had never, at any time, been an international expedition whose sole purpose was to observe a total eclipse of the sun.

"And certainly never," said Senator Thomas Hart Benton, leaning his substantial bulk back from the table so that the Willard Hotel waiter could refill his wineglass, "never an expedition with a female astronomer as part of the . . . team."

"Miss Cott is absolutely essential to us." William Henshaw

Pryce likewise leaned back on the other side of the table, in either parody or imitation. "Without her photographs, we should have no proof of the eclipse. Without proof, Mr. Babbage's Engine will not be vindicated, the royal government will not support him. Miss Cott is, there can be no doubt, our most brilliant and necessary . . . teamster."

Thomas Hart Benton of Missouri had been their senatorial guest at the demonstration, of course, and he had been described to Selena subsequently as a most important man to cultivate, the arbiter of all government projects in the West, the Washington City leader of the Andrew Jackson Democrats, although in the complex tortuosity of American politics he had evidently once fought a duel with Jackson. The Senator snorted now to show that he understood the peculiar nature of English humor, but he had a stubborn chin the size of one of Mr. Babbage's cowcatchers and he displayed, Selena thought, a thoroughly American refusal to be budged from his point. "My information is that you never went to the university, Miss Cott," he observed. "Not Oxford or Cambridge or any kind of school. Yet here you've won all these academic prizes in France, and the famous Mrs. Somerville says you're her protégée."

"Miss Cott, in addition, correctly calculated the return of Enke's comet in the year 1838," Pryce said, "when the Paris Observatory got it wrong." Next to him James Searle grunted and held up his own empty glass.

"Actually," Selena said, "in France and England girls are not allowed to attend university. I learned mathematics and astronomy exactly the same way Mrs. Somerville did. My brother was privately educated at home, and when his tutors came to our house I used to hide behind the curtains or sit in the window seat and play with my dolls. But really I was listening to every word of his lessons."

"I'll be a dog and a cat," said Senator Benton, admiringly.

"Not an uncommon trick for girls," observed James Searle.

Selena smiled and silently counted to ten. She was sorry if

she had upstaged Mr. Searle—but not very sorry. She had undoubtedly let her enthusiasm for science make her forget the myriad and manifest sensibilities of the masculine "ego" (another new word; the opposite, she thought, of "scientist"). But what was more important—the Expedition or James Searle's vanity? Besides, she decided, feeling her cheeks going dangerously red, it was hardly a "trick" and she was hardly a "girl."

"No curtains or dolls on the Santa Fe Trail," Searle added quite unnecessarily.

" 'I am ashamed that women are so simple,' " Selena quoted sweetly and insincerely, " 'to offer war where they should kneel for peace.' "

"*Taming of the Shrew.*" Senator Benton snorted in amusement and she transferred her smile to him.

It was the evening of the lecture and demonstration, and they were gathered, at Pryce's invitation, in the downstairs private dining room of the Willard Hotel. Outside, whenever the hurrying black waiters—*slaves,* Selena had belatedly realized that afternoon—opened a door, they could hear the general democratic uproar of the adjoining public boarding "spread." Inside the oak-panelled private room, if the food was no better, the atmosphere at least was calmer. Next to Senator Benton at the long table were three other congressional individuals, whose names she had not yet caught; on the other side, herself, Pryce, James Searle, and the tall, gold-epauletted army officer who had assisted Pryce with the maps, Lieutenant John Frémont, an American, despite his French name.

One dined early in Washington City. It was not yet seven-thirty, and the waiters were already clearing away the demolished remains of a massive flank of overcooked beef and a side table crowded with bright copper chafing dishes of potatoes, oysters, breasts of duck, brown rice, white rice, three kinds of stale bread. Senator Benton held his belly and softly belched.

"Yes, a wonderful meal," Pryce said, without discernible

irony. "Now, if you would all like to adjourn to my special suite—you, too, dear Miss Cott—I propose to show you something, Senator, something quite unusual. I considered making it a part of the demonstration today, but then—" he shrugged, smiled, pushed himself back from the table, "how pleasant always to keep something in reserve."

Amid the general buzz of curiosity he led them single file out of the private dining room and into the crowded lobby, between potted palms and gilded spittoons toward an exit.

The Willard Hotel was not a single, unified structure. Rather, it was a haphazard, barrackslike arrangement of six or seven unrelated wooden buildings of various sizes and architectural styles, all cobbled together around a large inner courtyard which was chiefly used, so far as Selena had been able to tell, to hang the hotel laundry and shelter sleeping pigs. They crossed the lobby and then the courtyard and began to climb the outside stairs to Pryce's large and expensive suite.

"You are, Senator Benton," Selena said, making conversation as they entered the suite together, "the leading spokesman in the government, I understand, for westward American expansion." A crew of the omnipresent Willard servants, materializing silently, began to draw curtains and set out decanters and glasses. Senator Benton, she decided, was essentially a good-natured man. But two bottles of fine claret at dinner had had the distinct effect of narrowing his eyes and lowering his brow.

"Miss Cott," he informed her with awe-inspiring simplicity, "I rise each morning at five and take a cold bath and curry myself with a pair of stiff brushes, and then I sit down at my desk and think of nothing for the rest of the day except how to bring about our national and manifest destiny."

"Manifest destiny," repeated Selena, guessing that a deferential echo was the best way to respond to this new senatorial note.

"Manifest destiny," he agreed placidly. The other Congressmen were gathered around them. James Searle deftly proffered a snifter of brandy. The Senator's big hand closed around it like a trap. "Southwestern desert or no desert," Benton said, "in a generation I see the American population stretching from coast to coast, across the golden prairies and the Rocky Mountains, from Atlantic to Pacific, an irresistible Tide of Progress. The Arkansas, the Platte, the Missouri Rivers will become for the people of the United States what the Euphrates, the Oxus, and the Cyrus were to the ancient Romans—lines of communication with eastern Asia, and channels for that rich commerce, which, for forty centuries, has created so much wealth and power wherever it has flowed."

"Powerfully stated, Senator," murmured Pryce. Behind him a servant was carefully placing a small, highly polished mahogany box on a table.

"Always the case, sir," demurred Benton, "always the case when I speak about the West."

"Where you have travelled personally, I believe, at considerable personal risk?"

"Senator Benton," said Lieutenant Frémont, "has actually gone pretty far up the Missouri River, with an army exploring party. He's too modest to tell you."

"We saw our Indians," Benton acknowledged, "our buffaloes, our terrible boiling wilderness."

"You understand then," Pryce said smoothly, "the greatest navigational challenge our little expedition will face, going without accurate maps into the trackless desert."

Benton frowned a thoughtful, claret-stiffened frown. Lieutenant Frémont, standing next to James Searle and so like him in height and beefy muscular physique as to be his twin, gave a tactful chuckle. "You mean, sir, the problem of longitude."

"I do indeed."

"You can find your *latitude* without a map very easily," Frémont explained to the three nodding Congressmen.

"Latitude," said Searle, "is simply your distance north or south from the equator. The equator is a natural constant.

You look at certain stars or shoot the sun with your sextant, and there you are."

"But finding your *longitude* by observation," Frémont reclaimed the conversational baton, "is virtually impossible. Until twenty years ago sea captains carried enormous libraries of logarithm tables and star almanacs, and even then ships, as you know, regularly missed their destinations by hundreds of miles. Same thing in the desert."

Searle cleared his throat. "I have had great experience in the African Sahara Desert," he said, and it may have been Selena's imagination that he looked directly and sternly at her, as if to establish their relative credentials.

"It is Searle's dearest dream," interrupted Pryce, "to return, in fact, as soon as possible, to that planetary furnace. Babbage and I have agreed, if all goes well here, to sponsor him and underwrite all his expenses."

Searle continued to regard Selena coldly. "In North Africa we sometimes had to calculate our position in the desert wilderness by studying the eclipses of the four moons of Jupiter, but that requires a perfectly clear sky for several hours and tedious yet highly complex applications of the calculus. You would not learn it by playing at dolls," he added in an undertone.

The Congressmen appeared dazed. Senator Benton extended his brandy snifter to be refilled. Pryce made a little half-turn on his heel to indicate the mahogany box on the table. "For the Expedition we therefore need, as you see, a more reliable method than the moons of Jupiter."

"The Thomas Arnold Marine Chronometer," Selena said, pointedly ignoring Searle.

"The Thomas Arnold," Pryce agreed indulgently.

He drew them closer to the table. The modern, infallible method of finding your longitude in an unknown place, he explained, whether on land or sea, had been brought to perfection in England only a few decades before. It merely required that a traveller carry with him a clock accurate to within a few seconds and set to Greenwich prime meridian time. Three or four relatively simple mathematical steps would then place you exactly on the map, anywhere in the world. The problem for about five centuries had been, of course, that accurate frictionless clocks that did not lose more than a second or two a month did not exist. They had been invented in England only in the middle of the eighteenth century. But those early chronometers were temperamental and expensive. General commercial production of such finely tooled clocks had become practical just in the last few years.

"The Santa Fe Trail proper," Pryce said, "is a known and travelled route, though no map places landmarks at exactly their correct longitude. But once we leave the Trail at the Cimarron Cutoff and head into the wilderness—"

He flipped two sturdy brass catches on the box and lifted the lid. Inside, resting like a crown jewel on a thick red velvet pad, was a gold-plated clock, little larger than an old-fashioned eighteenth-century pocket watch. It was ticking quietly and its three spidery hands pointed to 1:14 and 40 seconds, the precise time at that moment in Greenwich, England, longitude 0 degrees. The clock had been specially manufactured by the celebrated London watchmaker Thomas Arnold, Pryce told them, and was without question the single most important item of equipment the Expedition possessed. Because no matter what the Difference Engine predicted, if the Thomas Arnold were allowed to run down, or altered from Greenwich meridian time in even the slightest fashion, the means for locating the eclipse path in the Great Southwestern Desert were instantly lost. For good.

Senator Benton leaned forward. He touched the center clock with a tentative finger. "How do you wind it up?"

"It requires, like a safety-deposit box in a bank," Pryce replied, "two different keys operating at the same time. On shipboard coming over I wound it myself every day at noon in the captain's cabin—we made rather a naval ceremony of it, much sherry, some cannon fire. Then I locked it back in this special sealed and shockproof box. It is," he added, "a sobering responsibility. Once we're on the Santa Fe Trail, I plan to relinquish it gladly."

"You need one person with two keys. Or two people with a different key each."

"Yes."

Benton shook his head. "You want somebody scientifically trained."

"I do believe"—Pryce smiled and stroked the dial of the clock as one might stroke a kitten—"it is the manifest destiny of Mr. Searle and our dear Miss Cott to be partners."

CHAPTER SIX

President Van Buren and Professor Hollis

THE EXPEDITION'S FULL COMPLEMENT OF NUMBERS WAS not yet fully assembled, of course. The landscape artist Bennit Cushing had still to arrive. A western guide to see them safely off on the Santa Fe Trail would have to be found and hired, but not until they reached Missouri. And though Selena regarded herself as perfectly competent and capable of managing the purely scientific tasks connected with eclipse observation, she was secretly relieved that another, older scientist was due to join them quite soon: Professor Walter Josiah Tudor Hollis, of Harvard College in Selena's own native state of Massachusetts.

She had never met Professor Hollis—no one in the Expedition had met him, in fact. But Professor Hollis, as Pryce informed her, had two superbly important qualifications for the Expedition. First, he had written a book on the solar-constitution theories of Sir William Herschel and so was an expert on the sun. And second, Hollis had devised his own controversial mathematical procedure for predicting the location of a total solar eclipse, and to the supreme satisfaction of Babbage, his figures agreed almost exactly with those of the Difference Engine. (Regrettably, despite the fact that Hollis had published his formulae in a journal, no one else seemed able to duplicate his results.)

Hollis was, so Selena gathered, widely considered the most important professional astronomer in America, though how she came to have that idea she was hard-pressed to say. Perhaps, as Pryce drolly remarked, a man with four full polysyllabic names was simply destined for intellectual distinction.

"But I very much fear," he added, "that he will have all the usual academic virtues, especially Pride, Envy, and Incompetence. I already suspect him of Envy. In his letters the good Professor claims never to have heard of the Lanet Prize, or you, Miss Cott."

The heliograph demonstration had taken place on a Tuesday; the dinner at the Willard Hotel, Tuesday night. On Wednesday afternoon Professor Hollis was scheduled to arrive by the very same railroad and stagecoach connection that Selena had taken. Before that, however, Pryce, in his tireless drumming up of governmental support for the Expedition, had achieved a scientific-diplomatic coup: on Wednesday morning at half past ten he and Selena—James Searle would be away in Baltimore, collecting a special shipment of supplies—were invited to present themselves at the President's Mansion on Pennsylvania Avenue for an audience with His Excellency Mr. Martin Van Buren.

And so it happened that at nine fifty-five that morning the aged little comte de Broglie took two steps back from the mirrored dressing table in Selena's room, folded his arms across his vest, placed his right index finger on his right cheek, and soberly conceded that she looked very well indeed. Her blonde hair was much too short and boyish, of course. But her emerald silk dress with embroidered *mancherons* was just what he would have chosen; the vertical pleats of the bodice were excellent. The straw bonnet with lace trim would have to do.

"I would still have preferred a lower neckline," he mused, "and *le divorce*."

Selena eyed him reproachfully in the dressing table mirror. *Le divorce* was a French undergarment thus named because it separated the breasts and held them up, so to speak, for inspection.

"I am having coffee and a scientific discussion with the President," she reminded him, "not trying to seduce him." Though in fact Pryce had only half-joked the night before that the President was a bachelor, and the Expedition expected every man to do her duty.

It was no more than a five-minute stroll up Pennsylvania Avenue to the President's Mansion. Pryce and Selena exited the Willard lobby on Fifteenth Street, passed the Treasury building, then a row of rather shabby wooden houses, two of which were saloons, and paused in the grassy, pleasantly tree-shaded park just opposite the President's white house. From here they could see over the tiled roof of the Treasury Department straight down Pennsylvania Avenue toward Capitol Hill and the Capitol itself, massive and impressive as ever, though Selena had decided at first sight that such an enormous structure required a lofty Roman dome rather than the flat black roof currently in place.

The President's Mansion was surrounded only by a low bucolic wooden fence. A cow still grazed in part of its lawn, which stretched unimpeded by any other buildings toward the distant river. A gardener worked in the shade of a greenhouse. A guard leaned on his rifle near the gate. And under the handsome high portico at the end of the graveled carriageway, a small, beautifully dressed man of fifty waited for them, smiling.

"President Jackson had this portico added to the house," said Martin Van Buren when he had greeted them, shaken their hands, and courteously taken Selena's arm. "So we forgive him some of his architectural excesses. John Quincy Adams planted all those sycamore trees around the greenhouse. And Thomas Jefferson put in the Italian poplars along the Avenue. To be a President," he said, opening the front door for them himself, "one needs to be a bit of a tinker."

Martin Van Buren was very small indeed, not as tall as the comte and small-boned. In contrast to Pryce's black frock coat, he wore a snuff-colored jacket with outlined pockets, green trousers, blue lace-tipped cravat, yellow gloves, and morocco shoes. His nickname, Selena had already learned, was "the Little Magician."

Still murmuring pleasantries about the house, the President led them down a hallway toward the rear. To Selena's surprise the mansion seemed almost empty—an open door revealed a lounging clerk at a desk; two obvious political hangers-on rose from their chairs in the hall and smiled at them like a pair of alligators; a servant rolled a dish-covered cart through a side door. Except for the drowsy sentinel outside, she saw no other guard, no other state pomp or formalities. If she thought of France and the court of Versailles—

The Little Magician appeared to read her mind. "We err perhaps on the side of democratic simplicity here. I suspect that is Mr. Jefferson's legacy—he used to receive the English ambassador in his old house robe and slippers. Every Thursday afternoon, by custom, the President holds a reception and any citizen at all is welcome to come. John Quincy Adams told me that when he was President a man walked in from the street one day and sat down in front of his desk and asked to borrow twenty dollars."

Pryce and Selena laughed, and Van Buren flung open one more door. In his office, an unusual oval shape, were flags on upright staffs, chairs and tables, bookcases of law books, and two or three small army maps on tripods. The President offered them sticky sweet rolls and coffee from the rolling cart and glanced discreetly at the clock behind his desk. He made one last little pleasantry—Mrs. John Adams, it was said, had used this room to hang her laundry—then sat down, unbuttoned his jacket, and went directly to business. The Republic of Mexico, as they knew, had come into existence in 1821 in a bloody revolt from Spain, and there was considerable tension between the government of Mexico at Santa Fe and the United States, on account of its supposed expansionary colonial ambitions.

"We have no plans to go to Santa Fe." Pryce indicated a line on the nearest map marked simply "Cimarron Cutoff." "Our intention is to turn west here and go perhaps forty or fifty miles, no more, and fix our position and observe the eclipse. Not really so far off the trail or so dangerous a project as the newspapers might lead you to believe."

Van Buren nodded with the philosophical air of one who had long ago gauged the reliability of newspapers.

"It was our understanding," Pryce added, "that all of this wilderness is neutral or unclaimed territory."

The President shook his head. The Republic of Mexico claimed it now, he explained, and insisted that it owned every square foot of land up to the Arkansas River. But various other bodies disputed that, most notably the Republic of Texas, which the Mexicans therefore regarded with very deep-seated suspicion. The present governor at Santa Fe, they should know, was given to throwing undocumented American travellers into prison instantly as Texas spies. Some people had spent as long as two miserable years in the Santa Fe jail before they could buy their way out.

As for the Indians—the President ran a hand over his neatly lacquered hair and pondered the maps. "The Apache and Comanche tribes are here," he said, "all around the Cimarron River and north as far as the Spanish Peaks. Nomads, very, very fierce. You'll be crossing straight over their buffalo-hunting grounds. Worse still, the Indians here"—he tapped the right-hand side of the map precisely on the Cimarron Cutoff—"are the famous Kiowas." He paused to look directly at Selena. "They periodically capture white travellers and settlers, especially children and women, and force them to live as slaves with their tribe. Their hostility is impossible to estimate."

Selena concentrated on the map and said nothing at all. Indian captives, Mexican jails, spies—*What in the world had she done?* Her dress felt rough against her skin and her back was hot, but her eyes remained fixed on the map.

The President was glancing at the clock again and standing. Selena also came slowly to her feet.

"And what I have read is true, I suppose, Miss Cott. You have indeed discovered a way to take a daguerreotype of the sun in total eclipse?"

"It's not something I've been able actually to test, Your Excellency, of course. But certainly in theory everything works. On the other hand, my father keeps quoting Dr. Johnson that theory is only 'speculation by those unversed in practice.' "

"Your father is an American seaman, I believe."

"A merchant captain, yes, sir. I was born in Newburyport, Massachusetts. But he was so furious at Thomas Jefferson for his Embargo in 1812 that he moved us all to France. And he's so stubborn we've never moved back."

The President smiled diplomatically, made no mention of the portrait of Thomas Jefferson above the law books, and showed them with exquisite courtesy to the door.

"You were very good, my dear," Pryce said as they reemerged, blinking in the midday heat. He patted her arm in his uninvited, proprietorial manner. "Quite self-assured, quite bold."

But she didn't feel in the least self-assured and bold. The President's words were still very much in her mind. *A hostility impossible to estimate.* As soon as they reached the hotel, Selena excused herself and went to her room. After two minutes pacing by the window, she went downstairs again, through the perpetually crowded lobby, and out onto Pennsylvania Avenue.

It was true that in America an unescorted woman could go wherever she liked. Scarcely noticing her way, Selena walked first south, near the President's Mansion and lawn, then to the east along a path that skirted a gradually widening creek. Almost at once, and as if by plan instead of instinct, she found herself beside a row of docks and low warehouses and a double line of anchored sailing ships very much, she thought, like those that belonged to her father.

Inside her it was as if each component of her nature had gone to war with the other—the sheltered, cheerful French self who wore a *divorce* and shared her mother's pleasure in colors and clothes, pleading with her at this very moment to come to her senses and climb aboard one of the ships and hurry as fast as the wind would carry her, back to safety. And against it, scornful, the cooler, briskly competent American self who could calculate an azimuth heading twice as fast as her father and outrace her foppish brother the length of Rue Jacob.

In front of her a three-masted bark rocked gently in the water. A sailor climbing a sheet called down to her something familiar and jolly.

She watched his back arch and his bare feet grip the ropes and remembered that her father had taught her to climb like that when she was a fat little girl, barely out of the cradle. It would serve the sailor right if she kicked off her shoes right this moment and scampered up to the fore-topgallant studding sail and left him, so to speak, in the dust. But her French side, momentarily in control, made her smooth the civilized silk of her skirt with her fingers, shake her head, and walk on.

Her father was considerably gifted in what her mother sometimes called the art of accumulation. Silas Ephraim Cott had gone to sea at the age of eleven, as a cabin boy, and by the time he was thirty owned two square-rigger merchant sailing ships and minority shares in four others. His lack of formal education had not in the least inhibited his real intellectual curiosity—he was an unusually quick and proficient navigator and deviser of tools and instruments for shipboard. Nor did he lack the aesthetic "bump." He had a strong reaction to natural and verbal beauty. In the year 1821 he had actually met the great poet Lord Byron in Leghorn, Italy, and spent an afternoon, as he loved to tell, reciting his lordship's poetry, to his lordship's startled satisfaction.

Selena stopped at the end of the last dock. Downstream, in the casual and haphazard American manner, amid the scattered commercial structures someone had built a handsome brick house with gravelled pathways and double French doors opening onto a garden.

It was a sight curiously familiar in its outlines, and curiously strange in its setting. She took a few more steps along the muddy riverbank to get a closer view, and yet another of her father's good-humored, fearless sayings popped into her mind—You never know *what is enough,* little Mademoiselle, until you know *what is too much.*

She stopped and wiped her brow and thought of Parisians and Kiowas, covered wagons, equations, and jails.

Overhead, by a trick of angle, the fierce American sky was reflected in each of the numerous glass panes of the French doors, so that for one dazzled moment, before her eyes cleared and her mood lifted, she seemed to be staring at four brilliant ladders of western light, a terrifying mosaic of blazing white miniature suns.

PROFESSOR HOLLIS ARRIVED THAT EVENING, VERY LATE AFTER dinner.

When Selena answered the knock on her door at quarter past eleven, he stood in the dim gaslit hallway holding his hat in one hand and a leather-bound book in the other. By way of greeting, he made a quick, self-conscious and oddly repellent little bow from the waist that, she would afterward decide, perfectly summed up his personality.

"Miss Selena Cott, I presume. I am Walter Hollis. It's late, I know. I apologize. We had several concussions on the Philadelphia Line. But Mr. Pryce said you might still be awake."

"Well, I'm delighted you're here at last." Even in the poor light she could tell that Hollis was short, slender, badly dressed. He wore a shapeless green twilled woolen suit, brown shoes and dirty spats, and a sparse black moustache that Pryce would have said needed watering. Behind his rimless spectacles his eyes had a look of unmistakable but pained vanity.

"I was supposed to come down with Mr. Searle, but he's still in Baltimore, seeing to some special shipment on the docks."

"The Infant Engine, as Mr. Pryce calls it. Mr. Babbage's workmen have fashioned a miniature model of the Difference Engine to recalculate the eclipse's trajectory once we're in the desert."

The pained look sharpened. Hollis drummed his hat against his leg. "We will have, of course, my equations for that. Quite as accurate as the Engine, quite reliable."

"Well, yes, of course."

"I used to live in Washington City," he told her. "Mr. Pryce suggested you might be agreeable to a guided tour to-morrow."

"I would like it very much."

"Mr. Pryce is a charming man."

"Yes."

"But rather overbearing, I think. These are some cuttings from the Boston newspapers about myself and my career. The most recent concern the Expedition and my equations. They mention you as well, Miss Cott, but they've somehow mis-spelled your name. And in case you were finding it hard to fall asleep..." Professor Hollis paused and made the first and only joke Selena was ever to hear him utter. "If you have no other soporific handy, I have brought you a copy of my book."

CHAPTER SEVEN

A Curious Interlude

BUT AS IT TURNED OUT, JAMES SEARLE WAS DELAYED IN Baltimore an extra day, Professor Hollis was confined to his hotel room by a railroad-induced "megrim" headache. And Selena therefore, much to her surprise, found herself accompanying Pryce on a personal errand.

Judiciary Square occupied two city blocks north of the intersection of Pennsylvania and Constitution Avenues. Most of the buildings surrounding the beaten-down dirt square were, as the name implied, court buildings of one kind or another. But here, too, in a dingy brick annex to the Municipal Courthouse on Fifth Street, the United States War Department kept the bulk of its archives, mingled promiscuously with those of the court. And here for the greater part of her third day in Washington City, Selena and Pryce sat sweltering in a dusty anteroom while an assistant archivist searched his back-room files for information concerning Charles Babbage's great-uncle Richard.

"He came to America in '32," Pryce had told the archivist as he handed over a polite letter of request signed by President Van Buren's clerk.

"In the second administration of Andrew Jackson," the

archivist said. He peered over half-moon spectacles at Selena. "Hero of the Battle of New Orleans. He hated the English."

"Mr. Babbage's great-uncle also despised the English," said Pryce briskly. "That's why he came to America in the first place. This will save you considerable time."

He placed an envelope on the archivist's desk which Selena guessed must contain the somewhat celebrated and scandalous report of a private inquiry agent hired many months ago in London.

This report was far from confidential. The story of Richard Babbage was widely known in England: Charles Babbage, indifferent to family sensibilities, had actually allowed numerous friends and associates to read it. Selena had heard all about it herself over a cozy tea with Mrs. Somerville one afternoon last winter.

For his great-uncle Richard had been, from earliest youth, a very public and extremely determined Utopian. At Cambridge (the Babbage family university) Richard had imbibed the radical doctrines of Pantisocracy, the same universal scheme for social revolution that had so intoxicated the poets Coleridge and Southey. After Cambridge he had travelled extensively and financed a number of social experiments in communal living. When his third Pantisocratic commune had fallen apart, on the twin shoals of free love and women's rights, Richard Babbage had left England in disgust and travelled to Germany, which he soon found radical but uncongenial. (His Pantisocratic code did not, somehow, prevent his investing a certain sum of money in silver mines and porcelain patents and transforming a large fortune into an enormous one.)

From Germany he had gone to America. According to the inquiry agent's report, after renouncing the Old World and its stifling conventions, Richard Babbage had disembarked from the clipper ship *Hamburg* in New York City on May 24, 1832, and begun a long and permanent drift to the west. A tax report in 1833 showed him living in an ill-fated Utopian community in Ohio, said to have been founded by the notorious free-thinker Frances Wright. A year later he was in a

Quaker village in either Indiana or Kentucky. He was thought to have spent time with Sam Houston, now the President of the Republic of Texas, during that eccentric gentleman's self-declared exile among the Pawnee tribes on the western prairie. Was believed to have been in ill health for several years. Was known (by a newspaper account) to have died of a fever in St. Louis in 1837, but as a result of an untimely flood that destroyed a portion of that city's records, no official death certificate had ever been found.

"And that, of course," said Pryce, leaning forward in his chair at the end of this summary, "is the reason the Court of Chancery has never officially declared Richard Babbage dead and distributed his estate."

"Need the money, eh?" said the archivist. "Pretty damned expensive to go to Santa Fe and back." Though he held the report spread open on his desk, he continued to leer at Selena over his glasses. "You the scientific girl?"

Selena made her face stony, freezing her features in a special way learned from long experience in dealing with boorish and intolerant scientists. Men everywhere, as her father had warned her, would naturally assume that an unmarried young woman embarking on so daring an expedition was "loose" or "gay." But the coarseness of American men amazed her.

"Very," said Pryce, "damned expensive."

"Wouldn't let you go if you was my daughter."

"If you provoke her," Pryce said before Selena could respond, "she will quote Shakespeare to you without mercy. It is very damned expensive to go to Santa Fe, and it is also an open secret in England that Mr. Charles Babbage is sorely in need of money. But without official proof of his uncle's death—and a qualified witness as to the *date* of death—nothing, I fear, goes forward."

"Advertise?"

"The family have placed advertisements in all the important newspapers, yes. Our inquiry agent believed the United States Army might have collected information about foreign nationals on the frontier, especially those consorting and trading with

Indians. A remote chance, I know." He sat back in his chair and the light from the window brought out the spider's web of his wrinkles and a grim set of his jaw Selena had not observed before. "But Mr. Van Buren, as you see..."

The archivist rubbed his chin and reluctantly pulled his attention from Selena back to the task at hand. With an unexpected efficiency he began to open and shut cabinet drawers and extract folders. Frowning and snapping his fingers in front of his vest like a bandmaster without a band, he disappeared behind a high wire cage that evidently led to the rear of the building.

Pryce unfolded his copy of the latest *Niles' Register*. Selena opened her copy of Professor Hollis's book.

Just before noon the archivist returned with a discouraging shake of his head and the promise that, since the President was interested, he would continue to sift the records when he got an opportunity. On the other hand, Jefferson Army Barracks outside St. Louis used to keep a roster of foreign travellers. They might have written down something about the death of an eccentric rich Englishman.

"And from what I read in the papers," the archivist said, "you and your scientific girl go straight through St. Louis on your way to the desert. You could always stop and ask."

"The eclipse," said Pryce, taking back the envelope with a curt nod, "comes first."

LATE THAT NIGHT, AS SHE RUMMAGED THROUGH THE TRUNKS IN her hotel room, Selena came across a folded sheet of paper tucked behind a little leather case of telescope lenses.

She sat back on her heels, in a pose *de gamine* that would have had the comte pulling at his hair, and smoothed the paper across her knees.

Sweet Girl,
    Not sure when you will find this. I will be
thinking day and night about you and wishing I

could be there to help. Here are four lines of verse
I copied from a book.

Some are Born to Sweet Delight,
Some are Born to Sweet Delight.
When we see not Thro' the Eye,
God Appears, and God is Light.
You are my best girl.
Yr mother says Godspeed.
Father.

At the bottom of the note was a drawing of a tiny man in a
sea captain's hat peering through a telescope from France at a
line of covered wagons on the Santa Fe Trail.

Selena carried the sheet of paper to the window and read it
over three times. She memorized the lines of verse. Then with
the cool scientific objectivity of somebody's best girl, she
swallowed hard, twice; wiped both eyes, once; and gave a
crooked grin to her own reflection. She had already started to
refold the paper and place it beside her bed when the uneasy
thought brushed across her mind, as a candle brushes across
a dark doorway, that it would be no bad thing if somebody
like her father, and not a man with his mind on heirs and
death, were in charge of the Expedition.

CHAPTER EIGHT

Fishes in the Desert

O N THURSDAY, JUNE 13, THE DAY BEFORE THEY WERE TO
depart from Washington City, Senator Benton, the unofficial patron of all things having to do with the West, invited
the Expedition members to his house on C Street for a
farewell fete.

"Though I tender my excuses for Bennit Cushing," grumbled Pryce when they had all arrived in Benton's parlor,
where the evening's buffet had been "spread." "He's sent me
a message that he *may* join us here tonight. More likely,
he says he'll meet us in Wheeling, Virginia. The unpredictable
artistic temperament, I gather."

"End of the National Road, that's Wheeling. Smack on the
Ohio. You'll be catching your steamboat there. Magnificent
port." Benton made a host's rapid frowning survey of the
room—perhaps twenty guests in all, a butler, two Negro
maids, his wife and very pretty daughter Jessie. The ubiquitous Lieutenant Frémont was passing trays of Missouri ham
and peppered sausage. The Senator drained his glass of sherry
and gripped his big belly with both hands like a man, Selena
thought, picking up a wheelbarrow.

"To change the subject somewhat, Mr. Pryce," he said. "I
don't pretend to understand the higher mathematics. But I do

seem to remember that once you're out on the Santa Fe Trail, you have to recalculate some of your numbers."

"At the end of the Cimarron Cutoff," Pryce agreed. "About ten days before the celestial event. In the absence of maps and observatories, we plan to stop, as you say, 'smack' on the Cimarron River. There we'll recompute the path of the eclipse, to make sure we're going to be precisely in the center."

"And you mean to employ something you quite humor-ously call the Infant Engine?"

"It's a specially constructed miniature version of the great Difference Engine itself, yes. Mr. Babbage designed it for us. Miniature and portable and 'programmed,' in his odd phrase, to perform only this one sequence of calculations."

"The moon's umbra can be as much as a hundred and fifty miles wide," Selena volunteered, "but if we're just at the edge of it, the eclipse will only be partial, not total, and my cam-eras won't have enough time to work."

"We need to be where the light, so to speak, is darkest." One of Mrs. Benton's spiced sausages disappeared between Pryce's excellent white teeth.

"Should the miniature machine not work, of course," said Professor Hollis, using a finger to push his rimless spectacles back along his nose, "we will still have my own celebrated formula for calculating the eclipse path. *It* requires only pen-cil, paper"—he paused, smiled or grimaced at Selena, made his stiff little bow—"and brain."

Benton squinted down from his formidable senatorial height and nodded as if he had recognized a certain entomo-logical species. "Well, I would very much like to *see* this In-fant Engine before you go."

"Alas," said Pryce, "it's already sealed and packed away in ten pounds of Egyptian cotton. Mr. Babbage warned us not to unpack it until we're ready to use it, for fear of damaging its mechanism. The real Difference Engine in London whirs and clicks and makes a remarkable spectacle, as Miss Cott can tell you. Babbage is even experimenting with having it print its results instantaneously on pasteboard cards. But I fear you would be disappointed with our model. The Infant Engine is quite small and undramatic. Built mostly of brass. Still, it can calculate with amazing rapidity the logarithm tables our observation needs."

Senator Benton inclined his head in acknowledgment of the New Age. "The Indians will worship it as a brass Baal," he said, "and the lovely Miss Cott as its priestess."

At ten o'clock, as hired carriages began to arrive to take them back to the Willard, and all the guests crowded outside onto the Senator's wisteria-draped veranda, Selena looked about to make her courtesies to Mrs. Benton. Suddenly she found her arm taken and herself pulled firmly aside by her host himself. He had been waiting all night, the Senator explained (not quite releasing her arm), for precisely such an opportunity to "palaver" with her alone.

Selena was not unacquainted with such opportunities. But in Paris the rules for "palavering" between men and women were much clearer. She took one step backward. Senator Benton matched it with one step forward, then, to her relief, paused to draw on his cigar. She looked over her shoulder at the shadowy bustle of guests and carriages, moving about in the faint yellow light of C Street's single gas lamp. Oratorically, Benton lifted his massive chin and cleared his throat.

"My dear Miss Cott." He cleared his throat again with a forensic rumble.

He wished to speak with her like an old friend, he said.

He had grown up himself in the true frontier West, he informed her solemnly. He had fought his Indians. He had travelled his trails. (Like so many men, Selena thought, the Senator confused autobiography with conversation.) As a young man he had gone with a hunting party up the Missouri River two hundred miles, in the very tracks of Lewis and Clark.

This was quite far, he opined, from the elegant Parisian world Selena was acquainted with.

He could understand her desire to go west, on the Trail. It

sounded like a poetic epic, he knew, to hear of caravans of men, horses, and wagons traversing with their merchandise the vast plain which lies between the Mississippi and the exotic city of Santa Fe. The story seemed better suited to the steppes of Asia than to North America. But he was deeply concerned for an innocent young woman like herself out on the trackless deserts, without experience, without a *true protector*. The explorer person Searle was all very well, but Searle was only one man, and Searle had made no secret of the fact that he resented a woman's presence. William Pryce was a Londoner, the most citified kind of creature on earth. And as for that little striped chipmunk in spectacles, Professor Hollis, well... Who would look after her, he wanted to know? Who would be her loyal Vergil?

For a moment she felt the same sensation of icy coldness rise in her throat, just as it had in the President's office—a vision of murderous Indians, desert sand dunes, her own small, solitary figure on an enormous untravelled blazing plain. But the pleasant, familiar clatter of guests and carriages drowned out these secret terrors. "Well, of course, there may be risks," she conceded to Benton. "And certainly there are... personalities. But I've seen Mr. Babbage's Engine at work, you know; I have complete faith in his predictions. Really, I do it for Science."

But the Senator was persistent. He placed a cautionary hand on her wrist. "No, no, don't fall back on rhetoric and adverbs like a Whig. Ask yourself, Miss Cott, do you truly understand the risks? Are you prepared for the harshness of the climate, the unimaginable brutality of the western wilderness? The experience has terrible effects on sensitive persons. I have known of cases—this will astound you—where white men have become demented by the desert landscape and abandoned civilization itself to go and live with savages. That awful man Sam Houston in Texas actually did it for two full years before he finally came to his senses. He took an Indian squaw for a wife, painted his face red and blue, lived in a wigwam, wore a necklace of scalps."

"And stuck a feather in his cap," contributed a voice just below the veranda railing, "and called it macaroni."

Senator Benton whirled and glared into the shadows. "Who is that?"

A third hackney carriage was just then rattling up to the curb, and for a moment or two there was nothing to be heard but the clamorous racket of hooves and wheels and the drivers' shouts. Benton snorted and turned back. "There is also the question, Miss Cott, of the behavior of human nature on such caravans. You mentioned 'personalities.' I have been in the wilderness myself. On such a journey, personalities do not behave rationally. They grow treacherous and hostile. If you will allow the paradox, Miss Cott, in the arid and empty desert, people live like fishes, by devouring each other."

"Sand-dabs, no doubt," drawled the voice. A man's boot and leg swung over the veranda rail, followed in short order by torso, shoulders, face, and hat, although it was impossible to see anything clearly in the shadows except a long foppish red silk ribbon twisted around his neck like a mock cravat. "Walked up from the hotel," the newcomer said, bringing the other leg over the rail with a thump. "Got thoroughly lost, not a good sign for an explorer. Sand-dab is a fish," he said to the Senator, "kind of a joke." He extended a limp hand toward a slack-jawed Selena. "How do you do? I'm Bennit Cushing."

CHAPTER NINE

San Fernandez de Taos, Mexico

Two thousand miles from Washington City, on the western slope of the rocky Sangre de Cristo Mountains, the little town of San Fernandez de Taos, Mexico, was just beginning to sink into late spring twilight.

Most of its streets were empty. Virtually every window around the central plaza was already shuttered, and every gate and door was closed and locked. Even so, and despite the fading light, the lime-washed adobe houses of Taos had a lively dazzling whiteness that would have put Mr. Van Buren's presidential mansion to shame. A few miles to the west the Rio Grande del Norte wound gently southward and opened onto a great level plain, sprinkled here and there as far as the eye could see with cultivated fields. A few miles to the north the first candles and oil lanterns had begun to flicker under the flat mud roofs of the Indian Pueblo of Taos, a dismal and treeless enclosure that had been continuously inhabited, it was said, since the days of the Aztecs.

At almost precisely the same moment that Bennit Cushing extended his limp hand to Selena, Mr. Ceran St. Vrain of Taos glanced up at his pendulum clock and made a note to himself of the time. Seven twenty-four. His general store and bank would ordinarily be closed by now, like every other business, so that St. Vrain, a native Missourian, could sit for half an hour in his walled garden with his handsome Mexican wife and enjoy the last rays of the setting sun. After which he and his spouse would stroll inside for what was always a five-course meal including both fish and meat dishes and wine. Almost every other white man St. Vrain knew in Taos had long ago succumbed to the terrible informality and slovenliness of the Indian natives. But St. Vrain dressed for dinner. He insisted that his Indian servants wear shoes, shirts, and trousers. In the evening his wife wore handsome, feminine garments imported from as far away as New Orleans. He himself shot a game of billiards three times a week after dinner in his private study, where a genuine felt-covered English billiard table sat in regal splendor, carried all the way from Independence, Missouri, last year at an amazing and extravagant freightage.

St. Vrain tugged at his collar and leaned back in his chair and thought it would be hard to find a greater and more disagreeable contrast to himself than the man now sitting on the other side of his desk.

"Sign there, if you please. And there."

His visitor scraped his own chair a little closer to the desk and began laboriously to scratch his signature across the bottom of a printed St. Vrain & Co. receipt. He was an educated man obviously, but the way he gripped the pen and stabbed at the inkwell suggested a Mexican peasant much more than someone who had just withdrawn from his personal and confidential banking account the highly civilized sum of six hundred and fifty dollars, a full year's profit for most farmers or trappers. As a mere formality St. Vrain turned the receipt around and read the signature: Richard Hatcher Babbage.

"Cash and credit same as last year, Mr. Babbage?"

"Fifty dollars in gold coin now, sir. The rest in store credit. Wo-po-ken-ne is going to come by in the morning with a list."

His visitor stood up carefully and adjusted his clothing. Unlike St. Vrain, who was still in his banker's frock coat and wool trousers, Richard Babbage had attired himself in greasy buckskin pants, an old red blanket flung across his shoulder like a serape, and Kiowa moccasins. St. Vrain knew they were Kiowa because they had been crafted by placing the foot in the center of a piece of buckskin, not cowskin as the Pawnees and Comanches used, and bringing all the edges to meet on the top of the foot, where they were laced by *par-flèche* strings. The little fringed appendages on each heel showed they were riding moccasins. Without the appendage, they were widely regarded as the best footwear for walking over the cactus-grown plains east of the Sangre de Cristo.

"You will deduct your usual fee," Babbage said, part old man's grumble, part instruction.

St. Vrain, who had already done so, merely nodded and slid a small leather purse across the desk. The purse promptly vanished under the blanket.

"Would you like me to escort you to the end of the garden, Mr. Babbage?"

Babbage grunted, a sound that St. Vrain found especially offensive and degraded in a white man, and started toward the rear of the store. St. Vrain locked his desk and followed.

No one was in the garden, of course, not even his wife, because that was one of Babbage's several rather bizarre demands—no one in the bank, no one in the garden, all servants sent away until their transaction was completed, Señora St. Vrain to remain upstairs with her windows closed and shuttered. Any banker was accustomed to eccentricity and secrecy, as St. Vrain well knew, but really, Richard Hatcher Babbage's manias bordered on dementia. On the other hand, the account he had been keeping in St. Vrain's vault for the last three years was genuinely impressive, twenty-four thousand dollars in a mixed lot of United States banknotes and English sterling. Not a fortune in itself, but clearly Babbage had more at his disposal, somewhere at home or up in the mountains. Meanwhile the fees he paid for his eccentricity (and perhaps he was not fully aware of all the fees) would serve to buy many New Orleans gowns, many, many cases of wine.

When they reached the reinforced wooden door at the end of the garden, St. Vrain took out his set of keys and bent over the lock. Babbage bent close to watch, and for a moment St. Vrain was acutely conscious of the old man's foul body smell, his Indian smell in fact, and all its mixed odors of old smoke, animal fat, ancient and unwashed wool and leather. St. Vrain turned the key and pushed the door open. Babbage held out one dirty hand, and with a banker's heroism St. Vrain gave a little bow and shook it.

On the other side of the wall, against a full sweeping panorama of the Valle de Taos and the setting sun, St. Vrain watched two Indian braves approach on their ponies. The first helped Babbage climb lengthwise onto his own horse, Kiowa fashion. The second simply stared impassively at St. Vrain until his comrade made a deep guttural sound and then they wheeled about and cantered away toward the mountains.

St. Vrain hesitated a moment before going back in. The three men were now no more than dots and dust, rapidly disappearing. He had probably seen the Indian braves before, though he would be hard-pressed to say for sure—on any given day fifty or sixty Indians and mixed-blood Mexicans passed through his store. As far as St. Vrain was concerned, they were all of a type.

Babbage too, he decided, was of a type. Many was the eastern-born hunter or trapper who decided to spend a year or two living with some out-of-the-way tribe off in the mountains or up in the gorgeous Alpine valleys above the Raton Pass. They usually did it for a season or two, out of some sort of pastoralist-intellectual philosophy or just a plain, uneducated liking for Indian ways. But in St. Vrain's experience these were almost always young men, with time on their hands, and there was almost always a pretty young bright-eyed squaw involved.

What made Richard Babbage different was first his age—in his sixties at least, St. Vrain believed, and not a well or hearty man at all. And second, his fortune. Whatever else you might say about them, the Indians posed no threat to Babbage's money stock. The Kiowas were known for their honesty. Babbage bought them a few hundred dollars' worth of supplies once a year, and that was more than enough to guarantee their friendship and protection. They kept him close, kept his very existence secret because that was what he wanted—"tight as a tick" was the expression St. Vrain remembered from Missouri—so that virtually nobody else in Taos knew about the old gringo hermit who lived with the Indians over in the high country by the Cimarron River. But a few people did.

St. Vrain was a banker and therefore, as he liked to say, he understood thoroughly one half of human nature.

Sooner or later, he knew, somebody would come for the money.

CHAPTER TEN

On the National Road

THE EARLIEST RAILROAD IN AMERICA HAD EXISTED SOLELY
in the imagination of one Oliver Evans of Philadelphia,
who petitioned the Pennsylvania legislature in 1786—three
years before George Washington's first administration—for
the exclusive right to use wagons self-propelled by steam on
the highways of that state. The amused legislators doubted
Evans's sanity but granted him the privilege, as did the law-
makers of neighboring Maryland shortly thereafter, on the
grounds, as one of them chuckled, that such action on their
part could harm nobody.

Some four decades later, when the eastern coast of America
had over three hundred and fifty miles of working railroad
track and annual revenues of half a million dollars, nobody
was chuckling, everybody was scrambling aboard.

The Baltimore & Ohio Railroad had been established,
on paper at least, in 1827. It came into being because the
business leaders of Baltimore decided to respond to the eco-
nomic threat of New York's newly opened Erie Canal by
chartering a freight rail system between their city and the
Ohio River port of Wheeling, Virginia. The initial plan was
to use horse-drawn carriages over parallel wooden tracks—
the usual pattern in both England and America—and the first

thirty-six miles of track were actually laid down for horses. (One innovator built a locomotive powered by a mast and sail, but found that while he could easily go west from Baltimore, the winds rarely blew him back.)

By 1830, however, the Age of Technology had arrived. In Hoboken, New Jersey, an inventor named George Stevens took houseguests around a circular track in his sixteen-foot "steam wagon" at the breathtaking speed of twelve miles an hour. In England, George Stephenson had developed the great engine that would become his famous "Rocket." And in Baltimore a New York engineer named Peter Cooper demonstrated for the B & O his splendidly effective "Tom Thumb" steam locomotive.

There were problems with the Tom Thumb, naturally—exploding boilers were one, cascading ashes and sparks from the smokestack another. On an early trial run, passengers in the open carriages were issued umbrellas to protect themselves from the smoke and ashes; the umbrellas promptly burst into flames because of the sparks. But Cooper persisted, plans were redrawn, a branch was built to Washington, and the Baltimore & Ohio began to take its ultimate shape, though the process of surveying land and laying the cumbersome iron track (not wood) was slow. In 1840, passengers going from Washington City westward would first return to Baltimore on the branch system, then set out on the main line in a six-car train (three times a day) toward Frederick, Maryland; from Frederick the train would proceed northwest to Harper's Ferry, where the tracks temporarily ended. At Harper's Ferry, travellers booked a seat in one of the numerous stagecoach lines headquartered there and then followed the National Road overland to Wheeling. There, steamboats of every size and description were crowded two and three deep at the raucous, muddy docks, waiting to carry them down the Ohio.

This was precisely the route that William Henshaw Pryce had planned for the Expedition. He had worked it out months ago in England, in Charles Babbage's quiet study, with maps and timetables and city directories spread out in comfortable, logical profusion across one of Babbage's library tables.

And Pryce was pleased to see that, for the first few stages at least, the reality of American travel matched more or less the dotted lines on his map and the tables of figures in his notebook.

Thus it happened that early in the morning on Friday, June 14, the day after Senator Benton's fete, as the first rays of dawn began to etch pale golden lines across the eastern sky, the Somerville-Babbage Expedition set out for the Santa Fe Trail.

At five o'clock, servants in Willard livery knocked briskly three times on the hotel door of each Expedition member.

Thirty minutes later, a privately hired coach for the passengers and a luggage wagon for their numerous trunks and boxes rolled noisily up to the Pennsylvania Avenue entrance. A yawning Irish stablehand lifted the last of their personal kits onto the wagon, Pryce gave a sleepy signal, and while respectable Washington City, including untethered pigs and dogs of the street, was just beginning to come awake, the Expedition rattled up Pennsylvania Avenue past the President's Mansion and turned sharply right onto the Baltimore Road.

At Wheaton Mills a punctual descendant of the Tom Thumb locomotive waited patiently on a siding, puffing a fine plume of silver-gray smoke into a silver-gray sky.

At Baltimore Terminus there was a slight delay, no more than an hour, as cords of wood were loaded into the fuel car of their new train, but by noon they were "steaming" (the Great Verb of the nineteenth century, Pryce pointed out to Selena) past the last few straggling houses of the city, into the open country.

As a practical matter Pryce had tried to reserve an entire carriage for the Expedition and its equipment, but this had proved impossible. Their baggage was tied down on the open platform of the rearmost car, Searle and Bennit Cushing scattered to the front of the train, and the others found seats as near the baggage as they could manage.

Pryce settled back on the padded bench, fluffed his red beard, and lit what he announced was called a "stogie," a short black and very foul cigar much favored by drivers of Conestoga wagons. This passenger carriage was larger than the ones on the Washington-Baltimore branch and boasted at one end a squat little Franklin stove for warming and six brass oil lamps on the walls. The sight of the stove seemed to amuse Pryce, and to Selena and Professor Hollis, seatmates opposite him, he began to talk in a low, entertaining voice about the vagaries of American railroad travel.

The rugged terrain and great distances in America, he explained, had resulted in the very un-English lookout towers they would see at many rural stations, wooden poles about fifty feet high, with spars for climbing and a round seat on top where a station agent could perch and look up and down the track for miles, like the crow's nest on a sailing ship. Then there was the horror of American night travel—Pryce had taken the overnight train from New York to Washington City—during which a gentleman could only hang his coat and hat on one of the hooks on the wall, plant his feet on the part of the opposite seat not occupied by the head of a fellow sufferer, and await the morning. A woman, he said with a sympathetic nod to Selena, was strictly limited by American propriety to removing her bonnet and closing her eyes.

Even more peculiar, he told them, the first American locomotives had actually been manufactured without brakes, a manifestation, no doubt, of that remarkable national quality of rushing straight ahead at full speed, without any thought for the future. The earliest American locomotives were evidently brought to a halt at a station by teams of Negro roustabouts who would rush forward, grab the slowing chassis, and dig their heels into the earth, as if they were stopping a bull by the horns. Where horses were still used, in Pennsylvania, the horse was trained to pull the carriages to the top of a hill, then jump aboard as they coasted down. In England, however—

But Pryce's stream of information was irritating to Selena. She let her attention drift to the dense and tangled countryside she could see through the window, and the feeling of vast melancholy which she had experienced her first day returned with a rush. An enormous country, endless, a continent wide, and they were still only on the fringes, the very thinnest edge of the map. She leaned her forehead against the glass. Pryce's voice droned in her ear. From time to time as they rounded a long curve she could see the locomotive in front, a dark cylindrical shape wrapped in a trembling cocoon of smoke. If it reached the chrysalis stage, she wondered idly, what beautiful iron butterfly would emerge?

In the next row of seats the comte, who had decided to go on with her *comme chaperon* as far at least as Cincinnati, sat with closed eyes, chin on his chest, looking very old. Through the trees she caught glimpses of houses, once in a while a barking dog, a farmer in shirtsleeves, more emptiness. Despite every resolution to wring every drop from her adventure, slowly, rocked by the clattering train and lulled by American rhythms, she slept.

In the late afternoon, as they rolled into the village of Harper's Ferry (and saw indeed a crow's nest lookout pole just as Pryce had described), the emptiness of the landscape gave way to a controlled and miniature chaos. On the other side of the brick railroad station, alongside a wooden depot building, stagecoaches and freight wagons were lined up four and five abreast in the road, in a perfect bedlam of stamping hooves, curses, whip cracks, choking dust. Selena and the comte clambered down from their railroad carriage and waited beside the tracks, keeping a wary distance. James Searle watched the unloading of their baggage to the ground and then stood with his legs straddling the precious box with the Thomas Arnold clock. Meanwhile Pryce strolled calmly off in search of their coach. Selena watched him disappear, an elegant, incongruous figure in frock coat and top hat, between a wagon and a team of massive thick-bellied dray horses.

Seventeen different coach and freight lines served the terminus here. Their reservation, she learned when Pryce returned, was on the "June Bug Line," and their brightly painted red and green carriage had two colorful June Bug pennants flying from the top, the name "General Jackson" in gold on the door, and a friendly Negro driver dressed in a blue coat, shiny black June Bug gloves, and short trousers. Equipment and baggage followed in a flatbed wagon. They made their way past the parked coaches of the "Shake Gut Line," the "Good Intent Line," circled the village square, crossed a stone bridge over the Potomac, and with a sudden back-breaking jolt entered the National Road.

Almost at once, in the midst of nothing, in the midst of dark pine forests and vacant fields, they were part of an astonishingly busy, noisy, rolling torrent of traffic, like the Pall Mall in London or the Champs-Élysée, except in the American fashion twice as congested, twice as energetic. Nobody seemed to observe a lane. Selena counted a dozen four-horse passenger coaches shouldering up behind them; there were pack trains of mules and horses trudging along on either side, going in both directions; there were Conestoga wagons rolling and swaying alarmingly, drawn by six or eight horses and covered with hooped white canvas stretched as taut as sails. The National Road itself was almost eighty feet wide, but by law (Pryce shouted in her ear) only the central thirty feet was cleared of tree stumps, and even in the center the "General Jackson's" wheels kept striking half-buried roots and rocks.

It was the first day of the great trip to the eclipse. They crested a hill neck-and-neck with two Conestoga wagons and rattled into the setting sun at six or seven miles an hour.

CHAPTER ELEVEN

The Unpopularity of Bennit Cushing

THEY WERE TWO AND A HALF LONG DAYS IN THE "GENeral Jackson," from Harper's Ferry to Wheeling, a distance of 239 miles. They changed horses every four or five hours and stopped at taverns for meals and brief, uncomfortable snatches of sleep. As they pushed farther along the National Road, the landscape grew greener and more mountainous and the farmhouses and villages shabbier. Hour by hour Selena felt the familiar, comfortable half-European world of the eastern seaboard slipping away. In the last tavern before Wheeling, she found that the curtains in the dining room were simply strips of wallpaper nailed to the top of the window, the ladies' privy chamber a wooden finger pointing toward the woods behind the stable.

At the same time...it was easier to calculate the attractions and repulsions of the planets, Selena thought with a sigh, than the attractions and repulsions of human beings.

It was by no means unheard of, she knew, for a painter to travel with a wealthy patron or an exploring party. Why not an eclipse expedition? Only three years before, the romantic and adventurous Scot, Sir William Drummond Stewart, had commissioned an artist named Alfred Miller to accompany him to a Rocky Mountain "rendezvous" of fur trappers.

Earlier still, in 1833, Prince Maximilian of Wied-Neuwied
had hired Karl Bodmer to go with him up the Missouri and
record what they saw of Indian life, and Bodmer's paintings
had been prominently exhibited in Paris. Famously, in 1831
Count Mornay had taken the great Delacroix with him to
Algiers.

Bennit Cushing, however, was no Delacroix or Bodmer. He
was an American, a young man no more than three or four
years older than Selena. Cushing looked, Professor Hollis had
whispered to her, exactly like one of Mr. Thackeray's malicious caricatures in *Punch* of the Sensitive Modern Artist.
Day and night he wore the same green lounge jacket with velvet lapels and no discernible shape; a white shirt with cuffs
that extended three inches out of his sleeves like lacy snow-
balls and covered his hands to the knuckles. The red silk
mock cravat was a perpetual and annoying affectation. His
hat was low-crowned and flat-brimmed and dirty. His long
dark hair actually curled over his shoulders in the unkempt
and disheveled fashion that made other men growl under
their breaths and that was beginning to be called, on the Continent, "Bohemian."

Nobody, nobody at all could stand him.

Certainly not Selena—

"I don't approve of 'photography,'" Cushing had announced to her as they settled the first day into the hot,
crowded passenger compartment of the "General Jackson."

On the opposite bench, bouncing like a cork with the
bumps of the road, the comte puffed up his cheeks and blew
out air in an affronted moue. *"On vous a demandé?"*

"Why on earth not?" Selena reddened.

"Because I'm an artist." Cushing frowned with distaste at
Professor Hollis, seated directly across from him, knee-to-
knee, and clinging with both hands to the leather passenger
strap. Hollis was already suffering from another of his
megrims, brought on, he claimed, by the smoke and noise of
the train. His hair was plastered to his forehead with perspiration, his clothes were redolent with the strong scent of a

mint-green medicinal lozenge, and Selena was certain that at the next stage he should change places with Searle or Pryce outside next to the driver, for the fresh air. How, of course, he would survive three months on a primitive Conestoga wagon in the desert was another question.

"An *artist*," Cushing repeated with emphasis. "Not a mechanic. I've studied painting six years in Europe, you know. I've talked away my hours in the café with Horace Vernet, I've studied with Greenough and Nathaniel Willis. An artist's brush is an extension of his hand, part of his very self. An artist transforms what he sees into human terms, he chooses the colors, the patterns, he *creates* the picture."

"Rather a bold analogy. It makes you—" She meant to say something crushing like "godlike." But Cushing was deaf and rude and waved her silent.

"You don't see a poet using a *machine*, of course not. A poet employs a pen, ink, paper, nothing more. It's the same thing exactly with an artist. Look at all your trunks of chemicals and plates and apparatus. Look at your complicated and sterile daguerreotype camera—it merely records the cold, inert surface of things, not the *soul*. There's no creation, no artist's hand about it. I find something actually frightening about photographs of human beings, tiny dead unmoving figures trapped in a black-and-white world. Contrary to the usual opinion, Miss Cott, I think a daguerreotype picture is 'deathlike' rather than 'lifelike.'"

The "General Jackson's" front wheels struck a root or a rock or an elephant and they were all jolted left, then right, like puppets on a string. They could hear the driver cursing, the thud of somebody's boot on the roof.

"Dead and unmoving," Bennit Cushing said. "And a photograph of an *eclipse*, of all things, 'darkness visible.' Impossible. Can't be done. Not enough light. But I suppose you regard yourself as the Representative of Your Sex."

Selena made her face too stony to respond.

"*Elle a sa methode,*" muttered the comte. Then in English,

"She has a secret formula for the chemicals, her own invention."

"Ah," said Cushing. "Miss Cott's own secret method." He leaned back and closed his eyes (and the discussion) with maddening condescension. "Well, that's all right then."

The comte was far angrier than she. For the rest of the afternoon, as if determined to distinguish himself from the boorish and unscientific Bennit Cushing, the old man pored over Selena's copy of Mrs. Somerville's great book, *On the Connexion of the Physical Sciences.* "I am fascinated," he informed Selena, pulling his moustache, rubbing his rouged cheeks, ignoring Cushing with Gallic ostentation, "by the eclipse and Mr. Babbage's mechanical engine. *Every* thinking person should be." When they stopped for supper he persuaded the sickly-looking Professor Hollis to bring out one of his brass pocket telescopes, and while the horses and driver were being changed he strolled to a clearing and actually studied the new moon and wrote his observations in a pocket notebook.

Next morning he was still more interested. As dawn crept into the coach and the green Virginia mountains emerged from shadow and mist, he tackled chapter two of Mrs. Somerville. When he had finished he closed the book and turned with a little sniff to Professor Hollis. "What I still don't understand," he said, "having neglected to go to a university, is exactly why there's not an eclipse every month, when the moon goes between us and the sun."

Hollis sighed loudly and fumbled for paper and a pencil. As best he could between bumps and jolts, he drew a series of diagrams to show the moon's orbit and the sun's fixed position. Then he began an abstruse and complicated explanation of orbital "nodes" and the eclipse cycle of eighteen years, eleven days, which had been discovered by the ancient Chaldeans and called a "Saros," and which determined when, though not where, every eclipse took place.

"In fact," said the Professor, folding and creasing the paper sharply three separate times, "it's only by the most unlikely and providential coincidence that solar eclipses happen at all."

The man looked genuinely weary and unwell, Selena thought, and evidently the process of explaining what was so obvious to him, if difficult for the comte, had made him impatient and snappish as well. Poor students at Harvard.

"Well, I don't understand." The comte took the sheet of paper and turned it sideways.

"Oh, for heaven's sake," Hollis said. "The sun you see in the sky is in reality about four hundred times the diameter of the moon."

"Yes?"

"But it's *also* four hundred times farther away from the earth, so the disk of one is almost exactly the same size as the other. But if the moon were just two hundred miles smaller in diameter than it is, its disk wouldn't cover up all of the sun's disk, only a part of it, and a *total* eclipse would never occur, merely a partial." He sighed loudly again and looked out the window at the passing forest. "Someone living on Jupiter or Mars can never witness the kind of eclipse we're going to see three months from now. A total eclipse is a gift from the sky gods to earthlings."

"And yet you can see them every year, *n'est-ce pas?*"

"Good grief! Use your head, man—"

Selena turned the paper right side up. "If you stood on any one spot on earth," she assured the comte, "and simply waited, from that place you would see a total solar eclipse only once every four hundred and ten years."

And that, of course, in a nutshell, was the whole justification for the Expedition. One, sometimes two total solar eclipses were theoretically possible each year. But the shadow of the moon thus produced touched only a tiny portion of the globe, usually only ocean, and for only minutes. To see a total eclipse for certain, you literally had to follow the sun.

By now that sun had taken them nearly two hundred miles westward, far from the eastern seaboard with its paved streets and cities and railroads. On the folding map where their Official Journal tracked their progress, they watched themselves twist and coil through the narrow corkscrew valleys of the Alleghenies, following a path established more than forty years ago, in the great emigration "season" of 1795, when the solitary hunters and trappers in the northwest forests first began to hear the clatter of axes and wheels at their backs. In the early afternoon of the third day, the "General Jackson" climbed a series of wretched switchback curves over the spine of the Blue Ridge Mountains and then dropped, as Pryce drolly commented, like a piano pushed over a cliff, down to the banks of the Ohio River.

Here, at the port of Wheeling, high-pressure steamboats lay clustered together at anchor, dwarfed by the dense green mountains on either side of the river. The Expedition tramped down a swaying gangplank and onto the upper deck of the steamboat *Messenger*. Thirty minutes later, with little pomp and no ceremony, the ropes were cast off, the whistle sounded, and with a huge lurch and dip of the bow they were launched.

The *Messenger,* destined in a year to become the object of harsh satire from Charles Babbage's friend Charles Dickens, was an entirely typical Ohio River steamboat. It carried forty passengers in cabins and berths on the upper deck, a few miserable half-fare persons on the lower. It had no mast, sail, rigging, or discernible prow. Its shape was rectangular; its black roof was flat and covered with feathery damp ashes from the two very tall iron smokestacks in the front. Except for the pair of ceaselessly churning paddle wheels in the stern, Selena thought there was nothing boatlike about it at all.

One long narrow cabin ran the length of the deck, with a kind of private gallery accessible through a pair of glass doors toward the rear. This was the ladies' section, which Pryce was pleased to announce he had reserved entirely for the Expedition and its equipment. An especially desirable situation, he explained with sardonic understatement, because it was a well-known fact that steamboats "generally blew up forward."

Meals were served in the bar of the upper deck, in the same ravenous and democratic pell-mell they had grown accustomed to on the National Road. Otherwise, for the next three days until Cincinnati, they had nothing to do but sit on their private deck and watch the land drift by.

For Selena this was of more than superficial interest. If her father had marched off across the ocean eastward, to France, the other branch of the family, her mother's side, had left Massachusetts after the war in exactly the opposite direction. Some of her older cousins had settled first in a little town called Point Pleasant, Ohio. Later they moved on down the river toward the Illinois prairie. And then, so far as she knew, they had simply vanished one day into the Northwest Territory. In Paris she'd treasured the few Ohio letters that had reached her, with their brief, evocative descriptions of a landscape new to the cousins, utterly foreign to her. Alone in her *chambre* above the damp and gray-cobbled Rue Jacob, she had pictured beautiful snow-white steamboats on a cool, clear, fast-running river, rolling hills and azure sky, a canopy of emerald forest. As she read their letters, she was a counter-immigrant to her own country. Had there been no eclipse or expedition, she sometimes thought, it would have been necessary to invent one.

But now—well, the river was clear, certainly cool. And the landscape they passed—indeed, there were green forests and there were tiny romantic log cabins nestled on rising ground, just as she had imagined, and bright, unfamiliar birds could sometimes be glimpsed among the trees like flying flowers.

But at a closer look, the cabins were too often miserable affairs of logs and mud, broken windows patched with scraps of cloth, filthy blankets; homemade furniture decayed in the open yards, where the ubiquitous pig rooted among broken jars and plates.

Worst of all were the trees—for every stretch of beautiful green forest, they passed an equally long and depressing tract of badly plowed clearing, planted with wheat or stubble corn and pockmarked with burnt and broken tree stumps like the

ones they had seen on the National Road, or whole black-
ened forests, burnt for clearing and then abandoned, so that
skeletal charcoal trunks lay felled in every direction as if by a
wind of flames.

Once, on the second afternoon, the boat came to an un-
scheduled stop in the middle of an uncut forest, and while
Selena and the others watched from the deck, an Irish emi-
grant family waded ashore—two men, two women, four or
five small children. They carried a few chests and canvas bags
of possessions. One of the men hauled a wooden bed frame
on his back and a rocking chair on his arm. Someone from
the steamboat rowed in with a very old woman and helped
her ashore. When the whistle sounded and the *Messenger*
had rolled and bumped back into the current, Selena could
still see the old woman in her bonnet sitting in the chair at the
edge of the water, rocking. Then they rounded a curve in the
river and she was gone.

That same evening, walking on deck after supper, Selena
encountered Bennit Cushing alone, standing with his sketchpad beside the rail and looking out at the passing darkness.

"It must be hard to sketch without any light, Mr. Cushing."
Before she could stop herself she added, " 'Darkness visible,'
I suppose."

If he smiled she couldn't see it. He held up his pad so that
she could make out a quite wicked drawing of James Searle as
an enormous barrel-chested ox with a ring through his nose,
led by Pryce in a top hat. "Old habit," he said, "never go anywhere without my pad. Did I mention that I knew your
brother John in Paris?"

Since they had scarcely spoken of Paris at all, Selena
looked at him in genuine surprise.

"Tall fellow," Cushing said, as if to remind her. "Lean
chin, knock-kneed. When he walks he swags one side ahead
of the other."

"I remember my brother."

"Good teeth, wavy hair," Cushing continued. "Had a carriage, dressed French. He didn't like my art."

"I don't think I ever heard him refer to your art."

"Well, I didn't see him socially, you understand. When I was in Paris I lived in the Marais, on the Rue de Turenne." Cushing named the poor and unfashionable Jewish district, far from the Rue Jacob. "I had no money, of course. We met a few times at a salon for some of my friends, but he didn't understand their work. He's a scientific chap, like you."

I am not a chap, Selena thought. "My brother is quite interested in art," she said stiffly.

"Didn't buy anything," Cushing said, with an air of settling the point. He tore the drawing from his pad and stuffed it in a pocket. "James Searle has no money either, in case you didn't know. He depends entirely on Pryce. Pryce and Babbage promised to finance Searle's expedition back to Africa if he'd go on the Santa Fe Trail first. Otherwise he wouldn't be here at all, certainly not with you along, or me. It was your brother's Paris friend Cooper, by the way, who showed Babbage my work."

"Mr. Cooper the American consul?"

"He writes books too, James Fenimore Cooper. I happened to read one, just by chance, and it was his descriptions of the prairies that made me curious"—Cushing's hand made a gesture toward the shore, where a few lamplit windows could dimly be seen. "And then Babbage, Babbage really has the soul of an artist. Babbage said I should come out here, past where Cooper had been, and paint the landscape. He said there should have been an artist on every great expedition in history, starting with Marco Polo."

He spoke with considerable earnestness, and no condescension. But even as Selena began to think she had misjudged him, he went on, of course, and spoiled the effect.

"I told that to Searle and he laughed."

"I'm sure not."

"You think well of him," Cushing said, pulling his drawing out of his pocket and looking at it again, "because he's rude to you. First step in courtship. You'll be sweet on Searle before you know it."

"Mr. Cushing!"

"Pryce doesn't want me here at all. You must have noticed. He scarcely speaks to me. I'm just a deadweight expense to him, a ticket to buy and a mouth to feed. Same for Searle. Pryce thinks only of money, you know, filthy lucre. He's dead broke, I'm told, but he still has the soul of a merchant."

"My father is a merchant."

"Of course he is," said Cushing.

The next morning they reached the city of Louisville, Kentucky, and paused a few hours while the *Messenger* was resupplied. Then they set out again at noon.

As Pryce was the first to say, the landscape after Louisville was noticeably lower, flatter, stunted in appearance. They saw fewer farmhouses, fewer roads, fewer settlements of any kind. And yet, he added in what Selena thought a very un-merchantlike flight of imagination—and yet if America had been settled the other way around, from west to east, instead of east to west, think of the ironies! They would only now be entering the civilized portions of the country, seeing great cities and railways and churches and mansions. The wan and ragged farmer who leaned on his hoe in a half-plowed Kentucky clearing and stared up dully as they passed would be an industrialist or statesman! New York City would be a village of log cabins!

Travelling west in America, said Professor Hollis, was like climbing into a time machine and going backward.

On the second day out from Louisville, they entered the broad, swampy junction of the Ohio and the Mississippi, guarded by the baleful little port of Cairo, Illinois. Here they paused again to load more wood for fuel, then the *Messenger* steamed out into the yellow Mississippi current, seemed to take a deep, shuddering breath from stem to stern, and headed north toward St. Louis.

CHAPTER TWELVE

Recalled to Life

FROM CAIRO TO ST. LOUIS WAS TWO FULL DAYS BY STEAMBOAT, beating against the current.

It was a transit remarkable partly for the sheer size of the Mississippi—twice as big as the Ohio, sometimes two or even three miles wide; partly for the amazing amount of debris, especially floating timber and underwater trees, through which the *Messenger* had to navigate. Hour after hour one of the crewmen crouched in the front of the boat with his hand on a bell pull and scanned the ripples ahead for danger. And hour after hour, all through the night, the bell would peal, every five minutes, and the great boilers of the engine would snort and shriek, the paddle wheels would rattle to a halt, or spin rapidly in reverse. Then a long, breathless pause, a tremendous thump against the hull. And then the wheels would turn again.

Inside the cabin there was now a growing air of excitement. The river itself was muddy and monotonous, the land on either side as flat and desolate as before; but the horizon, Selena thought, had somehow changed, it had stretched and expanded, the sky around it had become taller, paler, huge and taut and concave like a filled blue sail. Bennit Cushing drew a single black line across the bottom of a blank sheet, then a caption: "The West."

St. Louis was a town of not quite sixteen thousand people, about half the size of Washington City. It possessed three English-language newspapers and two more in German. From its original French settlers it had inherited an air of European pretension. It had a college, three bookstores, and an opera house designed by the nephew of the explorer George Rogers Clark. It had boasted a jewelry store since 1819. A large rifle factory supplied the needs of the nonoperatic, and conveniently next door was said to be the only coffin manufacturer in Missouri.

But from the moment they stepped ashore it was clear to Selena—

"*Regardez!*" said the comte.

On the other side of the wharf, facing the steamboat, arms straight down at their sides, stood three rawboned, square-built men, the first Indians she had ever seen. Their complexion was dark red. They were dressed only in leather breechcloths. Their hair was long and black. They wore cloth bands around their temples, and a feather in each band. When Selena reached the bottom of the gangplank, the nearest of them turned his head slightly to stare at her, and she could see two small stripes of yellow paint under his cheeks and beads of perspiration on the hard muscles of his bare chest.

Between Front Street and the National Hotel at Third and Market she counted a dozen more Indians, some white fur trappers in greasy buckskin and moccasins, three women of the town, two priests in black, five nuns, some soldiers in uniform. She saw Creole women dressed like French peasants in white caps and crimson petticoats, black slaves in striped overalls. Almost lost in the pageant of color were the farmers and businessmen going in and out of the shops, wearing the usual drab American imitation of English town fashion.

While the men registered at the hotel, Selena walked to the town center. Here, the old stucco buildings were unmistakably European in their architecture, and she felt a piercing pang of nostalgia. There was a tiny café tucked into a shady corner next to the hotel. In a narrow alley of crazy tenements, a woman called to somebody in musical French. From a set of shuttered windows came the click of billiard balls, from another the jingle of a spinet.

Then she turned the corner and saw two young Indian boys, completely naked except for red bandannas around their heads. They were squatting on the corner of the sidewalk and picking carefully through each other's hair for vermin. One looked up at her, grinned, and popped something small and black into his mouth, and visions of home instantly vanished.

At dinner that evening Pryce seemed unusually thoughtful and abstracted. As the waiters (more black slaves) were clearing away the last of the dishes, he tapped his cigar ash in a coffee saucer and half turned in his chair toward her.

"An interesting city," he said.

"I like it very much."

"But far from the world."

"Yes."

"We are, it seems, a source of considerable excitement. All the newspapers are coming tomorrow to write about our heliograph demonstration."

"Mr. Searle reminds me that I'm to behave myself this time, unlike the demonstration in Washington City."

By now the other members of the Expedition were listening curiously.

"A somewhat theatrical moment, yes," Pryce acknowledged.

"You and Mr. Searle may have the stage to yourselves."

Pryce dismissed her sarcasm with a smoke ring. "Anywhere else in America, you know, in New York or Boston or Washington City—and certainly in London and Paris—a person can simply walk into a daguerreotype studio, right off the street, and have his portrait taken, for a grateful posterity."

"They sell daguerreotype prints of steamboats in the hotel," said Professor Hollis.

Pryce turned his head slowly toward him, then back to

Selena. "But it so happens—I've made enquiries—St. Louis is too remote from the rest of the country and commerce is so backward, there's no such studio here. As far as I can tell, no one in St. Louis has ever seen someone 'take' a daguerreo-type."

"Ah," Selena said, thinking that William Henshaw Pryce never seemed to "take" the straight and direct way about anything.

"It would create quite an additional sensation in the press," he said, "to see it actually happen, on the spot, so to speak."

"It would bore them to tears," declared Bennit Cushing.

Hollis inserted another of his mint-green medicinal lozenges in his mouth. "The press would be interested, I as-sume, in the comments of a Harvard Professor."

"The press would find them," Pryce said with a straight face, "irresistible. In any case, along with the heliograph demonstration, I propose that we also show the public how our daguerreotype camera works. Which demonstration could be arranged with ease by our Miss Cott."

How could she refuse? The Expedition was to remain three full days in St. Louis. The men were all going tomorrow morning to the big Hawken rifle factory on Laurel Street to purchase rifles and sidearms. Pryce wished to make one last effort to locate the death certificate of the vanished Richard Babbage. Her photographic equipment was ready to hand in their trunks; she would have plenty of time to prepare. And the eclipse, after all, was still more than two months away.

"Miss Cott has no academic standing," objected Hollis, and pushed his rimless spectacles higher on his nose. "None at all. I should be in charge of any public demonstration."

James Searle normally kept himself aloof from the vain lit-tle Hollis—and from everyone else, for that matter. Among the Expedition's personalities, he generally played the role of taciturn Brawn to Hollis's irritable Brain, total opposites. But the idea of a woman in their numbers was clearly a mighty irritant, strong enough to make him shift allegiances. He nodded almost cordially at the scowling astronomer. "We could always call her the Babbage Female Professor"—but his wit deserted his brawn—"of . . . of whatever."

"Eloquence," drawled Bennit Cushing.

IT IS NOT WIDELY UNDERSTOOD TODAY THAT THE INVENTION OF photography came about only because of the discovery of the element iodine. That element was first isolated in Paris in 1811, by the chemist Bernard Courtois. Almost at once other scientists remarked on what would now be called the "halogen" properties of the fifty-fifth element. Solutions of iodine placed on silver-coated glass or metal proved to be strongly light-sensitive: they captured the impression of objects held between the iodine coat and direct sunlight. This phenomenon of light sensitivity had been studied a full generation earlier in England, but through a series of chemical misadventures the "pictures" produced by the ceramicist Thomas Wedgwood and others could unfortunately be viewed only in darkness or by candlelight, and they had the further, quite spectacular disadvantage of vanishing completely within a few hours.

The first *permanent* photographs in the world had been taken in Gras, France, in 1826, fifteen years after the discovery of iodine, by a retired army officer named Joseph-Nicéphone Niepce—a "heliograph" of the view from his workroom. Exposure time was a full eight hours. A few months earlier a Parisian theatrical scene painter named Louis Daguerre had suddenly and inexplicably become obsessed with the same idea of forming lasting images by the action of sunlight. Daguerre began to devote his time, his fortune, and his considerable talents of showmanship to a partnership with Niepce, who was at heart a mild and retiring hobbyist and easily overshadowed by his flamboyant associate.

By now, Selena explained the next afternoon to the very crowded public drawing room of the National Hotel, by now, June, 1840, such was the speed of scientific progress, you actually had your choice of two quite different methods of taking a photograph. Daguerre's method, established and disseminated since the middle 1830s, worked by the use of sunlight on silver iodized copper plates, each one about seven inches long and five inches wide. These plates were coated beforehand, exposed in a camera, and then mercury vapor was applied to bring out the latent images. The images were fixed on the plate by washing the plate with a solution of hyposulfite of soda—"hypo"—which left the bare silver to form the dark parts of the picture. Exposure time had been greatly improved, of course, and varied now from four to five minutes to (at worst) several hours, depending on the light.

The other method, invented in England by William Henry Fox-Talbot, used sheets of paper instead of copper or some other metal to receive the image, which was "negative," not "positive." The "calotype," as Fox-Talbot called it, could be reproduced over and over, like a newspaper, but it was far less clear and detailed than a good daguerreotype.

"And therefore," Selena said, concluding her long presentation and sounding to her own ears much more like Professor Hollis than she liked, "this lack of detail makes the Fox-Talbot method not nearly so useful for scientific purposes. Now, if our volunteer subject will sit quite straight in the chair, I'll adjust the clamp."

The very stout, very mistrustful wife of the Mayor of St. Louis, Mrs. John F. Darby, folded her hands stiffly across her lap, lifted her chin as instructed, and closed her eyes. The comte de Broglie, muttering to himself in French, advanced and fastened a velvet-lined C-shaped metal clamp to the sides of her neck and the back of the chair. The clamp was necessary, Selena explained with an apologetic shrug, because during an eight-to-twelve-minute exposure most subjects, however patient, eventually began to move and fidget, and so, alas, they must be held in place in the posing chair like a prisoner in the stocks.

The comte wrinkled his brow in concentration and tugged at Mrs. Darby's collar.

"Perfect," Selena said. *"Très belle."* Mrs. Darby screwed

her lips tight, a smile. "*Maintenant,*" Selena murmured to the comte, "*le poudre.*"

Powder was rather too grand a term, in fact. The white substance that the comte now revealed in a little Limoges porcelain casket was in reality ordinary wheat flour, hurriedly purchased from a nearby shop after Selena had caught her first glimpse of Mrs. Darby's dark Creole complexion. It was standard practice to whiten the subject's face and create a contrast with the darkness of the background and, in this instance, the darkness of the clothes as well. (Itinerant Daguerreotypists in the South, knowing the French technique imperfectly, often produced photographs of slave-owners with completely black faces.)

The comte approached the Mayor's wife again, on the tips of his toes, powder brush extended delicately in front of him. Mrs. Darby turned her face ponderously in his direction like a dark moon.

"Meanwhile," and Selena gestured impatiently toward Professor Hollis, who stood beside the open window with a large square sheet of blue-tinted glass in his hands. His lips were pursed in disapproval. Nonetheless, at Selena's signal he attached the sheet of glass to the window sash and secured it in place with a set of elastic tapes. "This serves as a filter against the strong rays," Selena told the room, "of your western sun."

There was a murmur of pride for the strength of the western sun. Selena wiped her brow with the back of her hand—it *was* quite hot; sixty or more people had already crowded into the public parlor; more could be seen peering around doors and curtains, even from the street through the blue sheet of glass, until Professor Hollis waved his hands and shooed them away. When Daguerre had first revealed his invention, all Paris had been seized with "daguerreotypomania"—a famous cartoon in December 1839 had shown a mad throng pouring across the city in search of daguerreotypes for Christmas gifts. In Vienna the "Daguerre-Waltzer" was the dance rage. Last November, when the first daguerreotype was taken in the Plaza de la Constitucion in Barcelona, the camera operator had been escorted to his place by marching bands and soldiers.

"I use," Selena told her audience, "a Daguerre-Giroux portable camera. This is the very same instrument that will photograph the eclipse!"

She glanced at Mrs. Darby, her fat face now a ghostly white, suspicious eyes unblinking. The comte took one step backward and clicked his heels. Selena inserted a newly silver iodized plate in the camera box and tapped the button on her repeater watch. The great difficulty of a photography demonstration was that absolutely nothing happened, there was nothing whatsoever to do but stare (like the camera) for the next eight minutes at the plump, unmoving, deathly still form of Mrs. Darby.

In the central courtyard of the hotel, where the male guests gathered at a pump each morning to shave and wash, James Searle had earlier set up the helio-box and a telescope. Now some of the audience in the parlor drifted back outside to the telescope for a second look. Inside, others pushed even closer to peer openmouthed at Mrs. Darby or the camera. Some bent and studied the display daguerreotype of Selena's parents, mounted on a stand by the door. A fly buzzed in the silence. In the oppressive heat of the room, with its blue-tinted air and low, close ceiling, the smell of too much flesh and hair grew thicker by the moment. Mrs. Darby sat on and on, rigid as a corpse.

"Three minutes," somebody said, and the room gave a collective sigh. A few more spectators backed out of the door and headed for the telescope.

Selena tried to pass the time by answering questions in a low voice. But the questions were repetitious, and her mind drifted. She thought of the chemical formula for mercury vapor. She pictured the correct angle for the "development" cabinet, rehearsed how long to bathe the copper plate in distilled water. But all this was automatic, too. She had been taking daguerreotypes since 1838. She had an instinctive confidence in her arrangements, her knowledge. What she did not have confidence in— The minute hand of the repeater watch touched "seven" with a loud tick, interrupting her train of thought. Her eyes lifted to the window and she saw her own features reflected in the unearthly blue sheet of glass, and above her head a luminous green ball of fire, framed between strange buildings in a strange land. She thought of the sun and the moon rushing toward each other at ten thousand miles an hour, like demented lovers. How in the world could Charles Babbage's machine really know when and where they would meet? What in the world had she done?

She took a breath and her mind skipped a beat.

"Eight!" exclaimed the comte and clapped his hands under Mrs. Darby's nose. "Recalled to life!"

CHAPTER THIRTEEN

Ready to Begin

As Selena withdrew the copper plate from the camera, every eye followed her. In an atmosphere of strained silence she transferred the plate to a small wooden box on a table. Then while the comte officiously verified her measurement with an architect's drawing triangle, she tilted the box to an angle of 45 degrees and propped it on a wire rack.

With a mouselike rustling of skirts and sleeves, the crowd pushed closer, to the very edge of the table. The top half of the box was wooden, but the bottom half was made of copper and contained one ounce of liquid mercury. It had a glass thermometer on one corner. A copper panel riddled with pinholes fit like a lid between the top and bottom halves. To the low murmur of voices, Selena now lit a spirit lamp underneath the metal bottom. Within moments, mercury vapor rose toward the pinholes and the air around the table took on a sweet burning scent.

"When the thermometer shows 60 degrees centigrade," she said, "I'll put out the little spirit lamp. But it still takes almost fifteen minutes for the mercury vapor to condense on the glass plate and form the image. If you like, you can come up one at a time and look through the eyehole in the box." She smiled at four dozen frowning and impatient faces and felt like Mother Hubbard, who had so many children she didn't know what to do. "But I warn you, there isn't much to see."

She stepped aside. The comte stood rigid like a gendarme with his watch in the palm of his hand. Near the window, the forgotten Mrs. Darby slumped in her posing chair, comforted by her husband and fanning herself after her ordeal.

Precisely at the stroke of fifteen minutes, Selena pulled out the glass plate. Then, shielding it from the view of the hushed crowd around the table, she dipped a cloth in a basin and washed away the silver iodide on the plate with "hypo."

"A final rinse," she announced, and the comte handed her a second basin of distilled water, prepared earlier that day in the hotel kitchen. With her back still to the room, she dried the plate over the spirit lamp's flame. Then she slipped it under a glass cover to prevent scratching, turned dramatically around, and with a little curtsey presented her completely developed photographic portrait to Mrs. Darby, who promptly burst into tears.

It had been an absolutely standard and flawless daguerreotype session, and at supper that evening, in an alcove by the lobby that Pryce had somehow turned into a private dining room, Professor Hollis quite accurately put his finger on the problem.

"It took you eight minutes, at two o'clock in the afternoon, with a sunny sky, to expose the copper plate."

"The blue glass by the window," said the comte, who had passed on in expertise from astronomy to photography, "actually softened *la lumière*." Selena nodded.

"But," objected Hollis, "during an eclipse you'll have no sunny sky, no sun at all—"

"Rather the point of an eclipse," murmured Bennit Cushing.

"And the maximum length of time this eclipse can last—if Babbage's machine is correct—is six minutes, twenty seconds."

There was a long silence. Not six minutes and twenty seconds, Selena guessed, but long enough. The comte rubbed his moustache pensively. James Searle put his elbows on the table and frowned. Only Pryce smiled.

"*Ars longa,*" he said, quietly sardonic, "*memoria breva.*"

"Well, I do remember what the comte said," Hollis protested, "at Senator Benton's dinner or somewhere, about her new method of photography. I just hadn't worked through the actual complications then."

"It's not a method really," Selena said, conscious now that they were all staring at her and James Searle was still frowning. "In Paris people have been trying for many months to shorten exposure times by using different strength lenses or making the camera aperture bigger. What I do instead is add a special *accelerator* formula to the original silver coating on the plate. It takes a little longer to prepare, but it makes the chemical reaction happen at least three times faster."

"It wouldn't, by any chance," said Hollis, "be chlorine?" He thumbed another of his odoriferous mint lozenges into his mouth.

Selena permitted herself a small, tight smile. "Chlorine is a gas," she said. Hollis's face froze. "If I could use it the reaction might be even faster. But obviously it's hard to apply a gas to an open plate, and I would guess it's impossible to carry a supply of gas with us on the Santa Fe Trail."

"Is it bromine?"

Selena shook her head.

Hollis suddenly slapped the table with his fist. "Well, what the *devil* is it—and how do we even know it works?"

"It's my own private discovery," Selena said calmly, "and it's not for publication yet, and we know it works because I've used it dozens of times at my home in Paris. Mr. Babbage has seen the results. I can reduce the exposure time to twenty seconds in warm weather, and about a minute when it's cold."

A thoroughly gratifying moment, she decided, flushing with pride despite herself. She sat square-shouldered and composed, just as Mrs. Somerville would have done, and answered their skeptical male questions: yes, there were four different cameras in the trunks, Mr. Searle would remember listing them. Yes, she intended to install them in a row and photograph the eclipse, not merely at totality, but in a sequence, from first shadow to last. By the time the fourth camera plate was exposed, she would have inserted a new plate in the first camera and be ready to start again, and so on, one after the other, down the line. She was quite certain that the conditions of western heat and dust would not affect her formula. And indeed, the exposure today had required eight minutes only because, as Bennit Cushing (surprisingly) was the first to see, she hadn't wanted to waste her precious chemicals on Mrs. Darby.

"Though of ample charm she is," said Pryce with his usual dry mockery, "to chasten and subdue. Before we go, I have a second little matter to mention." James Searle, who had started to rise from the table, now sat slowly down again. "I've had no very good luck, as you might have guessed, in locating records concerning Mr. Babbage's deceased great-uncle. I went all the way to the Jefferson Army Barracks outside the city today, and of course no one could help. But I *was* successful in finding a guide."

"For the Santa Fe Trail," Professor Hollis said. For even with James Searle's extensive experience in Africa, from the first Pryce had made it known that he planned to enlist someone "local," as he put it, to guide them across the great prairie that led in turn to the Great Southwestern Desert.

"For the Santa Fe Trail," Pryce agreed. "His name is Webb Pattie. He's been a guide for the army; he's travelled six times to Santa Fe with trading caravans. Senator Benton recommended him. You may find him a trifle eccentric. I did not, but I am English, after all. No doubt I should have consulted you." He shrugged. "I found him satisfactory."

"Is he here?" Hollis levered himself a few inches higher in his chair as if to scan the lobby.

"He meets us in Independence, our jumping-off place. I hired him this morning, and he's already gone ahead to buy horses and wagons. As for us, we can now leave tomorrow, a day early, by steamboat up the Missouri."

It was not so much that she felt herself too abruptly shoved from the center of attention—Selena assured herself that she had been brooding about the matter for a week, every time she watched Pryce ostentatiously go into his cabin or room to wind up the Thomas Arnold clock. "And at Independence," she said, "if your intention still holds, Mr. Searle and I will become the joint keepers of the clock." She smiled sweetly at Searle.

Pryce looked at her, amused, and fluffed his raffish red beard. "*Memoria longa.*"

James Searle came peevishly to his feet. "I disapprove of women on an exploring expedition, I've said so many times. I certainly don't plan to share the responsibility of the clock with a French girl." He wore a loose-fitting tan cotton jacket today that showed his broad shoulders and chest to advantage. His face was tan, his big jaw strong in profile. In his holster was a heavy new Colt "Naval" pistol, created originally for the Republic of Texas Navy, purchased only that morning on Laurel Street. Around his collar he wore a leather lanyard with a red and white beaded Indian pouch at the end for his compass. He had never looked more competent and formidable, and yet somehow all Selena could think of was Bennit Cushing's cartoon of an ox with a ring in its nose.

"Then I presume," said Pryce, still sardonic and amused, "we're just about ready to begin."

BUT AS IT HAPPENED, NEXT MORNING—A DRIZZLY, UNPROPITIOUS day—when they arrived at the docks they learned that their steamboat had suffered an exploded boiler in the night, and the whole Expedition, packed and anxious to depart, was therefore obliged to return to the hotel until sent for.

Selena, truth be told, welcomed the respite from her companions. Impulsively she dropped her key at the desk and walked straight out again, alone. Despite the rain she strolled for more than an hour through the nearby French quarter, stopping twice for *une tasse de café,* relishing after so long a break the sounds of what was, after all, practically her native tongue. She treated herself to a simple noon meal of *salade composé.* Afterward, as if she were at a table in the Palais

Royal, she sipped a glass of wine and contemplated the unde-
niable truth that the French side of her character was thoroughly weak and sensual, even (*pace* Bennit Cushing)
romantic. It was the saving severity of her Anglo-Saxon side,
she thought wryly, that would soon drive her from her check-
ered tablecloths and green salad and wine—a cool, ambitious, logical machine—fearlessly out into the Great and
Trackless Southwestern Desert. She looked up at the gray sun
in the gray sky, made a round tart face like an apple, her
French face, and paid the bill.

At the hotel she found an impatient note from Pryce in-
forming her that the boiler was repaired, it had been repaired
since noon, and the others were already on board ("my dear
quite-at-your-leisure Miss Cott") *waiting.*

With a little cry of dismay Selena flew up two flights of
stairs, flung open the door to her room—and stopped at the
threshold and sniffed. Then, ignoring the ticking clock by the
window, she stepped forward and stared at the bedside table
where she had left her musette bag.

The bag was open. Her papers and books and letters were
spilled out onto the table, the bed, the floor, as if someone
had been hastily searching through them. At the foot of the
bed her portmanteau of personal effects had been pried open.
A notebook of equations was bent at the spine. Her ship captain's sextant had been tossed or kicked somehow onto the
carpet. Warily, she knelt and opened the side compartment in
her telescope case. The folded sheet of paper with her accelerator formula was still in place. She got to her feet with a half-
smile that was neither French nor Anglo-Saxon, she thought,
but grimly American, and reassured herself that the unmistakable scent in the room was of green medicinal headache
lozenge.

CHAPTER FOURTEEN

The Dancing Girls

*T*HERE," WHISPERED HOARSELY THE YOUNG WOMAN BE-
neath him, and though the light in the room was dim and
her pushed-up clothing dark, Charles Babbage understood
precisely—"there, *there*."

Babbage somehow managed to turn his head and glance at
the clock on his shelf, an ingenious device, purchased last
year at Turin, which showed not only the time, but the day,
the month, and the year as well: 8:41, Saturday, June 28,
1840.

"Faster, please, faster, *please*." The person beneath him,
Lady Ada Augusta Byron Lovelace, the twenty-five-year-old
daughter of the poet, began to arch her back and blink her
eyes at an astonishing rate, and Babbage, moving indeed
faster and faster as instructed, nonetheless thought for perhaps the hundredth time that it really was impossible to see in
her face any feature at all that suggested Lord Byron.

"My guests are arriving," he said, whispering himself, and
in fact he could just hear above the rhythm of her petticoat
and the springs of the couch the preliminary sounds of carriages outside in the street. "Hurry."

"You first," decreed Lady Lovelace, now moving so rapidly that Babbage felt himself to be drowning in a sea of

crinoline. He had, in fact, already finished his part two minutes ago by the Turin clock, but Lady Lovelace was so ardent,
so fleshly—his fingers gripped the rosebud nipple in the center of her plump right breast while his mind searched for the
word—so *pneumatic*...

"Oh," said Lady Lovelace. Her hips suddenly slowed. Her
face took on a new and solemn expression, as if she were
solving a particularly difficult mathematical problem. Her
very red tongue slipped out between her lips. She grew abstracted, frowning. Then her buttocks rose, her face was
frozen for an instant, not in thought, the answer arrived, and
her eyes opened very wide indeed. *"There."*

Some twenty minutes later, when she joined him on the
balcony with some of his guests, Babbage was both gratified
and annoyed to see that there was no trace at all of their earlier consultation visible on her person.

"Dear Mr. Babbage, good evening," she said quite calmly,
extending her hand to him and nodding to the others. "My
husband sends his regrets."

The woman on his right, Mrs. Mary Somerville, who had
come onto the balcony only a few moments before Lady
Lovelace, said in her soft Scottish burr, "They are making the
most unseemly fuss inside, Mr. Babbage, about your Dancing
Girls."

Babbage closed one compartment of his mind and opened
another.

"As well they might," he replied, and smiled complacently
at his guests. Charles Babbage's Dorset Street Saturday
soirées, he liked to think, were one of the great gathering
places of intellectual London. He prided himself on the enter-
tainment he provided. Sometimes he had even been known to
lead a select group of the scientifically minded into his workroom next door, to gaze at the Difference Engine, for conversation and mental stimulation. The Dancing Girls were quite
extraordinary, however, even for a *soirée* conversation piece.
When Babbage was a boy his mother had taken him to an

exhibition of machinery in Hanover Square where he had seen a remarkable automaton—two mechanical spring-driven statuettes of remarkable beauty. And just one week ago, by a curious and encouraging coincidence, he had found the very same statuettes at a Cockspur Street auction and bought them for thirty-five pounds, a trifle. He had repaired and polished them himself, and left them out tonight on the center table, without comment.

"Fox-Talbot is entranced," Mrs. Somerville told him.

"Ah, quite." William Henry Fox-Talbot was a clever and disagreeable man, tiresome on the subject of photography, which he claimed to have invented before Daguerre. Babbage bent forward and peered through the open French doors. The Dancing Girls were two silver nudes, each about a foot high. One of these glided along a circuit in an enclosed tray, with a music box attached to a corner. She used an eyeglass occasionally and bowed frequently, as if acknowledging acquaintances. The other danseuse carried a silver bird on the forefinger of her right hand, which flapped its wings and opened its beak as she moved in her sister's wake.

"He will be wanting to teach them the calculus too," Mrs. Somerville said to Lady Lovelace, who for some reason blushed at the allusion. The study of mathematics and science was not thought to be ladylike—females were not even permitted in the audience when papers were read at the Royal Society, with the exception of Mrs. Somerville—but Ada Lovelace had shown an impressive gift for such studies, and it was now a nearly public secret that Charles Babbage was giving her private lessons in the differential calculus.

"I'm almost sorry, Mr. Babbage," Ada said, "that the Difference Engine isn't on display tonight, because I've had an idea—"

But Babbage, never quite deliberately rude, but never entirely attentive either, had stepped inside the drawing room, where behind Fox-Talbot he had just caught a glimpse of his friend and banker Edward Kater, and since banks and money—and the painful shortage thereof—were much in Babbage's mind, he walked purposefully across the room, leaving the ladies on the balcony.

"Mr. Babbage," said Mary Somerville to the poet's daughter, "has more business with banks than he likes, poor man." It was not polite to speak of other people's private affairs, and it was, so rumor had it, entirely possible that Lady Lovelace suffered monetary difficulties of her own; something to do with horses. But still, she was Babbage's pupil, and his intimate friend.

"We were speaking just the other day of the Expedition," Ada replied. "He says he rather wishes now he had gone."

"With Henshaw Pryce?" Mary Somerville had grown up in a stern Presbyterian household and she could never approve of William Henshaw Pryce's red beard and raffish air. Despite his social standing, she had been heard to refer to him as a rogue male, in the precise zoological sense of a dangerous and solitary animal that has separated itself from the herd. "Doubtless Henshaw Pryce is entertaining the Red Indian beside a campfire even at this moment, telling him tales of the Alabaster City Across the Sea. Mr. Pryce was born to go on expeditions. I don't, somehow, see Mr. Babbage with his Dancing Girls in the trackless desert."

From the balcony, what the two women could, in fact, see was Babbage earnestly calculating something on his fingers for Edward Kater and the Bishop of Norwich.

"The government has refused another grant for the Difference Engine," Ada murmured.

"Sir Robert Peel," said Mrs. Somerville in a kind of gruff Scottish shorthand. The Prime Minister was known to dislike Babbage and to see no commercial or scientific advantage in continuing to support his work, and Babbage's money woes were generally laid at Peel's door. "I do not intend to vote money," Peel had informed the House of Commons, "for a wooden man to calculate incomprehensible tables."

"If only," said Ada Lovelace wistfully, "his great-uncle

Richard were still alive. Then Mr. Babbage would be his heir, and the Difference Engine could be finished."

"There is not a chance in the world," declared Mrs. Somerville, firmly. "We went into that most thoroughly, before the Expedition was formed. Henshaw Pryce had some fantasy, I believe, of finding him in a mansion along the Mississippi and bringing him back to England. He actually commissioned a private inquiry agent to search for him. He's dead, of course. But it turned out that most of the official records had been lost in a fire in 1838. Those that hadn't been lost in the fire were destroyed in a flood. He died in America in 1837 all right, but there is no official certificate."

"Fire, floods," said Ada, laughing. "What can be next? Locusts?"

"Lawyers," said Mrs. Somerville.

In the drawing room Babbage was shaking his head grimly at a question put by his banker Edward Kater. She watched sympathetically. Inheriting his great-uncle's fortune would of course, she thought, change everything for him. It would certainly make a perfected Difference Engine possible. But even if a proof of death could be discovered—and who knew what bizarre legal obstacles existed in the wilds of America—there was still the matter of Babbage's rival heirs in England. One was a quite determined and resourceful cousin, she knew, in Cornwall, with a large estate and many mouths to feed. The other, with a very strong claim indeed, was the uncle's own aged aunt in York. What was it Dr. Johnson said, let no man's happiness depend on the death of aunts?

"I believe in the ancient English practice of entail," Ada Lovelace said rather primly. "I wish Charles would stay away from lawyers."

"That will never happen; it's simply not in his character to give up money. But he'll never prevail."

Human nature, Mrs. Somerville liked to think, was quite simple. Find a man's obsession, wind him up, turn him loose. In many respects poor Babbage was a perpetual Innocent, a perfect babe in the woods compared to bankers and politicians, not to mention a wily and unscrupulous commercial person like Henshaw Pryce. Babbage's single obsession was his machine, which he quixotically believed would bring him incomparable glory. Pryce's obsession was the fortune he believed a perfected machine would bring *him*. And both of them needed the skills and photographs of her darling protegée Selena Cott to make their obsessions real.

Should she have allowed Selena to go off unprotected, with Henshaw Pryce? Mrs. Somerville's own obsession, her *idée fixe,* as she well knew, was the Progress and Rights of Women. Even so, for a moment a picture came into her head of the little band of travellers, her brilliant Selena in the lead, galloping on their spotted horses across a waving green western prairie, toward a furious gold-orange sun on the verge of eclipse. "I do have the most terrible premonition," she said aloud.

PART TWO

The Santa Fe Trail

CHAPTER FIFTEEN

The Church of the Horse

IN THE EIGHTEENTH AND EARLY NINETEENTH CENTURIES, despite the invention of the differential calculus and the universal availability of logarithm tables, astronomical predictions were widely considered the most complex and uncertain of mathematical exercises.

A cautionary tale was often repeated. Toward the close of the year 1753, a young French astronomer named Joseph-Jérome Lalande, full of pride in his science, invited his king and patron, Louis XV, to come to the Observatoire de Paris at a certain day and hour, no earlier, no later, and witness the transit of the planet Mercury across the face of the sun: a rare and spectacular event. Politely the monarch inquired how it was possible to predict such an occurrence with such precision. Lalande merely smiled, bowed, and repeated the invitation.

"Of course," Selena said, and she paused to wipe the perspiration from her eyes and silently curse the relentless Missouri sun. "Of course, Lalande was wrong."

"You amaze me," murmured William Henshaw Pryce. He shaded his eyes with one hand and peered across the steamboat rail to the other side of the river.

"No, really. The king waited six hours, until the sun went down, and there was no transit whatsoever. It couldn't be seen at all that year in Paris. Lalande was using tables that were fifty years old. He had a deviation of two minutes every three months in his numbers, an eight-hours and three-hundred-kilometers error. Mrs. Somerville told me the story herself."

"Mrs. Somerville knows many anecdotes of failure." Pryce rolled up the sleeves of his shirt. It was ten o'clock in the morning of their second day afloat, and even the fastidious Pryce had removed his coat and undone his fashionable collar.

Selena looked at him, looked at Bennit Cushing sketching on a bench farther down the deck. She wiped her palms on her skirt and sat back and thought, not for the first time, that one of life's great unfairnesses was the convention that women must at all times smother their bodies in three iron layers of cloth, whereas men—men could wear simple duck trousers and a white cotton shirt, no coat, and be quite acceptably dressed. On the Santa Fe Trail, she vowed, she would imitate the free-spirited squaw, she would become the Diana of the Desert and wear nothing but a buckskin skirt and a feathered hat.

"Your face is quite red, Miss Cott." Professor Hollis sniffed in the shadows behind her. "It doesn't become you."

Selena turned and regarded him with glacial collegiality. No mint-green lozenges in evidence this morning, *megrim* presumably cured. She had decided that there was no point whatsoever in confronting the pompous little man with his search of her bags, or in speaking to Pryce, or (worst of all) complaining to Searle. Grin, as they said in Missouri, and bear it.

"It's the heat," she told him. "It just ought to be cooler than this, by law, I think."

"One can hardly imagine," replied Hollis disagreeably, "how red you'll look when we get to the desert."

The desert, however, still lay some five hundred miles to the west. Independence, Missouri, their offical jumping-off place for the Santa Fe Trail, was three full days from St.

Louis, on the south bank of the Missouri, as far upstream as modern steamboats could navigate. Their vessel this time was the *General Burgoyne,* a much smaller and plainer craft than the *Messenger* (but with a more temperamental boiler), specially built, they were told, for the shallow draught of the Missouri. The comte, who had decided to go as far as Independence, had established himself in the forward saloon, engaged in an endless game of piquet with three other travelling Frenchmen. The other members of the Expedition passed the long hours staring over the rails at the passing countryside. Only Pryce, with his correspondence and his endless business accounts, seemed able to work.

"There's not much really to tell," he said with a sigh when Selena stirred herself in the heat and remembered to ask again about Richard Babbage. "The Jefferson Barracks census did have his name in a list of foreign settlers. Someone had put 'English' for his nationality and he had evidently crossed it out himself and written 'Utopian' instead. Very Babbage-like. The Army was not much amused."

Selena smiled. Charles Babbage had once signed a letter to her "*Citoyen du Monde.*" "But he did die in St. Louis?"

"Without a doubt. An undramatic, un-Babbagean exit due to what in St. Louis they call a 'summer fever.' Missouri is a place, one gathers, of seasonal perils. But a wretched flood destroyed the record office. One of the army officers knew of a witness to his death, a young Negro servant woman." Pryce paused and turned a page in his accounts book. His faintly lewd expression suggested to Selena that something more was meant than "servant." "But the person has disappeared, and in any case under Missouri law no black can serve as a legal witness to a document. Ergo, no death certificate. No death certificate, no inheritance. The case may stay in Chancery forever."

"Poor Mr. Babbage," said Selena.

"Poor," said Pryce, turning another page, "us."

*   *

FROM TIME TO TIME THE STEAMBOAT WOULD INTERRUPT THE journey by dropping anchor at some desolate point along the river where chopped wood had been piled haphazardly on the bank. The engineer would tug a lever on the boiler and whistle an ear-splitting signal, and after a few minutes a straw-hatted settler would stroll out of the forest, thumbs in his suspenders, and the boat crew would clamber down to load the wood into the fuel hatch. The vendor, Hollis pointed out to Selena, kept count of his sale by moving his hand down a series of notches cut in a long vertical pole. Then the whistle would blow again, the big paddle wheels would churn, and the *General Burgoyne* would swing its bow once more to the west.

At Franklin, Missouri, their halfway point, they made a longer stop to unload passengers and cargo. A quintessentially American town, Pryce informed them, reading with mock solemnity from his guidebook; named for Benjamin Franklin, founded by Daniel Boone's grandsons. They stood on the deck and gazed out at Franklin's handful of unpainted wooden houses, a general store with one end of its sign on the ground, a saloon, a dilapidated tin-roofed warehouse, and a single narrow dock for berthing the steamboat. Flags and patriotic bunting fluttered on the saloon roof, remnants of the Fourth of July celebration the previous day. Selena followed the progress of somebody's skiff, heading rapidly downstream. Beyond the treetops, where the river turned, low, dark hills stretched toward a silent horizon.

Ostentatiously, Bennit Cushing took out his pocket watch and shook it. "It must be broken," he told her. "Or running fast. It insists we're in the nineteenth century."

But if Franklin was a nearly deserted eighteenth-century village, the city of Independence, when they finally reached it in the weary, drizzling late afternoon of July 6, turned out to be a miniature version of modern bustling St. Louis, a noisy, smoky settlement of four or five thousand people stretching from the river into the absolutely empty plains.

They came slowly into the busy docks, rolling and bumping,

paddle wheels groaning and splashing in reverse. Ahead of them a dozen other steamboats were already moored. Off to one side, pulled up on a sandbar, was the bizarre and unexpected sight of an old wrecked hull whose sides had been painted green like the scales of a snake. Its bow was shaped like a giant serpent's head, with a fiery protruding tongue. At the stern a green tail arched high over the ruined paddle wheel. This, one of the crewmen explained, was the wreckage of the 1819 *Western Engineer,* the first steamboat to come up the Missouri. Its Welsh owners had decorated it that way to mystify and impress the Indians.

"So here in fact," observed Pryce, staring thoughtfully at the wreck, "be dragons." Selena shivered.

On the landing docks the Expedition watched while their trunks and telescope crates were loaded onto flatbed wagons; then they climbed aboard a roofless carriage themselves and jolted their way up a muddy bluff and into the town.

Efficient as always, Pryce had reserved a suite of rooms for them at the Independence Hotel, and there, perhaps as a sign of their exotic eastern celebrity, they were met at the door by the proprietor, a high-cheeked mulatto woman of indeterminate age named Emily Fisher, who shook them each by the hand and promptly disappeared. The men adjourned to the bar. Selena sat upstairs for five minutes in her solitary room, looking down through the rain at a team of miserable wet mules hitched to a fence. Then she made a face in the mirror, sprang to her feet, and went downstairs.

Independence was the last civilized settlement she would see for—who knew how many months? She ought to take an impression of it, a mental daguerreotype, so to speak, to carry with her into the trackless desert. If her mind were a camera, treasuring up impressions...

But, in fact, Independence offered absolutely nothing memorable for a mental camera. She strode up one side of the empty town square, back down the other, peering at the deserted streets. At this time of evening there were far more animals to be seen than people. She patted the damp flank of a tethered mule, stepped quickly past a team of malevolent red-eyed oxen in front of a parked wagon. Next to a water pump and trough, she paused to watch the windows in the nearest stores and houses as they began to glow with yellow gas lamps.

The odd thought crossed her mind that Bennit Cushing might have a right to be so defensive. Daguerreotypes and photography were going to change the nature of art, of that she was utterly certain. Until now painting had always had a certain archival quality; most of the time it tried to record precisely a scene or a person for the purposes of history. But daguerreotypes, so much more accurate and real, would soon take over such archival functions. In another ten years, the future of painting would lie only in its nonrealistic dimensions. A painter would have little left to do except manipulate light and perspective.

She reached the end of the main street and stopped. The last building in town was an unfinished one-story brick house that flew, on an immensely tall pole, an American flag. The light was failing now, what Mrs. Somerville would call the wet "mizzle" swung back and forth just overhead in strings of gray-white beads. Not a star to be seen, except on the flag. No Welsh dragons.

She shielded her eyes from the rain, propped her elbows on a rail fence and felt her mood grow darker. *A hostility impossible to estimate.* Most of the time, she thought, she was her father's daughter—the sheer thrill of the trip, of *doing* something nobody had ever done, kept her fears at bay. But when she was tired, when the weather was gloomy, when she was about to plunge off a cliff... She cocked her head and listened and sensed the French side of her nature coming gradually but surely into the ascendant. In Paris there would have been the sound of hoof and wheel on pavement, the claps and bumps of doors and windows, voices rising and falling, streetlamps, the faint but always palpable hum created by the sheer presence of thousands of human beings gathered together, social, civilized. Here there was only the bray of animals, the swish of the drizzle. Every voice she heard was male, masculine, foreign to her ears. She felt herself growing smaller, shrinking like a child inside her damp, heavy dress. A little civilization was far worse than none at all, she thought. She had never felt so far from home, so much alone.

"The Egyptians worshipped cats, didn't they, miss?"

Selena made herself turn slowly around; nodded.

"Well, I guess I worship horses," said the man in front of her, hard to make out clearly in the poor light, but tall, rangy, with one stooped shoulder, bearded; he wore the most nearly shapeless hat she had ever seen, and even six feet away, leaning on the fence rail, he smelled pungently of straw, wet cloth, animal. Water dripped from the brim of his hat. "I guess I belong to the Church of the Horse," he declared and nodded back at her. "Finest creatures on earth. Dogs are all right, too, dogs are priests and minor prophets in the Church of the Horse. Not cats. Cats are freethinkers and heretics. If I had a cat I'd name him Judas. You're the little astronomer girl, ain't you? The smart one? I'm Webb Pattie, gonna lead you out on the trail." He paused and showed his teeth in a friendly smile, quite like a horse. "Neither one of us smart enough to come in out of the rain."

CHAPTER SIXTEEN

Will It Be Dangerous?

THE CHURCH OF THE HORSE WAS NOT THE ONLY CHURCH to which Webb Pattie belonged. He was also a practicing Grahamite, as he explained early the next day to a fascinated Selena. It was half past six in the morning, muggy and damp, and there was a thick blue mist in the air almost like fog. The sun was a fat white worm scarcely higher than the dark hotel rooftop to the east.

"By Grahamite..." Pattie said. He stopped and stamped his boots in the wet grass of the field they had just entered. By Grahamite he simply meant that he was a follower of the great Sylvester Graham's revolutionary System of Physiology. He carried with him everywhere Graham's two-volume book *Lectures on the Science of Life,* which he would be glad to lend to Selena, a fellow scientist like Graham, and he subscribed wholeheartedly to Graham's belief that eating red meat and stimulating food was the root cause of America's constant national state of anxiety and nervous depression, not to mention cholera, yellow fever, and financial panic.

He paused to squint into the mist, searching for the rest of the Expedition. He himself, he told Selena as they watched first Searle, then Bennit Cushing come into view, had actually lived one year in a Graham-Principle boardinghouse in Indiana.

There they ate only two vegetable meals a day and drank only cold water. Even now, at breakfast he ate a healthful many-grained bread called Graham's Bread, or else a thin orange biscuit known as a Graham's Cracker. These he baked for himself or had made for him in town by a trusted cook. On the trail he ate nothing but vegetables, no meat if he could avoid it.

"Well, maybe buffler sometimes," he told her. The comte and the others began to appear as if through a blue curtain of mist. "When I have to." He shook his head and raised one sleeve to wipe his mouth. "Buffler is awful sweet and tasty, for the flesh of a dead animal."

Buffalo, Selena realized, belatedly.

They stopped beside a row of six unhitched Conestoga wagons covered on top with high rounded white canvas, like high fresh loaves (she imagined) of Graham's Bread. Close by, blurred in the mist, were four more wagons, turned to face in another direction. A crew of two or three men seemed to be on their knees, busy about the repair of a wheel. Similar groups of wagons were quickly becoming visible in the rising mist, scattered across the field and far to the right and down to the banks of the river, perhaps a hundred wagons altogether in various stages of preparation. Directly behind Pattie three horses grazed under the serious eyes of a thin boy who wore buckskin trousers and a red and yellow striped shirt and carried a whip. At his feet, regarding them with her head cocked, sat a little shaggy white dog that Selena identified with amazement as a pure- or nearly purebred West Highland terrier.

"Pearl of Scotland," Webb Pattie said. "My wife's dog." He planted his long legs wide apart in the damp grass and winked at her. "Acolyte in the Church. We're going to have to spend all day loading up these fine wagons," he announced in a booming voice as the last of the company caught up, "property since last night of our Mr. Pryce here." He pulled off his shapeless hat, found a receipt, and handed it to Pryce. "Normally we load out here in the field for about half a day, then hit the trail. But I need to see how to put all your telescopes and devices and magic wands just so, where you can get at them if you need to, but they won't be smashed to bits first bump we hit."

"Are six wagons enough?" Pryce, incongruous in his black frock coat and tall hat, was frowning at the crumpled receipt. "We expect to be almost three and a half months on the trail, coming and going."

"Four more wagons over there," Webb Pattie said laconically. "Belong to me, but you use them. Supplies for you people go in first, then where there's room left over I take a few personal goods for trading."

"And the crew?" Pryce asked.

"Some Canadians, mostly Mexicans. Fourteen altogether, not counting the higher management, which is me, of course, and eight spare mules and my strong and silent foreman, George." Pattie pointed toward the last wagon and a swarthy man who wore two gold rings in his ears like a pirate. "Got to be strong and silent to work with me. That's my wife, Lona." Next to George a slender woman in her forties looked up from a packing box. She had the straight black hair and dark, solemn eyes of an Indian, Selena thought, and her skin was mottled brown, not unattractive, but clearly not white.

"Half Pawnee," Webb Pattie said to Selena, with what seemed to be his unnerving habit of reading one's mind. "Lona goes along as cook, so you'll have a little female company, Miss Astronomer. Likewise Pearl of Scotland" (the dog gave a yip at her name) "goes along as, well, as dog."

It was Pattie's idea that each Expedition member should climb aboard an empty wagon, crawl about, sit down, stretch out, get a feel for the space that was to become their travelling home. James Searle, arms folded across his chest, silently demurred, but the rest of them, tentatively at first, then with growing enthusiasm, followed his suggestion.

The wagons were far more colorful than Selena had expected—their bodies were painted bright blue, their wheels a truly brilliant red, the taut canvas covers a shining white. The outside length of the wagon frame was about thirteen feet, width about three and a half feet; inside, under the canvas, the feeling was warm and snug, oddly childlike, as if they were about to play house with sheets and somebody's father's spare boards. But when Selena poked her head out the front again and swung her legs onto the high driver's bench, the scene was anything but childlike.

More horses and mules were now being led across the field; more men were converging on them, other wagons. She could see the back kitchen door of the Independence Hotel and women on the steps scrubbing dishes in a tub. Men were stacking wooden crates at the far end of the field. Wranglers had started to put together a holding pen for livestock. Blacksmiths' fires burned among the wagons, and the air was streaked with smoke and shaking to the thump and clang of hammers.

She pulled her knees to her chest. Hollis and Bennit Cushing climbed down from the next wagon on the right, George lifted a flour barrel in. From a nearby pasture sheep were calling in French, *"Mère, mère."* Her father or Mr. Babbage, with their great learning, would no doubt have said it was all like a passage in the *Iliad* or the *Odyssey*, hecatombs and smoke and oxen, an army stirring in its camp, preparing to move out. She thought of the last such point of bustle and business she had seen herself, Pennsylvania Avenue outside the Willard Hotel, or else chaotic St. Louis and its babel of races and tongues. But these were truly frontier American sights, she decided, unmistakable, not Greek, not to be confused with the languid energy of Europe. She shaded her eyes and peered at the thread of dark trees that marked where the Missouri River began its great broad thousand-mile curve to Oregon. Of course the wagons were painted red, white, and blue.

When she found Webb Pattie again he was engaged in a less than cordial discussion with James Searle about oxen and mules, and neither of them paused to notice her. The specification, Searle was saying with considerable heat, was for teams of oxen to draw the wagons, not the mules that were being led into the traces at that very moment. Oxen were

more economical; over sandy roads they had better en-
durance; they were far less liable to be stampeded than mules.
In Africa he had driven oxen for hundreds of miles across the
desert, even used them as saddle animals. Pattie leaned
against a wagon and drew his hat brim down across his face.
To one side Pryce pretended to study his receipt.

"Oxen are what we called for," Searle said. "Eight per
wagon."

"Africa," said Pattie mildly, and spat on the ground.

Selena felt a tug at her sleeve; she turned to find the thin
boy who watched the horses. He pulled her away toward the
rear of the wagons.

Here teamsters were unloading the telescopes from a flat
cart sent over by the hotel. Already on the ground was the Infant Engine in its special padded trunk. Next to it sat the
smaller box for the Thomas Arnold clock. As the boy led her
up, the teamsters stopped their work and stood with their
hands in their belts, grinning and waiting to see where she
wanted the trunks and boxes stowed, as if it were the most
entertaining thing in the world, out on the edge of the Santa
Fe Trail, to take orders from a female. Selena unbuttoned her
cuffs and took off her annoying, useless bonnet.

The next two hours she spent bending, lifting, pointing, rearranging—quite the little housewife, Bennit Cushing
mocked, passing by with his own load of boxes—until, with
Pattie's approval, the Engine was securely wedged to her satisfaction in the center of the wagon and the telescopes and
chronometers were tamped firmly and ingeniously alongside.
Then came the boxes and barrels of food: each and every
wagon, she was informed, carried flour in three 100-pound
double-sewn canvas sacks; 150 pounds of bacon; 100 pounds
of dried corn, hulled; 25 pounds of green apples; a barrel of
molasses; a keg of vinegar; another keg marked "beef suet,"
which George explained they would use for butter. Then blankets, clothing, gunpowder, soap, a pig of lead and a mold for
making bullets; phosphorous matches, pemmican, cooking
grease. Her photographic chemicals arrived on another cart,

and ruthlessly she sent the men back inside the wagon to re-
arrange yet again. She was a sea captain's daughter, she
thought, and it was just a matter of packing cargo into a hold,
jamming every nook and crevice. The medicine chest went
outside, pots and pans hung from the sideboards, as did lari-
ats and extra coupling poles, bolts, tar buckets, spare axles.
When she stopped to look about, the white-topped wagons in
every direction did in fact look like a fleet of sails. When she
squinted up and gauged the time by the sun, she pictured her
father out on the quarterdeck of his ship, staring up at the sky.
And she had always thought of herself as a rebel, original.

"The fruit never falls very far from the tree," she told the
comte de Broglie, who was seated, scowling under his little
umbrella, on a crate beside Pearl of Scotland.

"I plan to take the steamboat back tomorrow," he announced, "after you leave. Your first stop is Council Grove,
one hundred fifty miles into the dismal prairies. Mr. Pattie as-
sures me another caravan could bring you back from there, if
you change your mind. I shall write your father I have gone
well past the limits of friendship."

Dinner was brought out at one o'clock on still another hotel cart, and they labored on through the afternoon, loading,
unloading, heaving goods from wagon to wagon. The Conestogas were manufactured in Pittsburgh, Webb Pattie told
her on one of his roving tours of inspection. They were built
to haul as much as five thousand pounds each on eastern
roads like the National Highway, but he never allowed more
than four thousand pounds per wagon himself, because the
folks in Pittsburgh had never seen a deep ford on the
Arkansas River, or bogged down in the Sand Hills, or had a
little bit of a chase from a pack of Comanches.

"Mules it is, I take it," Selena said.

Pattie spat between the spokes of a wheel. "The semi-
saintly mule, yes. Some people do like oxen," he added judiciously. "They eat 'em when they're starving out on the trail
and can't find buffaler or deer. But an ox's hooves break up
on the rocks, they're hard to shoe. You can't sell them for

much in Mexico. Mr. Pryce tells me Searle actually did live in Africa."

"He means to go back after this, with the money he earns. That's the only reason he's coming, in fact. Mr. Searle's a dedicated African explorer."

"And you lived in France?"

"I was born over here."

"Let me show you something." Pattie hitched up his trousers and strolled between the wagons, and after a moment's hesitation Selena put down her box of copper daguerreotype plates and followed.

"This is *my* wagon," he said when they came to a stop at the last of the auxiliary four. He pushed aside the canvas flap and lifted out a small wooden box. Selena bent forward to read the stencil label: *"Légumes secs. Mis en boite par M. Chollet et cie. 46 rue Richer, Paris."*

"Dried vegetables," Webb Pattie told her proudly. "Recommended by Sylvester Graham. Rest of you going to be out there gnawing on a mule's drumstick and poisoning your mortal bodies. I just take one of these cakes"—he opened the lid and showed her tightly packed rows of what looked like hard brown soap bars—"drop it in the pan with a cup of water, instant vegetable plate."

She held a bar to her nose and smelled something like dried leather and lavender.

"What they do," he explained, "is cut your fresh beet or your carrot or whatever into slices about as thick as the Ace of Spades, slip them into a machine press, and squeeze out every last drop of moisture. Then when you're ready, could be two years later or fifty, doesn't matter, you just put the water back in and cook."

"It doesn't sound very French." She wrinkled her nose and replaced the bar, doubtful.

"Made in Paris." Pattie rubbed the label with a callused thumb.

Selena looked up at the sun. Some of the Conestoga wagons at the far end of the field had already moved out, heading west. Here and there men were laying down their tools. Other men were walking toward town. In their wagon group only James Searle was still working. Hollis and Bennit Cushing and Pryce were far off, at the edge of the grass, evidently returning to the hotel. As she watched, the nearsighted Hollis stumbled and Bennit Cushing shot out an arm to keep him from falling.

She wiped the perspiration from her palms. She thought of Paris and her father and a hundred little Frenchmen on the Rue Richer, pressing dried carrots with a hot iron, like washerwomen. Along the distant curve of the Missouri River, the western sun had set all the trees ablaze, obliterated them, as if the eclipse had somehow come early, in reverse, and was driving them all in anger toward an unbearable horizon of light, not shadow.

"Is it going to be dangerous, Mr. Pattie?"

"It's going to be the greatest trip of your life," Pattie said.

CHAPTER SEVENTEEN

Near the Cimarron River

THE MANNER IN WHICH THE KIOWAS CONSTRUCTED A TEPEE lodge, Richard Babbage thought drowsily, was most admirable, most pastoral.

Generally speaking, a tepee was built with about two dozen slender green pine poles, between eighteen and twenty feet long. The poles would be perhaps three inches in diameter at the butt, tapering to a fine point at the other end. The Kiowas tied them together in a cone, butts resting on the ground, and then fit a covering of buffalo skins around the outside. The hair of the skins, of course, had already been scraped away by a squaw, using an angular section of elk's horn or (purchased with the money Babbage supplied) a nice sharp piece of American iron shaped like an adze. They rubbed buffalo brains into the hide, to make it soft, and sewed the pieces in overlapping flaps with an awl and animal sinew. On a mild early July afternoon, such as today, there was no finer dwelling in the world.

Babbage stirred restlessly and lifted the unsewn bit of flap that served as his door, so that he had a better view of the village.

The Kiowas, with the Indians' unfailing eye for picturesque beauty, had chosen to settle this time in a secluded, narrow bottom, overrun with long, tangled grass, close to the river and sheltered by a hill. The entire hillside was covered with dark cottonwood trees whose long outspread limbs created a strong sense—Babbage groped for a word, felt the summer fever or whatever it was briefly cloud his brain again—a strong sense, he thought, of *protection*.

Near the base of the hill some of the *ki-kun,* the children, were playing noisily with their dogs. Boys mostly, very undisciplined. But of course the Kiowa never chastised or disciplined a boy, because it would break his spirit and render him unfit for war, and war was what a man did.

One of the squaws, O-ne-o, who was chopping wood at the next lodge, stood up and called to him.

"*Ten-o-wast?*" said Babbage gruffly. *What is it?* O-ne-o made a sign to ask if he wanted water, and Babbage, though he could feel the fever returning, perversely shook his head. Even at his age, he thought, the last true Pantisocrat could be quite as stern and self-denying as any brave.

In any case, O-ne-o was lazy and instead of bringing her drinking water in a bucket fresh from the river, she used the communal supply. This was a large buffalo intestine, one end of which was tied in a tight knot. It was then filled with water and hung from a lodgepole like an enormous filthy dangling sausage. When a drink was wanted, you simply put your mouth on the opening at the top and squeezed. It was one of the few points in which Babbage still felt himself to be an Englishman.

The thought snagged in his mind and reminded him of something else. At his feet was a small stack of *Niles' Weekly Register* newspapers, two and three months old, purchased for him by the village braves when they had gone back to St. Vrain's store in Taos last week. Although it was weakness, when you had figuratively "buried" yourself, and literally renounced the whole sad and infuriating world of white European civilization, nonetheless...

Babbage pushed the papers here and there with his bare foot until he came to the issue and headline he wanted:

"Somerville-Babbage Expedition to Set Out for Eclipse." He had already read it twice, but now he let his gaze travel curiously down the column once again.

The "Babbage," of course, was his great-nephew Charles, the mathematician. Charles was highly intelligent; Charles had some of the Babbage flair for gesture and drama. But Charles was hopelessly trapped, Richard Babbage considered, in the great smothering stone web of London and, unlike his truly dramatic uncle, would never, never escape.

Richard Babbage poked his head farther out-of-doors, in search of some relief in the mild air from the constant burning sensation that made his body so tired, his mind so lumpish. The poet Wordsworth had been an acquaintance of his once upon a time—Richard had even introduced him to Charles when the boy was a student at Cambridge. Wordsworth had a face like a sheep and a high-pitched disagreeable voice. But he saw through to the core of modern life.

> The world is too much with us; late and soon,
> Getting and spending, we lay waste our powers:
> Little we see in Nature that is ours;
> We have given our hearts away, a sordid boon!

Babbage rubbed his weary eyes and tried to focus on the boys piling up logs in a clearing for the cooking fire that night, beautiful boys, brown as berries, not really "red," hard of muscle, clear of eye, true descendants of the great creator of the Kiowa people, Sun Boy himself. Sun Boy, indeed. Babbage's favorite deity. According to the old women, he had called the first Kiowas into the world long ago, far away, by tapping with his fist on a hollow cottonwood log. Each time he tapped, another Kiowa emerged, until one pregnant woman got stuck in the log, and Sun Boy had laughed and laughed and left off tapping. A powerful, mischievous, jealous god. He was a spirit, of course, and there were no pictures of him. The idea of Sun Boy being eclipsed and "photographed" was far too risible for words. What did the poet say?

—Great God! I'd rather be
A Pagan suckled in a creed outworn ...

They would come by the Santa Fe Trail, of course. That was how Babbage himself had come three years earlier, with only a single guide sworn to secrecy, two extra horses, and a satchel of banknotes wherewith to get and spend.

He did not feel well, he was not a well man. He had been malarial and feverish for several days, although the racking cough that had come with the fever was now subsided. He kicked feebly at the papers. It might actually be a scientific expedition, who could say? It might have nothing at all to do with him. His mind was not working properly, he was aware of that. One of these days he would quite likely have to bring a halt to his little Pantisocratic experiment of living in the wilderness like a true Wordsworthian pagan. One of these days he would undoubtedly have to crawl back to the world of white men's hospitals and doctors and lawyers. Meanwhile, he thought, he was simply going to drag himself back inside his lodge and consume another bowl of his Kiowa medicine, a mush made from fungus growing on the side of decaying logs; it looked quite poisonous but tasted, strangely enough, though perhaps that was only his mind playing tricks, like the Brittany oysters of his youth.

William Henshaw Pryce. A sly, greedy man. But not physically strong or brave. Even in his present mental confusion Richard Babbage was certain of one thing. If Pryce knew where he was, if Pryce meant him harm, Pryce was too weak and cowardly to act on his own. He would bring someone wicked to do it for him.

CHAPTER EIGHTEEN

The Santa Fe Trail

IN ITS LEGENDARY HEYDAY THE SANTA FE TRAIL STRETCHED OVER nine hundred miles, from the new village of Independence to the already ancient city of Santa Fe, capital of the northernmost province of the Republic of Mexico. Parts of the trail followed old buffalo tracks and Indian hunting paths; parts had been created by Spanish explorers in the late seventeenth century as they moved north toward the Mississippi River. Only in the early nineteenth century, and thanks largely to Senator Thomas Hart Benton's vision of manifest destiny, did it come into existence as a single, defined route that could be taken by American traders eager to do business in Santa Fe.

A tourist today can cover the entire distance in a leisurely two- or three-day automobile trip. In 1840 the journey took two to three months, depending on weather and luck, although to win a bet in 1848 a single horseman named Francis X. Aubrey rode practically nonstop, west to east, in a record-setting and horse-killing five days and sixteen hours.

If you place your finger on a modern map, you can trace the Trail in a long southwesterly slant from Independence (now simply a suburb of Kansas City) across the southern third of Kansas and toward the high plains of eastern Colorado. A little past the present-day town of Dodge City, nonexistent in 1840, nineteenth-century travellers had a choice of routes. The longer but safer way (the "mountain route") was to continue west along the Arkansas River into Colorado, turn southwest again at an isolated settlement named Bent's Fort, and proceed over the high Raton Pass, down into northeastern New Mexico.

But at several points near Dodge City (the "Cimarron Cutoff"), wagons could ford the Arkansas, push seventy miles across the forbidding Cimarron Desert, which was Apache and Kiowa country, cut through the westernmost part of the Oklahoma panhandle, and finally rejoin the main trail below Raton Pass. From there, the Trail led due south until it reached the bottom of the beautiful Sangre de Cristo Mountains, where it curled north like a fishhook and entered Santa Fe. Near Raton Pass some travellers preferred to cross a narrow valley west of the Trail and ascend the mountains to the village of Taos, then as now a kind of magnet for certain artistic and mystical temperaments.

In the end it was this mystical quality that distinguished the Santa Fe from the other two great western highways. The Oregon and the California Trails, established more than two decades later, were longer, more popular, covered a greater variety of landscape. Certainly both stirred the imagination. But people spoke of the "lure" of the Santa Fe in a profoundly different tone of voice, as someone might speak of an enchantress. For one thing, the two northern trails led only to vague, undefined destinations—the Northwest, the long Pacific. No exotic city waited at the end, conjuring up, as Santa Fe did, romantic images of an arcaded plaza, a seventeenth-century Palace, strings of red peppers drying in the trees, brown babies dozing by old adobe walls.

For another thing, the Santa Fe was a merchants' trail. It had been established by men who wanted to make money fast, not by families of immigrants with their children and dogs and cats and household utensils banging along behind them. Its classic contemporary description, written by Josiah

Gregg in 1844, was called, significantly, *Commerce of the Prairies*. And far away as it may seem now, the revolutionary Technological Age of the 1830s and early 1840s was, exactly like our own time, an age absolutely intoxicated with the idea of *business*. Men found sheer poetry in the thought that they were part of the complex, shining web of international trade and that what they bought and sold in one place, no matter how obscure, sent vibrations all the way back the line to the golden spiders of New York, or London, or far-off Madrid. First and last, a trip to Santa Fe had something to do with *money*.

At six o'clock in the morning of July 8, Selena walked by herself down the little dirt road that led from the hotel to the wagon field. It was still dim, but the air was clear and warm and there was no trace of the gray mist that had hung over the grass and trees the day before. She listened to the rustle of her skirt and the crunch of her shoes on the dirt and yawned. She had been awake, she supposed, since midnight, watching the sky. Somewhere in town a rooster crowed. Over to the east the horizon was flecked with stars that looked like grains of sand floating in water. Automatically she named them in her mind: Vega to the left, Capella, blue-green Aldebaran just beyond the glimmering Pleiades.

Ahead of her the line of wagons was drawn up in the dim morning light like a school of sleeping fish. Nearby, Webb Pattie squatted on his boot heels and tugged or twisted some kind of chain rigging for the wheels. He looked like a scarecrow made out of damp rags and leather and a dirty black hat. A most unlikely guide, she thought, yawning again, certainly a most unlikely guide for the elegant and worldly Pryce to choose.

Pattie looked back over his shoulder. "Figured you'd be the first one up."

"The others are still sleeping."

"Lazy pilgrims."

On the other side of the wagon, she found a tiny fire and a big iron coffeepot. She poured coffee into one of the battered tin cups and walked back to the side where Pattie was working. Sounds were coming now, from the hotel. She heard the faint clip of mules somewhere. Departure Day, Pryce had grandly called it last night at dinner.

She sipped from her tin cup and looked at the silent field. Her favorite book as a girl had been a French fairy tale about a country mouse who had gone on a long voyage in a tiny carriage made of a walnut shell and wooden spools and pulled by crickets. And her favorite part had been the description of the morning bustle when the trip began and all the helper mice danced and sang and decked the carriage with ribbons. Who would have thought the real thing would be so quiet and chilly and dim?

Webb Pattie rose slowly to his feet and rubbed the back of his neck. Two wagons down the line, his foreman George appeared, wiping his nose with his sleeve. At the farthest corner of the field, somebody entered leading a pair of horses. Selena pulled her padded jacket closer about her and leaned against the wagon. She smelled wood shavings, grass, black coffee. Closed her eyes and drifted.

And then in a matter of moments, it seemed, though it must have been much longer, her eyes were open again and the whole field was covered with men, horses, wagons streaming toward them, and the red sun was lifting itself over the shingled roofs and dark treetops of Independence, as if the field were a great sloping stage and one of Mr. Babbage's brilliant theatrical lighting systems had suddenly been switched on.

Nearly at once all the bustle of the previous morning reappeared, intensified now by a noisy, raucous audience—two other wagon trains were also leaving that day, and most of the town of Independence had evidently come out to the field to watch. Hundreds of men and boys and a scattering of black slaves in farm clothes lounged along the dirt-road border, in a holiday mood. Women and girls were bunched by a gate at the southwest corner. A small brass band, more drums than brass, marched back and forth among the wagons, playing

"Turkey in the Straw" over and over. On the porch of the Independence Hotel curious guests lined the rails. Half a mile away, somebody fired an occasional blank round from the cannon in front of the courthouse, and at every boom the horses and mules shied and whinnied.

Toward eight o'clock the comte de Broglie came out to say goodbye, but in the confusion of whip cracks, shouts, and cannon fire they could barely hear each other.

"*C'est vraiment fou,*" he said, wincing at the noise and looking very much the old man, out of place, out of humor. "*Ce fou voyage. Mais comme votre père m'a dit, 'les enfants sont les flèches, vous êtes l'arc, et ils doivent partir un jour.'* "

Selena nodded. Her father spoke bad French, with a thick Massachusetts accent that would never improve. It didn't sound a bit like something her father would say. *Your children are the arrows, you are the bow. Someday they have to fly away.*

"I don't like that Bennit Cushing," said the comte abruptly. He glowered down the row of wagons toward the painter, who was standing uselessly beside a team of mules and looking, in his Bohemian costume and offensive long hair, quite as out of place as the comte. "Or the frail *professeur,*" he growled, turning back to Selena, "who doesn't like *you,* or *anybody. Bon voyage, petite fille.*" Then he stood on his toes, kissed her hurriedly on both cheeks, and left.

At nine o'clock, under the full, hot Missouri sun, Selena put her right foot on a wooden step and climbed up to the front of Wagon Number Four. Her skirt caught annoyingly on the brake lever and she yanked it hard. Then she took her seat on the bench, directly behind her driver, who sat, not on the bench as she had expected, but on a saddle on the nearest left-hand mule, the "wheeler."

For the first few days at least, the Expedition would travel with the other wagon groups in caravan. At the head of what seemed to be twenty-five or thirty identical Conestoga wagons, Webb Pattie lounged on a brindled mare, shouting instructions from time to time through the deafening noise.

Where the line of wagons curved, Selena could see George high on the passenger's bench of Somerville-Babbage Number One, with Pearl of Scotland seated beside him. Nearby, James Searle, mounted on a fine black gelding, was making short, impatient canters up and down the line. She craned around to see Pryce and Bennit Cushing clambering into Number Five. A white-faced Professor Hollis sat next to Lona on the bench of Number Six.

"Man's not well," Selena's driver mouthed over the noise and spat and picked up his reins.

A signal rifle cracked far in front. Webb Pattie stood in his stirrups and gave a shrill whistle between his fingers. Then he roared in a voice that could be heard in every corner of the field, "Catch up! Catch up! Roll up! Roll *away*!"

For a long moment absolutely nothing happened. The curving train of wagons sat motionless on the grassy field, a tableau. The wind stopped. The band stopped. The mules and horses stood in utter silence. Then the first white canvas top began to sway, and all along the line there was a low rumbling grind of wheels and wood. Selena's bench pitched left, then right, and before she could do more than grip the handrail and glance around, they were passing through a knot of cheering boys and through a double gate and out of Missouri and onto the Santa Fe Trail.

Days until the eclipse: 58.

THE NEXT TWO HOURS WERE, IN SELENA'S MIND, A KIND OF anticlimax. They rolled calmly and quietly enough along a well-marked road, in a forested countryside of gentle hills and valleys much like the countryside they had been travelling over since St. Louis. Once or twice they passed a solitary farmhouse and open field with crops growing. They stopped two or three times to adjust the harnesses or partly repack a wagon. Once during a stop a mule kicked loose from the band of "auxiliary mules" that trailed the last wagon and went skidding and dodging into a field while a band of teamsters ran whooping after him. Even then, mulelike, he would only walk backward, with two men pushing and three men pulling, all the way to his harness.

At the noon meal stop there was a second kind of anticlimax, Selena thought. As soon as the portable grill began to be covered with steaks and long slices of bread, Pryce led her and James Searle to the rear of Wagon Number Six and from a tightly packed cluster of telescopes and tripods pulled out the special mahogany box with the Thomas Arnold clock. Pryce had changed his clothes at the beginning of the day and was now dressed in teamster's garb of checked shirt, boots, and denim trousers. But his manner was still the familiar combination of urbane and raffish.

"As foretold in Washington City," he murmured. "Not being a scientific person myself, I yield the instruments of record to you two. You both will be checking our daily progress with your sextants and compasses. To establish the elusive longitude, it will be altogether neater if you wind our little chronometrical friend at the same time." He shaded his eyes and studied the sun. "Shall we say every day at noon, when we halt?"

James Searle took the key Pryce handed him. "I would strongly prefer to do it myself. Alone."

"I'm sure that you would."

"It's not a woman's kind of job or place or responsibility. On an expedition where she shouldn't be."

"You must try to rectify," Pryce advised, so smoothly that Selena smothered a laugh, "this over-tactful, over-delicate way of not saying what you think."

"I'm serious, quite serious, sir."

"Ah," remarked Pryce mildly. He studied Searle's face for a long moment, then placed the second key in Selena's hand. "But, Mr. Searle, *I* am master here."

Searle worked his jaw, opened and closed his fist, then turned abruptly and bent over the box.

"Six-twenty-one and fourteen seconds in London," he said, and Selena, holding her own key in one hand, took the leather-bound Official Journal Pryce held out to her and awkwardly wrote the date and time on the top of the page.

"Morning or evening?" said Bennit Cushing, who had somehow come up behind them, and so startled was she that for an instant Selena was actually unsure—the dial of the Thomas Arnold was an ordinary twelve-hour clock face, with three spidery hands moving in steady, almost imperceptible mechanical jerks. If you once lost track of morning or evening—

"Evening, of course," answered Professor Hollis. "Don't you know any mathematics at all, Miss Cott? You really are hopeless. Don't you think she's hopeless, Cushing?"

But Bennit Cushing merely scowled and muttered something about artists and scientists and walked away.

A LITTLE PAST THREE IN THE AFTERNOON, THEY REACHED THEIR first ford, a fairly gentle passage down a hillside, over a narrow pebbled stream that Pattie called "Blue Crick," and up a bushy slope again. Selena climbed down from her wagon and joined Pryce and Cushing under a tree. Clouds had been building in the western sky, and the air was now close and muggy. The sun was completely obscured.

Below them Webb Pattie had dismounted from his horse and was standing in the middle of the water with a whip in his hand. He waded back and forth, stamping his boots in the mud. Then he walked to the far bank and inspected the ground. He pulled away a root, kicked at a rock. Finally he turned back to the waiting wagons and waved his arm. Somebody whistled, somebody cursed, and after ten or twenty seconds of complete inaction Wagon Number One, loaded with four thousand pounds of food, clothing, and weapons, came bumping and rocking down the hillside, gathering speed like a huge white falling boulder.

The lead pair of the eight-mule team splashed into the water and stopped. The wagon tilted. Pattie shot his whip over their ears with a single crack like a gun. The driver shook the reins wildly and stood in his wheeler saddle, cursing. The red wheels sank six inches in the water, the mules brayed and twisted, Pattie raised his whip.

High on the bushy slope, Pryce was amused. "They should see this in London," he said to Cushing. Webb Pattie now had his shoulder to a mule's rump and was pushing as hard as he could. Wading up on the other side of the wagon was James Searle. The mule kicked, Searle dodged, Pattie boxed its long ears. Slowly the wagon began to roll forward. Somewhere far to the west, thunder growled, and Selena hugged herself tight in surprise. "Wonderful country," murmured Pryce beside her. "Wonderful country."

It took more than an hour to drive their wagons across the ford, and by the time they had all regained the rutted path on the other side, wagons were strung out over a mile and a half of forest. Selena walked for a time beside Number Four; rode; walked again. At dusk a light rain was falling, every trace of Departure Day's excitement had vanished: Pattie's signal to halt and set up camp was greeted with weary moans of approval.

In the open prairie, Selena understood, the wagons would be drawn together in a close circle at night, for protection from Indians; the animals would be staked or tethered inside the circle, under the eye of armed guards. Here, in the relatively safe forest, they made a rough formation in a beaten-down meadow, obviously used by many caravans before them. The animals were set out to graze with two or three teamsters to watch them. Meanwhile the other trail hands set to work strapping the wagon flaps shut against the rain and inspecting the wheels and axles. Others began to fashion lean-to shelters out of canvas strips and cedar poles. Lona the cook attempted halfheartedly to start a fire, but the air was too wet and the wind too strong. Even Webb Pattie could only keep the flames going just long enough to heat a pot of coffee on a miniature pyramid of coals under a little tarpaulin square.

Selena ate beef jerky and cold bread and sat with her back against a muddy wheel. In the growing darkness she could hear the Mexican and French-Canadian teamsters muttering. French phrases, not very decent, floated between louder outbursts of Spanish—*enfant de garce, sacré, une petite vide poche brunette à Québec*. She smiled to herself and tried hard not to translate.

"Tell us about the African desert," Pattie said nearby. "I'm interested in camels, probably a churchly beast." A long pause. Then James Searle's stiff, unfriendly voice could just be heard over the rain, something about Moroccan saddles, a khebir guide with only one eye he had known in Algeria.

Selena yawned. Near a stand of cottonwood trees one of the French-Canadians had set up a small canvas tent for her use alone, tall enough for her to stand in, equipped with a folding bed frame for her blankets. Pearl of Scotland had already gone in and out several times, leaving a wet doggy smell to blend with the general dampness, the slow, soporific pattering of rain on cloth. Selena crawled in; blinked at her watch; somehow struggled out of her dress and into a dry sleeping robe. She stretched her legs as far as she could, until rainwater soaked her stocking toes and she drew up her knees again. The air was warm and clammy. The tent was dark. Outside were the low, comforting voices of men going about their domestic tasks. She heard the hiss of the fire being put out. Somebody hammered a plank; once, twice. Just beyond the wall of the tent, the wind moved in the trees, making a sound like a broom on a sidewalk.

She was beginning to doze, close her eyes on her first night out in the open, on the trail. She thought of eclipses, daguerreotypes, her father and mother a world away on the Rue Jacob. Thought that tonight at least she was smart enough to get in out of the rain. Nearby, Pryce's indefatigable voice was saying something. His companion's voice was only a murmur. She heard the words "St. Louis," "ruse." Their voices drifted farther away, then returned. "Laws of nature as well," the other voice said indistinctly, which seemed a curious expression. She yawned and turned on the bed in the final, definitive motion we make just before sleep. "No laws out here," Pryce said suddenly, clearly, but she was already dead to the world.

CHAPTER NINETEEN

Prairie and Oasis

ON THE FIRST DAY'S TRAVEL THEY HAD COVERED SEVENTEEN miles—excellent for wagons on the Santa Fe Trail, where ten or twelve miles a day was considered a good average. Despite the rain and the mud they made another fourteen miles on day number two, and camped at a meadow called Round Grove, still in the midst of what seemed to Selena the same tame green Missouri countryside.

And then on day number three, two miles out from the Round Grove campground, they crested a hill, turned south through a stand of hardwood trees and scrub bushes, and abruptly found themselves gazing west, as if they had crossed a line on a map. Over an immense, endless plain, a vast hazy prairie of sunlit grass, there was not a tree, not a river, not another landmark in sight.

As they reached the turn, each wagon appeared to pause, hesitate on the crest. Some passengers and drivers looked back, involuntarily, toward the trees. The outriders wheeled about in nervous circles. Webb Pattie trotted along the crest, gave one of his shrill two-fingered whistles, and the first big wagon started to lumber down.

By ten o'clock they were fully out on the prairie, stretched back in a long line of white dots and dust, rattling slowly west. The grass that had seemed, from the crest of the hill, like a soft, plushy carpet of green and silver turned out to be, up close, tough and springy, waist-high for a man walking, and home to a whole civilization of flying insects and bugs. Selena sat on the swaying wagon bench, bonnet tied tight around her chin, one hand gripping the wagon, the other flapping steadily away at what Pattie informed her, riding by, were aphids, botflies, gnats, and jiggers. ("The light militia of the lower sky," said Pryce sardonically.)

At noon they stopped for a short meal in the middle of the grass. There was no spring or creek nearby, so for the first time they tapped some of the water barrels lashed to the rear of each wagon, and the drivers made a little dug-out fire, well cleared of the flammable vegetation, to heat their inevitable coffee. After she had eaten and wound the Thomas Arnold clock with Searle, Selena walked a quarter of a mile out into the prairie, swatting away bugs at every step. She intended to measure their latitude with her sextant, but the sun was so bright, the astonishing blankness of the landscape so distracting, that before she could finish, Webb Pattie was whistling again, the drivers were clambering to their feet, and in a matter of minutes the slow, rolling march of wagons had begun all over again.

By day five they had covered not quite seventy-five miles, about half the distance to the prairie oasis of Council Grove, and their trail routine was firmly established. Up at daybreak. A meal of fried bread or doughnuts and coffee, prepared by Lona. Then animals harnessed, wagons loaded and rolling by six or six-thirty. For their "nooner," which often came at eleven, the drivers would stop, have a light meal of more fried bread and coffee, and rest the animals for one or two hours. Searle and Selena would take their latitude and longitude and wind the Thomas Arnold. Just before breaking up camp at around two o'clock, the Expedition would take its principal meal of the day, a full dinner of meat, bread, dried fruit sometimes, potatoes, coffee. Then back into the wagons for another four or five hours of travel until Webb Pattie or one

of his outriders decided they had reached a satisfactory camp-
ing place for the night.

If they stopped by a creek, they forded it first and set up
camp on the other side, because mules in the morning, as
Pattie said, were just like people and refused to start their
work until they'd had their coffee and their breakfast, and
fording a creek was hard, slow, backbreaking travail. Then
the wagons would be drawn up into a tight circle, and the
mules and horses would be tethered nearby under guard.
Another meal of bread, coffee, fried meat; half an hour by
the campfire; bed. The drivers slept under the wagons, on
bedrolls. The Expedition men slept inside the wagons, tucked
between towering sacks of flour and coffee beans. According to an unspoken sense of Trail propriety, Selena spent the
nights apart in her canvas tent, in the center of the wagons.

The only surprise in the routine was the growing civility of
James Searle toward her. At first their daily noon sightings of
the sun and winding of the clock were sullen, wordless affairs. But a certain amount of conversation was actually necessary. Selena, the sea captain's daughter, was very quick
indeed with a sextant, and for longitude positioning could do
much of the complex logarithmic calculation in her head.
Searle was still gruff sometimes, but her calm, uncomplaining
competence had clearly begun to soften him.

"Just like a man," said the usually laconic half-breed Lona
one morning. "Finds out you can do his work for him, turns
all sugar." Then she brushed back her long black hair and
added with a shy grin, "Spends a fair deal of time sneaking
looks at you, miss, when he thinks you don't know."

Selena was far from the first woman to travel on the Santa
Fe Trail, Lona told her another day. White French-Canadian
épouses had gone with their trapper men over the Trail and
into the Rocky Mountains. Some Mexican women had come
to Independence last year all by themselves, in search of hus-
bands. Lona's own father had been a trapper and her mother
a Pawnee, and she had lived with them up and down the
Missouri, and since she married Pattie four years ago she'd

been out and back to Santa Fe twice. On the other hand, she said, frowning and holding up one of Selena's dresses to her lanky frame, none of those women had been fair and blonde and wore Paris, France, fashions.

On the sixth night the muggy prairie heat persisted long after the caravan had gone to bed. At some point after midnight, Selena sat up wide awake in her tent. For a moment or two she listened to the utter silence of the camp. Then she shrugged off her light blanket and crawled outside to look at the stars. Still there, as her father would say. Beyond the wagons, rising over the silver tips of the grass, arched the glittering, blazing blue-black bowl of the sky. Without thinking, she began to trace the familiar constellations, memorized when she was a girl of ten and never since forgotten. She was facing north, so there was Lyra in the east, Draco, Hercules, Boötes far to the west, with its bright reddish sky buoy Arcturus, bobbing in the night sea.

In ancient days, Mrs. Somerville had once told her in London, with all her wonderful imagination and learning, people felt much closer to the stars than we ever could now. A Babylonian priest would walk up a platform or ziggurat and believe he was almost in the heavens. The sky seemed very low to them. Daedalus flew only a thousand feet before he was next to the sun. Heraclitus thought the sun was the size of a shield.

Knowledge had changed all that, Selena thought. She hugged her knees and craned her neck for a better view of Draco. Science had changed all that. Now the stars were unimaginably far away. The universe had grown impossibly large. With his forty-foot-long reflecting telescope at Greenwich, Sir William Herschel had shown that the stars were all really suns, just like our own sun, blazing faintly away in infinite space, in millions of other galaxies, only Sir William went even further and called the galaxies, poetically, "island universes."

Pearl of Scotland was snoring and dreaming nearby on

the grass, but Selena couldn't see her. For all that celestial company, she supposed, human beings now probably felt lonelier than ever. She tried to picture a globe, Independence, Washington City, the Rue Jacob...island universes. She snapped a long stalk of grass and thought that the stars above her on the Santa Fe Trail were the biggest and brightest she'd ever seen; they looked as close to her as they would to a Babylonian. If she stretched out her arm full-length toward Arcturus, the stalk of grass would burst into flames. She was not a bit sleepy. Travelling west in America was like travelling back in time.

Some of the mules in the roped-off corral were pawing the ground. Over by Wagon Number Ten, Webb Pattie's silhouette could be seen sitting propped against a wheel. As best she could tell in the darkness, he was eating a Graham's orange cracker and looking out at the prairie. After a time she went quietly back to her absurd young lady's tent and dragged the little camp bed outside under the stars.

THOUGH THEY WERE STILL TWO DAYS AWAY FROM COUNCIL Grove, more and more trees had begun to appear along the trail. The creeks they forded now had steeper banks and stronger rushes of water. The clouds of insects, thick enough before, grew steadily worse, intolerable for mules and people alike.

Even more significantly, Indians, long discussed, long imagined around the campfires, now started to make their presence felt. Forty or fifty of them would materialize unexpectedly over a ridge, menacing silhouettes on horseback, watching and keeping their distance for miles. At other times they would simply ride alongside the wagons and stare impassively at the drivers.

Once a band of two dozen braves carrying bows and quivers of arrows halted in front of the lead wagon and formed a long, unsmiling barrier across the trail, until Webb Pattie, the picture of unconcern, rode his brindled mare into their midst and gestured broadly, as if he were shooing mosquitoes. Then the Indians, suddenly laughing and calling, wheeled their horses and galloped away.

Selena tried to make herself look detached and imperturbable, but inwardly her heart was shaking as if it had been struck by a hammer. Her mind flew back to the President's office, to Senator Benton's dire warning—*the terrible brutality of the western wilderness*. From the corner of her eye she could see James Searle studying her face. She held herself ramrod stiff on the wagon bench, for Science, and after an interminable pause the wagons resumed their noisy swaying passage.

Next day, at last, a dark line smudged low across the top of the horizon started to come into focus, first as treetops, eventually as thick groves and green brush, and finally, on day number thirteen, 148 miles from Independence, they rolled into a timbered island formed by a partially blocked river and a convergence of creeks, an island universe of leafy forest two or three miles wide that really might not have been out of place far back in Kentucky or Virginia.

The sparkling river that ran through the forest and created the oasis was called the Neosho, an Osage Indian word, Pattie told them, indicating that they were now in Osage country, not Pawnee. Two other caravans, heading east, were camped at the southern end, where the river curved out of the trees and into the prairie. Webb Pattie measured out a space at the northern end, and the Somerville-Babbage Expedition settled gratefully down for two days' rest.

The next morning Selena awoke abruptly with a feeling of strange uneasiness. She swung her feet over the end of the camp bed and listened for a moment. Nothing but the neighing of mules, the distant caw of a crow. When she turned her head, she could hear the Neosho River sliding through the grass nearby like a snake on its belly.

She pushed up the flap of the tent and found herself completely encircled—fifteen or twenty Indians, men, women, children, squatted on their heels in the cool morning dirt, staring. She snapped the flap down again and felt a cry rising in her throat. Then she forced herself to exhale slowly; inhale. There were fifty covered wagons camped in the Grove all around her, a hundred armed protectors. Absurdly, she unscrewed one of the short wooden poles in her folding bed and opened the flap once more. Pole in hand, lips thin and tight, she pushed her way through the squatting Indians toward the river.

Most of them came to their feet and followed her. As she knelt on the bank and splashed her face with water, they stood a few yards away and silently watched. When she finished her ablutions they pulled back in two lines, a gauntlet, to let her pass.

At noon, as she tried to nap in the heat, her tent flap suddenly flew open and seven Indian women in filthy buckskin tunics crowded in and darted forward like fish to touch her. Some spoke to her in their own language. She sat up and tried to answer, but their faces were blank and unfriendly, disfigured with thick vertical stripes of red and yellow coloring and what looked to her like wavy black tattoos, and the rancid smell of grease and dirt was so overpowering that she felt herself on the point of gagging. Brown fingers poked at her white skin and stroked her hair. Only when they began to unbutton her chemise did she spring angrily from the bed and (remembering Webb Pattie) shoo them out of the tent.

"Well, you're a public sight, that's all," Pattie drawled afterward, laughing. "People, even Indians, think they're just entitled to gander at a public sight. I'll never forget, my old Pap told me he lived in Virginia in the early twenties, down near Charlottesville, where Thomas Jefferson had his mansion. Jefferson used to come out and sit on his porch in the afternoon, and on the other side of the lawn, Pap said, there would be a dozen fancy carriages drawn up, full of people come to look at him. Just look at him. And so the old President would sit in his rocking chair and the people would sit in their carriages, staring and eating their picnic lunches, and nobody ever said a word, such was the price of fame."

"I'm not famous, and they weren't on my lawn, they were in my tent."

Pattie frowned at the cloudless sky and spat. "Never can make up my mind about Indians. These out here at Council Grove, the Kansa and the Kaws especially, some of the most degenerate creatures on God's flat earth. Lazy, superstitious, steal your boots off your feet. Don't even look good—never wash, and the river's right there, like a prairie bathtub. Smell to heaven. But then I go out past the big Arkansas River bend, I see Kiowa and Comanche braves so handsome and well formed you'd think they were your noble Greek statues come to life. And squaws that fine and womanly—I know white fur trappers married to Comanche wives, live in their tepees, hunt with the tribe, follow the Comanche way, and *they* say you can't get more civilized and happy. We call it goin' Injun."

"The search for Utopia," explained Professor Hollis, who had been standing nearby with Pryce. He spoke deliberately, with his eyes owlishly half shut behind his rimless spectacles, as if to a particularly dim-witted Harvard class. "Very much a civilized delusion. If it didn't begin with Plato, it began, I should say, with the French philosopher Montaigne."

Selena had long since stopped paying attention to Hollis's miniature lectures. The furtive little Harvard professor was interested, it was clear to her, only in academic poses, academic reputation—his treasured equations for predicting eclipse location, she had decided, were thoroughly impractical. Thank heaven for the Infant Engine.

"You married an Indian," she said to Webb Pattie.

Webb Pattie shook his head. "Half-breed. All the difference in the world. And she grew up around white settlements mostly."

"I wish us," said Pryce, ill-tempered for the first time ever in Selena's experience, "to keep our mind on the eclipse. Which is why we are here. Which is now less than two months away. How long are we to stay and wallow in this present Utopia, Mr. Pattie?"

"Pushing off tomorrow," Pattie said, "Mr. Pryce. As soon as the wagons are ready."

"See that they are," Pryce said curtly, and walked away.

But in the end, one of the wagons required extensive repairs to its rigging, and it was not until late the next afternoon that they set out again, heading westward.

The next two stages, Pattie warned them, would be longer and more arduous by far than the trip from Independence. First there were another two or three weeks of increasingly harsh, dry prairie from Council Grove to the Great Bend of the Arkansas River. There they would cross over the river and enter the suspicious and unfriendly Republic of Mexico. From this point on, they would be heading at a southwest angle along the little-used Cimarron Cutoff Route, with no reliable map or trail to follow, toward a vague and shifting spot called the Lower Springs. This was the dreaded *Jornada*, as the Mexicans called it, Apache and Kiowa country, the scene of innumerable Indian attacks and massacres, a truly desolate stretch of over seventy miles with no water source at all until they reached either the Springs or the Cimarron River, itself often bone-dry three-quarters of the year.

After which they would bring out the Infant Engine and recalculate precisely the longitude and latitude for the eclipse. And if the numbers were still as Charles Babbage predicted, they would then turn directly west and plunge straight ahead into the Great Southwestern Desert itself.

Two hours before twilight their wheels rolled out of the thick, moist grass of Council Grove and onto the dusty ruts of the Santa Fe Trail again.

Low on the horizon, against all logic, the sun looked hotter and hotter still.

CHAPTER TWENTY

The Theory of Miracles

O BSERVE, IF YOU PLEASE, LADIES AND GENTLEMEN, THE NUM-
bers on these three wheels."

On the other side of the world, in London to be exact,
halfway up the eastern and therefore shady and therefore
fashionable side of Dorset Street, Charles Babbage fixed his
teeth in a wide and rigidly insincere smile. About seventy
guests in all, he estimated, glittering with jewels, splendid in
evening dress, jammed into his drawing room so tightly that
those in front were actually bending down on their knees to
peer at the numbers, then rising and allowing the next row to
push forward and inspect. It was exactly 9:03, Saturday, the
26th of July, and the very high attendance at his *soirée* out of
season, Babbage decided, was a source of great social satisfaction. It was also doubtless due to the fact that he had taken
the unusual step of announcing on the invitations a formal title and theme for the evening: "The Theory of Miracles."

"They are all set at zero," grumbled his banker Edward
Kater, who was not professionally fond, Babbage supposed,
of the number zero.

"Is this the Difference Engine?" someone inquired from a
seat to Babbage's left. "No," Babbage said, turning with his
fixed smile in that direction. The voice, he thought, was

American. "This is the Demonstration Engine. The Difference Engine is in my workshop next door, in a special dust-proof hermetic chamber. This is much smaller and less complex, though perfectly suitable for our purposes."

The Demonstration Engine was, in fact, small enough to sit on an ordinary tea trolley, which Babbage's butler Simon had rolled in by himself, unassisted. It stood one and a half feet high, two feet wide, and two feet deep, a perfect bronze and steel manifestation of British precision. It consisted of four vertical steel columns, each with numerous cogs and gears and just below them two round, rather ocular wheels and a lever, six horizontal wheels continuously engraved with the numbers one through zero, counting right to left. It represented, Babbage thought, approximately one-seventh of the calculating capacity of the complete, true Engine, and in most ways it was very similar to the miniature Engine that Pryce and his astronomical caravan were carrying with them, at this very moment, into the trackless deserts of America. He glanced at the freestanding world globe in the corner and calculated. Five thousand miles away.

"If you were to paint in two eyes and a mouth," Edward Kater said, to the amused nods of those around him, "your engine would look rather like a human brain."

Babbage sniffed and let his gaze rise from the globe and sweep the room until he found the flatteringly intense face of Lady Ada Byron Lovelace over near the French doors. He would not have given Kater credit for that much imagination. He cleared his throat and held up his hands.

"If you have all had the opportunity to see...Every number of every wheel is set on the middle indicator at zero. I shall now proceed to demonstrate with the Demonstration Engine"—he paused expectantly, but only Lady Ada laughed—"my belief that the miracles testified to in Scripture are not fictions and superstitions disproved by modern science, as is so often alleged. They are, I feel certain, perfectly plausible events, and with the aid of the Engine they are comprehensible to every intelligent person."

"You are defending religion," said the American voice.

"I am," Babbage said brusquely. He gripped the L-shaped steel handle that protruded from the left-hand side of the Engine, waited until the room was completely still, and then turned the handle one revolution. The mechanism of the Engine operated with the faintest possible whisper or kiss of brass against brass. The first number on the right changed from zero to three.

"Observe again," Babbage said. He cranked the handle once more. The number on the wheel changed to six.

"Again," Babbage said. The number changed to nine. "Again."

"Twelve," said Edward Kater for the benefit of those in the rear of the room.

"Fifteen," said Babbage as he turned the handle yet again. "Eighteen."

"It's adding three every time," someone murmured. Babbage continued to smile and crank. *Twenty-one. Twenty-four. Twenty-seven.* Each time he turned the handle there was the same smooth, noiseless movement of the cogs and gears inside the brass "brain," and then the numbers on the bottom display wheel advanced by three. He turned, smiled, turned. The room grew restless.

"Not very thrilling, Babbage," said a new voice as the machine's wheels turned yet again and reached sixty. This was William Henry Fox-Talbot, the photography inventor. "Very boringly predictable and repetitive," he added, disagreeable as usual.

"Predictable and repetitive," Babbage said, still with the same fixed and rigid smile, "like the laws of nature, would you say? The sun rises each morning in the east by a predictable progression of seconds. Force always equals Mass times Acceleration—Newton's Second Law," he explained for the benefit of the ladies nearest him. "Two plus two always equals four."

"Don't see the point," Fox-Talbot complained. "What's this have to do with miracles?"

Babbage turned the handle. *Sixty-three.* Mrs. Mary Somerville was not present that night, he thought, looking again toward Lady Ada. More was the pity. *Sixty-six.* Fox-Talbot snorted. Someone he didn't know, a tall, lanky man with remarkably sunken cheeks, quite carelessly dressed, audibly cracked his knuckles. *Sixty-nine.*

"Now, Babbage," Fox-Talbot began, loudly, disagreeably. *One hundred and seventy-four.*

The whole drawing room gave a collective gasp and seemed to rise on its toes. The first few rows crowded forward. Babbage turned the handle once more, calmly, smile unchanged. *One hundred and seventy-seven.* One more turn. *One hundred and eighty,* and he released the handle, hooked his thumbs behind his jacket lapels, and made a slow, satisfied survey of his audience.

"Ladies and gentlemen," he said, "friends. You understand that you are the onlookers, that is your role. You observed a steady, regular, entirely predictable repetition, the addition of three, and you assumed or concluded that it was a 'law,' an event you could count on to happen every time I turned the handle. This unexpected leap from sixty-nine to one hundred and seventy-four seems to you a violation of this 'law,' because you had no way of predicting it, and of course you have no way of accounting for it now. But I had actually instructed the machine before I started that at the twenty-fourth repetition it would add, not three, but one hundred and five. So for *me* the discontinuity was not unexpected. Nor was it a violation of the law. Rather, it was the carrying out of a higher law, which was known all along to me, but not to you."

"In other words, a miracle," said the sunken-cheeked gentleman; unmistakably American.

"If you reason by analogy," Babbage said, "miracles in nature—the parting of the Red Sea, for example, Joshua's halting of the sun in the middle of the sky—are not necessarily violations of natural law, but the carrying out of a *higher* law, God's law, as yet unknown to us."

"And by the same analogy," the American drawled, "the

person who invented and programmed the machine would be a divinity."

"Albeit," retorted Babbage with an ironic little bow, "a minor one."

Afterward, as he talked with Lady Ada out on the balcony in the warm pink glow of an English summer night, the American gentleman simply strolled up to them, in the manner of his countrymen, and thrust out his hand. "Timothy Ferris," he said. "Came as the guest of—" he mentioned a name Babbage didn't recognize. "Curious because I'd heard about your machine back home. Also did some business with your uncle Richard a few years back."

"My great-uncle Richard?"

"Looked like you," Ferris said. "Taller, bushy-haired. Definitely eccentric." He wheeled abruptly and repeated his name to Lady Ada, who stared at his outstretched hand, then slowly took it, as if she had been given a dead fish.

"What I like about your machine," Ferris told Babbage, "is that you exert a *physical* force—you wind your crank— and you create a *mental* process. You add, you subtract, you get your logarithms, which is what the brain does, same exact thing."

Babbage leaned forward, blinking, to see Ferris better. The sunken cheeks were remarkable; they collapsed almost completely as he spoke, like a bellows, showing bone and jaw with perfect clarity, the result of some wasting disease, no doubt, yet they were not entirely repulsive, and what he said, of course, was indeed the great point: the machine *knew*. It exactly replicated a process of human thought. Foreigners were always more perspicacious about the Engine. Babbage's thoughts veered briefly toward the infuriating obtuseness of the Government, Sir Robert Peel's mulelike refusal to advance more funds.

"How in the world," Babbage said, "did you come to know my great-uncle?"

"Sold him leather goods," Ferris answered promptly, "in my store back in Kentucky."

"Did my great-uncle go to Kentucky?"

"Sure he did. Lived in the great city of Lexington three months, then moved on west. Told me he was a Pantisocrat— I made him spell it out—and the original founders fifty years ago always meant to come to Kentucky."

Babbage pursed his mouth thoughtfully. It was all quite true. The poets Coleridge and Southey and the radical philosopher Joseph Priestley had created Pantisocracy as a youthful "back-to-nature" scheme, and their earliest project had been a proposed emigration to Kentucky, twelve unmarried couples, where they would live in pastoral innocence and primitive freedom, like Red Indians. They had tried to persuade Wordsworth to go as well, but he was too sensible. Typically, of course, Coleridge had gotten himself unhappily married, Southey had wandered off somewhere, and the "commune" had collapsed.

"My father, Lord Byron," said Lady Ada to the sunken-cheeked Ferris, "thought they were all perfect jackasses."

"Don't know your father," Ferris said politely.

But before Babbage could rescue the conversation from Lady Ada's filial recollections, somebody in the drawing room had called him back to the Demonstration Engine, Fox-Talbot had put his hand on his shoulder and said he was better than a barker at a circus, and Timothy Ferris, when Babbage could finally look around again, had just disappeared into the second drawing room, where cold beef and claret were being served.

"Still don't agree with you, though, Babbage." Fox-Talbot stretched his neck and preened, all winks and nods to the little group of sycophants around him. Amateurs of photography, Babbage thought, not mathematicians. "Repeated numbers, Reason by Analogy, all that *stuff*." It was one of Fox-Talbot's peculiarities that at dinner parties he insisted on being served soup instead of meat. He was now sipping his abominable *potage* from one of Babbage's most delicate Meissen cups. "Don't believe in your 'Higher Law.' "

"Is the soup satisfactory?" Babbage asked.

"Delicious."

"Do you believe in a *cook?*"

In the second drawing room he found Ferris again, in a corner holding a pair of leather-bound books.

"About my great-uncle," Babbage said.

"Not much to tell, Mr. Babbage." Rudely, but then you couldn't always be sure with Americans, Ferris continued to leaf through one of the books. "I remember he bought two hundred and thirty dollars' worth of harnesses for his wagon rig. Had a Cherokee boy as a valet. Told me all about Pantisocracy and the beautiful pastoral life beyond the Mississippi. Seemed in pretty poor health even for a gent of—what would he be, seventy?"

"Sixty-five perhaps. He died a few years ago in St. Louis. No one knows the date or the cause."

"Ain't that something." Ferris stopped at a page toward the end of the book. "Money at stake, I guess."

His sunken cheeks *were* fascinating, Babbage thought. It was quite like speaking to a cadaver or the wax skull in a *memento mori.*

"Good-looking leather, calfskin. This is your article, I see." Ferris held up the topmost volume.

Babbage waved his hand dismissively. "An early exercise. I once worked for a life-assurance corporation, and I amused myself by calculating the numerical probability of resurrection from death. I estimated the total number of people who had ever lived since Creation and divided that into the number of times we have a record, verified by witnesses, of someone returning from the dead."

"Just one," Ferris said. "I'm a Methodist."

"I concluded the chances are two hundred thousand million to one."

"Long shot, all right," said Ferris with his skeletal, skulletal grin. "But not mathematically impossible, I guess." He flipped a page. "Funny thing, don't you think, Mr. Babbage? Your machine can find out the exact day and minute the sun's going to die and go out and then resurrect, but it can't tell you when your old uncle died."

Babbage felt a pang of discomfiture. He looked over his shoulder at his familiar guests, his familiar room. Simon was supervising the buffet as usual, there was Kater, there was Lady Ada with her mother, his paintings, his porcelain, good furniture, dozens and dozens of friends. "The other book in your hand," he heard himself telling Ferris, "contains the sermons of Tobias Swinden. A curiosity piece. The Reverend Swinden says the actual geographical location of Hell is in a corner of the sun, which accounts for the red flames observed during eclipses."

Ferris shook his head and continued to grin. "Myself," he said in his exotic American twang, "I would have put Hell somewhere west of St. Louis."

CHAPTER TWENTY-ONE

On the Trail

FIVE THOUSAND MILES WEST OF DORSET STREET, THOUGH not visibly closer to Hades or the sun, the Somerville-Babbage Expedition rolled across a seemingly endless prairie landscape, ten small white dots crawling over an enormous rumpled flag of dusty green and brown.

On July 29, the latitude reading at noon, taken as usual by James Searle and Selena, was 35 degrees, 6 minutes, 9 seconds north. Longitude was 106 degrees, 4 minutes, 20 seconds west. (The U.S. Army maps supplied by Lieutenant Frémont were quite badly off, also as usual, by one and a half minutes north, two minutes west.) The temperature, checked at the same time, was 94 degrees Fahrenheit. Winds were calm. High, thin cirrus clouds streaked the southwest sky. There was no rain whatsoever in sight. In the pocket-sized logbook she kept as a semi-official record, Selena wrote: *Approximate distance from Council Grove: 56 miles.* Then she squinted up at the sun and performed a quick mental calculation: *Days until the eclipse: 38.*

At two o'clock Webb Pattie made his shrill two-fingered whistle, rose in his stirrups, and called out, "Catch up, catch *up*!" One by one, with a great cracking and flourish of whips, the wagons inched forward again.

It is utterly impossible now—it was probably impossible then—to convey the true realities of life on a caravan of mule-drawn wagons, far out on the empty, wind-swept plains of western Kansas.

Day after day Selena woke in the darkness to the same sharp smell of roasting coffee, the crackle of burning wood; wet grass, mule hair, and musty straw; horses stirring. Through the opaque slant of her tent she could see the stiff white fingers of the dawn. Shadows moved back and forth on the canvas walls. Low voices, unmistakably masculine, quietly hawked and coughed and drifted about murmuring and making what her father used to call the daybreak sounds of nasal plumbing. If they had been on one of his ships at sea, she would have swung from her hammock down to a smooth tilting deck and the creak of wood and rope in the wind. Here, when she pulled aside the blanket on her cot and put her bare feet down, she touched unseen bristles of buffalo grass, cool earth. Before breakfast she and Lona walked back along the trail ruts, with Pearl of Scotland trotting beside them, the three females, and in the sleepy dim light, lifting their heavy skirts, went about their morning necessaries.

By the time the sun was level with the eastern horizon, they were already miles out along the endless trail, under the curved white eggshell of the sky, following the straight ruts straight ahead, as if they were driving methodically and directly toward the end of the world's great flat table. The ruts were not two-track grooves, such as a single wagon's four wheels would have made in the tall grass. They were wide square depressions in the earth, like dry creekbeds or a sunken road. And most of the time the wagons were not following them single file, as when crossing a ford, but were spread out in two or three separate lines twenty or thirty yards apart, rolling and swaying side-to-side like prairie pachyderms.

Up close, on top of a wagon, the noise of the caravan was loud and constant, the rattle and bang of the iron-rimmed wheels, the clatter-clatter of harnesses, the incessant clanging,

bouncing, metallic jingling of chains and pots and pans tied
to the sides of the wagon frames. From farther away, Selena
thought, from half a mile away, the prairie would swallow
this all and the noise would be little more than a low, grating
rumble. If she were suspended somehow high above, in
one of those hot-air balloons that occasionally came to the
Tuileries Gardens in Paris, the whole scene would be spread
out beneath her like a map unfolded on a desk. From such a
perspective she was sure it would all look exactly like the
cliché that everyone used, an immense, silvery-green sea of
grass, unmarred by trees or hills, rippled in long scythelike
waves by the moving wind. The caravan would be a tiny,
silent, mule-drawn flotilla sailing a dry sea, sending up narrow wakes of slowly billowing dust. If she could sail high
enough, she thought, the wagons would dwindle to specks
and disappear, dissolved in sunlight.

Unlike Professor Hollis or (she suspected) Bennit Cushing,
Selena was no very assiduous keeper of journals or diaries.
Even so, from time to time, especially at the long noon halts,
she would sit in the shade of her wagon, leaning against a
dirty wheel like one of the drowsing teamsters, and try to
write a few "memoranda" for her parents, on the busy cob-
blestoned and gaslit Rue Jacob half a world away.

Flowers, for one thing. For her mother she wrote down the
names, as supplied by Lona, of the numerous tenacious little
flowers that grew tangled and partly hidden in the tall grass,
or sometimes blossomed hardily on their own out in the open
ruts. There were places, she thought, she would remember all
her life. Places where for two or three whole acres the prairie
was like a Persian rug, thousands and thousands of lavender,
red, and yellow wildflowers mingling with the silvery weave
of the grass. Other places where wild grapevines ran riot, or
plums, persimmons, gooseberries, currants.

Or buffalo. The drawings she had seen in books had
scarcely prepared her for the sight of hundreds of the huge
shaggy beasts, big as one of the Baltimore & Ohio locomotives, grazing on the horizon. Occasionally the wagons came

close enough to a herd for her to make out the horns, the brutal black eyes and fist-sized nostrils, but usually Webb Pattie kept them at a far, safe distance. Nonetheless, running everywhere across the sea of grass, always in a north-south direction, there were buffalo trails, eight-inch-wide versions of the big wagons' trail ruts, trampled into existence by migrating hooves. Scattered along the buffalo trails were also buffalo wallows, small bright lagoons of rainwater, like turquoise beads strung on plain brown string. They were made, Pattie told her, by bulls fighting, pacing round and round and pawing up the earth.

And then there were the poppies, seen for just two or three days. These were a species of white poppy that bloomed only at night, and so irresistible were they that one day after the evening meal, while the men were tethering the animals, Selena ventured all alone out into the no-man's-land of the open prairie and filled her arms with their white fragrance. When she turned and started back, she had lingered so long that the stars were out in full force overhead, and the sky was a great black mirror of twinkling poppies. In the camp itself candles had turned the covered wagons into Japanese lanterns.

Eight days out of Council Grove, the southeast wind abruptly turned to the north and began to come whistling hard down the fields of grass. Black thunderclouds rose like warships over the western horizon, then the north, and climbed the sky with astonishing speed. In the lead with two or three of his scouts, Webb Pattie wheeled his brindled mare about and galloped back, shouting and waving his hat in his hand.

Before he was close enough for Selena to make out his actual words, thunder pealed far away, then almost instantly closer. The two sets of black clouds caromed into each other just above them. Rain started to fall in bursts of icy spray, driven like scuds along the top of the bending grass. For a moment the air smelled of electricity and had a taste of brass, and then the two black clouds were rent by the loudest explosion of lightning Selena had ever witnessed. Yellow zigzags forked again and again from the top of the sky to the endless black horizon; the air was full of unseen growling animals, hissing rain. Then the raindrops grew bigger, big as birds' eggs, plopping into the hard ground, hitting the taut canvas of the wagon tops with a sound like a stick raked along the spokes of a wheel.

By now Webb Pattie had turned the caravan 180 degrees, so that the mules were facing east, with their backs to the storm. The wet ground was already changing to mud. In a wild scramble of brays and shouts and whip cracks, the teamsters unhitched their animals and drove them together into a stupefied huddle. Other men, soaked and cursing, unloaded Selena's tent and two or three big rolls of shelter tarpaulins. The cook's crew frantically dug a fire hole. In ten minutes' time they were all drawn up in a cold, shivering camp, and a tiny fire was struggling to life under a lean-to tarpaulin. Then Webb Pattie, in an image of the Trail that Selena knew she would long treasure in her memory, walked out bareheaded, hands on his hips, a ruined cigar in his mouth, and stood on the tossing prairie, looking up defiantly at the tempest like a waterlogged Grahamite King Lear.

IT HAD NOT ESCAPED THE ATTENTION OF ANYONE ON THE caravan that, in the last few weeks, James Searle's attitude toward Selena had considerably softened. Indeed, it seemed now to have passed well beyond grudging civility toward something very like gallantry. He sometimes brought her, unasked, cups of coffee at the noon rest. He chatted earnestly during their latitude and longitude sightings, though chiefly about himself, not her, especially his adventures in Africa and his complete determination, when Pryce and Babbage paid him off, to return there for good. He *watched* her, she was becoming aware, constantly. Once when she was putting on her boots, she caught him staring at her ankle, and he had stammered and begged her pardon and claimed she

reminded him of his sister. She had begun, she realized belatedly, through no fault of her own, to excite certain tensions.

The American part of her character was rather grave in its
analysis of this new development. Opposites attract, she rea-
soned. Men were naturally drawn to what they could not
have. Her behavior, at all times, had been serious, chaste,
dedicated entirely to the pursuit of science; without a doubt
this was in and of itself provocative to a highly physical person like Searle. She had no intention whatsoever of giving in
herself to romantic, unprofessional, unscientific feelings.

The French part of her character was very pleased.

By the evening of the same day that the thunderstorm arrived, the whole camp had metamorphosed from a sea of
grass into a sea of glopping mud, and Webb Pattie had his
teamsters digging a ditch around their perimeter, to divert the
rising water. But soon enough the men simply threw down
their shovels and marched splashing and stomping back to
the wagons. A few tried to crawl under the wheels for shelter,
but the wind blew the rain up and down and sideways, in
stinging white sheets, and they were scarcely drier there than
out in the open. Most of them joined the Expedition members
who sat in the mud around Lona's miserable, tarpaulin-
covered little fire, wet blankets over their hunched shoulders,
waiting for food.

"If it rains like this on September 5," said Bennit Cushing,
to no one in particular, perversely cheerful, "awfully hard to
see the famous eclipse."

"Be quiet, Mr. Cushing," said Pryce. One of the Mexicans
repeated Cushing's remark in Spanish, to low grumbles.

"Certainly hard to take a daguerreotype, even with a 'special formula.' "

"I said be quiet, Mr. Cushing."

"Unless perhaps Miss Cott can operate her cameras in the
rain. Maybe Babbage will accept a drawing from me instead—watercolors, of course."

"The weather will be fine in September, the cameras will

work perfectly," James Searle told Cushing brusquely. "Keep your brainless criticisms to yourself, Cushing." To Selena: "We didn't finish calculating the longitude today, Miss Cott. Better see to it now, I suggest."

Selena felt her face color. For a long moment she sat stubbornly just where she was, silently fuming. What she did not need, she thought, was either Bennit Cushing's sarcastic condescension *or* James Searle's rather heavy-handed gallantry. What she did need was a dry bed and a cup of hot tea and milk and a long afternoon in the dressmakers' shops on the Rue Saint-Honoré.

"I have the notebooks in the wagon," Searle added, less peremptorily, getting to his feet and flapping water from his hat.

Selena shot her stoniest glance at Cushing. Wasted, of course, in the rain and the flickering light of the fire. Even the shadows were wet. "More like Noah's ark than a wagon tonight, I imagine, Mr. Searle. But lead on. It will be a mathematical pleasure." She smiled sweetly, drew her rain cloak tighter about her head and shoulders, and rose to join him.

Webb Pattie watched curiously as they walked away. Then he turned to Pryce and nodded thoughtfully. "Look like an old pair of turtledoves, don't they, Mr. Pryce? Heads all bent together. Pretty as a picture."

Professor Hollis snorted. "Doubtless she's pretty. But I assure you she is not a good mathematician. I've said it before. She has no university degree or training. She shows no understanding at all of the usefulness of my equations. I've had to correct her *twice* on longitudes already." To Bennit Cushing, whose expression had gone oddly blank, he elaborated with refined and academic malice, "If we depend on Miss Cott and her rote calculations with the miniature Engine, we'll be miles and miles off course for the eclipse, rain or shine." When Cushing made no response, he muttered petulantly, "So many things to go *wrong*. One almost wishes her ill success."

CHAPTER TWENTY-TWO

Minor Delays

AT DAWN THE STORM COULD BE SEEN LIMPING LIKE A THIEF in black tatters across the eastern horizon. Soon after, the prairie flared into light again. Then Pattie and his teamsters were up and busy, folding the big tarpaulins and storing them, hitching the mules, kicking mud onto the breakfast fire. By quarter to seven the storm was forgotten, the caravan was once more rolling and swaying in its monotonous rhythm over the slick, soupy trail ruts, moving west.

At noon the sun was as hot as ever; hotter. The swarms of insects that had disappeared after Council Grove now reappeared and followed them everywhere, almost as dense on the ground as in the air.

They had passed from the dominion of one great element to its exact opposite. The dark waterlogged thunderclouds of the day before were gone, but now in their place, all along the southern horizon, perhaps thirty miles away, thick dark clouds of another kind hovered low in the sky.

"Prairie fire," said Webb Pattie succinctly. "Smoke."

And it was true, as Selena found when she trained her telescope on them. The clouds were smoke, kept close to the ground by the heat of the day, and underneath them ran a long curling finger of orange that seemed to writhe and dart and coil like a living thing. She might have been watching, she thought, the very rim of the sun and its corona, an eerie prefiguration of the eclipse.

The fires were caused sometimes by lightning, Pattie explained, and sometimes by Indian hunters waving rag torches in the dry grass, though that usually happened later on in the year. The object then was to drive their game, especially antelope and deer, toward the edge of the creeks, where they could be hunted more easily. The object of a lightning fire, he said, was apparently just to burn the whole damn continent to the ground.

Hour after hour the fire drew closer. As the wagons slowly, imperceptibly swung to the left, the flames climbed higher into the sky. Acrid smoke stung Selena's nostrils and eyes. Flocks of birds, burnt out from their nests in the grass, would rise and whirl, screaming. Shrubs and trees danced in fantastic groups. Even from a distance she could hear the grass crackle and feel the blasts of heat. Toward late afternoon the scattered lines of the fire closed up and joined together, and for an hour or two the caravan seemed to be half encircled by a vast crescent of red.

The mules were pushed almost to panic—they kicked and shied constantly, especially the dozen or so auxiliary mules trailing Wagon Number Ten. The Mexican drivers wrapped their blue bandannas around their faces, as protection against the roiling smoke, and both Webb Pattie and Searle dashed ahead on their mounts to scout a stretch of burning terrain. But in fact, at this point the prairie was deeply crisscrossed with low creeks and gullies that served as natural firebreaks, and much of the grass was still damp from the previous day's storm and burned only partially, or not at all. The wagons moved steadily ahead, sometimes over beds of still-warm ashes and cinders. Snakes peered up from their holes in the burnt ground. Lizards, toads, mice of all kinds sat passive, with no grass or shrubs to shelter them. Pearl of Scotland, turned dusty black by the ashes, was in a kind of terrier ecstacy

of barking and pursuit, until at last she was completely exhausted and fell asleep, twitching and growling, in Lona's lap.

The caravan made its ten laborious miles that day and
camped at sunset beside a clear rushing stream and a stand of
cottonwoods, and over the whole long eastern horizon the
only sign that remained of the fire was a narrow band of
floating red light.

They were joined that night, to Selena's considerable surprise, by three Pawnee Indian braves, who materialized out of
the darkness, on horseback. Webb Pattie and Lona spoke to
them at length, warily, and after a time all three of them dismounted and came to sit by the fire. Selena watched in fasci-
nation.

The Pawnees were dressed in buckskin trousers and moccasins, no shirts. They were clean-shaven, but their hair (like
Bennit Cushing's) hung uncombed to their shoulders. They
spoke to Lona and Pattie in their own language, but otherwise sat in monumental silence as the food was served. They
drank coffee, however, with the relish of everyone else on the
prairie, and evidently praised Lona's special trail bread. And
then, after they had finished their meal, they stretched themselves before the fire and began to drum their hands rhythmically on their chests, making a low, hollow sound. This was
soon accompanied by a high-pitched chant that seemed to
consist of long, musical phrases, though each one ended
abruptly, with a sound like "Huh!"

When Selena made her way around the fire and asked
Lona for a translation, the half-breed cook gave one of her
rare smiles and said they were chanting about the way the
caravan looked, and the people and things in it. ("Rob us
blind if they could," Pattie grumbled beside her.) They
thought the young white woman was handsome, and also
brave to come out on the prairie. They liked Bennit Cushing's
hair and James Searle's pistol, and they said Professor Hollis,
with his rimless spectacles and ugly moustache, looked like a
horned frog and they would cheerfully roast him on a spit.

Sometime during the night the Pawnees vanished as mysteriously as they had appeared, although in the morning two of the auxiliary mules were also missing, and twenty pounds of coffee beans.

That day they covered twelve miles, the hardest yet, up and down steep, thorny, clothes-ripping, mule-torturing creek fords. The day after that, even Selena, without Webb Pattie's practiced eye, could tell that the grass was growing shorter and tougher, and the land somehow seemed to be tilting like a tabletop south. They saw more and more buffalo. Here and there grew another isolated stand of cottonwoods, but Pattie, out of fear of larger groups of Indians, steered the wagons well away from them. At night they heard wolves. Once or twice a scout brought in a freshly killed deer or antelope for dinner. Otherwise, meals at noon and night began to consist of water or coffee, fried bread, and a ration of "jerky"— tough ribbons of dried beef packed far back, long ago, in Independence, a world away.

On the two-page Topographical Corps map where Selena traced their path day-by-day, the Expedition was now gently turning in a southwest direction, toward a thin squiggle of blue ink that Pattie identified for them as the Great Bend of the Arkansas River.

Before that, however, they had to cross two bodies of water not on the map. The first was the Little Arkansas, a fairly easy ford, not more than eight or nine yards wide. The second was called Cold Creek or Cow Creek—Pattie and George disagreed—and thanks to the recent rains it was now almost a hundred yards wide in places, and wandered in several branches through sandbars and matted grass, and its gritty banks posed, Pattie warned them, considerable danger of quicksand.

They reached it at dusk on the fifteenth day out of Council Grove. And then at first dawn they crossed over in single file and for nearly twelve hours after that they plowed their way like a fleet of barges through a thick canebrake of shoulder-high reeds and astonishingly hard brambles—"green cast-iron," the teamsters called it. For half an hour at a time they were up to their wheel tops in mire and mud. The briars and broken reeds tore at the skin of men and animals alike. Again and again the drivers jumped from their wagon benches into the muck, lowered their shoulders to the wheels, and pushed and heaved till their hands were bloody and their clothes caked with mud and their faces black with crawling insects.

By late afternoon they had covered not quite three miles, but they were out once more on the flat, featureless plains, pointed west toward a pale golden-white sun that looked sympathetically, Selena thought, as weary and drawn as they did, an old rubbed coin in the sky.

THE NEXT DAY THEY COVERED PERHAPS EIGHT OR NINE MILES, then stopped for an early camp to make repairs to the wagons. An unexpected respite, the ideal opportunity, Selena decided, to bring out one of her daguerreotype cameras and experiment with recording the prairie landscape. For the first time since St. Louis she opened her photographic trunks and prepared two or three copper plates for exposure. When they were ready, she slung the developing box under one arm and a satchel with camera and chemicals under the other and half walked, half staggered all by herself to a sandy knoll just beyond the wagons. The crest was no more than a hundred feet above the trail ruts, but practically a mountain peak on the level grassland. It was already occupied by two or three curious rabbits crouching among some wild plum bushes. Occupied as well, she was not especially pleased to find, by Bennit Cushing.

His greeting was more or less what she expected.

"I thought your able-bodied admirer would carry that for you."

"If you mean Mr. Searle, he's gone out with the scouts to hunt."

"Ah yes, spreading slaughter and contentment."

Selena jammed the legs of her camera tripod into the dirt and wiped a strand of hair back from her forehead.

"I like your hat," Cushing said. "I've been meaning to tell you."

"Thank you." Three days ago she had thrown away her conventional cotton bonnet, such as even Lona wore, and adopted a man's brown slouch Stetson-style hat, purchased from an amused Mexican teamster. She took it off now and let it drop to the ground so that she could look through the eyepiece of the camera unobstructed. She was wearing a loose dress with three-quarter-length puffed sleeves, but like all modern women's dresses it had only one pocket, on the right-hand side of the skirt, and of course she needed half a dozen pockets for her copper plates and chemical phials alone. Tomorrow, she resolved, she would fashion a pair of men's trousers out of torn-up dresses and shock the world; then a practical vest of a thousand pockets. She would look like nobody's sister at all.

She was not going to use her special accelerator formula today—there was plenty of light, there was no point in wasting a single precious drop of it before the eclipse. As quickly as possible she set up an ordinary arrangement of chemicals around the portable developing box and inserted one of her already prepared copper plates in the camera. Then she focused the lens on the horizon and opened the shutter.

"Your photograph is looking quite sadly accurate and corpselike," Bennit Cushing commented some five or ten minutes later, coming over and peering down into the developing box.

"I would have thought, Mr. Cushing, that a painter was interested in accuracy."

"Then you would have thought wrong." He moved his sketching easel a few feet nearer her camera. Selena put her eye back to her viewer. Down below, the ten covered wagons of the caravan were spread out in a lazy semicircle, shimmering in the late afternoon heat, she thought, like so many white biscuits on a stove.

"If I were merely interested in copying nature," Cushing said, "I would invest in a physionotrace machine."

They were both facing the enormous western horizon. In her emerging photographic plate even a casual observer could recognize that the apparent flatness of the land was actually a rolling and irregular series of gentle billows, like surf, with here and there a deeper, darker indentation made by a creekbed or a crumbling ledge of earth and grass. A geologist would have noted that the creekbeds ran uniformly north to south. In the sharp black and white of the daguerreotype, the topsoil was thick and granular, while the buffalo grass had the wooly texture of a carpet.

"You see, of course, what I've done." Cushing nodded toward his sketch. (There were times, Selena thought, when Bennit Cushing was even more pompous than Professor Hollis.) But she did see what he had done. He had greatly exaggerated the darkness of the horizon and magnified the long billows of grass, so that the wind's breath seemed almost present on the paper. Belatedly she remembered her own musings, back in Independence, on the challenge of the camera and need for painting to do something more than record an image. The general effect of his drawing was one of immense, haunting loneliness, a feeling of emptiness—lostness—which, when she lifted her head to look up again at the sky, she reluctantly acknowledged to be true.

"You've put in Indians," she said, to object. Cushing had, in fact, in one corner drawn a pair of Indian braves, standing with their backs to the observer, bows and arrows in their hands. "And a moon."

She flipped the sketchbook on the easel back a page. The same horizon, colors, solitary clouds. But now a pale yellowish-green disk floated to one side, above the endless prairie. Delicately, Cushing's pencil had implied a human face on the moon, lovely and sad.

"I work by personal feeling," he said. "Your camera merely records chemical reactions. It would make exactly the same picture no matter who pulled the lever, if I did it or Charles Babbage or Pearl of Scotland. Even the mercenary and malign Henshaw Pryce. If I decided to paint the sun on this," he added, stabbing with his pencil at the easel, "I'd make it bloodred and huge, a big red blot of anger, as if somebody had shot a bullet through the skin of the sky. That's what you'd *feel*."

What she felt, Selena decided, was that Bennit Cushing had no tact or sensitivity whatsoever. The sun was what she knew about, the sun was her special subject. The sun was the reason she was journeying halfway across an empty, lonely continent. Her photograph would capture the true reality of the sun: the sun was simply a blazing white sphere of unimaginably hot gases ninety million miles away, which the cool orb of the moon would soon obscure and eclipse, according to the immutable laws of mathematics, and her camera would immutably record it all.

It would be pointless to say any of this, to say one word of it to someone as self-absorbed and illogical as Bennit Cushing.

She picked up her box and camera tripod and prepared to leave.

"I would have thought," said Cushing, "a woman would be more interested in art, feminine things."

"I'll send Pearl of Scotland up to you," Selena said sweetly. Then she turned and started to walk downhill back to the wagons.

Bennit Cushing watched her go. Almost of its own volition his pencil began to sketch her hair, her small shoulders; a few short lines suggested the sweep of her dress along the grass, the swell of her hip, which the dress did not quite conceal. He took up a darker pencil and drew an exaggerated solah hat, then a man's jaw as big as a cowcatcher. After a moment he ripped the page from the book and crushed it under his boot.

Next day, the wagons reached the north bank of the broad Arkansas River and began to follow its long green curve toward the southwestern desert.

Days until the eclipse: 22.

CHAPTER TWENTY-THREE

Dis-Astrum

THE MORNING OF AUGUST 15 BEGAN WITH THE USUAL golden-orange prairie sun climbing up, rosy finger by rosy finger, over the iron-gray rungs and ladder of the eastern horizon. Five-forty A.M. Temperature: 58 degrees. Wind: nil. An ordinary day.

Problems began almost at once.

The two "wheeler" mules in Wagon Number Ten, the closest animals to the wagon, were just being backed into their harnesses when a rattlesnake deep in the grass suddenly raised its head and struck the left-hand mule in the leg. In an instant, before the teamsters could react, the mules were kicking and rearing wildly. The wounded mule began to pull violently sideways. Its torque wrenched the front wheels over and around, an iron rim twisted and snapped, the wooden spokes flew apart, and the whole heavily loaded wagon tilted and sagged to the ground as if it were kneeling.

From the other end of the train Webb Pattie and George rushed forward, waving their hats and shouting. But the mules were now shaking free of their hitchings and starting to run. One bucked and blindly kicked and another wagon wheel broke into splinters. The second mule bolted toward the river, stumbled and pitched headlong, and disappeared into the current. Wagon Number Ten groaned and its front axle cracked with a sound like the bang of a gun.

It was, at first sight, merely another delay, a matter of jacking the wagon up and hammering the wheels back together. As for the mules—rattlesnakes in some parts of the Trail were as common as mosquitoes. One of the routine duties of the wagonmaster was to steer around them as they lay by the dozens in the sun, or else to treat and heal the animals and people they bit. The runaway mule was presumed drowned and would be replaced from the auxiliary corral. Meanwhile two teamsters tied down its yoke mate and scarified its leg with a hot knife to drain the poison. With a sigh Webb Pattie unloaded his box of tools.

But after an hour of hard labor, flat on his back in the dirt, he emerged grim-faced to announce that the whole axle-tree was hopelessly shattered. There was no possibility of repair. He and George would have to rebuild it with some of the spare lengths of timber they had carried out from Council Grove, slung under the various wagon frames like extra masts and spars for a ship. Half a day's work at least, in the boiling sun.

The rest of the caravan moved upslope to escape the swarms of insects rising from the river. Lona went off in search of hartshorn to rub on the mule's leg.

At one o'clock they set out again, but slowly, almost gingerly, to test the new rigging on Wagon Number Ten. The injured mule walked alongside its usual team, but soon enough began a pattern of staggering and falling behind, trotting for a moment to catch up, falling back again. By three o'clock its fetlock had swollen to the size of a bucket. At four o'clock it began to bray without ceasing, so that Selena, walking herself on the other side of Number Ten, had to stop her ears with her hands. Even as she was turning her head away, the mule galloped forward in a slathering frenzy, halted abruptly and stood trembling on three legs, then crumpled sideways and fell with a bone-hollow thud and died.

The loss of two mules in one day made their reserve of

only eight more mules, exactly a full team, look suddenly, ominously, small. Despite the blistering heat of the afternoon sun, Pattie and George took another hour to inspect and re-arrange the others and adjust the wagon loads ("muline dis-plomacy," Pattie called it). While they worked, Selena, with only her Stetson hat for shade, sat by Lona's little cooking fire with a tin cup of untasted coffee and stared wordlessly across the coals at Bennit Cushing and Pryce. Both men's eyes were red and swollen from mosquito bites. Pryce's smooth com-plexion was mottled and streaked with dirt, since he, like the rest of them, did not want to get near the river to wash, and his rakish Prince of Wales moustache hung sadly and unfashion-ably limp, gray with ashes from the fire. Selena stroked the whimpering Pearl of Scotland at her feet and decided not to look in a mirror that day, or the next.

Finally, just after five o'clock Webb Pattie smacked the last mule's dusty rump into its traces and walked back to them. Half-moon was rising pretty soon, he muttered to Pryce. They might as well make three or four miles in the moonlight before they quit.

Bennit Cushing came slowly to his feet and fanned his red face with his hat. "Three or four miles in Nebuchadnezzar's furnace is more like it."

For once, Selena thought, the Merchant and the Artist agreed. Pryce nodded to Cushing in almost cordial acknowl-edgment. "This has certainly been the worst day so far."

"Smooth as silk tonight," Webb Pattie said, chewing on a filthy Graham's Cracker, as wrong, Selena was shortly to think, as he could possibly be.

A crescent moon rose in the east just before seven, strangely glowing and hallucinatory. The ten wagons of the caravan were spread out across the open prairie in two un-even lines, first four, then six abreast. In the slanting twilight the trail ruts grew harder and harder to see. And then as night came on, under the eerie light of the moon, the land all turned to silver and shadow; every hump and dip of the ground seemed to be smoothed out and flattened. In the utter silence of the evening, the jingle of their chains and harnesses had a jaunty sleighbell-like sound. As if to recover lost time the wagons began to pick up speed.

They had never travelled at night before. On the bench of Number Four, just behind her Mexican driver, Selena watched the great vast landscape rise and fall in its new rhythm. It was a man's chest, breathing in and out, she thought drowsily, and they were Lilliputians crawling over it. Or they were a schooner tossing under a moonlit sky. She craned her head to find Arcturus. She thought of Mrs. Somerville, five thousand miles away in London, writing and studying no doubt or, if it was evening, attending one of Mr. Babbage's *soirées*. In her weariness the difference in time became jumbled. She pictured the little gold watch Mrs. Somerville had bought in Paris and carried on a black ribbon and always used for astronomical observations, and her mind made a sleepy leap of association to the very indelicate, very suggestive joke about a large key that opened her father's favorite novel, *Tristram Shandy*—"Pray, my dear, have you not forgot to wind up the clock?" She wondered if James Searle ever had read it.

With a start Selena sat up straight on her seat and looked for Searle. *Had* they wound the clock that day? She couldn't remember—smoke, heat, the miserable insects by the river. Had they walked out at noon to take their observation? There had been the rattlesnake, the dying mule. She swivelled in the other direction to find Webb Pattie.

But at that precise moment the lead wagons were coming to a wide, shallow ford, and Webb Pattie's horse she could just see clambering up on the other side. Speed was deceptive in the moonlight. They were all going fast, all the wagons were going fast. Pattie stood in his stirrups and looked back. He started to wave his arm to slow them down—Selena had a glimpse of the Arkansas River off to the left, coiled under the moon like a silver-backed snake. Then her wagon hit the ford with a stupendous wheel-dropping, spine-thumping jolt, a blinding geyser of water burst over her head, and the shallow ford turned treacherously deep.

The first line of wagons must have reached the ford at almost the same instant. They bounced, plunged, shot up again. Sheer momentum carried them halfway up the other bank and into a dense thicket of reeds. Selena's driver yanked his panicked mules to a wild careening halt.

On the other side of the ford, braking desperately, the second line of wagons was skidding sideways in a cloud of dust. She heard cries, whips, the nearest two wagons seemed to freeze in space, suspended over the grass, under the moon. Then the teams of mules collided, wheels crashed together with a shriek of iron, and the whole tangled, billowing mass of canvas and shadows collapsed in the ford like a sinking ship.

The day was not done yet.

For over an hour Webb Pattie directed a kind of makeshift salvage operation. On the far bank next to Lona, wet and shivering despite the warm night, Selena watched as the men heaved and pulled at the shattered Conestogas. Darkness and moonlight fractured them into white-shirted arms, flashes of skin. Sometimes they were chest-deep wading in the deceptively swift-running water, sometimes they were crawling on hands and knees in the reeds and grass, over a cat's cradle of ropes and towing cables stretched from bank to bank. Webb Pattie lashed his mules, cursed in English, Spanish, and Pawnee, and little by little, as the half-moon slipped out of sight in the west, the two wrecked wagons came ashore.

Wrecked they were, certainly.

Neither of them, the teamsters agreed, would ever roll again. All of the frames and axles were broken. Only two wheels had survived. Five of the sixteen mules were so badly injured that George and James Searle walked grimly from animal to animal with their long-barreled pistols. As the shots resounded through the darkness, Selena averted her eyes.

Two of the Mexican teamsters had probable broken arms.

One driver had evidently been crushed by his own wagon: he lay unconscious, blood seeping from his ears and one nostril. Another had a dangerous-looking gash across his head and a broken wrist. Selena tore a skirt into strips for bandages. Lona boiled a mixture of what she said was feverfew herb and mint. The other members of the Expedition sat or stood ineffectually by a fire while the teamsters stacked what they could save from the creek. Off to one side of the fire, hands jammed in his pockets, Pryce stood with an expression of pure, unchanging fury on his face. When Webb Pattie approached him with a question, Pryce turned on his heel and walked away.

Somewhere close to midnight, Selena crept into a wagon and lay down next to Lona and Pearl of Scotland. At James Searle's first rap she rose wearily on one arm, and Pearl of Scotland barked.

"We need to wind the clock," he said, stone-faced and grim as Pryce.

But at Wagon Number Four, where the Thomas Arnold clock and the Infant Engine were stored, they found the clock springs still so tight that they must have been wound at some point during the day, though in their exhausted state of mind neither of them could remember when.

At earliest dawn, with the eastern sun no bigger than a glowing coal in a bed of gray clouds, Webb Pattie was up and inspecting the wagons all over again. By the time the breakfast fire was lit and the three big iron coffee pots were on the flames, it was obvious to everyone, even the novice Expedition members, that a crisis had arrived.

The men with the broken arms could go on, of course— broken arms were as common as stubbed toes on the Santa Fe Trail. But the two badly injured drivers couldn't possibly survive the coming ordeal of the *Jornada* down to the Cimarron River, much less the cross-country trek, however short, to the eclipse. There was a hospital of sorts at Bent's Fort, eighty or ninety miles farther along the Arkansas. Another at Fort Leavenworth, north of Council Grove. Most likely in a few days or so a traders' caravan would show up on the main trail and, for a price, take them on. Lona was a skilled nurse. If George remained with her, and two wagons and their crews . . .

"Which would leave us six wagons," Pryce said. He had gotten up even before Pattie and washed his face in the creek and put on fresh clothes, so that unlike anybody else around the fire he looked almost as dapper as if he were about to take a stroll down Regent Street. But his tone of voice was unchanged from last night's fury. Instinctively, Selena shifted for a better view of Webb Pattie's homely Church-of-the-Horse face.

"You figure it was my fault, Mr. Pryce, go right ahead and say so."

"You lost two valuable mules in the morning. You decided to travel at night, and when the wagons were going too fast you did nothing at all. Yes, I say so. Sheer incompetence."

Lumbering, unshaven George stirred slightly. "Snakes are bad in the summer." He kicked one heel at the fire. "I've seen it worse. Can't blame Webb."

"Sheer incompetence," Pryce repeated.

"You want me to go back to Council Grove," Pattie said, "so be it. Mr. Searle there can handle any job you want done. Almost any job."

Pryce let his icy gaze travel from Pattie to Searle and back again.

"We're still three weeks from the eclipse," Searle said quietly. "He knows the trail." He was standing beside Bennit Cushing with a tin cup of Lona's breakfast coffee in his hand, and Selena was surprised by the mild, deferential tone of his voice.

"Do we have enough supplies?" Pryce asked.

"We prepared very well," Searle replied.

Pattie tipped back his old shapeless hat. "I remember in Independence, Mr. Pryce, you said we were 'brilliantly overpacked,' your very words."

Pryce worked his mouth. After another long, stony gaze at Searle he pulled out his gold pocket watch, studied the dial, then turned silently away.

"I take that as an English yes," Webb Pattie said. He stood and dusted his hat against his leg and started to walk toward the lead wagon.

"It was like a railroad concussion, really," prattled Professor Hollis, hugging his knees to his chest, "last night. I tell my students at Harvard that the word 'disaster' comes from the Latin, *dis-astrum,* 'against the stars.' An astrological term."

"Hollis," said Bennit Cushing, "you're a fool."

The day was relentlessly clouding over. For two more hours, as the air grew heavier and the sun grew hotter, the muttering teamsters repacked and transferred baggage. The five French-Canadians would stay with Lona and George and the injured drivers. The remaining seven teamsters, all Mexican, would go forward, though there was much grumbling and shuffling of feet and tobacco-spitting resistance and in the end Webb Pattie himself had to shout in Spanish and make a show of balling his fists. In the Expedition wagons, telescopes and cameras had first priority, naturally, and the padded trunk with the Infant Engine; firearms and ammunition next. Food and water barrels had to be divided between the two groups; coffee, dried meat, and vegetables rationed. Pryce stood by Wagon Number One and drew line after line across his master inventory and said not a word.

A little past noon, the unhappy Mexican drivers climbed into their saddles. Lona gave Webb Pattie a brief, stoic embrace, and Pearl of Scotland, who was staying behind, barked twice and lay down in the grass. Pattie swung into his own saddle and raised his hat. After a long moment, creaking and swaying, the six Expedition wagons began to roll west.

And then anticlimactically, half a mile along the trail they stopped again while one of the drivers shifted his ballast from front to rear. In the lull Selena lowered herself to the ground and walked out onto the prairie thirty or forty yards, to escape the dust.

She pulled the brim of her Stetson down to shade her eyes. In the chastened mood of the morning the caravan was formed in a single file parallel to the river. From where she

stood, it looked amazingly small and fragile. The two returning wagons and the wreckage-littered ford were already out
of sight, behind a low hump of silver-green grass. Even so,
men's voices reached her from over the ridge, in little knocks
of sound buffeted by the rising wind.

She was her father's daughter, of course, and just as if she
were a small girl again and he were with her, she oriented herself by the compass. To the north were lowering thunder-
heads, black and sullen. South and west, except for the sandy
glint of the Arkansas, the horizon stretched flat and clear and
utterly empty.

She turned to face the east and saw the enormous copper
orb of the sun smoldering in the clouds. A single bird, a
hawk, but too far away to identify, moved in a long silent
glide from north to south. As long as she lived, she thought,
she would remember this trail, not as trees and land, but sun
and sky.

Over the ridge now suddenly, barking frenziedly, appeared
the tiny white form of Pearl of Scotland. Selena took a step
forward. But then as abruptly as she had appeared, Pearl
came to a halt. She stood on her back legs and barked once
more. Someone called her name and the little dog whirled
and vanished over the ridge.

Long after she had gone Selena stood in the short grass, in
her mud-stiff cotton dress and floppy man's hat, watching. In
the unmathematical, unscientific part of her mind, she imagined that the rest of the country, Missouri, St. Louis, Washington City, all of it, had simply pulled away from the spot
where she stood and also vanished, like a ship leaving a dock,
like a departing planet. She might have been a figure, she
thought, in one of Bennit Cushing's drawings. She had never
felt so alone, so solitary and alone in her life.

CHAPTER TWENTY-FOUR

Rotten Row

B<small>Y NO MEANS SOLITARY OR UNPOPULATED, OF ALL THE FASH-</small>ionable spots in fashionable London perhaps the most glamorous—and paradoxical—was the long, tree-shaded riding path that curled in a graceful arc around the southeast corner of Hyde Park and was variously known as the Ladies' Mile or Rotten Row.

Here, throughout the spring and summer seasons, gathered the best-dressed, best-fed inhabitants of nearby Mayfair, hundreds of them, men and women both, trailed by their uniformed foot pages and waddling chaperons, splendid in their red and green riding costumes and polished leather boots and shoes, absolutely radiant (when the spongy English climate permitted) in the afternoon sunshine.

The paradox, of course, was that mingled among so many representatives of wealth and respectability was a very large number of the very poor and the very, very disreputable. These were, first, ladies of the demimonde, the bold, expensive courtesans who were so much a fixture of early Victorian life. To the practiced eye they were distinguished by a certain vulgarity of taste in their expensive riding habits and by a constant flirtatious working of their little knotted horsewhips, a gesture known to excite a not inconsiderable portion of their clientele. Some, indeed, could be observed from time to time actually halting their mounts on the riding paths, linking their hands behind their backs, and languorously stretching their chests and shoulders as if to relieve a kink. Everyone studied these free-spirited birds of passage more or less openly, men for the purposes of assignation or admiration, women for the longer-lasting pleasures of outrage or scandal. It was, however, an age of pragmatic hypocrisy, the courtesans were well dressed and mounted, and no one too loudly objected to their presence.

Not so with the other category of disreputables, the swarms of tramps, organ-grinders, Irishmen, pickpockets, and ragged street urchins who lent an ominous, scowling air of class division to the scene. These loitered on the Park's grass or strolled idly along the margins of the riding path, sullenly observing the parade. Now and again one of the urchins would dash jubilantly back and forth among the horses until a bobby, sighing heavily, would emerge from the trees and with a whistle and a nightstick restore the Ladies' Mile to order.

Charles Babbage, riding calmly along the central portion of the path, heading toward Kensington Gardens, was not an unworldly man. He knew, for instance, some thieves' slang, and had been heard to use it for the shocked amusement of guests at his Saturday *soirées*. He knew that the police constables in their tall blue-bottle hats and enormous black shoes were called "crushers." He knew that the small girls patrolling the opposite side of Kensington High Street, looking furtively over fences and down alleys, were "snowing," that is, watching for unattended laundry drying on lines in back gardens, which they could snatch in an instant and resell at an "uncle" shop for a halfpence per pound. He also knew, because he had once written a scientific paper on the subject of lock-picking, that specialists in that trade were called "screwsmen" and that pickpockets such as the one he now observed, bumping a gentleman spectator and deftly removing his apologetic cap with one hand and the unsuspecting gentleman's gold watch with the other—these were called "matchstick dippers."

Babbage snorted in a combination of disgust and admiration and watched the dipper disappear into the Park. Pointless to give chase or raise an alarm. People like that were gone in an instant. He was quite sure that the two attractive young women riding on either side of him had no idea at all that such was the world.

"I am still so fascinated, dear Mr. Babbage," said the woman on his left, Mrs. Amanda Creevy-Lee, leaning toward him across her saddle, "by what you say about hairdressers and mathematics in France."

Lady Ada Byron Lovelace, on his right, smiled indulgently. Babbage nudged his horse a step closer to Mrs. Creevy-Lee, whose elaborately dressed hair, he noticed, was bouncing rhythmically according to her horse's pace. "What I say," he explained in his usual gruff Devonshire manner, "is very well known, I should think. You've seen my collection of logarithmic tables and handbooks, of course."

"Three hundred and twenty volumes," said Mrs. Creevy-Lee.

Babbage nodded and went on, a shade less gruffly. Any precise reference to numbers and mathematics had a curious softening effect upon him. "Many of those were assembled and printed in France, you see, in the early part of the century."

"After the Revolution," said Mrs. Creevy-Lee brightly. Her ample and uncorseted bosom was also, Babbage concluded, bouncing in rhythm with her mount.

"Yes. And the computers—the term refers to the lowest level of persons who performed the actual calculations—the computers were almost entirely made up of unemployed hairdressers. This is an established historical fact. Hairdressing was once a thriving trade in France—"

"But after they guillotined so many aristocratic heads," put in Lady Lovelace, a poet's daughter and unable to keep silence long, "there was very little fashionable hair left to dress, and so of course the hairdressers were out of work and cheap to hire. Many of them went to special schools and learned rudimentary arithmetic"—Lady Lovelace was now herself proudly at work on volume two of *Behn's Differential Calculus*—"and became computers."

"I estimate," said Babbage, "that with the Difference Engine, I could have reduced the number of persons employed on any single volume of tables from ninety to twelve."

"Poor hairdressers," said Mrs. Creevy-Lee, pressing with one hand her auburn curls back under her riding bonnet. Lady Lovelace, perhaps recalling belatedly that she too bore an aristocratic head, looked thoughtfully over toward a group of ill-dressed, leering Irishmen sprawled drunkenly on the grass.

Their horses' hooves crunched and clopped. The air was rich and drowsy with the smell of warm horseflesh, leather, partially digested straw, and muck. Ahead of them, where the path turned gently uphill toward the Gardens, two men in top hats and frock coats cantered on a handsome pair of roan stallions, kicking up a muddy spray of earth and scattering squealing urchins in all directions.

"Illegal to race in the Row," Babbage remarked, though genteel racing was as common as could be.

"I am just imagining," said Lady Lovelace, "that we are, in our own way, quite like the members of your expedition, Mr. Babbage, in the trackless prairie."

"A parallel," said Mrs. Creevy-Lee, delighted.

"I see them in my mind's eye riding their great brown American horses down an open highway, the low horizon blue with haze and far before them." Riding sidesaddle, Lady Lovelace twisted rather dangerously to gesture at the gray stone facade of Apsley House at the other end of Rotten Row. "No tall buildings in sight, naturally," she conceded, "and doubtless not so green as Hyde Park is. But I *feel*, I *imagine* the sensation of setting out on their animals, heading west, as we are, toward the setting sun—such adventure!"

Mrs. Creevy-Lee clapped her hands in pleasure. "A poet *and* a mathematician both, my dear Ada! Don't you think so, Mr. Babbage?"

Mr. Babbage thought this was precisely the kind of sentimental twaddle that Ada Lovelace was inclined sometimes to indulge in. He blamed her awful mother. On his study wall, Babbage had the finest map of North America in existence, drawn up by the London cartographers Arrowsmith and Lewis, and he knew from it and from Henshaw Pryce's most recent communication that the Expedition was by now far out in the most arid and empty terrain imaginable. On the other hand, Ada Lovelace was an extremely wealthy woman; or rather, her husband was; and Babbage had just been presented with a bill for three hundred and fifty pounds from his chief machinist, who threatened to go to law if not paid promptly.

"Poet and mathematician both," he agreed with a smile and a very convincing semblance of good nature.

At the end of their ride, as grooms led away the horses and the two women adjourned to the Ladies' Dressing House, Babbage found himself standing somewhat apart, near the stables' entrance. He nodded neutrally to a group of men whom he knew by sight.

"Damned attractive, Babbage," one of them said, rolling his eyes toward the disappearing form of Mrs. Creevy-Lee. Babbage, however, was looking in the direction of a particularly handsome blonde woman with knitted horsewhip and lovely white teeth; his mind took a second to find its way back.

"Quite so," he said.

"Lucky horse," the man said, and the others laughed.

Babbage turned away. The woman with the whip and the white teeth, he now realized, reminded him very much of a person his partner Pryce used to see, in one of his rather sinister liaisons. But her "dab" had caught Pryce at it and in a fit of fury beat him and shaved all the hair from his head.

Babbage strolled a few steps farther, to escape the raucous and vulgar laughter of the men. Pryce on a horse. Pryce on the trackless prairies. Pryce had hinted just enough before he left to make Babbage anxious, determined not to hear more.

Babbage valued his reputation for integrity. He knew what people, some people, people like Mrs. Somerville and Edward Kater, thought of Henshaw Pryce. He had given Pryce free rein to pursue whatever the inquiry agents had turned up, on the condition that he, Babbage, was not to know anything of it. It was, he thought, rather like watching a dipper and turning your head.

Pryce, moreover, understood to a shilling how much money was needed to perfect the Engine. A share of a scientific prize, or one of the government's niggling grants, however pleasant, would come nowhere near the sum. What was needed was ironclad proof of Richard Babbage's demise for the Court of Chancery, witnessed by white men, not savages. Lady Lovelace had lately been asking if the Engine could calculate odds for a horse race, and of course it could, Babbage knew a very great deal about the subject of probability. The odds were that his great-uncle Richard was dead. If he was not, Babbage thought, doffing his hat as the ladies returned, surely he would be soon.

CHAPTER TWENTY-FIVE

Professor Hollis

FROM THE DIARY OF JOSIAH HOLLIS:
August 18, along the north bank of the Arkansas River, eighteen days until the Eclipse.

This morning Webb Pattie has declared a half-day of rest, in which rest his really quite wretched and stupid Mexican teamsters, who do not wish to be here at all, have actually labored two or three hours to repair "shackling" in some of the wagons. "Shackling" is the shrinkage of the wooden wheels in the heat, springing loose the metal rim that all of them illogically insist on calling "tires."

Not a grave or serious problem. It is a tribute to human resiliency how quickly we have recovered from the *disaster* at the creek, recovered and adjusted and resumed our tedious routine. *But a change is coming.* Everyone feels it. Everyone feels the shortness of time now, the importance of steady progress. This afternoon we push ahead to the Lower Crossing ford, which will carry us to the south bank of the Arkansas. After which, Pattie says, the dreaded *Jornada* begins, and then—

I do despise James Searle and Bennit Cushing.

Hollis balanced his little red leather octavo diary on his knees and wondered what pent-up impulse had suddenly seized his pen, to make him write such a thing as his last sentence. He should certainly blot it out. He fully intended, though no one else knew it, to publish his diary when he returned to civilization, under the title *A Professor in the Wilderness;* it was to be an exotic but factual account of the Great Eclipse, a vindication full and complete of his mathematical theories. The others had mocked and mistreated him, it was perfectly true. But in publication he would be generous-minded and fair. He would edit or delete what was ... merely personal.

He shifted position on the bench seat of Wagon Number Six in a futile effort to find shade. Perspiration ran down his brow and wrists. On the southern horizon was a black ovoid shape that five minutes earlier his pocket telescope had resolved into several hundred grazing buffalo, perhaps two miles away, on the other side of the river. Worth recording? They had been seeing buffalo every day since the wreck at the ford. Everywhere you looked the green grass was dotted brown with buffalo "chips." There were bleaching bones in the trail ruts, crisscrossing buffalo paths, broad white skulls and horns sometimes, gnawed and pitted by wolves. Even so, a herd of two hundred ... he scratched a new sentence in his diary and watched the heat dry his ink instantly to a purplish stain.

Too hot. It was too hot to write. He put down his diary and wiped his moustache with his sleeve. Wagon Number Six was at the easternmost point of their circle of six, facing west, facing the sun. The Mexicans were a few yards in front of him, finishing work on their "tires." Searle and the others were busy about their maps. Off to the left, despite the heat, near the tethered mules and horses a thin gray plume of smoke marked the Perpetual Shrine of the Coffeepot. A listless, grubby scene that in the last few weeks, amazingly enough, had become as familiar to him as Harvard Yard.

"Spent a winter once in Boston," Webb Pattie said, creating

his sometimes unnerving effect of having just crawled into one's thoughts. He put a tin cup of deep black coffee on the wagon bench beside Hollis. Then with one hand he jiggled Hollis's thermometer (98 degrees Fahrenheit, Hollis had just noted). With the other hand he waved away flies from his face in the one-two flapping motion they had all come to call the Santa Fe Salute. "Nearly froze my soul. Night, it got so cold it made the dogs sound like they were barking in a barrel."

They both turned their heads slightly, as if to find the small dusty form of Pearl of Scotland panting in the heat. But Pearl and her mistress were three days away, in the other direction.

"Year after that," Pattie continued, "I went on a ship down to Havana, Cuba, just trying to get warm. We roll out in half an hour, Professor. Brought you some coffee."

Hollis accepted the tin cup warily. He greatly preferred the prairie tea he had recently improvised from goldenrod leaves. Coffee made by the Mexican cook who had replaced Lona, he knew from experience, would have eggshells in it, and leftover grounds on the bottom, and miscellaneous bits of topsoil and grass deposited in the kettle by the wind. For the sake of science, he thought, for the sake of his scientific reputation, he must have already ingested several pounds of raw earth.

"Havana was a dangerous city." Pattie hitched up his belt and peered curiously at the leather diary. Hollis closed it firmly. "Had a row of tables behind the governor's palace where they laid out the dead bodies every morning, murdered the night before. People would walk along picking out their friends the way you'd pick out melons in a stall. There was an old Italian undertaker, bribed enough people so he had the exclusive right to bury any foreigners that died in Havana. He liked to stroll up and down the wharves with a yardstick in his hand, measuring the new arrivals for a coffin. You're looking much healthier these days, Professor, fit as a trapper. I meant to tell you."

"Apropos of coffins."

"Prairie air," Pattie said. "Clean prairie air. I call this the Lazarus Trail. Brings dead men back to life. Makes you stronger, makes Bennit Cushing nicer. Those your equations?"

"My revised equations, yes. I can now predict the ground path of the eclipse precisely within two miles."

"Don't really need the old Engine then, do they?" Pattie laid his hand on the flank of the wagon frame as he might lay his hand on a horse.

"It complements my work." Hollis lifted his chin and straightened his shoulders self-consciously. He had had this conversation almost word-for-word several times before with Pattie. The others were indifferent to or—in the case of Miss Cott—undoubtedly jealous of his mathematical reputation. But Pattie, though he was probably innumerate, actually showed intelligent interest. The first time he had broached the subject, Hollis had suspected the man of making fun of him. But there was no question, really, of the admiration and respect plain on his face.

"Well, they mean to pull it out of that box." Pattie nodded toward the back of the wagon. "At the end of the *Jornada,* two or three days from now, check their figures one last time. Pryce was just telling me. You can have a little contest, man against machine."

"Mr. Babbage is a very clever person," Hollis said. "His Engine is excellent for rote calculation. But nothing is as fast or profound as the human brain."

"You drink that coffee," Pattie urged him solemnly, moving away but pointing one long brown finger at the cup, "put hair on your brain."

Hollis watched him amble away, bowlegged as a sailor, to rejoin his Mexicans. Off to one side Bennit Cushing said something amusing evidently, and both he and Selena Cott burst into laughter. A loud laugh bespeaks a vacant mind, Professor Hollis thought; Oliver Goldsmith. Miss Cott was still wearing her absurd men's trousers and hat. He shaded his eyes and looked up into the hammered-copper sky. After a moment, careful not to spill his coffee, he slipped down to the far side of the wagon.

No one paid any attention to him. It was remarkable, as Pattie said, how fit and healthy he had become. He hadn't suffered a megrim in weeks. He rolled his neck and shoulders slowly, like a pugilist. Several of the assistant mules were tethered behind Number Six for some reason, and Hollis walked toward them. When the nearer one lifted his wide, homely face, he stopped to pat it. The miniature Engine—he would not stoop to call it the "Infant"—was kept in a trunk at the very end of the wagon, which end was open and yet, thanks to the stacks of other trunks and food crates behind it, invisible to the rest of the camp.

Hollis squeezed past the mule and placed his hand on the trunk lid, much as Webb Pattie had placed his hand on the wagon frame. The trunk, as he had observed on a number of occasions, was latched but not, strictly speaking, locked. There was a simple arrangement of three hook-and-clasp catches, perfectly secure against jolts and bounces, but easy enough to open. Hollis had remonstrated with Pryce about the absence of padlocks on their luggage, but Pryce had only smirked and said he thought there were very few burglars lurking on the Santa Fe Trail.

Hollis sipped his coffee and noted, as predicted, the presence of clumps of undissolved grit and dirt in the bitter liquid. In a less fit person they would certainly damage the internal organs. *Or gears.*

Professor Hollis stared past the wagon toward the buffalo herd on the horizon. The finest part of his book would be the chapter in which his equations, not the Engine, saved the day and placed them with unheard-of exactness in the center of the eclipse path. His mind moved, though he would not have liked the comparison, with the slow, single-minded tenacity of a farmer digging up a stump. A perceptible hardening came over his features. It had been absurdly easy to open Selena Cott's cases in St. Louis, he thought, though in that case he had simply been looking, examining. In a deliberate, trancelike motion, observed only by the mules, he lowered himself to one knee and scooped up a large handful of sandy earth. With the other hand he put down his cup of coffee and then, in an ominous variation of the Santa Fe Salute, he raised his thumb to a catch and opened the trunk.

CHAPTER TWENTY-SIX

Jornada

PAR-FLÈCHE" WAS THE ODD TRAIL WORD—ILLOGICAL CANA-dian French, Selena thought, something to do with "ar-row" lacing—for a kind of rawhide envelope folded over twice and held together by leather strips. It made a package about the size of an octavo book and it seemed to be chiefly used for holding dried meat, tallow, pemmican, or in the case of Webb Pattie, a mixture of dehydrated berries and rice that he could eat from the palm of his hand while he sat in the saddle.

Selena watched him close and fold his *par-flèche* carefully and drop it in the bulging double bag that hung from his sad-dle. In the cool pre-dawn air his brindled mare shivered her flanks and stamped her left rear hoof, making a hollow sound like a fist on a drum. Pattie stroked her mane and perhaps, Selena considered, in unconscious imitation stamped his own foot once against the ground.

"First one up again," he said over his shoulder to her, though in fact other shadows could be seen stirring and mov-ing among the dark wagons. "Just like in Independence."

Selena hugged herself against the chill and fought a yawn and thought that the silent, desolate, empty scene around them was about as unlike the gay crowds of Departure Day in Independence as she could imagine.

"*Jornada* has something to do with 'day,' " she said.

"Means 'a day's journey' in Mexican." Pattie finished buckling his saddlebag and turned now in his slow, easy horseman's way to look at her. "They use it for a long stretch that don't have water, so you ought to try to make it in one day. But of course you can't."

Selena nodded to show that she remembered. Last night around the campfire Pattie had explained that when they rolled out this morning it might take as much as two and a half days, if they were unlucky, a double *Jornada,* to travel from the banks of the Arkansas to the Cimarron. And between the two rivers, he warned, the landscape would change dramatically. For sixty or seventy miles there would be nothing but an immense barren plain—nothing at all, no wood and no water, not a stream, not a creek, not a puddle, not a drop of spit (he said) until they reached either the Cimarron River, which was itself often dry, or a spot just to the north of it called the Lower Springs. The Lower Springs, in fact, was what he meant to aim for. But their United States Topographical map was no longer any good.

Worse, their U.S. Army maps were practically blank as far as the *Jornada* was concerned. There were no landmarks, and very few trail ruts. So they would have to steer by compass and sun, like mariners on the sea. One risk was losing their way and perishing of thirst. A greater risk still was the presence of savage Kiowa and Apache Indians, who roamed this bleak and dusty ocean at will, like pirates.

"*Jornada del Muerto,*" Pattie added, "that's what some of the folks in Santa Fe call it."

Selena didn't ask for further translation. She stepped back to allow him to unhook the canvas sheet at the rear of Wagon Number Six and reach inside for a rifle. This was one of the Expedition's twelve muzzle-loaded Hawkens, purchased new from the factory in St. Louis, though in the gray light of the early morning its barrel already looked weathered and old. Because most men took nearly a minute to go through the complex process of pouring gunpowder, inserting the patch and the ball and ramming them home, the wagon drivers usually kept one fully loaded in a wagon holster next to a bench. And because they didn't want to damage the sights, they often stored the rifles, dangerously but efficiently, muzzle up.

Webb Pattie pulled his powder horn to the front of his vest and opened it with his teeth. Then with fingers moving so fast she couldn't really follow, he loaded a .50 caliber ball and tamped it home with a tiny wooden mallet. He slid it, muzzle up, into a slot in the tail of the wagon.

"Front and rear protection," he said, and winked at her. "Did you fill your canteen yet?"

"Just on my way."

"Should have brought camels instead of mules. Next time I'll ask old Searle."

But the joke was halfhearted and Pattie's face was solemn. He moved away quickly, with an air of frowning concentration, to the back of the next wagon. When Selena had first poked her head from her tent, he had been checking the water barrels fastened on the outside frames like ballast, two per wagon, filled at the river under his serious supervision last night. From his demeanor now, the palpable tension in his step, she had an idea he would recheck them all at least once more before they left.

The sun was glowing faintly now, small and flat over the eastern rim of the prairie. The tethered horses and mules were brushing against each other in the semidarkness with a familiar coming-awake noise of hooves and snorts. She made her way down along a pebbled bank to the edge of the Arkansas and filled her personal canteen to the brim. By the time she had clambered back uphill to the camp, the new teamster-cook Miguel had set out the first of his three black iron coffeepots and Bennit Cushing and James Searle were standing nearby side by side, sipping from tin cups. Searle looked muscular and fit in his checked shirt, his flared khaki trousers and spurs. Cushing's long Bohemian hair stood up in cowlicks and spikes. Two more contrary types of men... She let the idea trail away.

" 'Night's candles are burnt out,' " said Pryce behind her, " 'and jocund day stands tiptoe on the misty mountain tops.' "

"There are no mountaintops in sight," objected Professor Hollis, even more pedantic than usual. "None whatsoever."

"I was quoting verse," Pryce said. "*Bon Jornada* to you, Miss Cott. Shakespeare, *Romeo and Juliet*."

"Well, I wish you wouldn't." Hollis pushed between them and made his way over to the fire.

"Snippity," murmured Pryce, using a word Selena would not have guessed he knew, and watched Hollis hold out his hand to Miguel for a cup. "An intolerable little person, no? A learned imbecile. Perhaps we should offer him as a virgin sacrifice this morning to the gods of the *Jornada*. I feel sure that he qualifies." Pryce smiled at her and stroked his red beard. "I do beg your pardon, my dear."

Miguel served coffee, bacon, and fried bread. The drivers bolted their food and began to go sullenly about their tasks, and Searle and Bennit Cushing busied themselves with last-minute rearrangement of the trunks. Pryce and Hollis stood to one side, looking out of place. But as she often did, Selena joined the teamsters in untethering the mules. Then, already perspiring even in the coolness of the early dawn, she slapped the mules' flanks and kicked and shoved them into their harnesses, cursing in Spanish and French as if, she thought, to the manner born.

When the mules were hitched she walked around to the back of the rear wagon and took off her hat to wipe her brow. Half a mile away, on the south bank of the river, she could just make out a lone stand of cottonwood trees. As she watched, their silvery-green leaves flashed and darted back and forth in the rising light like a school of fish, and her mind suddenly jumped back to Senator Benton's phrase. *Fishes in the desert.* A moment later, Webb Pattie was swinging into his saddle and the brindled mare was trotting up to the head of the line.

The Arkansas River formed the legal border between the United States and the Republic of Mexico, though the nearest actual Mexican settlement was easily two hundred miles away, below the Raton Pass. It was a broad river, nearly a quarter of a mile wide at the ford, but shallow. Its maximum depth at this time of year, Pattie had told them, was a little over fourteen inches, and it would ordinarily have posed no problems at all for the bulky Conestoga wagons.

But unlike most of the other streams they had crossed, the Arkansas had a bottom composed largely, not of rocks, but of sand, often quicksand, as difficult to navigate as a bed of glue. One of Webb Pattie's many tasks before breakfast had been to wade out into the cold current and mark the best line of crossing with a series of wooden stakes. Now, under his watchful eye, the six wagons trundled over, in single file between the stakes, in a constant nervous racket of whips and curses, because stopping was not permitted or else wagons and animals both were liable to founder and start to sink. One after the other, to shouts and whoops of relief, they splashed out of the water at a gentle grassy slope on the opposite bank and turned right in a dead southwest direction.

THERE WAS A QUARTER-MILE-WIDE STRIP OF NORMAL GRASS AND scrub on the other side of the river. And then, with no transition at all, the caravan entered the first of the true *Jornada* obstacles Pattie had warned them of: a muscle-racking stretch of five miles up and down over a succession of high, bare sandhills, evidently formed over the centuries by sand blown up from the ever-shifting river bottoms.

These were not only brutally hard going in themselves—even the mules slipped and slid and lost their footing—there was also the renewed danger of rattlesnakes, which, Pattie had told them, liked to lie here warming themselves on the sand. And indeed the wagons now began to pass through a

veritable den of hundreds and hundreds of sluggish, half-
asleep snakes. Most of them crawled away at the sound of the
heavy wheels, but not far and not happily. Webb Pattie and
Searle rode or walked twenty yards ahead, firing their
Hawken rifles with a steady booming rhythm and flipping
aside the corpses with their barrels. Professor Hollis sat very
high on the bench of Number Two, heels tucked under, face
prim.

Halfway through the sandhills a wild mustang colt, apparently separated from its mother, came running through the
snakes and over the sand and forced its way in among the
eight assistant mules being led by their long tethers at the end
of the train. One mule snapped at it viciously, another kicked,
and the poor colt backed and stumbled away and then fell
behind, bleeding at its shoulders. As they reached a crest and
Selena looked back, it was standing unsteadily in the middle
of a black writhing mound of uncoiling snakes. *Fishes in the
desert.*

After the sandhills the caravan paused for an hour's rest.
Selena and James Searle took their sextants and notebooks
and carried the Thomas Arnold clock a little way out into the
prairie and faced south. From this vantage point it was easy
to see why Webb Pattie was anxious. In front of them
stretched a truly blank expanse of land and sky. Where the
prairie north of the Arkansas had been gently undulant, here
it was as flat and level as if it had been laid out with a
straightedge. There were no mountains, hills, or even ledges
so far as their telescopes and sextants revealed, and no trees
at all, not even an occasional bush or lone cottonwood, not
even a stump.

They took their measurements quickly and almost silently,
with practiced ease, like an old married couple, Selena told
herself wryly. But when she began to write down her numbers
in the daily notebook entry, Searle worked his big jaw in an
awkward way and then, dripping with perspiration, unfolded
their map on his knee.

"I thought we were one degree farther west." He looked at

the cheerful little Thomas Arnold clock ticking in its box on the ground. The dial read 8:24 P.M., Greenwich Meridian Time.

Selena frowned and swiftly calculated in her head—one full degree of longitude here equalled something like sixty-eight land miles, a nearly intolerable error in terms of reaching the eclipse. But she could see nothing wrong with her figures.

She knelt beside him. The map they were using now was a kind of composite, drawn for them personally in Washington City by Lieutenant Frémont and based on an incomplete survey twenty years old. The longitude and latitude grids were largely Army guesswork. On the blue line of ink she had so far traced with her pen they stood almost exactly at longitude 102 degrees, 48 minutes, in theory about thirty miles north of the elusive Cimarron River, perhaps a few miles closer to a short line marked "Sand Creek." Southwest of the Cimarron was a big cross for a place called Rabbit Ears Mountain, and another forty miles beyond it six red dots marked the main Santa Fe Trail coming down from the Raton Pass. West of the river and north of the mountain, where the eclipse path would fall, was nothing but an empty white square.

The clock glinted and clicked in the merciless glare of the sun. Searle wiped his brow again and folded the map. For once the African explorer seemed uncertain.

"Just as soon as we reach water," he said, jamming the map in his shirt pocket, "we need to bring out Babbage's Engine."

But they were still almost forty-five miles from water, assuming that Webb Pattie had read the nonexistent trail correctly. In another twenty minutes the complaining mules had been backed into their traces and harnessed, the six Mexican drivers had remounted their saddles on the wheeler mules, and the caravan was creaking and swaying forward again.

Now, however, with the rattlesnake dens well behind them, Selena decided to walk for a time and spare the panting animals her weight. She took up a position to the left of Number

Six, as far out of the billowing plumes of wagon dust as she could manage. Here, away from the shelter of the covered wagon top, the sun beat down unimpeded. Her eyes grew quickly dry and scratchy. Her daring black Stetson hat sat on her scalp like a hot iron lid on a stove.

"If he hadn't told us there was no water"—Bennit Cushing walked out of the dust and gestured toward Webb Pattie far ahead on his brindled mare—"I probably wouldn't be so thirsty." He uncorked his tin canteen and offered it to Selena, who shook her head.

"Buffalo over to the left." He pointed toward a long brown line, like a pencil smudge, on the eastern horizon, which might or might not have been buffalo. "First ones today."

It was obscurely annoying. If megrim-ridden Professor Hollis was growing stronger and healthier every day on the Trail, by the same token Bennit Cushing seemed somehow milder every day, less abrasive, less offensively opinionated. He did his part with the overworked teamsters; he helped with cleanup at every meal; he kept his disagreeable notions about Art and Science to himself. Childishly, Selena refused to lift her head to look at the buffalo.

"I thought you might be interested in my collection of clouds." They slowed to step around a low fissure in the grass, and Cushing handed her a little sketchpad from his pocket.

Selena accepted the pad, unwillingly, and began to flip rapidly through it, then she stopped and turned back carefully to the beginning. They were only charcoal sketches, clearly done on the run. Yet remarkably, he had managed to capture on the tiny sheets of paper not only something of the vast, haunting distances of the prairie landscape, but also, in the scientific sense, the exact and precise shapes and types of the clouds they typically saw.

"I thought an artist wasn't interested in accuracy, Mr. Cushing."

He ignored her tone. "I'm a great admirer of Luke

Howard's system. Besides, I rather like the poetic names he's come up with." He waved one brown hand across the southern quadrant of the sky. "Stratus, cirrostratus, fading over to the west into cirrocumulus. Agreed?"

Despite herself, Selena was impressed. For hundreds of years, from the Romans on, astronomers had been trying to devise a way to classify and describe the ever-shifting, ever-metamorphosing shapes of the clouds. It was one of the great, but obscure, scientific achievements of the nineteenth century that a young English Quaker named Luke Howard had recently perfected a system of universal nomenclature, starting with his invented categories of cirrus and cumulus. And it was still more amazing that the Bohemian painter Bennit Cushing would know anything at all about it.

Or perhaps, she thought, she was just being biased and unfair.

"You'll be taking daguerreotypes next, Mr. Cushing."

He smiled and slipped the sketchpad carefully back into his pocket. "*Ars longa,*" he said with a touch of his old acerbic self. "Art is permanent. Photography is going to be as transient as the clouds."

SOMEWHERE AROUND FOUR O'CLOCK THE CARAVAN PASSED through one of their infrequently seen prairie dog villages.

Selena had been much entertained by these "dog towns" when they had encountered them on the other side of the Arkansas, several hundred square yards of low dirt mounds and burrows in the midst of patches of buffalo grass, from which mounds popped up constantly, as if in perpetual motion, strange little brown yipping creatures about the size of full-grown rats. Pearl of Scotland had dashed furiously among them, barking and charging from one mound to another in a perfect frenzy of outrage, and the teamsters had often added to the uproar by pelting the prairie dogs with rocks or clods of dirt whenever they appeared.

Today, however, for no clear reason except perhaps the blazing sun, instead of throwing rocks, two of the Mexican drivers suddenly halted their wagons, picked up their Hawken rifles, aimed at the mounds and began to fire. Almost at once the others joined in. Even Hollis and Pryce could be seen kneeling on their benches and levelling their guns, and for three full minutes the empty landscape shook with repeated, rolling explosions of powder. The mounds erupted into sprays of dirt; the hot yellow air was smeared with smoke.

Then a shouting Webb Pattie was galloping back, waving his hat and cursing. Selena could make out the words "wasting bullets" and "Comanches." He jammed one of the rifles butt-first back into a wagon. The sullen drivers sat muttering for a time, then put away their guns and cracked their whips, and the caravan lurched forward again.

At six o'clock they stopped for a short, uncooked meal— fire might attract the Indians, Pattie warned, if the goddamn prairie dog shoot hadn't already—after which, despite Pryce's frowns, he decreed that they would push on at least another two hours before they camped.

"I hope you remember what happened last time, Mr. Pattie."

"The *dis-astrum*," said Hollis unnecessarily.

In the hazy twilight, covered with dust, Pattie looked ghostlike. He studied Pryce's expressionless face, then spat on the ground at Hollis's feet. "We'll go slow. But we've already slopped through half our water"—all eyes turned to the wagons, where the teamsters were now stowing away empty water barrels—"and I'd say we've got at least another day out here, maybe more."

Guiltily, Selena pushed the cork stopper back into her canteen and climbed up to the hard, sun-blistered bench of Number Six. Even in the heat she felt chill pinpricks of fear in her throat, her mouth. She watched the drivers mount their wheeler saddles again and raise their whips. What Bennit Cushing had said was true: they would never have drunk so much of their water if they hadn't been warned against it. Human nature. She licked her dry lips and clutched the side of the wagon.

Off in the distance, along the eastern horizon where the buffalo herd had been, she could see a few scattered stars and the curled tail of the constellation Scorpio. Small dark cumulus clouds were building. Fear was building. In the fading light, shifting back and forth with the sway of the wagon, the clouds appeared to be changing form slowly, as her imagination began to shape them, very like men on horses.

Days until the eclipse: 11.

CHAPTER TWENTY-SEVEN

Some Always Do

IN THE MORNING THE SKY WAS HARD AND BLUE AS AN INVERTED enamel bowl, and there were no clouds at all to be seen. The caravan resumed its rattling progress across the prairie.

Selena no longer walked now, but sat on the tilted bench of Number Six, hot and thirsty, limiting herself to a single quick sip from her canteen once each hour.

From time to time the whole train of wagons came to a dusty halt while Webb Pattie rode far out into the plain and scouted the invisible trail. Twice before the noon break a mule in the harnesses grew too weak and thirsty to pull and one of the assistant mules from the dwindling reserve had to replace it. At noon they stopped as usual to wind the Thomas Arnold clock and eat, and the thought came to Selena, as she turned a full 360-degree circle in the grass, that in all that brown and blue world, completely flat and visually round, there was nothing except the wagons higher than her head, nothing, in fact, higher than her knee.

Somewhere past two o'clock, in the scorching, brain-cooking heat, Professor Hollis climbed up to sit beside her. Briefly he was talkative and amusing about a colleague at Harvard, a botanist who had an attic office where he hid from students—to reach it, Hollis claimed, you had to climb a rope ladder—but soon enough he grew silent, overheated. After a time he climbed down and trudged ahead in the blinding sunlight to the next wagon.

Pryce likewise appeared, seeking change of place, different shade. But even his urbane energy was sapped by the endless, featureless landscape, which now seemed to Selena not so much like grass as tongues of flame. It was like travelling, she said to Pryce, pleased with the image, across the surface of the sun. She could hardly wait for the cooling shadow of the eclipse.

But Pryce had no interest today in the eclipse. "Pattie has been discoursing all morning on Comanches and Apaches," he grumbled. "He claims this godforsaken plain is often filled with moronic buffalo, and the Comanches and the Apaches each regard it as sacred hunting grounds, though not of course for the other."

"The President told us they were hostile."

"Little Whigs and Tories," Pryce said, evidently referring to Comanches and Apaches. The wagons creaked and groaned and the bare horizon seemed to stay perfectly still.

Selena sneaked a sideways glance at her companion. It was hard to recognize in the dirty, slouched form beside her Mr. William Henshaw Pryce of London and Oxford, doyen of bankers, maker of speeches. His raffish red Prince of Wales beard was puffy and untrimmed, brown with dust as much as red. His face was lined with dark rivulets of perspiration, like worms on a waxy mask; his dapper trousers were practically shapeless. He hadn't changed his shirt in days. He dragged his canteen to his mouth and took a long, undisciplined swallow, and the thought occurred to her that of all of them Pryce was giving in soonest, most completely to the *Jornada;* swiftly followed by the thought that Pryce was not a man to underestimate, Pryce had some hidden reserve of purpose she did not yet understand.

"Whigs, Tories, and Kiowas," Pryce murmured. "And Kiowas are supposed to be the fiercest of all."

"Mr. Pattie told me they should like us, since they worship the sun."

"Here be Druids." Pryce shook his empty canteen, then tossed it over his shoulder into the recesses of the wagon. "We're officially down to three barrels of water, Miss Cott," he said, "for six quite thirsty wagons."

TWO HOURS LATER, A WIND AROSE UNEXPECTEDLY FROM THE south and began to rip the sky into ragged flags of crimson and gold. Off on the southwest horizon, black dots appeared in a long shimmering line. In Selena's pocket telescope, even against the hard white glare of the sun, they took on the un-mistakable silhouette of riders, horses, spears.

For almost an hour the silhouettes moved along with them, never coming closer, never going farther away.

At five o'clock Webb Pattie brought the wagons to a slow, deliberate halt. James Searle and a bull-necked driver named Big Carlos maneuvered the Conestogas backward and side-ways into a box formation, closer and tighter than usual, and drew the assistant mules up to the eastern side and tethered them. Pattie sat on his horse and studied the silhouettes. Silently, one by one, the drivers and the men, even Professor Hollis and Bennit Cushing, took out their rifles and stood beside the wagons. It was, Selena thought, eerily quiet. The whole enormous prairie, from horizon to horizon, seemed to be holding its breath. Nothing moved or stirred. The wind it-self fluttered to the ground and crept under the wagons and died.

Then Webb Pattie was cantering out toward the silhou-ettes, followed by James Searle bouncing stiff and heavy-set in his saddle, and Big Carlos on a mule, with his boots scrap-ing the grass and a rifle across his arms cavalry style.

Selena and Hollis stood side by side with their telescopes to their eyes, but on the dry alkaline prairie even three animals quickly threw up an obscuring veil of gauzy brown dust. She had glimpses of Pattie's disreputable black hat, James Searle's sun helmet. Big Carlos shifted his rifle. The line of dark silhouettes dissolved slowly in the western light.

"Mirage," said Professor Hollis.

"Apaches," said one of the drivers and spat.

But in fact, as far as Webb Pattie was concerned, mirage it was. In less than twenty minutes he and the others came trotting back with nothing at all to report—if they were mirages they had vanished; if they were Indians they had no interest in white men or caravans today and had simply scattered over the horizon, which was their way. He passed from wagon to wagon, inspecting wheels and rigging, and then to a low, dry-mouthed chorus of groans, ordered them to hitch up the mules once more.

It was only then, Selena afterward thought, that the real test of the *Jornada* began. They had travelled seventeen or eighteen miles on the first day, a little more this second day. By now they should be almost in sight of ... something. Sand Creek. Lower Springs. The Cimarron itself, though Webb Pattie had warned them that the Cimarron in August was nothing more than a wide, mostly dry fissure in the grass. Unsuspecting travellers had been known to pass right over it.

She closed her eyes on the swaying wagon and pictured the prairie dwarfed to map-reading size. She placed imaginary pins to mark the Arkansas ford at the top, latitude 37 on the bottom, the long narrow swath of shadow above it where in ten days' time the eclipse would come. *Idée fixe*.

An hour before dusk they stopped for a rest. The drivers carried a bucket of water from mule to mule and Miguel squatted by his fire and ground his beans in a leather bag for the inevitable coffee. When they had finished, Venus was rising low to the east, the wind was stirring again, and they were down to one barrel of water.

Webb Pattie cracked a whip. The drivers climbed wearily back into their saddles. The wretched mules lowered their ears and heads and, stumbling and snorting, began to pull once more. Now, Selena thought, in the long twilight the prairie was presenting a new face. The returning wind bore a light-brown dust high into the air, which foreshortened the encircling horizon and tinted the endless low buffalo grass a soft, billowing purple. The sky around the red and setting sun was white as a shark's belly. The wind hissed and pressed against her with an invisible and mysterious force. She shifted on the bench; rode; walked; leaned forward in the baked air and tried not to lick her lips or swallow.

Mrs. Somerville was much in her mind for some reason. As she walked, plodded, one slow, heavy foot after the other, bits of memory drifted across her mind. Curiously for a great astronomer, Mrs. Somerville was afraid of being alone in the dark and always required her husband to be nearby. She had been afraid of a comet she had seen as a girl. She had a bad memory for dates, but never forgot a mathematical formula. In her girlhood in Scotland, she had told Selena, Liberals (men, of course) had worn their hair short to identify their politics, Tories wore it long, in pigtails. Mrs. Somerville thought of herself as a Liberal because she resented the injustices done to woman. But she was not a democrat; she believed in an aristocracy of the educated, she believed passionately in education for women. Her mother had required her children always to stand in her presence. From girlhood on she would never take sugar in her tea, because it represented the exploitation of slaves.

They were being followed, Selena thought. Two or three times, foolishly, she stopped and fell back behind the last wagon and stared to the southwest, into the darkness. Webb Pattie whistled angrily through his fingers and waved her forward. James Searle on his pony swung around in a close circle and watched until she caught up again. In the eastern sky Venus climbed a rope ladder of stars and disappeared.

At nine o'clock or ten o'clock—she was too tired to pull out her watch, too tired to read the stars—Webb Pattie finally gave the signal to stop again and make camp, and even then, while Searle and the drivers formed the wagons into a hollow box, Pattie rode out into the prairie toward what looked like a low, black depression of water, but of course was not. There was no water anywhere except in the single reserve barrel strapped to the side of Wagon Number Four, constantly regarded by every pair of eyes in the caravan.

Miguel made a low fire of buffalo chips and warmed a big iron skillet of dried meat, which they all ate with their fingers, drivers and Expedition members alike, sprawled together on the short, tough grass.

"Not the ideal time for my desiccated vegetables," Webb Pattie said to Selena. He sat on his boot heels and gnawed at the stringy beef like a dog. "Don't tell Mr. Sylvester Graham."

"How far to the river?" Pryce clearly meant to be brusque and authoritative, but the effect was spoiled by the gravelly rasp of his voice and, even in the flickering light of Miguel's little fire, the thoroughly shabby appearance of his clothes.

"Midday tomorrow," Pattie said slowly. "Maybe sooner. Place called Sand Creek sometimes runs eight or nine miles above the Cimarron this time of year. Be closer than Lower Springs. We might reach that pretty early." He turned his head until his gaze found Big Carlos, who nodded.

"Sand Creek." Hollis wiped his mouth with his sleeve. "What a name."

"Some of those mules are going to die," Pryce said, "of thirst."

"Some of them always do," said Pattie.

The drivers were to take turns standing guard, two at a time, though Pattie repeated, first to Hollis, then to Pryce again, that the Apaches of the afternoon, if they *were* Apaches, had long ago gone about their business.

Nonetheless, twice he mounted his brindled mare and rode out into the black prairie alone, rifle across his saddle. Once, Selena was certain she heard voices in the darkness. But it was only the wind. What she heard, she thought sleepily, lowering her head again to the ground and thinking of Mrs. Somerville on her white linen pillow in London, her father in long Tory pigtails, what she heard was only the wind.

In the morning, soon after dawn, Webb Pattie rode out again and stayed away for two hours, far out of sight somewhere to the east of the point where, sitting on the wagon bench and shading her eyes against the fierce white sun, Selena was certain the trail should be. When he came back one of the mules had indeed died, the last barrel of water had been opened, and even before he dismounted it was clear from his face that they were lost.

CHAPTER TWENTY-EIGHT

Sun Lodge

THE INDIANS OF THE WEST DID NOT RIDE THEIR HORSES bareback, as so many Europeans and eastern Yankees had originally and erroneously supposed. They made quite handsome saddles patterned after Spanish ones, or else designed their own simpler ones out of pads of matted animal hair covered with leather flaps. Similarly, they made eminently practical stirrups from pieces of wood pressed into triangles or, more often, from loops of thickly twisted rope. Bridles and bits were fashioned from wood and ropes as well, and also strips of buffalo hide.

Richard Babbage watched two or three of the older Kiowa boys, members of the Society of Rabbits, walk their saddled horses proudly (but quietly and respectfully) around the lodge of Chief Trotting Wolf and downhill out of sight, toward the clearing by the river where the Sun Lodge was being constructed. Kiowas, Trotting Wolf had told him once, had the most horses per person of any tribe in the world and were known to be strongest by far in horse virtues—bravery, audacity. Horses had come to the Kiowas hundreds of suns ago—during the first Spanish settlements in Mexico, Babbage assumed he meant—when the Kiowas, who formerly had no other domestic animal but dogs, had first left the northern woods of the upper Missouri, under the guidance of the great god Sun Boy, and descended to the prairie. Horses and the Kiowas suited each other perfectly, the Chief believed. Horses put a man's eyes and ears at a higher level, expanded his vision literally across the landscape, and made it impossible for the white man to conquer the Kiowa.

Babbage finished the delicious little cake of mesquite bean starch he had been chewing and wiped his hands briskly on his buckskin coat. He felt completely recovered from his three-week spell of whatever it was that had afflicted him with weakness and mental giddiness, back at their other camp along the Cimarron River. And of course he had to admit that part of his good spirits certainly came from the sheer energy and excitement that had seized the whole village as they set about their preparations for this year's much-delayed, much-anticipated Sun Dance Festival.

"White Hair," said one of the braves in greeting. Babbage had forgotten the brave's name. He too was leading a saddled horse past the old Chief's lodge. Babbage bowed and made a kind of Royal Guardsman salute with two fingers to his brow, which appeared to delight the young brave, who returned the gesture over and over, grinning broadly, until he was well out of sight.

Much more slowly Babbage followed around the Chief's lodge (Trotting Wolf was very old, older even than he, and rarely seen these days except at councils) and down the path toward the Sun Lodge clearing.

The village proper, his tribe, had located their new camp as usual in the shelter of a cottonwood grove. But for the public gathering, the great ceremonial Festival, a different place had to be used, level, bare, and open to the sun. At the bottom of the grove Babbage paused to drink in the scene and remind himself that here, concentrated in one square acre before him, was all the *vis vitae* a recovering valetudinarian like himself could wish for, not to mention a refugee from European corruption and effeteness.

Fifty yards ahead, close to a narrow brown stream he had

been told was the Canadian River, a noisy work party was in the process of erecting the Sun Lodge. This was not a typical Kiowa-style cone of lodgepole pines and stretched buffalo hide. Instead it was a large rectangular structure rather like an English barn. It had a single door facing the east and a sacred tree, cut down two days ago by purified braves, rising through a flat roof of leafy cottonwood branches. When finished, Babbage estimated, it would be capable of holding perhaps two hundred people. In concentric circles around it, to the water's edge in one direction, the cottonwood grove in the other, were several dozen traditional tepees. Most of these were already covered with buffalo hide. Some were occupied by Kiowas, others were set aside for guests from those two or three friendly Apache tribes who regularly sent their goodwill delegations to the Sun Dance.

"Topadok'i," said another passing brave. "White Hair."

Babbage bowed gravely. *Topadok'i* was the title reserved for an important chief. It may have been used ironically to him, or then again, Babbage thought complacently, he had certainly brought, if not scalps, considerable white man's wealth to his little band of Kiowas: no doubt he merited some special title of respect.

The noisy, chattering work party building the Sun Lodge was all women, of course, all squaws; all squaws as well down by the river pounding buffalo hide and grinding beans and roots in their mortars.

"Topadok'i," said one of the prettier squaws, looking up, then she giggled and showed perfectly dreadful rotting black teeth and added, *"ko-da-u,* uncle."

Babbage bowed with the same easy gravity and accepted from her a little gift of wild grapes. He could not decide, he thought, strolling now among the tepees, nodding left and right as he passed, whether he most resembled, say, Robinson Crusoe, shipwrecked in the western American desert and ruling his wild kingdom of Fridays; or else perhaps a truly eccentric and sunburned lord of the English manor inspecting his Druids.

The lord inspecting his Druids, he decided, and made his way on through the chattering women and over toward the far side of the clearing where twenty or thirty men were gathered together by the water, mixing red and yellow paint in clay bowls and decorating themselves.

"Our uncle," said one of the handsomest of the boys, a member of the *Kingep,* or Big Shield, group. He handed Babbage a *cigaritto* fashioned in the Spanish manner and with a good deal of flattering bustle sent one of the Rabbit lads off to fetch a burning stick to light it.

Babbage sat down, finished off, he considered, a full day's work of benevolent nodding to his subjects, and prepared himself to admire the decorations.

These were most savage, of course, and most pleasing—stripes of red, yellow, and black on every face; chests adorned with leather breastplates and elk's tooth necklaces; hair beplaited and befeathered and behung with ribbons—a wonderful sight, no less wonderful for the unashamed delight the Kiowa men took in themselves, in their own bodies.

Last year on his semiannual visit to that unctuous banker in Taos, Babbage had purchased half a dozen small mirrors, which had proved an inspired gift indeed. In Babbage's youth English men of good breeding had worn makeup and paint in abundance. He could remember his own uncles covered with face cream an inch thick, rouge, large black beauty patches on their cheeks just like the women. As a boy he had loved to sit on a little stool beside his grandfather's toilette table and watch the old man daub on layers of cream with a silver trowel, then spray white powder from a horn; next came the faery's work of the powder knife, which cut off the lines of the forehead and temples; then the magnificent, towering wig, more powder, and finally the critical operation of the six-folded jacconot neckcloth, which could consume a full and fussy quarter of an hour of his grandfather's time (and that of two hovering servants).

Babbage was in a very good mood. He watched a young man named Stumbling Bear admire his painted brow in the mirror, then proceed with his bowls of colors over to his tethered horse, which horse he proceeded now to paint and decorate, red, yellow, and black just like himself, a wonderful sight, wonderful, Babbage thought. If they had painted their horses red and yellow in Grosvenor Square, perhaps he would never have left old England.

Babbage was in a splendid mood, really, with only the faintest possible touch today of lingering illness to make him feel languid and dreamy. He stretched out full-length in the grass beside the stream, an unmapped pastoral stream in an unmapped country, and watched his boys. His tribe, he thought, the Kiowa-Pantisocrats. One of the older braves was holding forth, a man called simply and always "The Hat" because he was the proud possessor of a tall black silk hat, acquired who knew how, which he wore at all times, with no other clothing except his breechcloth.

"Smit," said The Hat, nodding at Babbage. "Smit was an Englishman."

"American," murmured Babbage, though The Hat paid no attention; all Indians told stories rigidly from start to finish, no digressions or interruptions allowed. The story in question today, he noted, was the well-worn business of Jedidiah Smith, a celebrated Santa Fe Trail guide who had nonetheless gotten himself lost some years ago between the Cimarron River and the Arkansas and had wandered about with his train of wagons for three full days, on the brink of dying from thirst. Smith, however, had been a seriously determined and capable person, and had finally managed to break away and reach the elusive Cimarron on his own. He had just been digging through the dry-sand bed of the river, down on his hands and knees to scoop out a little seeping water, when a party of twenty Comanches on horseback had thundered up.

He tried to stand and reach his own horse. The Comanches drove it away. They shot him with their arrows. Smith pulled out his pistols and killed two braves outright, then dashed at the others swinging his ax. Still on their horses, they slashed him to bloody ribbons with their knives, pierced him with a lance. When they dismounted to scalp him, he suddenly rose up and stabbed as many as he could with his own knife, so that in the end, though Smith was certainly dead, so were thirteen Comanches and Smith was regarded, by the survivors at least, as a kind of demigod. This was in 1831. If they had been Kiowas, The Hat declared to general howls of approval, none of the braves would have died.

There was much excitement following the story. The guest Apaches apparently had some story of their own to contribute, some news, though Babbage did not understand the Apache dialect well and in any case was now quite definitely feeling the effects of the drowsy-making *kinick-kinick* pipe and the warm afternoon sun, which, after all, they were there to worship.

The Apaches began to play on their war drums; some of the older squaws, over by the Sun Lodge, began to chant. Nothing could be sillier, Babbage thought, than the idea that Indians were unemotional, dour, silent. They were truly the most excitable of people, as emotional as Sicilians. It was the supremely best thing in his life to have renounced old England and buried himself in the West. Poor Jedidiah Smith, shot full of arrows. Doubtless he had been up to no good and deserved it.

That night Babbage ate with some Apache guests and a number of Kiowa braves, crowded together in a tepee. It was a meal of strong fermented drink, buffalo rib, crushed roots, and a small, tasty bean that the children found stored in nests by meadow mice (they always left a few beans for the mice, to show "good heart"). The Kiowas would not eat fish or bird, but Stumbling Bear had actually been willing to catch a nice trout from the Canadian River for Babbage's exclusive use. At the end of the meal a bowl of water was passed to drink and to wash fingers with, which was done by filling the mouth with water and spitting it out on the hands. Another hygienic test, Babbage thought, that he was not quite ready to pass.

Outside two of the handsomer braves offered to help him

back uphill to his own tepee, and Babbage found himself asking, perhaps to distract from his stumbles, what the uproarious news of the Apaches had been.

"Wagons out in the prairie," replied one of the braves. "Gone wide off the trail, miss the river."

"Easy to happen," said Babbage, oddly enough in English. He was thinking, however, not of Jedidiah Smith, but his own guide three years ago when he had come out the same way. Then he stiffened and stopped in his tracks. The fermented drink had been strong, but not so strong as to cloud his mind completely.

"How many wagons?"

"They say six."

"Were they carrying—?" There was no Kiowa word for telescope. He squinted at the sky in frustration and tried to recall what he had read in the other camp, in *Niles' Register*, about his nephew Charles's absurd expedition.

"Plenty of rifles," said the second brave. "Apaches stay far away."

William Henshaw Pryce, Babbage thought. He hadn't seen Pryce in years; he had no idea how to describe to a Kiowa a stylish English gentleman banker. "Was there a woman?"

The brave on his right shrugged.

But surely six wagons was not enough. Surely *Niles' Register* had said the caravan was twice that size. The two Kiowas had lost interest in the wagon train. They started to walk uphill again, pointing and telling him something now about Sun Boy and a group of stars. But Babbage scarcely heard them. His mind kept swivelling back, like the needle of a compass, to the threat of the wagons, the greedy and cowardly Henshaw Pryce. Then he paused and gripped each of his strong young escorts by the arm and relaxed. If by some amazing chance it was Henshaw Pryce and his expedition, of course they would never find him here, in the Sun Lodge camp, not without help, not without expert assistance, which no Kiowa would ever give.

At the top of the hill one of the Rabbits was leading a pony, and even by starlight you could see that it too had been painted red and yellow and decorated from head to tail with streaming ribbons and feathers, like some sort of four-footed idol. Out of Babbage's memory rose a curious phrase, unbidden but somehow provoked by the sight. "Church of the Horse," he said out loud.

CHAPTER TWENTY-NINE

At Sea

SHE WAS, SELENA THOUGHT, A HUMAN TORCH, A WALKING human comet made out of burning sand.

It was necessary to be scientific, observant.

Off to the right, mounted on their horses a few hundred feet ahead of the six wagons, Webb Pattie and James Searle were picking out a path, tenderly and gingerly and much too slowly it seemed to her (not a scientific observation), between low clumps of sagebrush, bearing roughly north-northwest, into a fiercely blinding sun.

They had gone past Sand Creek yesterday without knowing it, that much was clear. Webb Pattie had announced it when he dismounted that morning. And by doing that they had somehow missed the Cimarron River too. Now they were far to the south of both of them, out in a vast triangular patch of arid land, not quite desert, not quite prairie, out of water, with no hope at all unless they could find their way back.

He had sketched the triangle in the dirt, then rocked back on his heels and shoved his hat up and looked from one face to the other with a flat, blank expression impossible to read. After which, without a word, James Searle had pulled out his sextant and his compass and swung into his saddle and ridden out of sight back along their trail, gone for over an hour. When he came back he told them he knew where the river should be.

Selena wobbled in the hot sun and adjusted her hat for shade. There was no shade. It was somewhere between eleven and one o'clock, day three of the *Jornada,* and they still hadn't found the river and there was no shade anywhere in the world west of St. Louis. She kicked a bone-white stone out of the way and half expected it to burst into flame, like the head of a phosphorous match.

They were all walking now, no one was riding except for Pattie and Searle. Even the Mexican drivers trudged along in the dust, wearily cracking their whips at the wretched and dying mules. Pryce was up ahead of her, by Number One. Hollis and Bennit Cushing were off to her left. She could only tell them apart in the plumes of dust by Cushing's long Bohemian hair, the occasional flash of Hollis's rimless spectacles.

It was amazing country, Selena thought. If she were not so horribly hot and thirsty, she would actually be interested in the scientific phenomenon, the geological oxymoron, so to speak, of its ever-varying monotony. They had gone too far to the east evidently, that was their mistake, and now they were in the process of cutting back cross-country, over their own ruts, toward the *Jornada* trail.

But without the sun for guidance, she thought, she would have no idea which direction they were really travelling. The horizon, treeless, level, and brown, stretched for miles and miles in a perfectly smooth and flattened circle, not a single hill or gully or valley to fix the eye upon. And yet up close, as the wagons creaked and swayed and the mules staggered and kicked in their rigging, they were constantly struggling down little depressions and unseen ravines, up small hillocks that came upon them with a cruel abruptness that never failed to surprise her. It was the refraction of the atmosphere, she decided when she could turn her parched thoughts away from her thirst, an optical illusion of flatness produced by a deflection in the perspective of the plains.

At two o'clock Webb Pattie called the wagons to a brief halt.

Selena flopped down in the dirt and fanned her red face with her hat and stared mindlessly at the mules, standing exhausted in their traces, exactly where they had stopped. Most of their backs and sides were streaked up and down with bloody running sores and cuts from the whips, and crawling with flies, so that they looked like bizarre red-and-black-striped zebras.

She was still staring, watching the flies and a cow bunting bird, *Eberiza pecoris,* which had landed on a mule's back and was pecking away at a sore, when she realized that James Searle was speaking to her.

"Going to have to jettison one wagon, probably two," he said, and she made him repeat it because his throat was so dry, or her ears so clogged with dust, that she scarcely understood a word.

"The mules can't do it," Searle said wearily. "We're down to just working teams, without any reserves. We have to drop one wagon completely and lighten the others."

"Not the cameras!" Selena scrambled to her feet and looked wildly down the line of wagons. Three of the Mexican drivers were already tossing boxes and canisters into the sagebrush. "Not the *cameras*!"

"Be reasonable, dammit." Searle's eyes narrowed. "Everybody has to sacrifice, even the famous Miss Cott." His face was red and flushed. He started to turn away.

Selena caught his arm.

"The *cameras* are the reason we're here, you fool!" She knew she was shouting, making a scene—the others were gawking, openmouthed, but she paid no attention. "Why else are we *here* except for the cameras and the telescopes and the eclipse?"

She gripped his arm and held on as hard as she could.

"Irrational female panic," Searle said, intolerably.

Down the line Professor Hollis was picking up a jettisoned box. Selena swung her gaze toward him. "Hollis! Tell him no!"

Searle shook off her hand. Cushing and Pryce and even the Mexican drivers came crowding up, and for a short incendiary minute Selena and Searle were literally snatching cartons and bundles out of each other's hands and tossing them into the dirt or back again into the wagons. And then, of course, heat and thirst resumed their dominion. Searle threw up his hands and stalked away. Selena sagged against a wheel. Carefully, silently, the Mexican drivers began to pick through the litter of boxes and deposit the discards off to one side, under the blazing sun.

They threw out three of the six telescopes.

One of the five cameras. Two full heavy boxes of precious photographic chemicals and one of her three canisters of special accelerator formula.

Ten big boxes of dried corn and beans. Two barrels of flour. Half their blankets. Half their clothes. Selena's tent and bed.

Bennit Cushing tossed away most of his sketchbooks, a third of his paints and rolls of blank canvas. Hollis, petulant and complaining, gave up a box of astronomical books.

When they set out again, now two wagons less, it was past four o'clock, they had had no water for more than thirty hours, and Webb Pattie himself had begun to wonder out loud if they were going in circles.

At six o'clock Selena had entered a new phase of thirst and fatigue, clearheaded, almost calm. Equations came into her mind, which she solved easily and swiftly, as if on a screen; and odd facts and expressions—Sir William Herschel had tried to build a reflecting telescope once, Mrs. Somerville had confided to her, giggling like a schoolgirl. He used dried horse dung for the mold of the mirror, and it had exploded in his hands and covered the great man with manure. Tahitian women, she had overheard her father say to her mother, were known to trade their favors for any shiny metal object. Captain Cook had ordered his men not to give them any nails, which the women particularly fancied, but the sailors disobeyed so often and enthusiastically that their ship almost came apart.

A line of poetry wandered through her brain—"Water, water everywhere, / Nor any a drop to drink"—and she thought of the irony of a sea captain's daughter perishing of thirst. The added irony of all her comparisons, weeks before, of prairie to ocean.

It was almost dusk when she looked up from the bristly field of blue-tinged sagebrush across which she was hobbling. Far overhead the sky seemed to have caught fire from the sun's hot trail, and a long swath of high-flung dust was weaving back and forth in the invisible breeze, beautiful draperies of scarlet and gold. Then her eye dropped to the horizon, where a dark line now floated softly just above the dry blue rim of sagebrush. And slowly, step by step, as the sun sank and the great western belly of the land rose and rolled toward them, the line grew darker still and split in two and turned into trees, and between the trees Selena was the first to see the glint of water.

IT WAS, IN FACT, AS IT ULTIMATELY TURNED OUT, NEITHER THE Cimarron River nor the Lower Springs, but a small prairie creek completely unmarked on anybody's map, a trickling brown streamlet no wider across than a man's arm could reach, fed by a spring somewhere off to the north. Where the side of a ravine had crumbled in on itself, a shallow pond had formed—Selena's glint of water—perhaps thirty feet long and bordered by a belt of spiky weeds and a few small chokecherry bushes that had long since been stripped clean of their fruit by birds and rats. Six or seven scrawny cottonwoods on the north bank were the only trees anyone could see in the whole flat circle of the plain.

But water it was. To Selena and the others, in the furnace-like heat of the twilight, under a few dim blistered stars, it might have been the great Mississippi itself. The Mexican drivers, whooping hoarsely, led their staggering mules up team by team to the lower end of the pond. There they unhitched them one at a time and allowed the miserable animals just two minutes each of frenzied drinking—otherwise, a grinning Miguel explained to Selena, with a broad gesture at his paunch, their shrunken stomachs would bloat and burst. The drivers themselves waited until the animals had drunk.

At the other end of the pond the Expedition members tried to imitate the drivers and mules in self-discipline; failed utterly. Professor Hollis sprawled facedown in a long narrow puddle, lapping like a dog. Bennit Cushing and Pryce sat side by side in the brackish water, splashing their bare heads and laving, in Cushing's oddly hilarious phrase, "their oozy locks."

Webb Pattie attributed the find to sheer luck, Pryce to the desert skills of his personal "explorer"; the rest of the Expedition had no interest in the debate. The four remaining wagons were rolled up into a crude corral for the mules. A guard was posted out in the prairie, off to the west. Miguel was too spent to do more than hand out cold jerky and coffee. By eight o'clock, for all intents and purposes, the whole exhausted caravan was asleep.

Selena herself could scarcely move. Her throat was raw. Her legs still trembled with nervous fatigue. She rolled up on the dirt in her single blanket, all that was left to her after the jettison, and listened to the faint, delicious ripple of the little stream. For a time—she had no idea how long—she let her gaze drift across the bare sky. She found Jupiter, very close to the horizon, and thought of its moons and the old-fashioned way of finding longitude. She located Kappa and Upsilon in the tail of Scorpio and by some buried process of mental association thought of sand dunes and oxen. After another long moment she stood up, still clutching the blanket around her body, and walked softly between the sleeping Mexicans to the far end of the wagon corral, where she found James Searle, sitting on a wagon bench and scanning the black horizon.

"The very first Latin word my brother taught me," she said, clearing her throat, "Mr. Searle, was *apologia*. I behaved quite badly about the jettisoning of our goods. You were right and I was wrong. I apologize."

In the dark, even with the stars so thick overhead, it was impossible to read his expression. But the smell of leather and perspiration and horsehair on him was very strong and pleasant, and by no mystery of association at all, for the first time in three months she thought of her old Welsh pony when she was a girl.

"Accepted," he muttered. "Apology accepted. Of course."

"I like to think of myself as objective and self-controlled, a 'scientist' through and through. But I suppose my brother knew better."

If he had said one word about irrational females, she thought, or women's fragility or the wise policy of the Royal Navy, she would have exploded again. The Latin for that kind of man was *mulus,* mule-headed, impossible. But Searle sat where he was and said nothing at all.

"You saved us, you know," Selena said. "I don't think I could have lasted another day without water."

"Experience in the African desert," Searle replied stiffly, continuing to scan the horizon. "You look for what I call wrinkles in the topography. Streams out here, I think, always run to the southeast sooner or later. Still, hard to believe we could have missed an entire river, walked right over it."

"Pattie says it's happened to people before. He says some years the Cimarron goes completely dry by July."

"Very likely." They sat in silence for a moment, then it was Searle's turn to clear his throat. "Well, you care about the eclipse, Miss Cott; more than anybody else, you care about it. If you were not quite 'scientific' today, that is because you have...passion." He turned and lowered himself from the bench to the ground, so that they were standing beside each other in the desert night, not six inches apart. "You would make a splendid travelling companion, you know, even in Africa." He started to say something else, stopped again.

And then so swiftly that she scarcely had time to know it, he raised her hand to his lips, pressed once, and slipped away.

Back beside the little streamlet she rolled herself tight in her blanket; made a pillow of her battered hat; permitted herself one very small, very French smile. She had no intention of changing anything in her life, certainly no intention of abandoning her science for . . . Africa. But still, it was quite pleasant, she thought, to be told one has passion; it was quite pleasant to have one's hand kissed by James Searle; it was pleasant indeed (she would tell Senator Benton) to have one's faithful protector.

Overhead the leaves of the cottonwoods looked like black feathers brushing the stars from the sky. A prairie breeze drifted down from the northwest, carrying hints of distant mountains and pine trees and cooler air. In the morning it would be six days until the eclipse.

In the morning they would bring out the Infant Engine.

CHAPTER THIRTY

The Infant Engine

IN THE MORNING, HOWEVER, NO ONE ELSE, NOT EVEN Pryce, seemed to care.

They washed their foul clothes twice, even the drivers; they drank from the hospitable little stream and filled their canteens and water barrels and drank again.

"Not a bad idea," said Webb Pattie as he sat by the breakfast fire with his coffee, "rest the mules one more day right where we are." He looked over his shoulder and translated it for the squatting Mexican teamsters, all of whom nodded and spat in unison, like a Greek chorus.

"We just have to go from *here*," said Professor Hollis, who had spread out a clutter of maps and papers on the bench of Number Four, "to *here*. If this little stream runs into the Cimarron River—" He paused and wiped his brow with the back of his hand. He seemed strangely, curiously nervous, Selena thought. "Then this line, this one, is the start of longitude 103. By my calculations we can't be more than twenty-five miles due east of the eclipse path. Two days' travel."

Selena stood and brushed the dirt carefully from her skirt. Hollis had removed, then replaced his rimless spectacles, and now he was holding up the large Frémont map on which, however blank and useless it was, she and James Searle entered the midday longitude and latitude.

"Here," Hollis said. "Here's where we must be. And here's where my equations place the westward regression. Getting lost actually brought us closer."

She frowned at the map. Despite the early heat and her raw throat, a good night's sleep had done wonders; her mind at least was relatively clear. And the part of her that was the sea captain's daughter intuitively calculated or felt or simply *knew* that the point where Hollis's finger hovered had to be a mistake. The eclipse trajectory was going to be farther west than that, Babbage had firmly predicted it. The little nameless stream was farther south. She had only to look at the sun through the trees.

"It really is time," she said slowly, "to bring out the Engine."

But that, of course, was easier to say than do.

In the first place, as the sun climbed in the sky, Webb Pattie was more and more anxious about the Indians they had seen two days before. The Indians would know the stream even if the Army maps didn't, and the wagons were exposed and visible for miles. James Searle was already standing guard somewhere on the other side of the cottonwoods. The weary drivers were muttering among themselves and preparing to join him.

And in the second place, the Infant Engine was packed away in the center of Number Four, buried under heaps of repositioned trunks and boxes after the great *Jornada* Jettison. It would take an hour of painstaking work just to find it.

"It was our *plan* all along," Selena said stubbornly. "At the end of the *Jornada*." Hollis was sitting with one of his logarithm books in his lap and she could barely resist shooing him onto his feet, like a farm girl with a chicken. "Those equations look wrong."

"I have a megrim headache," Hollis murmured. He stayed

where he was. Webb Pattie drank his coffee. Pryce fluffed his beard mechanically and looked almost as weary as the Mexican drivers.

Selena took a deep breath and put her hands on her hips. Then she walked to the back of the wagon, braced her feet and squared her shoulders—and suddenly bent and *heaved* the nearest box onto the ground with an earsplitting crash.

Pryce dropped his coffee. Miguel jumped for a rifle.

Selena turned back around and smiled her sweetest smile and finally got results—"Move the bloody *boxes,* Mr. Pattie!"

And even then it was not so simple as merely unpacking Number Four and cracking open the special padded trunk with the Infant Engine.

To calculate precisely where the moon would cross its ascending node and eclipse the sun—where precisely its shadow would fall in the uncharted, unmapped Great Southwestern Desert—had taken Babbage's original Difference Engine an enormous number of individual computations (twenty French hairdressers' worth, he had joked to Selena, ten lords a-leaping) over a course of several months.

The Infant Engine was designed, not to repeat this whole complex process, but simply to adjust, if necessary, the longitude reading of what was called the moon's westward orbital regression. Yet for this quite limited operation they still required a set of Napierian logarithm tables, which Selena kept in her personal box of books. From those someone had to prepare the numbers to feed into the Infant Engine. And someone else had to calculate by hand the angle of the sun's ecliptic path on that day, in that place.

Webb Pattie directed two of the drivers to unload Number Four Wagon gingerly, box by box like cartons of eggs, and stack the contents on the ground. Slowly, with a furrowed expression of pain on his thin face, Hollis began to study the logarithm tables Selena handed him.

"Just to be useful," said Pryce with a touch of his old sardonic humor, "Mr. Cushing and I will sacrifice a lily white mule to the Infant Deity."

Selena ignored him.

There were two kinds of mathematicians in the world, Mrs. Somerville had often told her, walkers and divers. Walkers were like Hollis, they proceeded cautiously step-by-logical-step, they plodded down a straight, narrow line toward a predictable conclusion. Divers, on the other hand, skipped and sailed over the logical steps, like arithmetical acrobats. They arrived at their conclusions much further down the line, unexpectedly, by intuition, as Babbage did.

Hollis's figures were wrong, she simply knew it, there was no point wasting time on them. Done her way, she thought, using Babbage's original numbers modified by her own longitude sightings, the calculation of the westward orbital regression of the sun would take the Infant Engine no more than two hours, three at the most. After which she could realign the map and see precisely where the center of the eclipse path would fall, where her cameras could have totality long enough to do their work—that was Babbage's genius, if the world would only give him credit, to let his Engine (and its progeny) do the plodding and free his intuition to dive and soar and predict far, far ahead how the numbers would turn out.

She shielded her eyes against the sun (and registered the irony of that) and fought the momentary return of thirst and fatigue. Then she squeezed her mind into a ball and began to figure the ecliptic angle of the sun.

It was almost two hours later when she realized that all of the men—Webb Pattie, the drivers, Pryce, all of them—were standing in a semicircle some thirty feet away, staring at her. She blinked and looked down at her equations, up again at the staring men.

"When Babbage is doing mathematics," commented Pryce dryly, "he always closes his eyes, pinches the bridge of his nose with two fingers, and purses his lips in and out like a carp. You make a much more attractive, if less entertaining sight, Miss Cott."

Selena frowned at the sheet of paper in her hand. She had been double-checking her earlier longitude figures, this time using Krafft's method for "clearing the distance," which required no logarithmic tables, only natural versines. But the result was not nearly as crisp as Babbage's original prediction. With an effort she pulled her thoughts away.

"Had the machine out for half an hour, little lady," Pattie said, "just waiting for you."

The line of men parted slightly in the center to reveal the back of Wagon Number Four, where the unprepossessing red and black trunk that housed the Infant Engine sat on a burlap sack of coffee beans.

"It's been locked away and sleeping for two thousand miles, like Rip Van Winkle," Pryce announced to no one in particular.

Hollis worked his jaw and took off his spectacles. He did look like a carp, one in a checked shirt. "There's no reason *at all*," he said with an increasing shrillness in his voice, "to use this foolish machine. I say we're almost in the path already."

"Actually," Searle reminded him, "according to your figures the eclipse won't hit land until Chihuahua, Mexico."

"I still have revisions to make." Hollis unfolded a much-folded version of Selena's map.

No one paid the slightest attention.

Webb Pattie himself walked back to the wagon and lowered the Infant Engine's trunk to the ground. Hollis rubbed his eyes.

The three hook-and-clasp latches on the front of the trunk glinted in the sunlight. Pattie got down on one knee beside it. The Mexican drivers came closer. Even the tethered mules by the stream stopped bobbing their heads and seemed to inch forward. Pattie undid the first and second clasps. Hollis sat down in the dirt and gripped his knees.

"Put it up on the boxes," Pryce said, "so we can all see it."

Pattie took off his disreputable hat and wiped his chin with his sleeve. Big Carlos came around to kneel on the other side of the trunk.

"*Dos, tres,*" Pattie grunted and they lifted the trunk

together and set it carefully on top of what Selena recognized as their last remaining barrel of flour.

"All right," said Pryce, rubbing his hands, "all right."

The Infant Engine had been wrapped in London in ten pounds of white cotton padding, like swaddling bands. These bands had been cleverly arranged by Mr. Babbage so that, while they protected the delicate mechanism against all bolts and bumps, it was possible to pull them away in an easy two-step motion, as a conjuror might produce a rabbit. This was intended to allow the travellers easy access for inspection. Twice on the road Selena had opened the trunk to make certain all was well, once in St. Louis after the long voyage up the Mississippi, once in Independence. Since Independence no one had disturbed it.

"Take it out of the trunk," Pryce ordered.

Webb Pattie and Big Carlos reached inside and lifted up a thickly padded rectangular shape whose top was covered by a single felt pad, like a lid on a vase. This also could be pulled away in an instant. James Searle drew the trunk away and the two men lowered the Engine to the top of the barrel, where it sat like a square, chubby white baby.

Pryce put his hands on the felt pad and lifted it.

Selena was puzzled to see a thin stain of dirt on one side of the padding.

"Miss Cott, Gentlemen of the Prairie, may I present, at long last, the sixth member of our Expedition?" With a flourish, Pryce tugged at the swaddling bands.

The Infant Engine was slightly smaller than Babbage's Demonstration Engine in London. An orange-colored protective varnish along the frame made it look like a very strange, very rigid jack-o'-lantern. Its four vertical metal columns enclosed a dazzling complex of tiny brass wheels and golden cogs, backed and braced by strips of the finest mahogany veneer. Across the front, flickering in the sunlight, were two small round gears and a straight lever that resembled human eyes and a nose. Underneath the lever was a wide central slot that would have been the mouth and the teeth and should have contained six circular brass wheels of numbers.

"Gone!" Pryce bent forward and jammed his fingers into the empty slot. "All the numbers are *gone*!"

Selena pushed him aside. From the top she could see straight down into the mechanism. The number wheels had been on tiny brass axles, no bigger than threads, deliberately easy to rotate and lift if the Engine needed adjustment. But those number wheels were the only way the Engine recorded its calculations. Without them, no one could read what the Engine thought.

She took the top of the frame in her two hands and pulled it forward, gently. Directly out of the center slot, where the mouth should be, flowed a fine brown stream of sand.

In the stunned silence that followed, only Professor Hollis moved. He swallowed hard and wiped his hands compulsively on his shirtfront. He turned the gear crank with his finger, and Selena, standing beside him, could hear the cogs faintly grind against each other and then the plink of a gear tooth slipping out of line.

Hollis drew back his hand and looked miserably away. A dreadful surmise began to form in Selena's mind.

"We still have the clock," Hollis said at last.

PART THREE

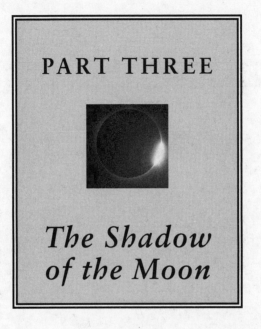

The Shadow
of the Moon

CHAPTER THIRTY-ONE

Clubs, Pantisocracy,
and Money

WELL, I KNEW YOUR UNCLE RICHARD, OF COURSE. ONE OF Nature's perfect dunces, what?"

Charles Babbage thought that there were, after all, degrees of perfection. He smiled insincerely at his two companions now lounging across from him, side by side in their great leather chairs, nearly perfect dunces themselves. Edward Kater, his banker, was completely bald and exceedingly white in complexion and resembled nothing so much as a giant egg in a faultless satin waistcoat. His ancient uncle Erasmus Kater, who had just spoken, was, contrary to nature and logic, furnished with abundant black hair that had been obviously treated with some kind of cosmetic coloring. *He* quite resembled, Babbage thought, still smiling, Humpty Dumpty under a wig.

"I knew Richard at Cambridge," Erasmus Kater added. He cleared his nasal passages with an enormous, moist, nostalgic snort. "Trinity man he was, two years ahead of me, quite a noted college character—you look like him, Babbage, same horsy teeth. He once introduced me to the poet Coleridge. Very tall, thin person, I was surprised to see. Always pictured him as short and fat."

"I am," said Edward Kater, who had been murmuring

snatches of Coleridgean verse (Babbage presumed) under his breath, "the same way about Benjamin Franklin. Always think of him as short and fat, but I'm told he was actually five feet ten inches tall."

"The American Rebel," said his uncle, and both eggs nodded in perfect idiotic unison.

At which timely moment the waiter arrived with three glasses of port wine on a salver and three fat cigars already clipped and guillotined. While he was laying out these items on the table between them, next to a neatly bound but untitled folder of papers so far unmentioned by anyone, Babbage took the occasion to glance around the so-called "library" they had now settled into. The Diogenes Club found itself, as the French liked to say, on Pall Mall, just two doors down from Babbage's own club, the Reform. He had passed by its massive oak double doors a hundred times, but never before stepped inside. Every room so far was, of course, precisely as stifling and conservative as he had imagined.

"Your uncle Richard," Erasmus Kater informed him from behind a rising cloud of blue cigar smoke, "was a kind of rebel himself. He was a Pantisocrat."

Babbage took a moment further to contemplate the gloomy dark-panelled walls, the obsolete gasolier suspended from the ceiling, the inevitable long central library table piled with newspapers and magazines. From several other clusters of chairs rose more blue puffs, rather like, he supposed, the smoke signals the red Indians were supposed to have devised in America.

"Indeed, before he disappeared my uncle left the family a number of privately printed treatises on the subject," he said quite neutrally. He rolled his unlit cigar between his fingers, squinted at his left sleeve cuff where he had penciled the word "smile," and smiled.

"Used to tell me England was soft and decadent," Erasmus Kater snorted.

"And rife with corruption." Edward Kater gave the neatly bound folder a little push with his index finger.

"Wanted to get away from monarchs, aristocrats, factories, and dark Satanic mills. Wanted to live pure and free in Nature," Erasmus said, "like a noble savage."

"Speaking of factories," Babbage began.

"Coleridge wrote a poem once in the *Morning Chronicle* about Pantisocracy," Erasmus said. "Called it a 'poor innocent foal.' Next week the satirists ran a cartoon of Coleridge and Southey as jackasses."

Babbage consulted his sleeve once more. He had come to dinner only in the poor innocent hope of interesting Edward Kater's quite wealthy uncle in investing in the Engine. But the old man belonged apparently to the genteel school that never discussed money over food. Babbage had already suffered through undercooked game pie and boiled Dover sole and two solid hours of autobiography, beginning with Kater's most recent and noteworthy industrial triumphs and working chronologically backward. At coffee and dessert they had reached his trip to New York and Philadelphia after the War of 1812. Now at port and cigars they were at Cambridge and Pantisocracy, with boyhood, infancy, and birth presumably still ahead, and not a syllable yet about the Engine.

But old men, old men with two bottles of first-rate Hock in them, were never altogether predictable, not even to the creator of the Difference Engine. Erasmus Kater peered at the high-panelled wall for a moment himself, as if recalling exactly how the poet Samuel Taylor Coleridge looked as a jackass, and then abruptly changed the subject.

"Met your friend Searle last year," he said. "Wanted me to subsidize his next African exploration. Plans to go south in the spring, he said, on a camel safari from Rabat to Tamanrasset, looking for diamonds, opals, whatnot. Caoutchouc."

"He's in the trackless deserts of America right now," Edward Kater put in helpfully, "assisting Babbage's astronomical expedition."

"Did you promise him," Babbage made an effort to keep his voice low and calm, "money?" For Erasmus Kater had made his fortune with a series of Midland factories that produced, among other things, highly profitable rubber "erasers"—so named because they could be used to wipe out pencil marks on paper. He might well be interested in exotic African sources of caoutchouc. How galling, indeed, if James Searle were to be subsidized, and not the Engine!

Erasmus Kater wrinkled his egglike brow in an egglike frown and launched predictably into a long-winded reminiscence of his own days in Africa, the politics of empire, the bright future (given the human propensity for error) of rubber erasers. Babbage did his best to give the impression of listening intently. In fact, his mind had already begun to drift irresistibly toward the gas streetlamp just visible through the window, partly veiled in a London drizzle. He had been reading that very morning some of the lectures of Humphry Davy, who had extended remarkably the uses of Alessandro Volta's *pile,* or chemical battery. If instead of gas to illuminate the streets, one substituted electrical batteries and some sort of phosphorescent coil—

"Your numbers," Erasmus said and tapped the folder on the table, and Babbage, as always, came to attention when numbers were mentioned. "Gone over your budget for the machine, workers' salaries, bank rates, everything."

"Most grateful," said Babbage rather stiffly. He was not very good at this sort of negotiation, he knew. Pryce should *not* be half a planet away.

"Talked with the Duke of Wellington," Erasmus Kater said.

"The Duke has been kind to me."

"Says he could see using your machine in navigation and naval gunnery, military operations."

"Yes."

Erasmus Kater studied the ash on his cigar and for a fubsy man of seventy-plus, with an egg-white complexion and implausibly black hair, looked actually very businesslike. "If a total eclipse *really* happens in America," he said, laying stress on the word "really" in what Babbage thought was a most offensive manner, "as your machine predicts, and you have incontrovertible *proof* of it—"

"The daguerreotypes," observed his banker nephew.

"The daguerreotypes, yes. Well, then I would be willing to invest," Erasmus Kater said, and paused to draw noisily on his cigar, "four thousand pounds."

Four thousand pounds was a very satisfactory sum. Four thousand pounds would allow Babbage to finish the prototype model of the Engine. The prototype was only the beginning, of course; he was already thinking of how he could sell that to the army perhaps, use the resulting funds to build a larger, more complex machine, one that could—

"With *proof,* mind you," said Kater through a blue puff of smoke. "The daguerreotypes are absolutely necessary."

"Proof, of course."

"No daguerreotypes, no money."

Despite the coolness of the room, Babbage found himself suddenly perspiring. "Do you mean to say that if something happened to the cameras—" He found the sentence awkward and started over. "Do you mean to say that if circumstances arose and the only proof of the eclipse—" This too was awkward. "Do you mean to say you would not take the word of Mr. Pryce?"

Erasmus Kater was very dry and businesslike indeed. "I would most certainly not," he said, "take the word of William Henshaw Pryce."

HALF AN HOUR LATER BABBAGE SLIPPED INTO THE THIRD CARriage down from the streetlamp outside the Diogenes Club and flung himself into the rear seat next to Ada Lovelace. He gave a sharp rap with his cane against the front partition and the carriage began to splash and roll onto Pall Mall.

"Oh dear," she said, reading his face even in the imperfect light of the passing lamps. "No money."

"Not quite that bad," said Babbage grimly. He took off his

top hat and wiped it with a cambric handkerchief and proceeded to give her a quick and concise account of Erasmus
Kater's insulting offer, his rigid conditions, his utter refusal to
budge.

"Sir Robert Peel's work," said Ada when he had finished.
Sir Robert Peel, soon, as everyone knew, to be Prime Minister
again, had almost entirely on his own created a widespread
distrust of the Difference Engine. In the last three months he
had blocked all further government subvention, poisoned the
minds of the bankers, and actually denounced Babbage in
the House of Commons as "that wooden man."

Babbage grunted and allowed himself to concentrate on
the pressure of Ada's body against his arm. The carriage
swayed as they turned up Picadilly and increased the pressure. He felt her small breast move in its silk cup and found
himself recalling the famous announcement of Lord Byron,
Ada's father, when he took his last Italian mistress: "I am living now in strictest adultery."

"My mother has gone off to the country, ill again from
overeating." Ada leaned very close in order to be heard over
the rain on the roof and the clatter of wheels on pavement.
Babbage was aware not only of breast and shoulder, but also
thigh. "She wants to be by the sea, where her footman can
row her out at a moment's notice, as she puts it, to unload her
stomach."

Babbage grunted again. They were rolling quite fast, con-
sidering the weather, in light carriage traffic past the Burling-
ton Arcade, and his mind was partly preoccupied with the
rigidity and shortsightedness of Erasmus Kater's offer and
partly with the interesting idea of streetlamps and electrical
batteries. "And your husband?"

"Gone to the country as well."

"Then your house—"

"All to myself."

"Ah."

Ada shifted on the seat and adjusted her skirts. In the rainy
darkness, by the stroboscopic light of the passing lamps, as if

from a distance Babbage saw his hand lifted by hers and like-wise adjusted, and then felt the sudden touch, not of silk, but warm, bare flesh. "A woman's role," whispered Ada gravely, "is to comfort."

"I am thinking," said Babbage, who liked to follow his own abstract thoughts at such a time, as a delaying distraction, "of your mother at the seaside." The lights were like a rapid series of miniature eclipses. His voice sounded quite hoarse. His hand moved on its own, higher. "The irony, I mean, of my expedition in the trackless desert and us here, on an island, in a rainstorm." His voice trailed off.

Ada was calmer, preoccupied in her own way. "They have a woman with them, yes?"

"Perhaps," Babbage said, recalling the very attractive but very cool and single-minded young Miss Cott, "not such a great comfort."

He thought of deserts and red Indians. Thought of western landscapes, paintings, photographs. Of course the cameras would work, the photographs would serve as proof, of course. And yet, and yet—

His mind came full circle back to the Engine, its expenses, its glorious future. "My uncle Richard," he said aloud to Ada. Earlier in this thoroughly wasted day he had sat in his solicitor's office and read once more the inventory of his great-uncle Richard Babbage's fortune, which, if proof of death could only somehow be established, would fund the Difference Engine a hundred times more richly than Erasmus Kater or the unspeakable Peel. "My uncle Richard's fortune," he said again, rather plaintively.

"There is really no other source of money," said Ada wisely, "that you can count on."

There is really nothing, Babbage thought, not quite hearing her, so completely erotic as the swaying rhythm of a London carriage at night, though perhaps an eclipse in the trackless desert...

"I picture the Expedition," he said, and realized too late that he sounded exactly like Ada herself, "ten white covered wagons strong, the Miniature Engine, a party of guides and workers, rolling smoothly westward—"

"Yes, yes," said Ada ambiguously.

"I have every confidence in Pryce," said Babbage as she turned toward him and the carriage swerved providentially right, onto Half Moon Street. "Pryce is a supremely calm and deliberate individual."

CHAPTER THIRTY-TWO

Into the Desert

THE FOUR BATTERED AND FILTHY CONESTOGA WAGONS, which were all that was left of the original Somerville-Babbage Expedition, pulled up single file to the top of a bare ridge and hesitated, one after the other, for a long, silent moment while Webb Pattie inspected the brakes and axle-trees. Then at the sharp crack of a whip the mules in their harnesses began a cautious, jangling, swaybacked descent to the floor of the Great Southwestern Desert.

In truth, the landscape so far was not remarkably different from the prairie to the east, though the grass was very sparse indeed and only lightly dotted now with sagebrush and tumbleweed. Farther off on the western horizon, the change was much more obvious. There, forty miles away perhaps, but as clear in the dry air as if they were painted on canvas, out of the flat horizon rose thick, massive buttresses and buttes, sheathed in red stone armor. In front of them lay a wide, rolling plateau, scarred everywhere by dark ravines and tree-lined gorges. Closer up, where the wagon wheels were following alongside the nearly invisible bank of the Cimarron River, the rocks under the mules' hooves were iron black at times, or a rich leathery brown, or even sometimes a shimmering glaucous green that suggested the sea.

It was possible, Selena thought, that God had created the world in stages, not all at once.

France was an experiment in greenery and grayness. The forests west of Washington City must have been an early experiment as well, so lavish of trees and vegetable growth that it was amazing there were seeds left for any other place. And the unmapped, unexplored desert west of the Cimarron Cutoff must have been a very late stage indeed, when seeds and water had run disastrously low and the divine temper had grown irritable and impatient. Parts of the arid, sunburnt landscape ahead of her now, she thought, looked as though it had been crumpled up in a gigantic fist, like a sheet of brown paper, then tossed contemptuously aside. It was an angry god who had made it, or his unskillful apprentice.

She shifted uncomfortably on the bench of Number Three and gripped her rifle. It was late in the afternoon, and they had been following the sandy dry bed of the Cimarron River for almost two hours. And for almost that long they had been followed themselves by three Indian braves on horseback, keeping stealthily off to the north, bobbing up from time to time for a minute or two, half a mile away, then vanishing again behind a hillock or a shaggy rise.

"Nothing for twenty-two minutes." Professor Hollis braced his back on the wagon bench and held out his pocket watch for Selena to see. "They must have gone away."

Selena rebalanced the heavy barrel of the Hawken rifle on her knees and regarded him balefully. For a full hour after the Infant Engine had been unveiled, suspicions had whirled about the repellent little professor—the machine had been sabotaged, *that* was clear. The six brass number wheels could not have vanished into thin air; the incapacitating sand could not have penetrated into the gears without somebody's helping hand. And who else had a motive except the vainglorious Hollis, with his rival equations, his Harvardian pretensions, his unbearable academic ambition? But nothing could be proved; Hollis was adamant, tearfully indignant. In the end,

muttering and cursing, they had loaded the useless Engine
back in its trunk and set out on the original path, half a day
late, silently furious.

"Hunting buffalo," Hollis said. "They were undoubtedly
hunting buffalo, that's all." Which was just likely enough the
case to be annoying.

Selena made a noncommittal grunt and readjusted the rifle. What she should do, she thought, was swing the barrel
around to her left and blast the ridiculous little professor all
the way back to Boston. She should probably do it just for the
aesthetic satisfaction.

Up ahead, twisted sideways on his saddle, Webb Pattie was
holding up his hand in a signal to stop.

Hollis said something else, but it was lost in the racket of
the iron-rimmed wheels on the rocks and the jingling of the
mules' harnesses as they came to a halt. Selena jumped to the
ground, holding her rifle at what James Searle had told her,
back on the nameless cottonwood creek, was "port arms."

She moved off to one side to have a clear view east and
west. No Indians, no buffalo.

"Got to water the mules." Big Carlos appeared with a
bucket in each hand and started to stumble down to the dry
bed of the Cimarron.

Selena watched in puzzlement while he joined the other
teamsters down on the sand. The creek yesterday had had a
little water in it, of course, but once they had abandoned the
hopeless job of repairing the Infant Engine and started to
trace the creek back to the south, the Cimarron proper had
turned out to be almost totally dry, a shallow gully winding
like a snake out of the western desert.

They had missed it on the *Jornada* because for half a mile
at a stretch even the gully disappeared into the dry grass and
crumbling dirt, and as Webb Pattie said, a train of wagons
passing over it at night or twilight would never even know it
was there. Already today, under a brilliant sun and cloudless
sky, they had lost its trail twice and been obliged to stop and

stand guard while Pattie scouted ahead to find where the gully surfaced again.

" 'Thus Alf the sacred river ran,' " said Pryce as he came up beside her, " 'through caverns measureless to man, down to a sunless sea.' I suppose they're going to wring water out of the dirt. Someone should really breed a mule that drinks sand."

"We haven't seen Indians for almost half an hour."

"I'm an optimist," Pryce said, though he was in fact holding loosely a naval revolver pistol like James Searle's in his right hand. "I'm like the man who told Dr. Johnson he always wanted to be a philosopher, but somehow cheerfulness kept breaking in."

In the gully the seven Mexicans were now kneeling in a row and digging in the sand with their hands. Bits of clattering harsh-sounding Spanish drifted up to Selena, and it occurred to her that the teamsters looked more than usually sullen today. Why not, of course? Why, in the name of bad maps and dead mules and incompetent academics, not?

Below her one of the drivers stared silently up at Webb Pattie, who sat astride his mare on the opposite bank, rifle cradled in his arms.

"The idea," Pryce said, "is that the river actually does run *under* the sand along here, one or two feet down, or so Lord Pattie insists. He evoketh the name of one Jedidiah Smith, to be lamented and mourned, I gather, as the first white man to find that out." Even as he spoke another of the Mexicans began to scrape his bucket into the sand and Selena glimpsed a quick silvery splash of water.

"The fish, I suppose," Pryce said, "will have miners' candles on their hats and crawl on their bellies."

Selena shaded her eyes and looked up at the burning sun. "Recalculation of the eclipse path isn't *absolutely* necessary," she said. *Idée fixe.* "Even without the little Engine we can still use Babbage's original figures. We really *have* to push on."

Pryce had started to clamber down the crumbling riverbank to join the Mexicans, but now he stopped and regarded her with an unfriendly curiosity in his face that she had never seen before.

"Did you ever for a moment, Miss Cott," he said coldly, "imagine that I would turn back? From anything?"

Digging water from the sand was a slow and tedious business. Selena occupied herself first by rechecking their latitude once more with her sextant and repacking the camera boxes in the back of Number Two. Then she used her pocket telescope to peer out toward the red-shaped buttes. No Indians, none. At the head of the little four-wagon caravan Webb Pattie sat with his rifle across his lap, looking in the same direction. At the rear, wearing his solah sun hat and Arab-style neck cloth and holding his rifle braced on his thigh, James Searle walked his horse in tight, vigilant circles.

By five o'clock the last mules had been watered from the buckets and the wagons were once again in motion. Clouds had come up, high, thin cirrus clouds, and though they seemed to do nothing to lessen the oppressive heat, the landscape ahead was now sinking under their purple and black quilt of shadows and promised, in an hour or two, coolness.

Selena was walking beside Number Three. Bennit Cushing was walking; the three Mexicans who weren't drivers were also walking. Only Pryce was riding on an open bench. Somewhere under the canvas sheet of Number Two, Professor Hollis had disappeared, either to reformulate once again his stubborn equations or else to nurse a resurgent megrim, and yet it was Hollis, surprisingly enough, who first spotted the Indian horsemen again.

The caravan had just rounded a curve on the sloping hillside above the sand-dry Cimarron and was picking its way across a field of rocky splinters protruding from the golden sand. From the back of his wagon Hollis suddenly shouted. Pattie wheeled his horse. The Mexicans and Bennit Cushing scrambled for their rifles.

For an instant Selena, tumbling and scrambling herself into a wagon, actually stopped to look down at her watch and up at the sun, as if to remember the time. Then she was over the side of Number Three and yanking the big Hawken rifle from its slot by the barrel.

For another instant she thought that this alarm was merely a repetition of Council Grove, where the lazy Osages had lined up before the wagons in a show of menace, only to pull aside laughing as Pattie shooed them away.

But these Indians, straight in their saddles, bronzed, splendid, with magnificent black hair down to their shoulders and glittering breastplates made of reeds and bright feathers—these were warriors, not Osage boys. One by one, like disciplined cavalry, they rode slowly up and formed a stern, silent half-circle along the right side of the caravan. There was no intention in their faces either to move or to laugh.

She counted fourteen. They were armed with bows and arrows. They wore leather breechcloths. Their bare feet were hooked in triangular stirrups made of leather and wood, and oddly, irrelevantly, she noted a great raw cut in one brave's ankle, crawling with black flies that evidently he did not feel. Alone in the group, this brave carried a rifle. In the still, hot air of the afternoon she could hear the clink of a horse's hoof against rock. A mule snorted and raised and lowered its head rhythmically like a seesaw. Pryce drew back the hammer on his pistol with a loud ominous snap.

"Kiowas." Webb Pattie's voice was low and unexcited and in the general silence carried all the way back to Selena. She looked at the nearest brave, who stared back at her as indifferently as he might have studied a rabbit or a sleeping dog.

At such a time the mind falls apart into different fragments of thought; the eye sees different motions, simultaneous, delayed; bits of memory bob up into consciousness like corks in a stream.

She was aware of Pattie advancing his mare toward the center of the Kiowa line. Part of her mind registered that he still had his rifle cradled peacefully across his arm. Another part saw James Searle turning his horse's head slightly and searching for her with his eyes. Years ago she had visited the room in the Palais Louvre devoted to the old king's collection of medieval armor and weapons, and she remembered that she had actually been allowed to pick up and handle one of the battered jousting helmets, and the picture had flooded into her mind of hard masculine faces, ruthless eyes behind a slit barrier of steel.

These were Kiowas, not Apaches or Pawnees, she thought, recalling one of Pattie's campfire lectures, because they wore their hair long, but cut back over the right ear to ease their aim with a bow, and because they were so handsome.

In front of Number One, Pattie was saying something now in a guttural language she assumed was Kiowa. The brave to whom he spoke made no answer, but the man on his left slipped his bow over his shoulder and began to hold out his fingers as if he were counting or playing a child's game. Pattie responded the same way and they both rose a little in their stirrups to point toward the southern horizon. At the same moment precisely, the brave next to Selena's wagon leaned forward and snatched her rifle.

CHAPTER THIRTY-THREE

Another Surprise

A GIFT, GODDAMN IT!" WEBB PATTIE SHOUTED. "HE JUST wants a goddamn *gift*!"

He wrenched his mare's head around and kicked his spurs and reached Selena before she or anyone else could move. In a spray of stones and sand he wheeled again, nose to tail, and grabbed the rifle back.

Behind him, at the rear of Number One, two more Kiowas were probing and poking at the trunks visible under the canvas sheet.

"They just want gifts!" Pattie shouted again. He thrust the rifle into Selena's hands. "Don't interfere, don't do a thing—leave it to me!"

All of the Indians now except the sign-language maker were pushing their horses' flanks hard against the wagons and shaking them as if to dislodge anything loose. One brave had dismounted and started to untether the last two remaining assistant mules. Professor Hollis pushed his head out like a turtle from his shell, then vanished again. The man with the cut ankle appeared on the other side of Selena's bench and caught up the little leather-covered English pocket telescope she kept strapped to the frame. In the wagon ahead someone held up a bright tin coffee cup. One of Miguel's big cooking skillets materialized in the hands of a ferocious-looking warrior with a long black cicatrix across his cheek.

What they wanted, Webb Pattie explained, riding up and down along the wagons, shouting at the Indians but still cradling his rifle, all they wanted was gifts, that was their custom, that was what they expected, gifts—the shinier the better. To Selena he said in a gruff voice, "Stay seated, don't take off your hat, keep your head down. Good thing you're wearing those pants." To Bennit Cushing—"Give them some paints and colors, anything that glitters." William Henshaw Pryce put his hand over the trouser pocket where he kept his gold watch. James Searle blocked the two untethered mules with his horse.

In the end they took one mule anyway, and a half dozen cups and pans, two or three blankets, the telescope, and to Selena's amazement a whole carton of dried-out Graham's Crackers that Pattie had stashed away like a mouse inside his bedroll. But the cameras and big telescopes were untouched, locked out of sight in their wooden trunks and boxes, and the precious Thomas Arnold clock, which would have been disastrously irresistible glitter, likewise remained unseen and unmolested in the back of Number Two, saved, as Bennit Cushing reported with a grimace, by four sacrificial jars of cadmium yellow Ackerman paint.

It could have been worse, Pattie informed them afterward. Three years ago, when he last came out on the Santa Fe Trail, a band of sixty Apaches had carried off "gifts" of tobacco, calico, fine woolens, lead and powder, and one English-tailored suit of men's clothes to a total cost of upward of a thousand dollars, though as it happened his employer that year could easily afford it.

"Tribute goods," he said with a nod at James Searle, "tribute for passage, just like your Arab sheiks in Africa."

"We might have offered them the Infant Engine," said Pryce sardonically, "with a funeral pyre of quadratic equations."

As the hard desert light began to lose its glasslike edge,

they clattered to a halt beside a high butte of red-and-brown-layered rock, overlooking the dry river. Pattie ordered the grumbling Mexicans to pull the wagons around, up against its sheer side, for an illusion at least of protection on one side. Then he sent out guards and set another, smaller party of diggers, including the cook, to work refilling the water barrels.

Selena took it on herself to prepare four loaves of trail bread in the tiny twig and sagebrush campfire that Pattie permitted them. She picked through Miguel's foul "kitchen" kit and found a black tin baking box, perforated rather like her developing box, which she scoured with sand and rinsed with water from a mule's bucket. The dough she made from nothing more than white flour, salt, water, and Miguel's canister of starter yeast. The baking box fit into the gray ashes of the fire like a sleeping cat, and while the bread cooked she made coffee and roasted buffalo meat *en appolas,* as the Mexicans called it, on sticks.

"Will they come back?" the shrill-voiced Hollis wanted to know. "Tonight? Tomorrow?"

Pattie was eating standing up, frowning out across the bare back of the desert, where two red-gold crowns of pillared rock glimmered in the last sinking rays of the sun.

"Going to their medicine festival," he said tersely. "That's what the sign-talker told me."

Bennit Cushing looked up curiously from his meat and bread.

"Annual dance they have," Pattie said to him. Like everybody else, Selena noticed, Pattie avoided speaking at any length to the little professor. "They used to hold it a few months earlier, but the smallpox got in among them two or three years ago and now they think it's safer to wait till September. Kind of a dancing tribute to the sun. The Kiowas run it, down by Rabbit Ears Mountain, but they let the Apaches come as their guests."

"Sun dance," Cushing said and laughed.

"Same as us, yep." Pattie walked a few steps closer to the dry river and frowned even harder. "What the hell those

Mexicans are up to I don't know, pardon my French, Miss Cott." To James Searle he said, "Mules that get used to white men don't like the smell of Indians. Another point for mules, Mr. Searle, good as an extra set of guards."

When they had laid out their blankets for sleep, Selena crept to the edge of the boulder wall and gazed out over the starlit desert. There was a planet rising far to the south, Jupiter, near the spot Webb Pattie had pointed out as Rabbit Ears Mountain, where the Kiowas had gone. Or should have gone. Or might have gone.

Her mind was still too churned up and busy for sleep.

Automatically, without thinking, she began to calculate the path the new moon would take in daylight, high up in the western sky, to block out the dancing, cadmium yellow sun. In her mind's eye their three reflector telescopes were already on their tripods, dark eclipse filters snapped into place, lenses focused.

Step by step she rehearsed the sequence. Her four cameras would stand in a row nearby, developing box and chemicals behind them, a watch to time the exposures. At precisely two-fifteen in the afternoon—but a sudden thought made her muscles stiffen. The little telescope case the Kiowas had taken—did it still contain her precious accelerator formula? Twice on the Trail, as precaution against the meddling hands of Hollis, she had moved it about, from telescope case to camera case to . . . pocket. With a sigh of relief she patted the inner pocket of her trousers and found the sheet of paper. Another disaster averted.

Just beyond the wagons a mule snorted and she felt her blood jump. Her fingers crept from her pocket to close around the barrel of the rifle. Then the mule was quiet again and the shadow of one of the Mexican guards passed silently by. Galileo in the sixteenth century, she remembered for some reason, had had no chronometer more accurate than his pulse. He timed his experiments by that—something takes two pulse beats to fall; the moon needs forty pulse beats to cover half a degree of sky. Over by the coals of the fire she recognized James Searle's big shoulders in profile. In some ancient myths, she thought, growing sleepy now and yawning, the sun and the moon are lovers and an eclipse is their modesty in love; she hadn't brought that up at the demonstration in Washington City. In another version the moon is the sun's eternal enemy and once every hundred years tries her best to devour him.

She crept back closer to the coals and rolled up in her blanket and listened to the camp's silence. The sky was filled with a thousand candles. Light fell to the ground in soft, white burning drops. They were, by her best reckoning, not more than thirty miles from the path of the eclipse, as first predicted by Babbage's Engine. Even without the Infant Engine they should reach it easily. Her cameras were safe and intact. The weather was perfect. They had two, perhaps three more days of travel. There was no reason in the world they couldn't make it.

Today was September 2, 1840. The eclipse was exactly three days away.

In the morning when she awoke every one of the Mexicans had vanished.

CHAPTER THIRTY-FOUR

West

THIRTY-FIVE MILES TO THE SOUTH, JUST HALF AN HOUR BE-
fore sunrise, the Kiowa rider who suffered from the long,
raw cut on his ankle and who was known as Many Bears held
up his right fist and brought his party of thirteen braves to a
remarkably silent halt.

Even on his horse he carried his rifle in a particular manner, characteristic of Indian caution. The barrel sat tight in
the crook of his left arm. The butt, trigger, and breech rested
against his right hip, in easy reach of his fingers.

Richard Babbage looked up calmly. Like most of the
Kiowas he was a very early riser. He had already had his
breakfast of boiled coffee and bean cakes. Now he was simply sitting in front of his tepee watching the smoke rise from
the Sun Lodge sweat houses downhill, on the other side of the
trees. One of the visiting Apache women, who found his
white skin and whiter hair objects of endless giggling fascina-
tion, was brushing his scalp. She used, as the Kiowa women
also did, a hairbrush fashioned from a section of porcupine
tail attached to a wooden handle, and Babbage had often
considered that he could make a small fortune selling such
brushes in the fashionable shops of Picadilly and New York.
That was, however, thinking like a merchant, a capitalist.

By the condition of their horses the little band of braves had obviously gotten up even earlier. They had been out for the past two days, he knew, over near the dry Cimarron, hunting buffalo for the Sun Dance. But rather than buffalo horns, Many Bears, he was more interested to see, carried a fine leather-covered pocket telescope, clearly of European manufacture, attached by a cord to his scalp belt. He dismounted and walked toward Babbage while the other riders backed their horses toward the downhill trail and stopped at a respectful distance.

The Kiowa sign for a deer was made by raising a forefinger and imitating the bobbing motion of the deer's tail when it runs away. Curiously, the same sign was also used to indicate strangers or trespassers, and the Kiowas often employed it to denote white men who might or might not be enemies. The Kiowas as a people had sworn eternal hostility to citizens of the Republic of Texas, authors of two or three truly horrifying attacks in the past few years on Kiowa hunters. But the Indians were not always certain which white men were Texans and which were merely Americans.

Many Bears said something low and stern to the Apache woman, and she stood up hastily, put down her hairbrush, and disappeared behind the tepee. The Kiowa brave took her place. And then, because he was young and perhaps ill at ease speaking directly to such a venerable old man as Babbage, Many Bears cradled his rifle and made the sign of the running deer.

Richard Babbage was very good at sign language. All the men in his family had excellent visual imaginations; that was a key, he had always thought, to his nephew Charles's success with his mathematical machines. He watched the Indian's hands intently. Many Bears was telling him something of great importance. He pointed repeatedly to the north. White men in wagons, but far off the Santa Fe Trail, well armed, carrying valuable goods—the Indian detached the telescope from his scalp belt and handed it to Babbage to examine—except that they were hard in their manners and refused to give good gifts. When they talked among themselves they didn't sound like Texans or Americans, they sounded like Babbage, which was why Chief Trotting Wolf had sent Many Bears to Babbage's tepee.

Babbage turned the telescope over in his fingers and studied the manufacturer's tiny engraved brass label: *Chance Brothers, Birmingham, England;* a very expensive grade of instrument, a scientific telescope, not a toy; and rather an ironic name, if his growing suspicions were correct.

"Were they off the Trail," Babbage asked Many Bears, "because they were lost?"

The Kiowa considered the idea in the slow, deliberate Indian way that always made Babbage think of a cow placing a wager. "No."

Babbage turned the telescope over one last time and gravely returned it to the young brave, who looked, Babbage thought, relieved to have such a costly geegaw safely back. Babbage's whole chest was drawing painfully tight with tension. His heart was a hard knot of wood. The fatigue and perspiration of last month were returning with a vengeance. It occurred to him, not for the first time, that it was really his money that the deeply pastoral and Utopian Indians valued. If he lost his money for any reason and could no longer supply them with gear and precious trinkets from St. Vrain's piratical store in Taos, they would abandon him, he was quite sure, like a worn-out and useless dog.

"You think we should kill them?" Many Bears asked him.

Babbage rubbed his chest and considered. "No."

"Easy to kill them."

"Catch them first," Babbage said, "bring them to see Sun Boy. Then sell them for money to the Mexicans."

Many Bears put his hand on his belt and smiled. "You think like a Kiowa now."

CHAPTER THIRTY-FIVE

Farther West

G ONE?" SHOUTED WILLIAM HENSHAW PRYCE AT ALMOST exactly the same moment, and spun about on his heel like a dervish—"where the *hell* gone?" He lifted his naval revolver, stabbed it furiously at the rising sun, and fired three booming rounds of bullets into thin air. Then he spun around to Pattie.

"How *many?*"

Webb Pattie was standing with his arms crossed over his chest beside Wagon Number One, at the edge of the protective red wall of the butte. In front of the wagon the long eight-looped hitching rig lay limp and flat on the ground. Its chains glinted faintly in the early dawn light of the desert. The guide pole for the rig had been pushed to one side, up against the front left wheel. Behind Number One the other three wagons were still in the semicircle arrangement of the night before, but their canvas covers were undone at the rear and flapping slowly, vacantly in the breeze.

"How many Mexicans or how many mules, Mr. Pryce?" Pattie made no move to uncross his arms.

Pryce reached him in three quick strides. "Do not provoke me, man!"

Pattie let his eyes fall to the gun at Pryce's side. He turned his head slightly to the right and spat into the dust.

"All the Mexicans," he answered. "Half the mules. Must have snuck out one at a time while I was asleep. Took just about as much gear as they could haul away on their backs."

"*Why?*"

Pattie brought his gaze back around to the bench of Number Two, where Selena, Hollis, and Cushing stood in various stages of dress and shock. Selena wore her man's trousers and heavy cotton shirt because she always slept in them now. Hollis, like Pryce and Webb Pattie, was in shirtsleeves, but wore no shoes. Bennit Cushing had on a dust-smeared shirt with no collar and trousers, and his long black hair lay uncombed on his shoulders. Fifty yards away, standing in the makeshift corral with the mules that remained, James Searle stood quietly stroking his gelding's neck.

Pattie turned back to Pryce and rubbed his homely face hard with one hand, so hard that Selena thought she could hear the bristly scratch of morning whiskers on his chin.

"If I had to guess, Mr. Pryce, I would say all those Kiowas yesterday just scared them right off."

"And your miserable incompetence on the *Jornada*."

"Maybe that too."

Pryce looked down at the gun in his hand and made a low growling noise in his throat. Then he stalked over to the bench of the lead wagon and shoved the pistol back in its side-mounted holster next to the brake. When he turned around once more he seemed, by an extraordinary effort of will, to have composed his features into a kind of glacial calm. He fluffed his red Prince of Wales beard and placed his hands on his hips, like a gentleman of the city about to look around for his cane and kidskin gloves. Only the trembling of his fingers betrayed emotion. One of the mules brayed. On top of the butte a raven perched and cawed, come from who could guess what part of the arid and desolate landscape around them.

"So," he said in a normal voice, "our loyal brown-skinned drivers have deserted us. We have five able-bodied men, counting generously the cerebral Professor Hollis. One charming female. Sufficient four-legged friends to draw two wagons."

He paused and squinted at the pale-yellow sun, climbing sluggishly over the rim of the world and casting striped shadows up and down the gullies and over and across the sandy bed of the dry Cimarron River below.

"Would you be so kind, Miss Cott, as to boil us some coffee and warm a few slices of your incomparable ash-fire bread? Perhaps the Professor will make himself useful with silver and crockery."

"You mean to go on?" Hollis looked, not at Pryce, who had begun walking toward the back of the wagon, but at Selena and Cushing. "Go on *now*?"

Pryce stopped and regarded him coolly over his shoulder. "We have to go *somewhere*, don't you think? And I've come this far to see—we've all come together this far. Since there are only six of us we can carry everything we need in one wagon easily, two if need be. Mr. Searle and the expert Mr. Pattie can find us game to eat and water to drink—how far have we come from the cutoff trail, Mr. Pattie?"

"Forty miles back to the Lower Springs maybe."

"Where our drivers have presumably—what was your odd little word, Pattie—'vamoosed'?"

"Vamoosed," Pattie agreed, "took French leave, skedaddled."

"We're still miles and miles from the center of the eclipse path," Selena said. "Almost half a degree of longitude, I think, maybe more."

Pryce nodded gravely, as if this were precisely what he thought too. "And that would present a serious problem indeed, Miss Cott," he said as he picked up a rifle from the back of the wagon and slapped its barrel into his palm, "if I had ever had the slightest intention of observing the eclipse."

CHAPTER THIRTY-SIX

Decision

WEBB PATTIE HAD A RIFLE TOO. HE CROSSED QUIETLY BE-
hind Pryce and into the shadow of the butte. The only
sound was the faint crunching of his boot heels in the dirt and
the distant caw of the raven, now far overhead, turning
south.

For some reason Selena looked at her hands. Then she
lifted her head and blinked over her right shoulder at the rising sun, and despite her sternest and most disciplined effort,
her mind became suddenly foolish and girlish and she found
herself wondering if it was the ancient Egyptians who had
thought the sun was inhabited. If there was someone up
there, some inconceivable flame-tossed creature standing on
the burning solar surface and looking down with his telescope, how would their little caravan appear—brave specks
in a maze? Five men and one woman scattered around four
battered canvas-topped wagons, some indifferent, grazing
mules.

"Actually," she heard Pryce saying now in his weary, elegant London drawl, "I overstate the case considerably. Blame
it on our vanished Mexican friends. If they hadn't stolen
away in the night like the Assyrian cohorts with our mules in
their pockets, we would certainly have gone on as planned.

We would have seen our total eclipse, and afterward, while you and the gifted professor were busy developing your photographic plates, Miss Cott, I would have simply slipped away and taken care of my particular...business. Such was the master plan, right from the start."

She peered to her left and saw Professor Hollis sitting on the ground. Bennit Cushing had not moved at all, not a muscle, not a step. She looked around for James Searle.

"On the other hand," Pryce continued, "you are a rather difficult person to fool, Miss Cott. Two or three times when you asked quite persistently about Richard Babbage, I thought perhaps you had tumbled, as our Babbage, Charles Babbage, would say, to the 'flash pull.'"

She shook her head and looked again toward the mules for Searle.

"Robbery." Pryce's voice was heavy with exaggerated patience. "A flash pull, Miss Cott, is a daring robbery job. Babbage is fond of thieves' slang, you know. You must have heard him use it at one of his foul *soirées*. Doubtless he'll invent a mechanical translator for it one of these days, after the Difference Engine is perfected and he and I are leisured men of wealth."

"Then Richard Babbage..." Selena began, and faltered. James Searle appeared at the corner of a wagon.

"Is quite alive," Pryce finished, "at last report and somewhere close by, and I intend to find him." In one smooth and practiced motion he hoisted the rifle to port arms and cocked the hammer with a loud, ominous click. "Mr. Searle, kindly see to it that the professor and the artist are not burdened by any weapons. Miss Cott, I believe you were about to boil our coffee."

It was Bennit Cushing, of course, who lowered his head and charged like a two-legged bull and actually came within ten feet of Pryce before Searle took one step forward and simply knocked him down. And when Cushing stumbled to his feet and made as if to charge again, the bigger, stronger Searle shoved him backward with both hands once, twice, until the painter was jammed hard against a wagon frame. Webb Pattie casually raised his rifle and pointed it at Cushing's chest. Cushing wiped a trickle of blood from his mouth with the back of his hand and stayed where he was.

"The coffee please, my dear," Pryce told Selena.

IN THE END, AS ANYONE WHO KNEW HIM MIGHT HAVE PREdicted, Pryce had to talk. Had to talk, as Pattie sourly put it, a red and blue lightnin' streak.

While Selena knelt by the little twig fire and prepared the coffee, therefore, he paced back and forth, rifle in hand, and kept up a smug and entirely self-satisfied monologue.

The master plan, he asserted, was almost childishly simple.

What was required for the Difference Engine was obviously a massive infusion of cold, hard, English cash, one that would free Babbage's irascible genius and allow him to finish the damned machine and thereby allow Pryce the privilege of applying that finished machine to the commercially profitable life-assurance business and to the equally profitable world of mechanically computed ship navigation.

But there was no such infusion forthcoming in England. The government was resistant, commercial investors hidebound and wary. The only possible source of cash was the vast untouched fortune of Babbage's great-uncle Richard, who had vanished without a trace, in search of the pastoral life of the noble savage, leaving his money tangled in the toils and webs of the Court of Chancery.

The eclipse was a perfect godsend.

The eclipse was a perfect excuse to send, unknown to any rival heirs for the Babbage fortune, two very capable white male witnesses, English citizens as required by law, out to locate, cajole, and ultimately shake free from his fortune the very eccentric and doubtless very feeble old Pantisocrat.

"You're frowning quite hard, Miss Cott."

Selena stirred the coals. "Webb Pattie knows where he is," she said.

"Webb Pattie does indeed."

"You didn't hire him by accident."

"A private inquiry agent in New York located Webb Pattie for me. Our archival research in Washington City, I'm afraid, was merely for show. You're very clever, my dear."

"And when you find Richard Babbage you're going to kill him."

Off to the side James Searle, in the process of loading Wagon Number One, stopped and squinted up at the sun.

"You're the sort of person who would give euphemism a bad name, Miss Cott. Webb Pattie guided Richard Babbage out to the Kiowas three years ago, for a handsome fee and a solemn Grahamite promise, carelessly broken I fear, never to reveal his whereabouts. When we find him, we intend, according to the strictest rules of Chancery, to have him rewrite his will—"

"And then die."

"It's a pity about your eclipse," Pryce said, shrugging, and moved a few steps away.

Selena turned her head. "Do you happen to know the Howard system of cloud names, Mr. Searle?"

Searle shook his head.

"I thought not," she said. She set the coffeepot on a flat rock next to the fire and dropped Miguel's palm-sized box of phosphorus-tipped matches into her right trousers pocket.

Pryce leaned his rifle against the wheel of Number One, well out of the reach of either Cushing or Hollis, who both sat nearby on the dirt, cross-legged, under Pattie's watchful gaze.

"Don't be too hard on Mr. Searle, my dear." Pryce picked up a tin cup from the pile at Selena's feet and wiped it against his sleeve. "Mr. Searle likes you very much. But Mr. Searle is poor, quite wretchedly poor. And much as he likes you, he wants even more to go back to the promised land of Africa— who can think why? Mr. Searle's as obsessive about it as you are about your beleaguered eclipse, or our Hollis over there about his pathetic reputation. Mr. Searle intends to explore and explore and explore till his fame has circled the globe. A most expensive proposition. But when his name is signed as a witness to Richard Babbage's last will and testament, Mr. Babbage and I have promised that Mr. Searle will have plenty of, as the poet calls it, wherewithal."

Pryce filled his cup and sipped from it. He surveyed the four wagons, the mules, the rising white sun. "The great theme of the nineteenth century, I'm afraid, Miss Cott," he said, reaching for his rifle again, "is actually the triumph of money over—" He smiled and shook his head sadly. "Over everything."

THE MEXICAN DRIVERS HAD LEFT THEM EIGHTEEN MULES, BUT five of these were in such an exhausted state that for all practical purposes only one fully loaded wagon could be hauled. A second wagon might possibly be drawn by a half team, Webb Pattie thought, if its load were drastically lightened and the driver walked.

Pryce ruled against it. Everything would be carried in one wagon, he said, every Expeditionary egg in a single basket.

As the day grew hotter and hotter, James Searle and Pattie worked to redistribute the water barrels, filled once again to the brim from the river; the boxes of dried food, blankets, one change of clothing per person; all the heavy, jangling equipment for repair and maintenance that had first been heaved aboard so lightheartedly back in Independence, in another country.

The wagon sat patiently, Selena thought, like an old dusty nag as the two men worked over it. There was not a trace anywhere of its original gay red and blue paint.

The sun had grown unbearably hot. Even in the shadow of the red butte, where she was sorting Miguel's cookware, she felt herself growing dizzy with heat. Nearby, Bennit Cushing and Hollis, under orders, were lowering telescope crates to the ground. Neither Searle nor Pattie seemed to pay much attention to them. The thin, bespectacled little professor moved with abrupt, strange jerks, as if he were still in shock. The cut on Bennit Cushing's mouth was still bleeding slightly. "You're free to go, my dear fellow," Pryce had said when Cushing had balked at unloading the wagon. He had gestured in a wide, mocking circle. "East, west, north, south, go any direction you choose, my friend, walk as far as you like."

Selena let her fingers close around the little packet of phosphorus-tipped matches in her trousers pocket. There was this to be said about obsessions, she thought, hers or Searle's or William Henshaw Pryce's. Obsessions didn't melt in the sun.

She backed out into the heat and tugged her hat brim as far down as she could to shade her eyes.

Just beyond the empty traces of the nearest wagon, the sandy bed of the dry Cimarron curved back around to the east like a hook. Straight ahead, all across the western horizon, the mysterious and massive buttes rose from the sunburnt grassland, stark, close together, dozens and dozens of them.

Out there, she thought, not a whole day's journey, the center of the shadow of the moon would almost certainly fall.

Of course, if they stayed exactly where they were, exactly where the Mexican drivers had deserted them, she was sure she would witness something. In any eclipse the width of the moon's total umbra was never less than a hundred and fifty miles, and as best she could determine without the Infant Engine, somewhere a little to the west of their nameless stream they had entered that band. But on the edges of that band, on either side, an eclipse was always partial, incomplete. In order to witness totality, an observer would need to be, not at the edge of the shadow, but deep into the center. And in order to see a total eclipse at its longest duration—long enough to permit a daguerreotype camera to expose its copper plate and take an image—an observer had to be in the very narrow part of the shadow where the surface of the rotating earth came closest to the moon and the lunar disk was at its maximum.

She would know she was there by the ticking of the Thomas Arnold clock.

"Mr. Pryce?"

Pryce's pocket telescope was trained on a thin column of black smoke that could be seen rising far to the south, where the sky was the color of burnished silver. He didn't bother to turn his head to her. "Yes."

"If I took my cameras, just my cameras, in one of the other wagons and went west, by myself...I could still see the eclipse."

"Nonsense."

"I don't care about your plan," Selena said, "or Babbage's inheritance—or *any* of that." She looked to Bennit Cushing, as if for confirmation. Cushing nodded his head slowly. "None of us does. I only want to see the eclipse."

"No."

"If I take my photographs back to England, you not only have your inheritance, which still might be years in settling, you have immediate *proof* the Difference Engine works. People will finance it, the government will, the Navy will. Not as much money as the inheritance, maybe, but sooner, right away. It would be like taking a policy of assurance."

She started to say more, but the word "assurance," she realized, was Pryce's kind of word, Pryce's world.

Pryce was looking thoughtfully at James Searle. "They'll be more hindrance than help," he said, musing aloud, "in finding Babbage, down there with the Kiowas. The professor, the artist, a mere girl. We can go faster on our own." His waving hand took in Searle, Webb Pattie. "The three of us."

There was a long, precarious pause. The sun beat down unmercifully. Flies crawled over Selena's face, over her nose. She kept her gaze fixed on Pryce.

"I would need Mr. Searle's key," she said.

"To wind the clock?"

"Without the Thomas Arnold I don't know where exactly to stop. We're close to the center band, but I don't know how close. I need to check the longitude one more time."

Pryce turned his head to examine the buttes in the distance. "Mr. Searle?"

James Searle avoided her eye. He would be splendid in the African desert, she realized, if Pryce didn't somehow cheat him out of his money. He would be perfectly splendid, handsome, *gallant,* breaking every brainless heart in the harem. Searle folded his arms across his chest; he shrugged.

"Give her your key," Pryce told him. After a moment, Searle reached in his explorer's jacket pocket. He was extending his palm toward her, the brass key glinting bright in the sun, when a shadow passed in front of her, like a hawk swooping, and Webb Pattie's big callused fingers covered her hand.

"They come with us," Pattie said. He slipped the key back into Searle's jacket pocket and fastened the button.

Pryce took a step toward him, one eyebrow raised, about to speak.

"Don't know exactly how you mean to pull old Babbage out from all those Kiowas." Pattie's voice was so flat and calm that Selena half expected him to extract another of his Graham's Crackers from some hidden recess of his clothing and begin to have a pleasant horselike chew. "I'm sure you've got a plan. But she's too smart and he's too mad." He pointed his rifle barrel at Bennit Cushing. "And even the Mexican government, if it comes to that, might pay attention to witnesses."

Pryce worked his tongue around his lips, then stretched his neck and fluffed his beard. His mocking smile came nowhere near his eyes.

"I think we had all better hang together, my dear," he told Selena.

CHAPTER THIRTY-SEVEN

Pryce

IN TRUTH, WILLIAM HENSHAW PRYCE HAD NOT YET worked out a plan for seizing Richard Babbage from all those Kiowas.

This was of no concern to him whatsoever.

From the very moment he had first conceived his scheme, the moment Babbage had first started to speak of the eclipse, he had refused to concern himself with the minutiae of the Endgame in the Great Southwestern Desert. The vital climax, in which he would confront and manage, one way or another, Babbage's great-uncle and bring back sad but indisputable proof of the old man's demise—this he had left open to possibilities, improvisation, circumstances. He intended to rely on his mental gifts and, as he always did, on the one moral quality above all which he considered he possessed in the extreme. Audacity.

In this Pryce liked to think he was very much a man of his time.

Only a few years earlier, in a much admired and celebrated London crime, three clever and supremely audacious thieves had climbed the sheer outside of Mr. Laurence Chubb's safe-manufacturing establishment near Picadilly—four stories of slippery stucco-coated brick walls, punctuated by outcroppings of broken glass shards and rusted spikes. These obstacles the thieves had dealt with head-on, hoisting themselves up in the middle of the night by means of alpine ropes, loops, and grappling irons. They had clambered over the top of the roof, which bristled with still more broken glass and spikes, and, defying gravity, lowered themselves through a skylight into the great safe-maker's sanctum, where a month's payroll for the London-Brighton railroad line had been deposited, in an advertising and publicity scheme, as if in a bank vault.

Their total haul was almost five thousand pounds, about three hundred thousand dollars today.

And remarkably, as it was later revealed, the thieves had carried off this extraordinarily bold feat by deliberately imitating the exploits of one Horace de Saussure, the well-known Genevan scientist who had, at the end of the eighteenth century, virtually invented the new and daring modern sport of mountaineering.

More remarkable still was the fact that not one of the thieves had ever seen an Alpinist climb, or studied climbing techniques, or taken a single lesson in mountaineering. They had simply read about it in the papers and assumed that what the Swiss adventurer had done, they could do too.

At the subsequent trial—for they were audacious in their spending as well, and quickly captured—the flabbergasted prosecutor had only been able to shake his head and murmur, "But, sir, you could have fallen fifty ways to your death or impalement—you must have been *mad*."

Pryce had actually attended the Chubb trial as a fascinated spectator. He had identified quite cheerfully with the bravura and unparalled self-confidence of the defendants. But certainly *he* was not mad. He was in full control of his faculties. He considered himself extremely well informed about the exigencies of British inheritance law, he had no fear of ignorant, unlettered savages in the trackless desert, and he had depended on his own skills of improvisation all his adult life. Like the Chubb thieves, he was audacious. Unlike them, however, he was subtle and adaptable.

"What is required," he said to James Searle, leaning side-ways to make himself heard over the rattle of the wagon wheels, "is a white man who can testify in Chancery to date of death and also as to the subject's sound mental state."

"An English citizen, yes," Searle muttered. "You've told me a hundred times."

Pryce was driving the wagon from the bench, a skill he was pleased to discover he had almost unconsciously developed in the last few weeks. Searle was riding next to him, a few feet away, on his brown gelding. He wore his white explorer's sun hat tightly strapped to his chin, and he carried his rifle with the butt on his hip, angled upward, the very picture of a guard on alert.

Except that this guard, Pryce had noticed, was seriously distracted. Searle glanced constantly over his shoulder, not toward the horizon east or south, where danger might indeed lurk, but backward toward the bedraggled group some fifty yards behind the wagon. There, braying and snuffling as usual, plodded the six wretched fly-bitten and ladder-ribbed assistant mules Pattie had insisted on bringing with them. Bennit Cushing was walking to the left of them and driving the mules, less ineptly than one would have expected, by means of a long prod and a whip. Next to him trudged Pro-fessor Hollis. Next to him, striding calmly in her man's trousers and hat, as if the heat of the afternoon were nothing, as if her predicament were nothing, came Selena Cott.

"I don't think she bears much resemblance to a threatening Kiowa brave, Mr. Searle," Pryce said dryly. Then, because he thought Searle was potentially a weak and calflike person where Miss Cott was concerned, he added sharply, "Go up ahead to Pattie."

Searle glowered and rose in his stirrups. But after a mo-ment's hesitation he spurred his horse forward.

Pryce snapped the reins of his mules and picked up speed himself. He let his left hand grip the reassuring shaft of the ri-fle in the gun box beside him. Methodically, through the dust from the mules' hooves, he surveyed the grassy range before him, left to right. Even he, not an outdoorsman, could tell they were entering a dangerous kind of landscape, no longer flat and open, but made up of increasingly steeper hills, lower valleys, dips, shadowy clumps of pine and cottonwood where anyone might hide, anyone at all. Off to the west the strange red buttes still lay scattered and shimmering in the heat, like huge fiery boxes tumbled from a passing giant's wagon. It might have been the burning surface of the sun. But they were not going there. They were going south.

They stopped in the shade of a cottonwood grove to rest. A stiff breeze had come up, making the dry grass ripple and the leaves of the cottonwoods shake. Selena laid out cold strips of beef and tin cups of tepid water from the barrels. Others tended to the mules. Pryce and Webb Pattie walked to the top of a nearby ridge and looked downhill, across two or more sets of rolling valleys, toward a dense, dark line of trees where Pattie thought the North Branch of the Canadian River or some tributary of it probably lay, though neither he nor any other guide he knew of had ever ventured this far west of the Cimarron Cutoff, off the Santa Fe Trail. Two or three lines of silver smoke curled in the wind above the distant trees.

"Those would come from their sweat houses, I reckon," Pattie said in a low voice. He was anxious, Pryce thought scornfully. The man was anxious. His foul old clothes had a rank smell that came from more than dust and heat, and he insisted that they squat low on their heels while they talked, out of the line of eyesight or bowshot. "What they do," Pattie said, "is build a big dance lodge down by a river. Then they put up three or four little sweat houses off to one side for the medicine men. Some of the tepees will be right around the lodge, but most of them are off somewhere back in the trees."

Pryce shaded his eyes and stared. Anxiousness was contagious. His mind had been preoccupied, in some sort of defensive process no doubt, with what to do *after* they had found Richard Babbage. Taos and Santa Fe were the nearest towns on the map, places where there might be some sort of rudimentary officialdom. The Court of Chancery liked to see paper, many sheets of paper with stamps and dates, testimonials to the date and manner of death. Better if they were in English, of course, witnessed by English speakers. And the Mexican government was deeply suspicious of all foreigners; they had been warned often about that. But still—

"Once the dance starts," Pattie was now grumbling beside him, shifting his lanky underfed body in his awful clothes, "everybody goes inside the big lodge."

"Would they know about the eclipse?" Pryce suddenly wondered. "You said they worshipped somebody called Sun Boy. Sun Boy is their god."

Pattie squatted even lower on his heels and, annoyingly, chewed on a long dry blade of grass. Part of the Grahamite diet perhaps. What he had liked at once about Webb Pattie, Pryce thought, was the quasi-religious air he affected, his absurd dietary fanaticism, his homespun theories. A perfectly American combination, in Pryce's experience. Mind-numbing professions of pseudo-faith, ruthless devotion to self-interest.

"Who knows?" Pattie replied. "Matter of fact, *you* don't know for sure there's an eclipse."

"One keeps the faith." Pryce had brought along a little pocket telescope, the twin of the telescope the Kiowa brave had taken from Selena Cott. Though the wind was making his eyes water, he lifted it up with both hands and focused. One had to have faith in the processes of one's mind; in audacity. Off in the haze to the south, not that far away, he could see through the telescope a party of men on horseback. Kiowas; hunters, no doubt. A thought tickled his memory, a vaguely uncomfortable thought. He lowered the telescope and studied the curling streams of smoke above the distant river. Hunters.

"If you want Babbage alive," Pattie said, "you have to wait till all the braves are inside the lodge."

"I want him alive long enough for two English white men to witness his death, officially, and sign a certificate."

"So you said. Too damn quiet around here."

An idea, not a memory, was beginning to stir in Pryce's mind. "They all go into the lodge for the dance? All the Kiowas?"

"Every man jack one of them. Women and children too. And once they go inside, everybody has to stay and dance, or watch the dance. Whole thing takes most of the day."

"And Richard Babbage?"

Pattie's face had the beginnings of one of his slow, dishonest grins. "The middle of the dance is when they worship the ten Grandmothers' sacred medicine pouches. Those are gifts from Sun Boy himself, after he created the Kiowas. No white man in the world has ever been allowed to see that."

"So whatever happens, all day tomorrow Richard Babbage will be left alone outside, unguarded."

Pattie spat out the disgusting blade of grass and then, despite his earlier insistence on stealth and caution, stood straight up and put his hand on his gun.

"Imagine," Pryce said, and his contempt for Pattie dissolved in the pleasure of contemplating his idea, his audacity, "imagine the consternation when Sun Boy's eclipse begins."

"Somebody's set the goddamn grass on fire," Pattie said.

CHAPTER THIRTY-EIGHT

Race to the Buttes

THE NOTION HAD BEEN IN SELENA'S MIND ALMOST FROM THE moment she had sat down that morning at the little twig fire to make Pryce's coffee, moving like a dark shadow below the surface of her thoughts—Indian hunters, dry grass and wind, the great writhing coils of smoke on the prairie where the Pawnees had deliberately set the land on fire to flush their game.

As soon as Webb Pattie and Pryce were started up the hillside, she had seized Bennit Cushing's mule prod and stepped quietly out of sight, behind the wagon. Hollis was sitting slack-jawed on the ground with a tin dinner plate in his lap. She ignored him. She ripped with her teeth a long strip of cloth from the old, discarded skirt she kept as her one last change of clothes. This she wrapped like a little turban around one end of the mule prod. In Miguel's cooking boxes she found the can of buffalo fat he used to grease his skillets. She smeared the cloth with it and laid it across a flat stone. Reached in her trousers pocket for the box of phosphorus-tipped matches...

The match caught at the first swipe, and the little turban of cloth and fat burst into flame with a sound like a loud *whomp*. Selena sprang to her feet and began to wave the mule prod backward and forward, ankle-high, as if she were swinging a scythe; all around her the dry grass leaped up, orange and blazing, and she started to run.

It was Bennit Cushing's job (settled in whispered French as they walked between the mules) to distract James Searle—hold him, wrestle him, do whatever he could until the fire was burning. But neither Selena nor Cushing had imagined the fanning power of the wind.

Searle was twenty yards from the wagon, among the trees, when the torch ignited. Instantly he swung toward the flames. His hand fumbled for his pistol. Cushing shouted, pointed uphill; Searle spun again toward the top of the grassy rise where Pryce and Pattie had gone.

"Up there!"

Searle took three or four steps in the wrong direction, broke into a run, then stopped on his heels and swung himself wildly around.

From the back of the racing fire Selena made a dash toward the wagon. She stumbled, fell to one knee in the grass. For a single tick of a clock she was lost in a black cloud of smoke and ashes, flailing blindly. Then the wind moved, she reached the wagon, vaulted over its side like a sailor, and kicked the brake lever loose.

Searle had started downhill slowly, in disbelief. His pistol was in his hand, but pointing to the ground, almost dangling, and whether he would ever have raised it or fired was not to be known, because at that moment Bennit Cushing flung himself forward with a shout, and the two men tumbled over and over, legs and arms flying, downhill toward the blaze.

At the top of the rise Webb Pattie appeared in silhouette, then Pryce.

Selena yanked up the reins of the eight braying, kicking mules and gave them their head.

Mules, like horses, like oxen, like every animal, will turn and run from wildfire in a panic. Selena could already see rabbits and other low, dark shapes bounding ahead of the flames, which had now, astoundingly, climbed almost a hundred yards up the southern hillside and across the dry grass slopes to the left, a curling, twisting rope of terrifying black and red. A deer flashed by, out of the trees. The unhitched mules by the trees began to run.

"Stop them, Searle! Stop the goddamn mules!" Pattie was half falling, half sliding on his back and his heels down the grassy slope, rifle held high over his head.

Selena's mules had perversely jumped at first exactly toward the curve of the fire, into the choking black smoke. Now they dug in their hooves and actually skidded sideways, and before she could do anything more than lean the other way, her front left wheel slammed into a cottonwood trunk with a jolt that almost knocked her off the bench, and she came to a shuddering halt.

On the right Bennit Cushing, somehow on top and straddling, plunged his hand into Searle's jacket pocket. Then he was up and free and limping toward her.

At the base of the hill Pattie, hatless, wreathed in smoke, raised the barrel of his long Hawken rifle.

Half a step before Cushing could reach the wagon, or Pryce could cry out, or Pattie's finger could squeeze the trigger, Walter Josiah Tudor Hollis dove toward the rifle barrel and hit it, and his right arm flung the tin dinner plate of meat and bread into Pattie's face. And then Cushing was sprawling headfirst into the back of the wagon, Selena was cracking her whip, and the white Conestoga top, like a hare down a hole, was disappearing into the smoke, back toward the buttes.

When they reached the next rise north, three-quarters of a mile away, the trail swung hard to the left. Selena craned to look back.

No one was following them, no one at all, no wagon, no rider on mule or horse. The hollow where they had stopped to eat was lost to view under a swirling canopy of smoke. Flames made a huge semicircle at the edges, running south and east before the wind, and more flames were shooting up the sides of trees, to the very tops. As Selena watched, two cottonwoods, one above the other, burst into crowns of crimson and gold. Trunks and branches exploded like distant gunfire. Far to the left she could see Webb Pattie loping out of the way of the flames. For an instant, less, she saw a line of redskinned horsemen strung along the farthest ridge, looking down, beginning to descend.

Then Bennit Cushing scrambled through the canvas flap and onto the bench beside her. Grinning, he held up a small brass key. And in sheer scientific exuberance, nothing else, Selena kissed him hard on the mouth and grabbed the reins and they were off again.

The eclipse was exactly twenty-three hours and nineteen minutes away.

CHAPTER THIRTY-NINE

Two Hemeralopes

B Y FOUR O'CLOCK THEY HAD REACHED THE EARLIER CAMP-ground, where they had long ago begun the day, next to the sandy bed of the dry Cimarron.

If the vanished Mexican drivers had ever come back, or a Kiowa party had found their stacks of discarded supplies, there was no evidence of it. In the shadows of the tall red rocks, everything was just as they had left it. Selena steered the wagon as far into the shade as she could. And then, while Cushing tended to the mules and hastily scrabbled up water from beneath the sand, she climbed into the back and started to toss out bundles, one after the other, higgledy-piggledy—extra boxes of food, tools, all but two blankets, Pryce's London frock coat and Lock Brothers hat, James Searle's other boots.

By the time Cushing had finished watering and rehitching the mules, the big Conestoga wagon was reloaded, trimmed down to the bare essentials, and Selena was sitting on the bench, with an unapproachable frown of concentration, rewinding the Thomas Arnold clock.

Peering through the rear flap, Cushing counted four cameras and tripods in their crates, two telescopes, a large box of copper daguerreotype plates, another box of protective glass covers for the plates, the developing box that had been used in St. Louis, six or seven bottles in a half-opened crate labelled "Hypo." Next to the Hypo was another carton of bottles and canisters; next to it a smaller wooden box marked simply "Accelerator Chemicals."

Cushing ran his hand through his long hair. Then he walked over to the base of the red rocks, to a jumbled stack of paintings and drawings that Pryce that morning, rifle in hand, had made him cull. He picked up an armload and carried it back to the wagon. He made a second trip and deposited next to the cameras a square drawing board and a set of paints and brushes.

"*Ars longa,*" Selena said with a faint smile, and turned away to replace the clock in its padded box. She wrote down the time in her notebook, and Bennit Cushing heaved himself onto the wagon and handed her the reins, and at six-fifteen exactly their wheels began to turn and the Somerville-Babbage Expedition, what was left of it, started west toward the setting sun.

THEIR GOAL WAS SIMPLE, OF COURSE—THEY HAD AGREED ON what to do almost without discussion, either in French or English. They would travel as far as they possibly could until just before noon the following day, toward the invisible point, surely not too far distant, where the Thomas Arnold clock would tell them they had reached the center of the moon's umbra, the heart of the path of the total eclipse. And there they would halt and set up the cameras. Afterward... afterward they would think about afterward.

For well over an hour they steered directly into the western horizon, following no trail, rolling steadily, with a strange, silent absence of rattling pans and jingling chains, out across the scrub grass. The sky ahead of them was an enormous blue-orange dome, hung with ghostly white ribbons of cloud. All around them the mysterious buttes, two and three hundred feet high at times, rose from the brown grass into the fading sunlight, glowing a deep mahogany red and showing their humped backs, dolphinlike, above a sea of shadows.

Selena had never been so utterly tired and filthy in her life. Smoke clung to her skin and clothes. Dust and dirt were caked on her hands and face. Her legs were burning hot wires. She walked, trudged, stumbled beside the lead mules, encouraging them, stroking their ears, pulling their halters. On the other side Bennit Cushing walked with his rifle and his whip in hand. They kept their eyes on the ground six feet ahead and forced themselves and the shuffling, panting animals forward step by step until at last the sun disappeared for good, and providentially, to their grateful surprise, they found they had halted beside a tiny, sweet-tasting stream where the mules could drink and they could drop to their knees and rinse their faces.

Briefly, Selena looked up and considered whether perhaps they could still push forward in the gathering darkness for another two or three miles. But a solar eclipse, total or partial, can only occur at New Moon, or as her father had long ago taught her to call it, Dark-of-the-Moon, an old seafaring term. There was no moon tonight, nor should there be if an eclipse was to take place tomorrow. And the brilliant white tree of stars beginning to spread out over their heads was far from bright enough to guide the wagon safely.

She sank down in the prickly grass next to the right front wheel. "Mrs. Somerville likes a word," she told Bennit Cushing. " 'Hemeralopic.' It means 'day-blind,' unable to see well except by night. She thinks astronomers should all be hemeralopic."

Cushing was squatting on his heels, a pale, slender form in the darkness. She could barely see his long hair. Vaguely she watched him pile up a little pyramid of twigs and grass and strike a matchhead against a stone. Abruptly, like a goblin, his face and body materialized.

"Not a camp without a fire," he murmured, which was one of Webb Pattie's sayings.

She frowned and turned to scan the southeastern horizon,

but there was nothing, nothing at all to see, and for a moment in her exhaustion, until she oriented herself by the constellation Cassiopeia, she couldn't be sure which was south, which was west. Bennit Cushing was methodically hammering something at the rear of the wagon. The tethered, unseen mules pulled noisily at the grass along the stream. A hoof stamped.

She leaned back against the wagon wheel and watched the tiny fire wriggle and fidget. Her mind drifted. Somewhere back in the twilight she had already marked out part of the route they would have to take after the eclipse—southwest through the maze of buttes and hills, down toward the place where the main branch of the Santa Fe Trail came out of the mountains, the Raton Pass, and curled around to the town of Taos, civilization. This time of year there would surely be dozens of caravans, coming and going. They had enough water; they had a rifle.

She yawned. She could almost see the map in her head, Lieutenant Frémont's map, like a photograph in her memory. Her thoughts made a worried skip backward to the cameras, the sequence of chemicals tomorrow for proper developing. Had she forgotten anything? The special accelerator required bromine, but also a measured application of gold chloride (her personal discovery), which had performed to perfection in the cool, temperate climate of France. How much the heat, the six weeks of incessant jolting in the wagons had damaged it, she had no idea. Surely it would work, surely the cameras would work.

She was her father's daughter, Selena thought. She would do exactly what she had set out to do.

She shifted her back against the wagon wheel and for a moment her mind went back to Pryce's description in Washington City—was it only three months ago?—of the glorious spectacle of the coming eclipse, and she felt her instincts stir, felt the sheer sensual pleasure of science flicker and come alive. What else was an eclipse but the brief, dramatic, utterly stupendous embrace of the masculine Sun and the Lady Moon?

"You'll be warmer in the wagon," Bennit Cushing told her. "I've laid out your blanket in there." He spread his own blanket on the grass. "I'll watch the mules."

She yawned again and held up her watch and saw a silver meteor streak through Cygnus the Swan. Belatedly it occurred to her that there was something far more scandalous about sleeping and travelling in the Great Southwestern Desert with one man only, instead of six or twenty.

"Or forty or a hundred and fifty," she said sleepily, just to be counting something. She sounded like Mr. Babbage. She would invent a Difference Engine herself, and program it to count sheep for insomniacs. The wagon was right behind her, much too far away. She let herself slip down in the grass and yawn one last time, and after a time she felt a coarse blanket gently draped around her.

CHAPTER FORTY

The Shadow of the Moon

WHEN THE SUN CAME UP, SOFT AND HAZY PINK OVER THE rippling brown North Fork of the Canadian River, Richard Babbage had already been awake, fitfully, for hours.

He sat in a kind of wooden frame chair made of lodge poles, propped against a borrowed tepee. The tepee was located in the first of a series of concentric circles of tepees around the central Sun Lodge, and it had an unobstructed view not only of the sunrise, but also of the large trampled field between the Sun Lodge and the riverbank.

For a long time there was really nothing to be seen. Babbage ate a few bites of a fish and herb cake one of the old squaws brought him. Then two more old women came to tend his feet, which were still slightly blistered from the fire yesterday, when he had been slow getting out of its way and a burning cottonwood had come down next to him like a torch. He closed his eyes and let the sun play on his face, and he must have dozed for an hour at least, because when he woke up again it was hot.

"Buffalo dancers," said one of the two old squaws who were still busy about his injured feet. Babbage stirred uneasily in his chair. He looked toward the river where she was pointing.

"Pretty bad terrible buffaloes," the old woman added, giggling, and bobbed her head up and down like a cruel little long-haired bird.

What the Kiowas would have done to their white hostages, what horrors they would have performed if he hadn't spoken out so firmly, Babbage shuddered to think. What they were doing now, in any case, was more than sufficiently bad enough.

All four of the white men captured at the grass fire yesterday were now huddled together in a makeshift corral between the river and the imposing bulk of the Sun Lodge. Around the corral fence, shouting and jeering and throwing rocks, were gathered fifty or sixty Kiowa braves as well as most of the young Society of Rabbits. At the center of the enclosure, just out of arm's reach, Pryce, Webb Pattie, someone named Searle, and a pathetic little specimen who seemed to have lost his glasses—every one of them was dressed in a complete and heavy buffalo hide, including all four legs and hooves, head and horns, and a stiff tail.

They must be sweltering, Babbage thought, looking up at the sun.

He started to gather his strength into his legs, preparatory to standing up. Meanwhile some of the bigger Rabbits had already, predictably, dodged under the fence rails and were thumping the four "buffaloes" mercilessly with sticks, as someone might beat a rug on a line. Some of the young girls were joining in, too, heaving more rocks and clods of clay and kicking the bare and bloody feet of the white men.

"Old, old fellow," said the old, old woman, dabbing something cool and pleasant on his injured feet.

"His name is William Henshaw Pryce," Babbage intoned, and the two women nodded solemnly. Pryce was just then being toppled slowly into the dust by several quite husky Rabbits, and what could be seen of his dirty hair and beard did look old. He moved stiffly like an old man, too, as he tried to stand. The Rabbits knocked him over again and started to drub his sides with their sticks. The two ancient nursemaids showed Babbage a pair of toothless grins.

Webb Pattie, Babbage was oddly pleased to see, was bearing up better under the thumps and blows. But Pattie was a tough, philosophical person. Another one—not the big quiet fellow, but the one who had apparently lost his eyeglasses—was curled ridiculously under his buffalo hide, resisting all attempts to make him get up.

Over by the two sweat houses some of the medicine priests had emerged in their painted robes, and crowds of men and women, Apaches and Kiowas, were gathering around them. From inside the Sun Lodge, where neither Babbage nor any other white man would ever be permitted, the rhythmic pounding of drums could be heard now. It was accompanied by the "hi-yeh, hi-yah" of the sacred chanting.

Briefly, Babbage considered going down to the field and the herd and speaking to Pryce again, or his old guide Pattie, but it was much too hot and crowded down there, and his chest really hurt quite badly and in any case what was there to say?

Nonetheless, he heaved himself to his feet. Pryce, he thought, Pryce and his nephew Charles and his dreadful calculating Engine. Yesterday Pryce had tried to spin some trumped-up story about coming on a scientific expedition, not in the least aware that Babbage was here. But Babbage had seen through that. Babbage understood the magnetic lure of money. Either Pryce had come to drag him back to civilization, where his greed-crazed relatives would doctor him up like poor old insane King George and throw him in a private madhouse, or else Pryce had come for a far worse reason.

Babbage's mind was growing hazy.... Something else about Pryce's mission. He couldn't remember. He squinted up at the sun again and saw that the sky had begun to tilt and turn in slow blue wheels. Everywhere he looked, white-puffed clouds appeared to encircle the sun, like tepees around the sacred lodge. Babbage felt quite childishly pleased. He believed that people all over the world tried to align their cities and their temples with the sky and arrange their lives according to a perceived cosmic order. Exactly like the dome of St.

Peter's in Rome, the Sun Lodge and its circles were a miniature universe to his people, the Pantisocratic Kiowas. Pryce
was a negligible fellow. He scarcely disturbed the cosmic
order.

The old women were tugging at his arms and Babbage
shook them away and took a single tremulous step toward
Many Bears, now emerging from the haze. Then the pain in
his chest stopped him dead in his tracks. He wouldn't let
them kill the four white men, he thought. In the end he was
still too civilized. He had already made Chief Trotting Wolf
agree to turn them over to the next patrol of Mexican soldiers—six months or a year in a Mexican jail, eventual ransom from the white sepulchered city across the sea—a
wonderful plan, excellent. What had he left out? What had he
forgotten?

Richard Babbage took another step and watched the world
spin over in a cerulean cartwheel, as if he himself and not the
sky had tripped and was swooning and falling, and he
clutched his chest and screamed and tumbled head over heel
into the blazing sun.

FIFTY-TWO MILES AWAY, SELENA PULLED BACK HARD AT LAST ON
the reins, and her weary, panting team of mules sagged and
clattered to a grateful halt.

Almost before the wheels of the wagon had stopped rolling,
she was marching out into the scrub grass. When she reached
a level spot clear of where she estimated the wagon's shadow
would eventually stretch, she stopped and planted the first of
her four camera tripods. Behind her, Cushing unhitched the
mules and led them downhill toward the shade of a few old
gray pines made hunchbacked by the desert wind. Selena
turned back to the wagon.

The great question all along, she decided, as she carried the
next load of cameras out, the great question all along for her
had always been, not would the eclipse actually take place, but
in what kind of country would it be located: deep, inaccessible

canyons, high mountains, or even long rolling dunes of pure white sand like James Searle's Africa? Now the answer was in front of her, and on every side.

She lowered her boxes to the dirt and made an anxious survey, full circle. This part of the Great Southwestern Desert was not nearly so flat and sublimely dull as the western reaches of the Santa Fe Trail prairie. Nor was it anything like as arid and blank as the desolate brown triangle of space where they had wandered when they missed the Cimarron River—she had lost track of how many days ago. Since dawn she and Bennit Cushing had covered almost ten more miles, due west. Little was really different. On the north and the west they were bounded by low brown hills, and here and there a stark bare cliff that loomed above the scrub grass floor like the gray ramparts of a ruined castle. To the south and east the undulating land grew flatter. The mysterious red rock buttes, closer together than ever before, rose a thousand feet or more, huge fixed sails in a great stone armada.

It was 11:21 in the morning. The eclipse was predicted to begin at 2:15. She got down on her knees and opened the padded box that contained the Thomas Arnold clock.

At some point in the previous night she had awakened suddenly, bolt upright in her blanket, convinced that the clock had stopped. For five minutes she had tried desperately to pick out the moons of Jupiter with her naked eye, since it was possible in theory, if you had the proper charts and equations, to figure out longitude that way. Galileo himself had devised the method. But she lacked the right charts, Jupiter was invisible in the clouds, and it was too late now to trust anything but the Difference Engine and the clock.

She opened the lid, took a tremulous breath, and noted the time. Six twenty-one in the evening in London. No slippage since she had wound the clock with her two precious keys that morning. She wrote the time on her pad. It would take ten or fifteen minutes to calculate their longitude exactly—an academic exercise, she realized; they were where they were, right or wrong. Latitude was far easier. Latitude was reassuring in its simplicity.

She put the clock to one side and stood up with her sextant. Then, after she had found her place in her book of altitude correction tables, she put the sextant to her eye. She swung the index arm out and adjusted the screws once, twice, until the lower limb of the sun in the sextant's mirror dropped to the eastern horizon. This was called, in nautical parlance, "shooting the sun," and her father had taught her to do it when she was eight years old, in the Jardin des Tuileries, sighting over the rooftops beyond the Place de la Concorde in the most beautiful and faraway city in the world. She brushed desert flies from her cheek and wrote down the sun's declination from the correction tables and did a simple quadratic equation in her head.

Then she picked up her pad and pencil and began to calculate their longitude.

"Cosine P over two," she muttered when Bennit Cushing's shadow fell across her lap. She didn't look up. "Sin s times the sum of sin s_2, minus ZX. This is a formula from Mrs. Janet Taylor's *Principles of Navigation*, 1837 edition, the best navigation manual there is, and written by a woman with a husband and seven children."

"And lived in a shoe and had so many cosines she didn't know what to do."

Selena drew two thick lines at the bottom of her pad. "We're at longitude 104 degrees, 57 minutes. We're almost half a minute short of the maximum."

"Will it matter?"

She stood up wearily and dropped the pencil and the pad of paper to the ground. It was furiously hot. Her shadow was no more than a small black moon at her feet. She hadn't imagined it would be so hot, and for a moment she tried to think what such heat might do to the bromine in her accelerator formula, even in its specially designed and insulated phials. As for the mercury and the gold chloride . . . She shook her head. "We'll have about four and a half minutes of total-ity instead of six," she said, "but if everything goes well, it should be enough."

She left him arranging the cameras in a straighter line and returned to the Conestoga wagon, where her chemicals were stored. The sheet of paper with the special accelerator for-mula had been folded and refolded so many times that it was almost illegible now. She crawled into the back on her hands and knees, smoothed it over the top of a wooden crate, and began to mix what Hollis would undoubtedly call her witch's brew. The fumes of the bromine were awful. With her nostrils about to burst into flame, she hunched over a little makeshift workspace, sweltering, shrouded under the hot canvas top of the wagon, and one by one she prepared her forty-eight cop-per plates for exposure. She had just under three hours to do them all.

The first step was to polish and brush them with silver io-dide. Then, off to one side, she stirred the bromine into a chemist's glass basin. Next came the other ingredients of her hypo mixture, read off through watery eyes from the formula sheet; finally the gold chloride. By now her hair was plastered to her scalp with perspiration. With sore, stained fingers, un-packing her box from front to back, she lifted the daguerreo-type plates up by a corner heel, like little baby Achilleses, and laid them in a slanted line on the wagon floor to dry. At quar-ter to one, scarcely looking up to thank him, she nibbled at the fried bread Cushing brought her and continued to pour and mix her chemicals.

At one-thirty, when she had prepared all but the last few ounces of hypo, she took a moment to step down from the back of the wagon and breathe. In the scrub grass she stopped and stretched her aching arms and legs and noted the thin cirrus clouds drifting slowly to the east. As if it were any other day and they were out in their leisure on the Santa Fe Trail, Bennit Cushing sat a few yards past the row of cameras and the telescope, sketching.

She put on her hat and walked a little closer. He was

drawing the low hills and bluffs to the north, and despite the
fact that his back was bent low in concentration, over his
shoulder she could make out a graceful whorl of black
crayon, white space, a whole landscape conjured up by his
fingers and somehow possessed by light.

She liked her phrase. If you were a painter, an artist, you
might by your very nature be possessed by light. Or if you
were an astronomer too. Cushing's long black hair was now
well below his shoulders, but like a mountain trapper's hair,
not a city fop's. In the last six weeks his arms and shoulders
had grown muscular. His face had lost its sneer. When had
she first noticed? She turned toward the wagon again and
brought her mind firmly back to bromine and hypo.

It was one fifty-five, and she was rinsing her hands at one
of the water barrels when she felt the change in the air.

There was, in fact, no obvious change at all. Everything
was the same, everything was normal. The sun was its usual
burning yellow orb, the sky close around it was pearl-gray,
then blue, then azure. But the mules were standing with an
odd, stiff tension. Bennit Cushing was slowly getting to his
feet. Selena dried her hands on her trousers and kept her gaze
on the sky.

When she reached the telescope she snapped in the darkest
filter and tapped the viewing box to the left. On the slanted
mirror the sun looked utterly normal. She fumbled in her case
for a lighter filter. Still no change. She looked at her watch,
which could, of course, be fast. If she had time she could go
back to the wagon and check the Thomas Arnold clock.

But she had no time.

In the viewing box, at two-fifteen in the afternoon, just as
Charles Babbage had predicted, at odds of nine hundred to
one, a tiny nick appeared on the right-hand side of the sun.

She could detect nothing else different. The sunlight pouring down on the Great Southwestern Desert was exactly the
same. The mules had not changed their watchful posture. A
trio of ravens circled the nearest bluffs unconcernedly.

And then gradually, inch by inch, a sense of uneasiness

seemed to steal over the landscape. The ravens cawed and flapped about noisily. The grasshoppers were silent. The blue of the sky grew pallid. On the ground the light began to diminish and the tawny hillsides and dry brown grass took on a steely metallic cast. Overhead the black nick on the sun became a crescent.

By the time the sun was half covered, Selena was moving purposefully among her cameras, with scarcely a moment free to look upward. At her side Bennit Cushing followed her quick, brusque instructions—they opened lenses in sequence, timed them, closed them, slipped the plates from the cameras, inserted new ones; started again.

She was reaching for the fourth full round of new plates when Cushing touched her shoulder. Toward the northwest the half-covered sun was still fiercely bright, just as before. The bleached blue of the sky was darker at the edges, otherwise unchanged. She shook his hand impatiently off her shoulder. And then, far out on the horizon, she saw what she could never in the world have imagined, what no words could ever communicate. The shadow of the moon was on the ground and coming toward them.

It approached with terrifying speed. It advanced like a flying wall of blackness.

It was a vast moving presence, swifter than imagination, darker than night, utterly silent. Moment by moment the world around her, hills and trees and gully, turned ash-gray and died.

As if in a trance, she opened the lenses of the next two cameras, then knelt beside the viewing box.

The moon had almost covered the entire disk of the sun. In another few seconds it would be safe to raise her eyes from the filtered image in the box. At the left-hand edge, the crescent was now disintegrating into sparkling dots of intense white light, and these, she knew, though she had never seen them before, were Baily's Beads—the final rays of sunlight passing through the mountain-framed valleys on the very rim of the moon.

Then the dots of light combined suddenly into one glowing protrusion on the left-hand side, like a celestial diamond on a ring, and the sun went dark. In the great and beautiful mathematical order of the universe, the sun, the moon, and the earth were absolutely, precisely, perfectly aligned, and she was standing in the umbra of the moon, the center of its shadow. All around the black disk were now flashing radiant streamers of silvery, unearthly light, the sun's corona, its crown. She saw a solar prominence, bright crimson, tens of thousands of miles long, dart out from the streamers, and then another and another, in soundless glory. She heard herself utter the simple word "Totality."

And then almost before she knew it an arrow of pure sunlight from the right-hand edge struck the distant hills, and the corona and the prominences began to fade.

On the western horizon an orange band below the darkness announced the end. Green and brown earth began to reemerge. The shadow of the moon slid out from under her feet with frightful and accelerating velocity.

If it could be repeated every day for a year, Selena thought, she would never budge from where she stood. She was vaguely conscious that tears were running down her cheeks. She felt Bennit Cushing's arm around her shoulder and heard him murmuring something she couldn't hear. She was as certain as it was possible to be that her cameras had caught it all.

CHAPTER FORTY-ONE

Epanalepsis

TWO WEEKS LATER, IN THE MIDDLE OF A LONG, LAZY MID-September afternoon, Ceran St. Vrain strolled to the front door of his prosperous general store and bank and looked out across the south side of the tree-lined Plaza de Taos.

Coming down the road from the north, still three or four blocks away as you measure distance in a true city, was a Conestoga wagon much the worse for wear. It was drawn by a full team of prancing mules and followed at a little distance by a dozen other wagons of similar make and disrepair. A normal sight, the arrival of a wagon train from Bent's Fort off the Santa Fe Trail, of no special interest or novelty. At this time of year it happened two or three times a week. Except that the first wagon appeared half empty. On the driver's bench a man was holding the reins. Next to him, St. Vrain presumed, was the famous young lady of whom he had heard so much in the last two days, though because of the distance and the low glare of the sun it was hard to be sure. On the other hand, even at a distance one saw very few blonde heads in Taos.

St. Vrain said something over his shoulder to one of the clerks, who scurried away to find the Señora, who would, of

course, already be running down the stairs anyway, having
been on the watch for the wagon train since noon and surely
alerted by the curious shouts of the trappers on the street. By
now a bedlam of little boys was scampering alongside it, the
azoteas—red-tiled roofs—were covered with women and
children, and doubtless the strum of guitars would soon be
heard. It was St. Vrain's unshakable opinion that the first
word any Mexican learned was *fiesta*.

To distinguish himself quite clearly from what his old
mother back in Missouri called the "vulgarity," St. Vrain
struck a phosphorous matchhead and lit a shuck *cigaritto* inserted in the end of an elegant gold tube. Then he turned and
strolled casually back to his office.

He had thought a good deal about how to receive his
guests—there had even been some rumblings of advice from
the governor's palace in Santa Fe, where the foreign prisoners
were held—but St. Vrain liked to do everything in his own
style. *Nil admirari,* he thought, the old Roman advice not to
stare and gawk, was his way.

His wife had prepared two guest rooms upstairs, and in the
garden courtyard she had instructed the servants to set out tables and lanterns as well as several barrels of ice from the ice
shed to cool the wine. The ice was a recent luxury and inno-
vation—St. Vrain had read in one of Richard Babbage's
newspapers about the so-called "Ice King of New England,"
who had lately perfected the shipping and storing of huge
quantities of ice to Cuba and thereby made an astonishing
fortune from the sweltering population. Intrigued, St. Vrain
had ordered six hundred pounds of ice brought down from
the snowy heights of the Sangre de Cristo Mountains and
packed away in straw-lined dugouts behind the stables. But
he was sure there was specialized technical knowledge needed
to ship it any great distance.

A question for his scientific guest, perhaps? Though from
what he had read, Miss Selena Cott was much more interested in the melting agent—he glanced through the window
at the red September sun—than the cultivation of ice.

His wife and her sister came dashing down the stairs together. There was a predictable outburst of imperative Spanish in his direction. Five seconds later they were out on the Plaza with the rest of his staff and household. St. Vrain heard the shouts growing very close.

He had prepared a little speech of welcome, in fact, which he thought he would deliver with bankerlike dignity from behind his desk, a gracious summary, in English, of what everyone in Taos had heard about their great adventure and what the governor in Santa Fe proposed. He inhaled tobacco smoke, hooked his thumbs in his waistcoat, and took up a pose. But just then the lead wagon rattled loudly past his window, somebody on the street blew a trumpet, and a cheer went up, and the ineradicable Missourian in St. Vrain thought, "Oh, what the hell." He hurried outside to join the others.

THE SPEECH OF WELCOME WAS NEVER MADE, OF COURSE. SELENA watched in secret sympathy as the tall, slightly built and rather overdressed man, obviously American, held up his hands and tried to clear a space and quiet the crowds—but the children were too much for him, the imperious Mexican wife was oblivious to his oratory, and before he could do much more than shout his name, Señor St. Vrain, and declare them welcome to San Fernandez de Taos, the wife had sped Selena inside the store like a rocket, upstairs to the living quarters, and safely into the ladies' sanctum.

Not until dinner that night, when they were all gathered in the enclosed and lantern-lit garden behind the store, a flickering oasis of wonderfully scented mimosa and acacia, could she finally sit down properly and make the acquaintance of her host.

"I have definitive news of your expeditionary friends," Ceran St. Vrain announced as warm Spanish brandy was served to the men, hot chocolate to the ladies.

Selena bent forward to hear him better over the guitars,

which seemed to be a feature of every corner of Taos, and wondered if her face showed quite the right mixture of concern and relief.

"The governor has arrested all of them, I'm afraid," said St. Vrain, "as proven Texas spies—"

"They're from England, for heaven's sake, two of them," Bennit Cushing put in before Selena could shush him.

"The Mexican government is not always delicate in its political distinctions, sir," St. Vrain told the artist dryly.

"What will happen to them?" Selena asked.

"I would guess about one year in prison and eventually the discreet acceptance of certain fees in exchange for freedom. Long before they're released, alas for us, you'll be back in Washington City, Miss Cott."

But before she could open her mouth, whether in explanation, protest, or approval, a pair of earsplitting trumpets joined the guitars. The Señora and her sister presented themselves and pulled her away to judge the children's dancing.

Nonetheless, slowly, in fragments over the rest of the long, noisy evening, Selena was able to piece together what had happened. After the eclipse, she and Cushing had travelled a day and a half due west, between the great red buttes. They had been rescued, just as Cushing predicted, a few miles below the Raton Pass by the first wagon train they saw. As it happened, the train was headed southwest, to Taos rather than Santa Fe or east toward Missouri. They had been given more mules, amply supplied with food and blankets, and cheerfully adopted by the trading crew as rather entertaining visitors dropped from another world.

As for Pryce and the others, however—from what Ceran St. Vrain could tell her, a band of Kiowa Indians, in a considerable state of panic, had deposited four English-speaking captives in an abandoned shack near Rabbit Ears Mountain and then sent off a messenger to the nearest *barrio* of Mexican soldiers, farther down the Trail. The panic was occasioned by what the Indians claimed was the unbelievable and wicked extinction of the sun—for a full *day*, the savages claimed—a terrible omen clearly connected to the white men they had innocently captured the day before. The Kiowa tribe was washing their hands of them, relinquishing all four to the Mexican government, and moving away to the upper reaches of the Arkansas River, as far as possible from the ill-favored spot where the supposed Texans' evil medicine had caused a raging wildfire, and then an unparalleled assault on the Sun Dance ritual itself.

But it was not the fairly typical fate of suspected spies that really interested St. Vrain. He was much more curious about the remarkable total eclipse Miss Cott and Mr. Cushing and some two thousand jabbering Kiowa Indians all claimed to have witnessed.

"I say 'claimed,' because here in Taos and in Santa Fe it was raining furiously that day, and as far east as the Cimarron Cutoff nobody else seems to have seen it. Nor did anybody else experience the great lightning storm you say started the wildfire."

"A very local storm," said Bennit Cushing, in a voice almost as dry as St. Vrain's.

"Indeed."

"We were in the last wagon," Selena said, embroidering only slightly the story they had agreed on to protect Charles Babbage's reputation, "and the rain was so hard everybody else was separated from us almost at once. I thought we'd never be found. Or else the Indians would find us first."

"And in all this," St. Vrain asked, "did you also hear of *another* white man, living with the Kiowas?"

Selena glanced at Cushing. They shook their heads.

"*We* hear stories," St. Vrain explained. "From time to time some susceptible and Utopian-minded person from the East goes off and lives with the Indians for a while. The latest is apparently an old white man up with Chief Trotting Wolf and the Kiowas, not in good health, pays his own way." He regarded Selena thoughtfully over his *cigaritto*. "Whether he's alive or dead, I suppose we'll never know."

At the end of the evening, as Señora St. Vrain was herding

them all indoors, St. Vrain stopped and peered up through the lanterns and leaves at the starlit sky. "You'll stay a few days as our guests, of course, before we send you back to the United States."

"You're very kind," said Selena.

"As harmless repayment," murmured the banker, "since we missed the eclipse here in Taos, perhaps in the morning you would be willing to show us your pictures."

AND SO IT HAPPENED, NOT THE NEXT DAY, FOR THERE WERE A hundred errands to run and formalities without end to arrange for the government in Santa Fe, but on the second morning, around ten o'clock on a beautiful, cloudless, and very sunny day, Ceran St. Vrain, his wife, her sister, and a dozen or so dignitaries of the village gathered in his back garden to see the exhibition.

It was a memorable occasion on several counts, and despite his philosophy of *nil admirari,* St. Vrain had gone to some considerable trouble to do it justice. There were benches and chairs in four neat rows; refreshments, of course, guitars unavoidably; and against the thick adobe background of the western wall of the garden, the *pièce de résistance:* a ten-foothigh wooden latticework of shelves for the photographs, put together by St. Vrain's personal carpenter.

At ten o'clock the shelf was still concealed behind a very large blue and red cloth that had been strung up before it like a stage curtain. Behind it, under a second awning, Selena Cott and Bennit Cushing could dimly be seen arranging the photographic plates in order on the shelves. The effect, she had told St. Vrain, would be like the unveiling of a statue—she would stand to one side, Cushing on the other, and at her signal he would pull aside the red and blue curtain to reveal, in one sweeping motion, the entire marvelous exhibit.

And marvelous it would be, she promised. After the eclipse was ended, she and Cushing had labored far into the night developing their exposed daguerreotype plates. A certain number, she regretted, had not produced useful images, but that was to be expected—mistimed exposures, insufficient mercury vapor, a camera accidentally bumped; normal mishaps, anticipated and unimportant. She herself had inspected each five-by-seven-inch plate with extreme care after it had emerged from the developing box. And thereafter they had all been doubly protected by a glass cover and a padded carrying box lined with cushioned velvet. They had not been out of the box—or out of her sight—for fourteen days.

At half past ten or thereabouts, when the last guest had settled onto a bench and an expectant quiet had descended over the garden, Selena stepped forward. Had St. Vrain or the others been present four months earlier at the United States Topographical Corps auditorium, they would have recognized her unconscious tribute to William Henshaw Pryce's manner of public speaking. She was calm; she smiled confidently at her audience; she told the history of the expedition, the odds against it, the determination of their little crew.

Off to one side, in what appeared to be an excess of good humor, the long-haired Bennit Cushing had prepared a large and quite impressive crayon sketch of the sun in total eclipse, an effort dashed off late last night and presented now on an easel tripod as an artistic tribute.

"But what you are about to see next," Selena said, gesturing to the closed curtain, "are actual daguerreotypes, not paintings. Real pictures, not imaginary. These are the first photographs ever taken of the sun in eclipse—complete and historic vindication of Mr. Charles Babbage's genius and his amazing Difference Engine!"

Smiling broadly, she turned and nodded to Cushing. The artist stepped away from his painting. He rubbed his hands slowly and carefully together, directed a wry look at Selena, then reached up and pulled smartly at a rope in one corner.

The curtain dropped to the ground.

And there before them, propped at a slant on the wooden latticework shelves, glistening dramatically in the sunlight, stood six separate rows of photographs.

The audience came to its feet. St. Vrain shouted, "Bravo!" The guitars struck two triumphant chords, and for one remarkable moment the eclipse lived again. In strict, beautifully calibrated order, thirty-two daguerreotype plates showed the swift, inevitable, utterly hypnotic movement of the shadow of the moon across the face of the oldest of all the gods.

And then, one by one, the daguerreotypes started to turn black.

Too late, Selena leaped for the fallen curtain. Too late, Bennit Cushing pulled the awning down—over the eastern wall of the garden, as if jealous of its own image, or furious at the shadow once again devouring it, the sun poured its fierce, angry beam on the copper plates. And also, as Selena suddenly realized with a loud cry of dismay, poured its transforming rays on the special bromine formula, disastrously and chemically altered from accelerator to metallic acid by two weeks of heat and dust.

Relentlessly, second by second, every speck of photographic whiteness was consumed by the radiation of the sun. Moment by moment, from top to bottom, each and every plate lost the brilliant silver-mercury amalgam that formed its patterns of light against darkness and, with the slow inevitability of a ticking clock, eclipsed and metamorphosed into sullen umbra.

In the end, while the Taos audience could only stand helpless and aghast in front of the shelves, all that was left were thirty-two bare and empty jet-black plates, each one reflecting from the sky overhead, like a celestial golden eye, a diminished and passing image of Sun Boy himself.

CHAPTER FORTY-TWO

Coda

CHARLES BABBAGE WAS IN THE MIDST OF ONE OF HIS FAMOUS Dorset Street Saturday *soirées* when he received the final word, at least as far as he was concerned, on what had happened.

It was late November and the weather rainy and chill. Attendance was considerably sparser than usual that evening; indeed, by nine o'clock Babbage had counted no more than a dozen guests altogether, scattered and milling about in the great spaces of his drawing room. He himself, although the host, was in no particular mood for conversation and had retreated with Ada Lovelace to a corner by the window, where his mechanical Dancing Girls had been relegated. He had just bent over the table, thinking how to repair one of their misaligned silver legs, when Edward Kater, his bald and unimpressive banker, strode up.

"For you," Kater announced and handed Babbage a fat brown envelope covered with foreign stamps and markings.

Babbage cocked an eyebrow and held the envelope up to the light. "Republic of Mexico," he read aloud, then translated the official return address. "Bureau of Prisons, Palace of the Governor, Santa Fe."

"It contains," said Kater, nodding at Ada but poking

rudely at the Dancing Girl's leg, "an ill-written appeal in Spanish on behalf, you will not be surprised to hear, of one Señor William Henshaw Pryce, held at the moment in durance vile, or 'calaboose' as they would apparently say. They want money for ransom."

"For *ransom*," Babbage repeated in a tone of disgust. He opened the envelope and scanned the letter.

"And also more money for fines, customs levies, and jailer's fees. Six thousand dollars in all. And since you still have no inheritance to borrow against, and probably never will—"

"Pryce appears to have bungled everything, with everybody. Disgraceful." Babbage jammed the letter angrily back in the envelope.

"A high price for a Pryce," Kater agreed with irritating good humor. "And alas, along with Miss Cott's regrettable report about the daguerreotypes, this rather puts an end to any hope of government support." He glanced, not subtly, toward the wing of the house where the Difference Engine resided. "Everyone assumes that Miss Cott, of course, is merely protecting you and that the noble machine's prediction was somehow off the mark."

There was something patently offensive in Kater's tone, Babbage thought. Pryce in jail, an English gentleman in a Mexican jail, was a shocking thought, not to be joked about. On the other hand ... Babbage thrust his hands stiffly behind his back and stared at the fire. He could not help being reminded of the one aphorism of La Rochefoucauld he had ever committed to memory. *There is something in our best friend's misfortune,* the cynical and sardonic Frenchman had observed, *that does not entirely displease us.*

"You'll have to pay, of course," the old banker said cheerfully, since it was not his money. "Somehow."

"Miss Cott insisted there *was* an eclipse." Ada, who had never looked more lovely and pneumatic, pressed her left breast delicately, artfully against Babbage's arm.

"It is well known," replied Kater, "that Miss Cott lives in Paris, with a Bohemian painter."

"Very shocking," said Ada Lovelace, primly.

Babbage was tired of Kater, the *soirée,* even the Dancing Girls. He nodded curtly to the insufferable William Henry Fox-Talbot, strolling by at that moment with his tedious cup of soup. What Babbage desperately wanted was to leave them all to their own devices and disappear into the next room with Ada, to seek philosophical consolation. "The Engine-computer will prove itself one day," he said to the banker, "government or no government. The great theme of the nineteenth century," he added rather grandly, recalling now another aphorism, though for some reason not its author, "is the triumph of Science over Nature."

"Or else," murmured the warm-bodied and beautifully scented Ada, stroking his hand behind his back, "vice versa."

NOTE

Charles Babbage was a real historical figure, and the Difference Engine did exist. Portions of it, including one of the sections used in the demonstration on miracles, can be seen today in the Science Museum in Kensington, London. But, alas, it was not used to predict an eclipse in 1840, and the adventures of the fictional Selena and Pryce are all invented. Other historical characters like Ada Lovelace, Thomas Hart Benton, and President Van Buren, are drawn from biographies, journals, and letters.

Readers interested in learning more about Babbage will enjoy *The Difference Engine* by Doron Swade (2001). Babbage's memoirs, *Passages from the Life of a Philosopher* (1864), give something of the tart flavor of his personality.

There are hundreds of books about the Santa Fe Trail. Two very good recent histories are David Dary, *The Santa Fe Trail* (2000), and Stephen G. Hyslop, *Bound for Santa Fe* (2002). The firsthand voice of experience is heard in *Down the Santa Fe Trail and into Mexico: The Diary of Susan Shelly Magoffin, 1846–47*, edited by Stella M. Drum (1926). The single best book I know about the Trail is *Land of Enchantment* (1954) by Marian Russell, the memoirs of a wonderfully adventurous young woman who first travelled to Santa Fe in 1852. It is available in paperback from the University of New Mexico Press. I have adapted several descriptive sentences and phrases from her book, and much information.

Many people have helped me in writing, especially Tom Allen, Charles Nash, and Harold Weaver. My friend John Lescroart is a terrific novelist and generous counselor. My beautiful wife, Brookes Byrd, read (and improved) every page. Diana Essert has most patiently typed the manuscript. And finally, with every passing year I am ever more deeply in debt to Virginia Barber of the William Morris Agency and to the best editor I can imagine, Kate Burke Miciak.